DEADLY MISTAKE

ROB SINCLAIR

Boldwood

First published in Great Britain in 2025 by Boldwood Books Ltd.

Cover Design by Head Design Ltd.

Cover Images: iStock

A CIP catalogue record for this book is available from the British Library.

Paperback ISBN 978-1-83703-193-1

Large Print ISBN 978-1-83703-192-4

Hardback ISBN 978-1-83703-191-7

Trade Paperback ISBN 978-1-80635-321-7

Ebook ISBN 978-1-83703-194-8

Kindle ISBN 978-1-83703-195-5

Audio CD ISBN 978-1-83703-186-3

MP3 CD ISBN 978-1-83703-187-0

Digital audio download ISBN 978-1-83703-188-7

This book is printed on certified sustainable paper. Boldwood Books is dedicated to putting sustainability at the heart of our business. For more information please visit https://www.boldwoodbooks.com/about-us/sustainability/

Boldwood Books Ltd, 23 Bowerdean Street, London, SW6 3TN

www.boldwoodbooks.com

1

Over an hour since the sun had disappeared beyond the frazzled fields on the horizon, yet the temperature had barely dropped. Sweltering. The choking air remained thick with moisture and Simon Peake's T-shirt and shorts clung to his body as he sat back in the wooden porch chair, his skin glistening in the faint glow of light from the flickering bulb above, the incessant drone of cicadas all around him.

He sighed and took a swig from his beer. Not as chilled now as two minutes before when he'd pulled it from the freezer. He downed it. Nothing else to do tonight so he decided to go get another. He stood up from the chair, his bones creaking as much as the warped wood beneath his feet, a stinging discomfort pulsing across recently healed wounds where the scars told only a tiny part of that story. Sometimes he felt several decades older than he was, the amount of punishment his body had taken. Particularly from most recently, in New York.

He headed inside, the screen door slapped back into place and the superheated air hit him. Close to a hundred outside. Probably 130 inside given there was no AC in a ramshackle home like this. Before he reached the fridge, a beeping noise caught his attention above the muffled din of the cicadas.

He took his phone out and navigated to the camera feeds. Had expected – hoped – that the camera 300 yards away at the boundary of the property had picked up the movement of a nighttime creature. A coyote, most likely.

But no. A car.

Peake spun around and dashed toward the back door and flicked the switch for the porch light then did the same with the kitchen light, plunging the house into blackness. For all of a couple of seconds anyway, until the beams of the car's headlights crested the hill on the south side and swept down toward the house, the light twisting and morphing across the floors and walls of the open-plan space around Peake.

He went to the cupboard by the front door. Checked the shotgun. Loaded. Checked the handgun. Loaded too. He left that in place behind the toolbox and took the shotgun and a handful of extra shells which he stuffed into the pocket of his linen shorts. The house went momentarily dark again as the car continued its approach on the twisting, undulating dirt lane. A slow approach, no revving engine, only the sound of tires on the rough surface, getting louder all the time.

Shotgun in hand, Peake moved back to the kitchen, away from the front door. He crouched down beneath the counter to look at the camera feeds again. Split screen, so he could see both the front stoop and the back porch. The car came to a stop at the front. The lights flicked off which threw him into darkness once more, except for the glow from his phone.

Three men stepped from the car, their forms only just visible in the moonlight. Maybe he should have gone for the much more expensive night-vision cameras after all. The men stood side by side at the front of the car, staring toward the house. He could hear their muted, gruff voices through the thin walls of the house, but couldn't make out any of the conversation. After a while they walked in unison toward the house, the taller and lankier of the three eventually breaking away as they neared the porch.

The front security light flicked on and the man at the front flinched and whipped a hand up to his face to shield from the glare.

But not before Peake got a glimpse of his face.

What the fuck was he doing here?

The other two paused. One of them reached his hand behind to the waistband of his jeans.

So he was armed, although he didn't pull the gun free. Peake wondered about the third man. No obvious sign of a weapon on him, but a small bag was hanging off of one shoulder.

Peake remained rooted as the heavy thuds shook the front door, vibrated through the whole front of the old wooden house.

No words accompanied the hefty knocks. Peake's eyes stayed glued to the phone screen. The camera looked directly down on the three men, giving a not-so-great view of their faces, but he was sure he didn't recognize the two at the back. Both were white average-looking guys. The one with the bag had a shiny bald head, the other had a muss of hair on top and a thick, bushy beard like a Viking warrior.

The man at the front... younger. Dumber, perhaps.

'Peake, it's me. Adam. Open up,' he shouted out.

Peake didn't move.

'Peake. Please. We need your help.'

The thuds came again. Not from Adam this time, but from the guy with the bag who'd stepped up to the door and shouldered Adam aside. When he finished he stared up at the camera. Kept his gaze there a few seconds.

'Simon Peake,' he shouted. 'We know you're home. Open the damn door.'

'Peake, please,' Adam shouted. He looked over his shoulder toward the car, his edginess clear. 'I know you're home. Your truck's here. And who the hell would go out for a walk on a night like this in the middle of nowhere.'

Fair point, but Peake still didn't move.

The three men had a brief hushed exchange, cupping their mouths to further muffle their voices.

Then the bag-guy looked at his watch, glanced to the car, then back up to the camera.

'Your friend here said you were the guy who could help us. A bit of... cleaning work. If you catch my drift.'

Peake gritted his teeth.

'There's ten g here for you. Up front.' He pulled the bag from his shoulder, opened it and pushed it toward the camera. Sure enough, four bundles of notes were stuffed inside.

'Ten g,' Beardy said. 'Fuck, if this idiot doesn't want it we may as well clean up ourselves and keep the money.'

Baldy nodded in response and zipped the bag back up but neither of them moved from the spot.

'Ten seconds. Then we're gone. The money too.'

Peake kept his focus on Adam, who looked even more jittery now.

'Ten...'

He hadn't seen Adam in several days. Apparently he'd headed down to Florida, for some work.

'Nine...'

It looked like he hadn't learned much from his previous life lessons, given he'd ridden back up here with these two no-good goons.

'Eight...'

'This asshole...' Beardy said, shaking his head with obvious disdain. Disgruntlement too.

'Seven...'

'Why don't we just bust the door down?'

'Six...'

'If he's inside, hiding from us...'

'Five...'

'...fucking get rid of him too. Messing us around like this.'

'Four...'

'No, he's good for it,' Adam said. 'Trust me.'

'Three...'

Thud, thud, thud. 'Peake, you asshole!' Adam said. 'You're making me look real bad here!'

'Open the door or I'm just gonna break it,' Beardy shouted. 'And then I'm gonna break you.' Out came the handgun.

'Two...' Baldy paused. The three men stared at each other, then glanced to the camera. Beardy pointed the gun toward it, mimicked firing a shot as though doing so was supposed to intimidate Peake, or make him more likely to open the door or something.

'Let's get outta here. We need to get this done tonight,' Baldy said to his buddy.

'Guys, no, he's—'

'Not here, is he?' Baldy said, slapping Adam's shoulder.

'Yeah, but I might just come back another time,' Beardy said. 'Wasting our time like this...'

'One...'

A few seconds' pause again before, heads shaking and grumbling under their breaths, Baldy and Beardy retreated down the steps. Adam eventually turned and scuttled behind them.

Peake rose from his position. Tiptoed to the front door. The car engine grumbled to life, the headlights flicked on. Peake thought a moment more.

He knew Adam. He didn't know the other two. He didn't like that Adam had brought them here. What had the kid told them about him? Anything at all, even his name, was too much.

Cleaning work.

Peake thought he knew what that meant. It meant Adam's loose tongue and his willingness to please his two chump companions had got the better of him. At what risk to Peake?

Could he take the chance of them leaving without knowing the full story?

Plus… the money. Whatever the situation, ten grand was a lot of money.

His money, really.

Peake opened the front door, pointed the shotgun toward the car. The engine shut down again. The lights turned off. The two front doors opened and the men half stepped out, shielding themselves behind the metal and glass.

Adam got out of the back, seemingly not as bothered about the threat of the shotgun as he took two steps clear of the car as he approached Peake.

'Jesus, I knew you were home! What the fuck?'

'Show me your hands,' Peake shouted.

Adam paused in his step.

'What the hell is this?' Beardy shouted over.

'I said, show me your hands.' Peake took a step forward. 'All of you.'

The three men each brought their empty hands up above their shoulders. Peake was a little surprised.

'Step away from the car. Bring the money with you.'

'The bag's in the car,' Baldy said. 'You want me to lower my hand to get it?'

'Do it,' Peake said.

Baldy slowly reached for the bag then both men stepped out into the open.

'Weapons?' Peake asked.

'What do you think?' Baldy said.

'Toss them to me.'

'Fuck you.'

'Peake, come on,' Adam said. 'We're not here to—'

'You want this to end in anything other than a firefight? Get rid of your weapons. All of you.'

Adam lifted his shirt to show he had nothing stashed. Surprisingly the other two men slowly pulled out their handguns, holding them pincered between two fingers to show they weren't about to turn the weapons on Peake.

'But we're not giving them to you,' Baldy said. 'We'll leave them in the car.'

And before Peake could suggest otherwise they both gently tossed the guns in through the open car doors.

'Satisfied?' Beardy asked.

'Enough,' Peake said.

All three men remained on the spot, looking from one to the other. Peake's finger remained on the trigger of the shotgun as he moved the barrel slowly back and forth between the targets.

'So?' Baldy said, sounding fed up with the situation more than anything else. 'Are we doing this or not?'

Peake finally took his finger from the trigger and pulled the barrel of the shotgun down, toward the ground.

'Come on in,' Peake said, stepping to the side and beckoning the men over with a wide smile forced on his face.

2

Adam's companions moved inside first. Peake momentarily grabbed the youngster before he joined them.

'What the hell?' Peake mouthed.

Adam shrugged his shoulders, a pleading look on his face before he headed on in without a word in response.

Peake followed the three into the house, turning on the lights across the hall, kitchen, living room before he closed the front door. The men remained hovering in the small, open space.

'Take a seat,' he said, indicating the threadbare brown sofa.

'Some place you got here,' Beardy said mockingly.

Peake said nothing but glared until all three men had edged toward the living room area, though none of them bothered to take a seat. Peake didn't blame them. He hated the crappy sofa too. Adam remained closest to Peake, that pleading look still plastered on his face, as though he couldn't understand why Peake was making this situation hard.

'You gonna put that thing down?' Baldy asked, indicating the shotgun still hanging lazily in Peake's grip.

Peake did so, but not because he felt the need to do as he was told, simply because he knew he didn't need it right now. He placed the weapon on the kitchen counter. Still far closer to him than it was to them should he need it.

They'd left their guns in the car. Supposedly. He had to expect they both remained armed. Another hidden gun. A knife. Something, somewhere.

'So, I know Adam, but who are you two?' Peake asked.

Baldy raised an eyebrow; Beardy kind of grunted.

'You're a Brit,' Beardy said.

'Kind of.'

'Kind of?' Baldy asked.

'I've been around.'

'Don't sound like you've been around here much.'

'Not for long.'

'So how'd a Brit end up in south Georgia then?' Beardy asked.

'I came for the weather.'

Baldy very nearly smiled. Beardy looked nonplussed.

'I asked for your names,' Peake said.

'You don't need to know our names,' Baldy said.

'The start of a long and prosperous business relationship,' Peake said, with just enough sarcasm to see the agitation in both men in front of him rise a little more.

'McGinty recommended you to us,' Baldy said with a glance at Adam. 'Told us you were the man to help us here.'

Peake caught Adam's eye but the youngster quickly looked away.

'This is stupid,' Beardy said to Baldy. 'Should never have listened to the kid. Let's do it ourselves. Keep the ten g. Hardy's gonna be pissed if we're not back soon.'

'Hardy?' Peake said. 'Who's Hardy?'

All three stared at him.

'Your boss?' Peake asked.

'The man who put the money in this bag. Who wants someone else to do this, not us. Separation or something. So if you screw us here, you're really screwing him. And you really don't wanna do that.'

'Peake, seriously, listen to them,' Adam said, but Peake waved his interjection away.

'Ten grand for what?'

The men exchanged another quick glance.

'Cleaning,' Baldy said.

'You want me to mop your floors?'

Beardy snorted and shook his head. 'Funny guy.'

'You know what we mean,' Baldy said. 'McGinty said you're the guy for this.'

'I'm guessing you've done this shit before. Otherwise I'm not sure why we're here.'

Adam was doing everything to avert Peake's gaze – glare – now. What the hell had he told these two men?

'Look, we just brought the body. The money,' Baldy said. 'We'll leave both with you and you don't need to see us again.'

'It's here?' Peake asked.

'Yeah, it's here,' Baldy replied, sounding more irritated by the second. 'Slowly cooking in the trunk. If you take any fucking longer it's gonna turn into a feeding frenzy for every damn maggot in the state.'

'One body?'

'You saw the car. How many you think we got in that trunk?'

'Depends on the size of them. And how many pieces. Takes up less space if they're all chopped up.'

'We ain't the butchers. Apparently you are. Although I'm starting to wonder 'bout that now.'

He glared at Adam as he said that. The kid was becoming more and more jittery. Not just at the agitation and threat from his buddies, but probably because his whole master plan was now unraveling before his eyes.

'So you want me to get rid of a body for you?' Peake asked.

Baldy squirmed a little at Peake's brazenness, as though he thought someone would overhear even though there wasn't another property within two miles.

'No, we don't – Hardy does,' Beardy said.

'Hardy, who I don't know.'

'Who gives a crap who you do and don't know? Are you doing this, or do we got a problem?'

Both men tensed as though Beardy's ultimatum might turn the situation into a bloody confrontation. Well... that was down to them.

'Who is it?' Peake asked.

'You don't need to know,' Baldy said.

'Do you know?'

'Yeah, we know, but you don't need to,' Beardy said.

'I say I do. Ten grand for getting rid of a corpse? Not so bad if it's a nobody. If it's a cop? A politician? The president?'

'You think we have the dead president in the trunk of our car?' Beardy said, disdain now dripping with every word, and spread across his face too.

'Do you?'

'No. We don't,' Baldy said. 'It's a nobody. Ten grand for a nobody. You don't need to know nothing more than that.'

'Did you do it?'

'What?' Baldy said, sounding fed up, like he'd really had enough of the whole conversation now.

'Did you kill them?'

'What does that matter?'

'Just trying to figure out who I'm working with here.'

'You're doing this for Hardy.'

'Who I don't know.'

'This is fucked up, we should get outta here,' Beardy said, taking a couple of steps toward Baldy, closer to the exit, as though hoping his buddy would turn and head out too.

But Baldy stayed on the spot.

'Do we have a problem?' Baldy said to Peake.

'Show me the money.'

'I already did.'

'Toss the bag to me so I can check it.'

'No,' Baldy said. 'We go outside. We get the body out of our car. We give you the money as we leave.'

'You want my help? That money is mine. Toss the bag now or I'll come over and take it from you. Then this ends with me having to get rid of four bodies tonight, not one.'

'Peake, please—' Adam butted in.

'And that's no big deal for me. After all, Adam told you about me, didn't he?'

Peake sent daggers but Adam's eyes were to the floor. He knew he'd fucked up coming here.

The room fell silent, except for the hum of the cicadas drifting in from outside.

'Okay, Mr. Tough Guy,' Baldy said, raising his hands. 'We didn't come here for trouble.'

'This time,' Beardy added, clearly not wanting Peake to forget that he was the edgiest of the two.

'Here.'

Baldy underarmed the bag toward Peake who caught the strap, his eyes not leaving the men in case the move was a distraction for them to launch an attack.

It wasn't. They didn't move as Peake diverted his eyes to the bag and unzipped the top and felt around inside. Cash. Ten grand? That, or something close.

He put the bag down on the counter, next to the shotgun.

Peake smiled. 'Let's go see what you've got for me then.'

All three men glanced toward the money bag and the shotgun as they made their way to the exit. Peake left both in place to follow them outside.

Cool air. Cooler than inside, anyway. Peake got a good look at the car as they approached, the arc of the security light reaching past the vehicle's front end. A battered old sedan. Perhaps dark red or a mucky brown, or maybe that was just the rust; it was difficult to tell because the metalwork was so badly dented and the paint mottled and peeling. Too many years without attention. Too many years out in the baking sunshine.

The old vehicle looked like it belonged in the dusty grounds of Peake's home.

The men walked past the front doors of the car to the rear. A good sign – they'd decided not to reach for the weapons that lay on the seats inside.

A Florida plate.

Real or fake, it told a story.

Peake caught Adam's eye for a split second as Baldy took a key from his pocket.

Florida. Adam had gone to Florida for some work. He'd come back with two grunts and a dead body and in a whole heap of deep shit.

Peake kept a couple of yards away from the three, one eye on the men, one eye on the trunk lid as Baldy stuck the key in the lock and used a bit of force to pop the likely rusted mechanism.

Baldy yanked open the creaky trunk lid and stepped back toward his companion, as though giving space for Peake to move forward and take a look inside. A dark space, given the angle of the car to the light at the front of the house.

'She's all yours,' Baldy said.

She.

Peake stared into the darkened space as his eyes adjusted, moonlight creeping over the form inside. Clothing, dark and glistening with wet blood. Flesh, similarly stained.

A face. Tucked into the corner of the cramped space, too far into the dark for him to properly make her out. But no reason at all why he'd know this poor woman anyway.

She.

'Come on, lover boy, you get to do whatever you want to her once we've gone. But let's just pull her out of there so we can leave you two in peace.'

Peake ignored the jibe and reached inside to pull on the dead woman's shoulders to bring her head out of the crevice at the back of the trunk. Eyes open but unmoving. Dark hair. A face spattered with blood. No, he didn't recognize her.

'Seriously, Peake, get her out so we can get outta here,' Baldy said.

'You take her legs,' Peake said.

'Do it yourself. She only weighed about 120 pounds even before she lost all her blood.'

Peake grimaced at the heartless words.

'Just give me a damn hand here, will you?' he demanded.

Baldy grumbled but was soon by Peake's side. Peake still had his hands around the woman's shoulders and Baldy took hold of her ankles. But still Peake didn't make a move to pull the body out.

'She's a looker, eh?' Baldy said. 'You should have seen her before this.'

She wore jeans. A simple strapped top. Her watch, necklace, rings remained in place. Everything tainted with her blood. Coming from... where? Gashes to her torso. Arms. A large puncture wound in her gut and another in her chest where blood had gushed out over her clothes.

A frenzied attack. Not a quick, clean kill.

A kill?

'Peake, what the fuck are you doing?' Baldy said. 'Come on!'

A kill...? No.

Not a kill.

As he leaned in further he felt it again. More sure of himself this time. Not the lightest of light nighttime breezes but definitely cool air moving against his cheek.

Coming from her...

Peake turned to Baldy. The look on his own face must have tipped the guy off. Baldy knew – Peake could tell by the sudden worry in the man's eyes. A worry which exploded when Peake let go of the woman and sprang into action.

'Fuck, Evan!' Baldy shouted as he reeled back.

Beardy reached down to his ankle. A knife. Baldy had nothing and found himself caught between Beardy and Peake. He chose to fight rather than back down and swung a meaty fist Peake's way. Peake swiveled to avoid the blow, lifted his foot up and crashed it down onto the side of Baldy's knee. The guy squealed in pain as his leg buckled and he collapsed onto his good knee. Peake lunged toward Beardy who thrust the knife forward, aiming for Peake's abdomen.

'Peake, no!' Adam shrieked.

Peake took no notice. He blocked the knife, forearm to forearm, grabbed the wrist with his other hand, twisted the guy's arm unnaturally until the elbow socket popped. Beardy didn't scream but clenched his teeth. His eyes popped like his elbow just had as he stared at the knife still clutched in a hand that was now entirely useless to him.

Not useless to Peake. He grabbed the fist and squeezed and turned the knife upward and thrust the tip up. The metal plunged into Beardy's neck, right under his chin. Three inches of blade disappeared and Peake pulled the knife free, taking the weapon from Beardy's grip before kicking the man away. He plummeted to the dirt, gargling his last breaths.

As Peake turned he noticed the metal in Baldy's hand.

Peake ducked and dodged as the guy hobbled on one leg and opened fire with his handgun. Adam yelled in pain.

Shit. The kid was hit.

Peake didn't look to see how bad it was. Kept moving. Kicked up dirt which caused Baldy to cower. He swept up behind and wrapped his forearm around the guy's head, pulling his face up to expose his neck. He fired off everything in the gun, nothing more than desperation as Peake drew the edge of the knife across Baldy's skin, the blade cutting long and deep, easily penetrating the carotid artery.

Blood hissed out as Peake let go and Baldy crumpled down in a heap next to his friend. Both lay there drawing their last breaths – neither would survive.

Adam...

Peake swiveled. Expected to see a body sprawled on the floor...

Nothing. Adam was gone.

Peake looked into the darkness, pinched his eyes together as though the extra focus would help.

'Adam!' Peake yelled out.

No response. No sounds of him breathing or scuttling away into the night.

Peake knelt and touched the dark, wet patch in the dirt. Blood. Adam was hit. How badly, Peake didn't know.

He rose up to his feet.

'Adam! I'll help you. Don't make this worse.'

Still nothing.

Peake thought for a moment. No point in trekking out into the darkness. He had more immediate matters to deal with.

Peake went back to the trunk and peered inside at the woman. She certainly looked dead enough but...

He pushed two fingers against the side of her neck.

A faint pulse.

Unlike the men who'd put her in there, she was still alive, whoever the hell she was.

Looking at the space now, Peake realized it was easily big enough for more than one body, despite Baldy's earlier assertion there was only one in the trunk.

He should know. He had enough experience of these things, as Adam McGinty well knew.

Peake would find out exactly what the hell Adam had told them when he caught up with that idiot.

For now, it was time to get started on clean up. He had a long night ahead of him.

3

The cold water of the shower felt like heaven on his skin, helping to soothe every aching muscle. He tipped his head back and closed his eyes, letting the water cascade over his face for a few seconds, initially enjoying the sensation. But after a while... gory images. Not only from the last couple of hours, as he'd cut the trash down to size, but from his often violent past. He shivered, opened his eyes and looked down to his feet where dirty water swirled. Mud. Blood.

No, seeing that didn't help at all. His heavy heartbeats aligned with the rhythmic thudding of the water on his back. His eyes tracked the liquid running along the grout lines as his mind was pulled deeper and deeper into the memory. Blood. Pain. Gun shots to his back, chest, gut to go along with the gory gashes and slashes from a horrific beating he'd somehow fought his way out of. Somehow survived.

But not without lasting damage, both to his body and his mind. Neither would fully recover from his ordeal in New York.

He'd headed south after that, on the run, but mainly simply for a fresh start at life.

Not the first time he'd tried that.

And it seemed like not much fresh was left about this new life already.

He turned the water off and pulled himself back to reality before sliding back the grimy, yellowed shower curtain. He grabbed the towel from where he'd left it on the sink. He quickly dried himself, leaving smudgy brown marks across the fabric showing he'd too hastily turned off the water. It was fine; he was cleaner now than before, more refreshed. Even if by the time he was pulling on some clean clothes, sweat droplets were already popping up across his clammy skin, not just from the heat but from the exertion. He wanted to be outside in the relative cool as soon as he could.

He hadn't intended to say goodbye to this place tonight, but he didn't have much choice now. Next time... air conditioning. Or a different area altogether. Somewhere not as hot.

He'd have to leave town. He knew that.

But not yet. Not until he had some answers.

Where the hell was Adam?

Peake thumped the wall in frustration, ignored the throbbing in his fist as he moved into the bedroom.

He quickly packed some clothes into a holdall. He had a second bag and box too, for the few other things he wanted to take with him – a small cache of weapons, ammo, the wireless security camera system. Medication. He had the basics but he'd need more if he was to take care of this woman, revive her, figure out who she was and what to do with her. He'd have to wait until morning to get supplies. Only a few hours away in reality. Sleep? At some point. But not right now.

Someone – Hardy? – wanted the woman dead. But she wasn't dead... So sooner or later, her being alive was going to cause Peake a problem. Not to mention the issue of Adam. Peake needed to find him before he caused even more trouble, and regardless of whether he was now friend or foe. That all probably depended on who caught up with him first.

Peake placed his things in the back of his truck then opened the rear passenger door to check on the woman sprawled across the back seats. Still unconscious. Her pulse remained slow but steady. He'd done what he could for her for now. Stitched the worst of her wounds. Put some clean clothes on her – his clothes, which were big and baggy on her small frame. He'd cobbled together a makeshift saline drip to help combat the effects of blood loss, dehydration. For now, she was stable enough, even if he still had no idea if she'd ever wake up. Even if she did... brain damage was a real possibility given the state she was in. Adam and his friends had thought her dead. Perhaps she even had been at some point before somehow getting a second chance. It didn't take long for the brain to become permanently damaged through lack of oxygen when the heart failed, even for a short time...

No way of knowing yet.

Just like he still knew nothing about her. No identification in the car at all. Just her and her clothes and the jewelry she still wore.

Something he did know now: the names of Beardy and Baldy. Evan Huggins. Tyler Kittle. Not much left of those guys now, but like Adam, both men had carried their wallets, IDs. The sedan they'd driven to Peake's place had a Florida plate. He'd check the registration, but his best guess was that it was a fake. Still, their IDs... He'd memorized the information. Two names, two addresses. Both local. At least, within fifty miles of here.

He'd check out both places soon enough.

Like the men, the IDs were no more. He'd left those in the car which was most likely still burning in the wooded area five miles south of Peake's home. No, not his home. Just a place where he'd stayed a while.

There'd be little left of the car by morning. As for the remains of the men? Peake had done the best he could given time and available tools, materials. Ideally he'd have buried the bodies – the pieces, at least – with lime which would have helped to quickly decompose the flesh and bone. Or used a strong acid to turn everything into a mushy pulp which could be discarded here and there. Fertilizer, animal feed, whatever.

Instead he'd hacked the bodies apart in the bathroom and dumped the parts in shallow graves across the farmland and woodland. Most pieces would be scavenged within a few hours – vultures, coyotes the main carnivores out there who'd be grateful for the easy meal. If a person came across the remains and the police got involved... they'd still have a hard time figuring it all out any time soon.

Peake shook his head to erase the gruesome images.

The biggest risk for Peake right now wasn't what remained of Huggins and Kittle, but Adam McGinty and the building in front of him.

He'd find Adam sooner or later. This house? A problem. Hardy had sent those men out to kill and dispose of the woman. Sooner or later someone would realize those men were missing and sooner or later others would come looking here. Police possibly, too. Which was why he had to destroy as much evidence of his – and their – presence as he could.

He walked back toward the house, up the stairs, pushed open the front door. He held no emotion to this place. It had served a purpose.

He lit the match and tossed it toward the puddle on the floor. The fuel ignited with a whoosh and quickly sucked the available oxygen toward it causing air to pulse against Peake's face. Within seconds, flames had taken hold of furniture, drapes, and were licking up the walls to the ceiling.

Peake backstepped to the door, then turned and, feeling nothing at all, carried on to his truck.

* * *

Peake looked from the twisting lane ahead and to the orange glow in his rearview mirror. The structure had gone up like a matchstick house, the abundant wood, varnish, paint, and the already superheated dry air providing the perfect conditions for an all-consuming fire. By daylight nothing of the structure would remain. No fire engine would make it out in time to save the old house. For starters it'd require someone actually calling 911. Unlikely, as by the time Peake reached the road, the building, the flames, were already out of sight beyond the hill.

He glanced in the rearview just one more time. Not even any smoke visible yet in the night sky, the fire was burning too hot and clean.

He momentarily looked to the woman spread across the back seats before returning his focus to the road. She was fine. As fine as she could be, anyway.

He turned left, heading toward the nearest town in that direction. Prenticeville, some five miles away. A rundown place with only a few hundred houses and little by way of jobs or prospects. Did that explain why young men like Adam McGinty were drawn to the supposed easy money of criminal life? Yes, and no.

Regardless, at a little before 2 a.m. on a Friday night, there was still a good chance that the town's only bar – Slug's Tavern – remained open. If people wanted to stay and drink, the owner generally let them.

Six other cars remained in the parking lot of the bar when he arrived, but Peake guessed there'd be many more people inside. Five of the vehicles were big pickup trucks, beloved in this part of the country where size and macho manliness were important to so many. The other car was a tiny battered old thing. Jenn's car. A pang of guilt jostled inside Peake's gut, but he shut it down as quickly as it'd come.

He was too damn good at doing that.

Peake parked up, cracked the windows open to let some fresh air in, quickly checked the woman before heading to the bar. A burly guy stood outside. Travis. Six foot seven, 275 pounds of mostly muscle. Mostly, because over recent years the natural aging process had taken over and the simple fact was that he was past his peak as an athlete or a fighter or whatever he'd been in his early twenties.

Still, he was perfectly big enough and strong enough and well-rehearsed enough in brawling to be a good bouncer in a small town like this, where generally everyone knew each other anyway.

'Evening,' Peake said with a relaxed smile.

Travis checked his watch. 'Couldn't stay away even on your night off, huh?'

Nothing untoward about the man's reaction to seeing him. Which meant Adam hadn't arrived here bleeding, crying foul about Peake.

'Can't get enough,' Peake said, though apparently not with the right amount of sarcasm as Travis looked a little unsure for a second.

'This place? Or you mean a certain someone inside?'

Travis winked. Peake carried on past.

Loud rock music from the jukebox played inside. Boisterous chatter fought for control of the airwaves and took on a whole other level of rowdiness the moment Peake pushed open the door to go inside.

He clocked Jenn first, behind the bar. She didn't take notice. Too busy wooing a couple of bulky tattooed guys who had empty shot glasses in front of them to go along with their beers. She leaned over toward them, whiskey bottle in hand, her eye-popping cleavage resting on the bar right in front of them. She really knew how to work the tips out of these suckers. Which explained why the owner, a local businessman called Frank Booker, had her working as much as possible these days. Often on her own even on a weekend night as there simply wasn't another barwoman in this town who could compete with her, and none of the punters wanted to be served by a guy. Oh, and Frank took 50 percent of her tips, of course. Win-win. Or something like that.

Peake quickly scanned the rest of the large space in front of him. A classic small-town bar. Wood paneling. Tables, booths. Neon signs on the walls, Americana. A couple of pool tables. Which was where most of the noise was coming from. A group of about fifteen were over there – all men except for three. Rowdy, but they were enjoying themselves, at least for now.

Peake recognized most of the faces. It wasn't really the kind of town that tourists or business visitors came to. That said... a man and a woman at a booth in the far corner weren't regulars. At least not to Peake's knowledge. And as he neared the bar and caught a glimpse of their faces he realized he didn't know the two gruff-looking men who Jenn had been serving either.

She fixed him with a wide smile when she spotted him and the two guys looked his way too, clearly a little disgruntled that he'd stolen her attention.

He found a stool a few spots away from them and Jenn soon came over.

'Hey, handsome,' she said. 'Didn't expect you here tonight.'

Like Travis, she didn't seem at all rattled to see him. So Adam hadn't been in touch with his sister. Was he lying dead in the fields somewhere?

'Yeah. It's unexpected for me too.'

She leaned over toward him and he kind of wished she hadn't tonight, with eyes already on him, but still he moved forward too and kissed her cheek. Her smile widened even further, if that was possible.

The two tattooed guys looked really sullen now and turned away from the bar, beer glasses in hand, as though to signal they'd had enough of Jenn now they realized her friendliness hadn't meant she had any real interest in either of them. Their fault for being deluded in the first place.

'What're you drinking?'

He really wanted another beer, but would it do any good at this point in the night?

'Beer and a chaser, please.'

'You got it, babe.'

She fixed the drinks while Peake looked around again. No one paying him any attention. Why would they?

'You look like you've had a rough night,' Jenn said, putting a large beer and a whiskey down in front of him.

'It's not exactly gone as planned.' He downed the whiskey then sank half the beer in two big mouthfuls. 'Damn, I needed that.'

She looked at him a little dubiously. 'Something happen?'

'Kind of.'

'You wanna talk?'

Which was exactly why he'd gone to Slug's. He didn't know many people in this town well. He knew Jenn. And her brother. For good and for bad. Out of anyone here, he trusted her the most. And knew she'd help him. After all, he'd helped her out in the past. His first night here he'd pulled three drunk out-of-town bikers off of her, around the back of the bar. They'd lived, but they'd not come back to this bar, this town again.

And then the second time he'd helped her, her brother too, was...

No, he wasn't dwelling on that tonight.

'When'd you last hear from your brother?'

Immediate suspicion on her face, but he had to ask.

'Not since he went to Florida. Why?'

Peake shrugged. 'He wanted my help with something. So if you see him, tell him I can do it, yeah?'

'What's he getting you mixed up in this time?'

Peake laughed, a bit too forcedly.

'It's nothing. But...'

'But what?'

'I kind of need a place to crash,' he said.

'Kinda?'

'Not kind of. I do need a place to crash.'

'Just tonight?'

'Maybe a few nights.'

'Frank found a buyer for the farm? He didn't say.'

Frank Booker. The local businessman. He owned the bar. The farm too. The majority of every business in Prenticeville had Frank Booker's stamp on it one way or another.

'No. No buyer yet. Just... I'm not sure it's gonna work out for me there now.'

'More to handle than you thought? I could kinda tell you weren't the farming type.'

She laughed at that and the two big guys looked over momentarily, still looking disgruntled. Peake didn't respond to the joke, but he'd never pretended to be the farming type anyway. And Frank hadn't wanted that. Just someone to keep the place in some sort of shape while he worked on selling it. The house – well, the soon-to-be charred shell – had been pretty much worthless anyway but the forty acres of land had value. What Frank didn't have was the capacity to realize full value from it, nor did he have a line of interested parties to take it off of his hands. So Peake had been a bit of a go-between. Free board for him, and for Frank a part-time bouncer at the bar getting a reduced rate of pay because of the favor, plus someone to do the basics of looking after the land while he tried to figure things out. Which basically meant Peake doing what he could to not let the land go to complete shit, keeping squatters, meth-heads and the like away, while Frank worked favors with the town and county to try and get clearance for a development which would see the land value sky rocket.

Frank certainly wouldn't be pleased with how Peake's custody of his land had turned out...

'You OK in there?' Jenn asked, snapping Peake from his thoughts. He noted the even more dubious look on her face now.

'Yeah,' he said.

'You can crash at mine, if you want?'

A slight glint in her eye at that suggestion. And it wouldn't be the first time he'd stayed there with her. But that really was the last thing on his mind tonight.

'It's not... That's not gonna work this time.'

She looked more pissed than disappointed at the rejection.

'Jenn, it's not like that. But... something came up. I need to lay low. I don't want you to be involved.'

'Then why are you asking for my help?'

Fair point.

'Wait. This has something to do with Adam, right? What the hell are you two up to?'

'What about your dad's place?' Peake said, hoping she would take the bait of the change of subject.

'You want to stay in my dad's house?' Her disdain at his suggestion was clear.

'No. But... he has the stables? And the horses have gone already.'

'You'd rather sleep in a barn than with me?'

He put his hand on hers. 'That's not it. I just need somewhere quiet. Away from... anywhere. I can explain another time.'

'You're really giving off some creepy vibes right now. What are you running from?'

'I'm not running.'

'Hiding, then.'

Peake didn't say anything to that.

'You know he's outta town for a few weeks,' she said, looking around as though she expected someone was listening. 'But the house is off-limits. If you really wanna sleep in the stables...' She shrugged.

'Thank you.'

'But the fact you'd rather stay there than with me...' She shook her head at him, then responded when a group of three guys the other side of the bar signaled to her. She went off without saying another word.

Peake finished his beer. He wanted to get out of there.

'You two look pretty cozy together,' one of the burly guys at the bar said to Peake.

'Yeah.'

'Do I know you?'

'Don't think so.'

'Huh.' He turned back to his friend and the two of them leaned in to one another to whisper.

Jenn was soon done and strode back toward Peake, but the guy who'd spoken moments before reached across the bar and grabbed her wrist. Peake flinched but then remained rooted. Unless this was about to turn really ugly he didn't need any more problems tonight.

Jenn whipped her arm free and tried her best to smile and look easy.

'Another drink, fellas?'

'Yeah. Same.'

She got to it.

'What? No chit-chat this time?' the one who'd spoken to Peake said when she put the drinks down.

'And she put her tits away too. Fucking cocktease.'

Jenn, her low-cut top riding higher now than before, moved away from them and the guys followed her movement, eventually locking eyes with Peake.

'What?' the guy nearest him challenged.

Peake said nothing, just continued to glare.

'You wanna say something?'

Peake did. But he decided not to.

'Leave it, they're fine,' Jenn said, gently pulling on his arm.

'Yeah, lover boy. Do what your little bitch tells you.'

'Please,' Jenn said to him.

Peake relented. 'OK. I'll see you soon, yeah?'

She paused a moment then sighed. 'Why do I feel a little used here?'

'Sorry, Jenn, I'll explain another time. Tonight... I just need—'

'It's OK.' She leaned over and pecked his cheek. 'And when my brother surfaces, I'll tell him you're looking for him.'

'Please do.'

He saw the glint in her eye. Nothing suggestive about it. Sadness. Regret. He understood why. He wanted nothing more than to forget about the last few hours, take her out of there and wrap her up in his arms for the night.

'Can I ask you something?' he said to her, pulling himself back to grim reality and well aware the guys were still looking over.

'Shoot.'

He beckoned her closer.

'You know a man named Hardy?' he whispered. 'Local scumbag, maybe.'

She pulled back from him. He really couldn't read the look on her face. Unusual as she usually sold her feelings pretty openly.

'Do you?' he prompted.

'No,' she said. Someone else was wanting a drink, so she took the opportunity to rush off.

'Ouch, bet that hurt,' came the call from one of the two men.

Peake got up from his stool and dragged himself away from the bar and the hecklers, even though he could still hear their insults all the way to the door.

'That was quick,' Travis said as the bar door closed behind him.

Peake said nothing as he scanned the parked trucks. Not too hard to find. There was only one Chevy. He'd spotted the tattooed guy's key on top of his wallet on the bar.

'You see the two guys who arrived in that thing?' Peake said, indicating the top-of-the-range truck, a huge thing that towered over the other vehicles.

'Yeah,' Travis said.

'They're giving Jenn a hard time.'

Travis kind of snorted.

'You know them?' Peake asked.

'Know of them. Frank's doing some business with them. Apparently. Something he and McGinty had going on together.'

Thomas McGinty, Peake assumed – Adam and Jenn's father.

'What business?'

Another shrug. 'I'm just the dumb doorman.'

Except Travis was anything but dumb. He had a decent degree from a decent college, but he'd been dragged back to Prenticeville five years ago to look after his ailing mother. Here, a college degree did little for him and he took whatever money he could. Apparently he had a long-term plan, but thoughts of that were for another time.

'When'd they get here?' Peake asked.

'The bar?'

'Town.'

'A couple days ago.'

'You know anything about what business?'

'Didn't I already say?'

Kind of, though Peake hadn't been sure whether the previous response was only one of petulance.

'Like I said, they're giving Jenn a hard time. Can you do me a favor?'

'You want me to turn them over?' Travis said. 'Not sure Frank'd like that.'

'Just look out for her. Make sure she gets out of here tonight.'

'I always do.'

'Bruh! There's a girl in the back of here,' came a voice from across the parking lot.

Peake looked over to see two scrawny youngsters – early twenties perhaps – over by the bushes. One was smoking and on the lookout while the other relieved his bladder. Apparently the bush was a better option than the bar's toilet. Well... Peake had seen that place too many times, so maybe they were right.

'Hey!' Peake shouted, walking toward them.

'Seriously,' the smoker said to his friend, nudging him in the side. 'There's some woman passed out in there.'

Both moved closer to Peake's car. He glanced back to Travis as he moved. The bouncer had taken interest too, had moved a couple of steps forward.

'Get the hell away from my truck,' Peake shouted, finally getting their attention.

'You kidnap her or something?'

'Bet he's a serial killer.'

Though they both thought it was funny.

'Get outta here.'

The guys headed back to the bar as Travis approached.

'What was that?' he asked, a questioning look on his face.

Peake simply shrugged and turned his hands out.

'Remember what I said about Jenn.'

'Of course.'

Peake looked through the glass to the woman inside his truck. Still not awake. But at least now he had a place to take her to.

His gaze switched again to the Chevy. He could imagine the satisfaction of going over there. Slashing a tire. Breaking a window... He pictured the two guys spilling out of the bar in response. The brawl that would likely follow. The looks on their faces when they finally realized they'd made a big mistake. When they got what they deserved...

Tonight wasn't that night, and a part of Peake hated that fact.

'You sure you're OK?' Travis asked. But then the sound of heightened shouting from inside took his attention. Breaking glass, too. 'Shit.'

He dashed off for the bar. Peake opened the driver's door and sank down into the seat.

By the time he'd started up the engine, several people had piled out of the bar to the parking lot. No brawl there – they'd escaped whatever melee was taking place inside. Among the people who'd come out... the two men from the Chevy.

One nudged the other and both looked at Peake's truck. He reversed the truck then swung it around toward the exit. Travis emerged from the bar dragging a man with him, who he tossed to the tarmac. Another man clattered out through the door and to the ground and soon, despite Travis's efforts, the fight continued outside.

Better out than in.

Within seconds, everyone was consumed by the ruckus.

Everyone except the two men who continued to stare Peake's way.

He took a left onto Main Street and they were soon out of sight.

Although he already knew, whoever they were, he hadn't seen the last of them.

4

Peake opened his eyes but didn't move as he stared at the woman, lying there on the blanket on the floor of the otherwise empty stable. She looked strangely peaceful, content almost. The opposite of how he felt after a horrendous few hours trying – and mostly failing – to find a sleeping position that he could stay in for more than a few minutes.

At least he hadn't drank too much at the bar last night, as a hangover really would have made everything worse. Yet as he pulled himself up, his head nonetheless throbbed as though angry with him. He sighed and quickly gathered his thoughts. Peeking outside and across to the house it all still looked quiet over there. Jenn's family had owned the place for more than twenty years, but recently – ever since the death of his wife a little over two years ago – Thomas had spent more and more time on his new business ventures in California. He hadn't been seen in Prenticeville for several weeks. His long-term plan was to sell up here and move out west permanently, if he could just get out of all his business interests in the south.

He'd got rid of the horses not long after his wife had passed in a car accident. The horses were her passion, not his, apparently. The stables had been empty ever since. The large, detached home was way too big for a man who lived on his own now his kids had left.

Anyway, no one was home, and Peake saw no one else around the place – no threats to him following the events of last night. No one lurking on the road either which lay only a hundred yards away and in view from Peake's lookout.

Peake moved over to the woman. He checked her pulse. Same as before. Her drip was running low. He needed to head to the pharmacy and stock up on various supplies to help keep her alive and recuperate. The saline would be essential for now, but if she remained unconscious – in a coma? – for a prolonged period... What was his plan exactly?

He needed to find out who she was. Doing that would hopefully give him options.

He lifted her shirt and removed the dressing from the gut wound. The other major wound was high in her chest. The smaller gashes and scrapes were healing fine and wouldn't need much more treatment. What he hadn't noticed last night was the ugly bruising all over her arms, legs, and torso. Around her neck he could practically make out the indents from individual fingers.

She'd been beaten, savaged. Choked. Stabbed.

But not killed. A mistake on the part of Adam and those two clowns? Or had someone else attacked her and those three were just the grunts tasked with delivering a corpse – or not – to Peake?

He redressed the wound on her gut, then the one on her chest, then pulled her shirt back into position. The whole process, working on her like that, her oblivious, made him feel so... awkward.

Did she even realize she was still alive or in her last conscious moments had she thought herself dead?

He slumped down next to her, back against the stable wall and sighed.

'Who the hell are you?' he asked.

And he was sure he saw the slightest of twitches in her eyelid. He stared more intently... nothing at all now.

Was she dreaming?

He got up from the floor and headed for his truck.

* * *

Supplies first. He hit the pharmacy early before many other people were out and about. Next up he paid a visit to Frank's farm, first performing a drive-by from the front where there was no sign of activity at all. No people, cars, police, fire engine, anything. No noticeable smoke even from the building further afield. He drove around to the north side where a dirt track wound to within half a mile of the property. He completed the recce on foot, ending up right outside what used to be the farmhouse. Now it was just a smoldering pile of ashes. Nothing of the structure remained except for a few feet of the stone chimney, the rest of the building having collapsed into and been consumed by the fire. He saw no sign that anyone had attempted to put the flames out at any point, or that anyone had been here at all.

Which was good from two standpoints. Perhaps it meant no one had come here looking for the dead men – or Peake – yet. And secondly, Frank likely didn't yet know the house was destroyed. Peake would have a further think on what to do when the news inevitably broke.

What he didn't like was that he also found no sign of Adam. He'd half expected to find the guy's corpse not far from last night's battle. But he found nothing. He'd already cleaned up the blood around the outside of the house in the night, and he found no other trail in the daylight to show Adam's escape route. The guy had simply vanished.

He tried Adam's cell as he traveled back toward Prenticeville. It didn't even ring out, meaning the phone was likely out of juice or Adam had turned it off. Peake parked up outside the small condo building where both Adam and his sister lived. Their dad had bought them both a place when the building had first been put up a few years ago, a venture that Thomas McGinty and Frank Booker had both had a hand in and made a tidy sum of money from. Yet even after only a few years, the shoddiness of the structure was now becoming clear with patches of roof tiles missing and siding that was rotting and hanging off. Windows were severely warped – or just misfitted – with gaps big enough to fit fingers between the frames and their surroundings, some of them sloppily filled with expanding foam.

Yeah, Booker and McGinty had made a tidy sum, largely by cutting costs everywhere they could, all at the expense of the poor people who'd shelled out real money to buy the units.

Peake glanced up to the second floor as he moved across the parking lot, to the windows for Jenn's condo. Maybe she'd be there right now, still sleeping after her long shift at the bar. Unless she'd already had to make a quick turn-around to get to the diner for an extra shift and some extra cash. Either way, he saw no sign of her looking out, noticing him, which was a good thing.

He carried on to Adam's door on the ground floor and knocked lightly, not really expecting a response, and he kept his eyes busy on the outside as he waited.

Nothing.

He moved to the window and peered through. Dark inside, but he could make out the open plan living space of the studio. As messy as always but nothing looked untoward. No signs of someone who'd been shot up having come back to tend to his wounds. No sign of anyone having come looking for Adam either, the place certainly wasn't ransacked.

Peake tried the door. Locked. He could break in but saw no point. Adam wasn't there, and it didn't look like he'd been back since the fight last night. Since he'd returned from Florida with those goons? Hard to tell.

Peake didn't dwell. He walked quickly back to the truck then set off to the first of the two addresses for the dead men. They lived within five miles of each other, close to the border with Alabama. One in a town called Granton, the other in Paleridge.

Peake knew nothing about either town, but as he neared the first address in Granton, he felt he had a good read of the place. Considerably bigger than Prenticeville, Granton had everything he'd come to expect of towns in this part of the country. Which meant it had most things except real wealth and prospects. As in Prenticeville, agriculture was likely the largest industry here, but it was an industry where the national conglomerates and a few billionaires made all the money while hundreds of thousands of workers across the country did the grueling work for pennies. And there often weren't even enough of those jobs going in towns like this, which only led to further problems. Unemployment for too many. No way out of the hole for a lot of people who were often forced to turn to crime, drugs, gangs.

As for Evan Huggins and Tyler Kittle? Peake didn't know their stories yet but most likely they were low-level gang members, and the gangs around here most likely followed simple ethnic and racial lines. Peake wouldn't underestimate that if he stopped at the wrong house and asked the wrong person the wrong question... he could be in some serious shit.

Wouldn't be the first time, though, would it?

A mile away. Road after road consisted of small single-story homes, some neat and tidy but many looking seriously sorry for themselves. No center as such in the sprawling town, just basic-looking strip malls here and there with a ubiquitous choice of fast food chains and thrift shops.

He took a left and slowed the truck. Huggins's house was coming up on the right. A group of kids were throwing a baseball on the road further afield, but he otherwise saw no one about. He stopped outside the house and glanced in his rearview mirror where another vehicle had just turned into the street. A truck – a Ford, like Peake's old Ranger – but the F150 was a much bigger, newer model than his, and this one rode on rugged, oversized tires, and beefed-up suspension, hoisting the cabin a good couple of feet higher than normal.

The F150 crawled past Peake, the windows too high up for him to get a view of the occupants as it went past. It took the next right and was out of sight. And Peake was soon out of his truck and walking up the weed-covered slabs to the front door. No sounds from within the house. Peake rapped on the wood. Still nothing. No voices, footsteps, TV. He put his face closer to the grimy frosted window of the door. No movement beyond. He glanced over his shoulder to the street. The kids continued their game, not paying him any attention and he still saw no one else around.

He could break in. Wouldn't be hard. The house only had a basic three-foot fence to scale to reach the backyard. He could get around the rear and be inside within seconds. Once inside he'd search top to bottom, looking for clues to the man's life, how he knew the woman he'd brought to Peake's door, who the hell she was. Hardy, too.

Peake moved away from the door and toward the fence, but he hadn't quite made it when movement caught his attention further along the street. Just past the kids. That same Ford truck again. Pretty damn obvious it was the same one given how conspicuous it was.

Peake stood at the front of the house staring over as the truck slowly approached. Two figures up front. Any behind? Hard to tell. But the passenger window was wound down and as it came closer Peake got a good look at the faces of the two men in the front – they were kind enough to stare his way for several seconds, after all. He didn't know them. Hispanic-looking. Whether or not they knew Huggins, Peake had no clue. But the looks they gave him as they drove on past... They knew Peake didn't belong.

But neither did they. He'd figured on the way here this was a white neighborhood – the Confederate flag dotted here and there and the yard signs displaying the names of the local hard-right politicians gave it away.

So where were those two men from?

He watched the truck all the way to the end of the street where it hung on the corner a few seconds. Peake took the opportunity to dash across the front yard to his vehicle. Only when he was inside and with the engine on did the Ford turn and move out of sight once more.

Definitely a warning sign. But warning of what? Regardless, he wasn't going in that house right now, not while someone was watching.

On to the next.

Peake drove away on heightened alert, wary of every person, every vehicle that came and went. No sign of that F150 again though, and it would have been pretty damn obvious if it'd followed him.

Tyler Kittle's home, the street, the town of Paleridge, was like a mirror image of Huggins's place in Granton. In fact, the two towns had no real boundary, one merging into the other with no defining changes in the scenery. The main difference on this street? No kids playing, but there were other people about, and this place had much more of a melting point of cultures – no Confederate flags here, the minorities wouldn't stand for it. He spotted a group of three Black women with strollers heading away from him. Two Hispanic men stood smoking by a car in the opposite direction. A couple other people – white – sat in chairs on their front porches. A lot of eyes potentially on Peake here.

He couldn't decide if that made him feel more safe or more nervous.

Depended on what happened when he knocked on the door, he guessed.

He already knew the outcome here would be different as he could hear a baby crying inside. A cry which grew louder before the door opened and Peake found himself staring at a redheaded woman bouncing a baby in one arm.

'Good morning—'

'What do you want?' she demanded, clearly not happy about the intrusion.

A quick check over his shoulder. No one watching. Not overtly, anyway.

'You're Tyler's wife.'

The woman snorted. 'You a cop?'

'No.'

'He in trouble?'

He's in several pieces, being nibbled on by critters.

'He's not answering his phone, but you know what he's like,' Peake said with a chortle. The woman merely glared at him.

'Where you from?' she asked.

'Prenticeville.'

'Don't sound like it.'

'England. A long time ago.'

'That fits... Will you be quiet a minute!' She turned her glare to the baby who immediately turned his volume down a few notches at the barked instruction.

'Sorry, I'll get out of your hair,' Peake said. 'I just needed an address from Tyler.' Peake went to turn away.

'What address?'

He faced her again. 'I got some cash I need to get to Hardy. You know, for some errands we were running. Only Tyler didn't give me his address.'

Nothing from the woman now, the look on her face cold and hard.

'You know Hardy?' Peake asked.

She shook her head but didn't say anything.

'No? Then I'm sorry to have wasted your time. You have a good day.'

'Yeah. You too. What did you say your name was?'

'When you see him, just tell him Simon came by.'

He moved away, back to his truck, but hadn't made it before he spotted the police car coming his way. No lights or sirens, it crawled toward him and he already knew he was the target before it slowed to a stop right by his door. The window wound down to reveal a balding, heavily tanned officer wearing big aviator sunglasses. Peake scanned the car. Morrison County. The next county along from Fallcreek where he lived. Kind of lived. But where he knew the majority of the cops, at least in his neighborhood. Here he didn't have a clue about them, nor them about him.

'How are you doing, sir?' the officer asked.

'Very well, thank you.'

A pleasant, relaxed start.

The officer put his car in park and shut the engine down and stepped out.

'Is something wrong?' Peake asked.

'Is there?'

Peake looked back to the house where Tyler's wife remained with the now quiet baby, as though he too was interested to see where this was going.

'Fallcreek,' the cop said, after a quick look at Peake's license plate.

'That's me.'

'What brought you over this way?'

'Work. Sorry, is there a reason you—'

'Sir, I need to see your license and registration, please.'

Which Peake could have stood and argued against, but what would be the point? For whatever reason this cop had targeted him and the best thing to do was to play along. Had someone on this street called them? Why would they?

Peake gave the officer what he'd asked for and he went back to his car and on to his radio to check the details. He came back to Peake's side less than two minutes later.

'Did I check out?' Peake asked, taking back his documents.

'Where you from?' the cop asked. 'And don't say Prenticeville.'

'England.'

'Thought so. You're a long way from home.'

'England hasn't been home for a long time.'

'Still.'

Still what?

'Why you over here harassing people?' he asked.

'Harassing? I—'

'You were over at Granton, snooping, now over here.'

Peake didn't say anything. Those guys in the truck? Had they called the police? That didn't fit with the type of people he'd assumed them to be at all.

'He told me he's working with Tyler,' the woman shouted over.

'That right?' the cop asked Peake. 'And what kinda work would that be?'

'He said he was looking for some fella. Hardy, was it?'

He really wished she'd shut the hell up.

'Hardy?' the cop asked.

'You know someone by that name?' Peake asked.

Although the flash in his eyes when Tyler's wife had said the name had already given that answer away.

'You can leave the questions to me,' the cop said, then stared at Peake for several seconds, holding his eye, as though waiting on Peake to say something in response. 'Probably time for you to get back home now.'

'Prenticeville or England?' Peake said with a smile on his face that wasn't reciprocated at all. 'You know what, I'm not even sure this guy was called Hardy. Could have been Harry, Haversham. I still sometimes have a hard time understanding your accents.'

The cop said nothing.

'And like you said, you don't know anyone called Hardy, right?'

'Did I say that?' the officer responded.

Silence. A standoff. After a few seconds Peake relented and nodded and moved over to his door and grabbed the handle.

'And if you come back this way again, asking about... anything, just know I'll be watching you.'

Peake said nothing more as he sank down into his seat, fired up the engine and set off.

Hardly a treasure trove of new information from the two house visits, but one thing he did know – both Tyler's wife and that cop knew Hardy.

Whoever the hell he was.

5

The sun was too damn hot, his skin prickled with heat, and he probably should have put more lotion on top of his head which seemed to attract the sun's rays more than any other part of his body, but Lance Hardy didn't really care. He would only stay out here a few more minutes and those few minutes would be time well spent, because sitting here by the edge of the pool he got to watch Ivanka's ridiculously sexy figure glide up and down the water. And, as usual, she'd chosen to take her morning swim wearing nothing but her goggles. For his benefit, obviously. She just kept going. Lap after lap. Front crawl, where his eyes fixed on the rise of her buttocks. Breaststroke where he watched her legs parting over and over. Backstroke where her nipples pointed up to the sky, enticing, like two—

'Boss.'

'What!' he slammed, sitting up in the lounger and spinning around to see Wyatt standing by the open patio door.

'Sorry,' Wyatt said, looking down at the ground, rubbing at his straggly beard like he often did, the way a kid toyed with a comforter. He was tough as nails, but that damn beard and the way he played with it irritated the hell out of Hardy. 'You told me to get you at ten.'

Hardy looked at his watch and sighed. Time up.

'You don't have to avert your eyes,' Hardy said to Wyatt, who was looking anywhere but at the pool. 'She won't turn you to stone.'

He turned back to his wife who hadn't yet taken any notice, although as Hardy got to his feet she looked up at him and then came to a stop at the edge of the pool facing him. She lifted her goggles up.

'You're going?' She sounded disappointed.

'Not for long. You carry on. You didn't get that figure by accident.' He winked at her and she smiled that dirty little smile that sent a rush through his groin.

'He can stay and watch if he likes,' she said.

'I... I...'

'Jesus, Wyatt, this is why you don't have an Ivanka in your life,' Hardy said. 'You have to win a woman like that.' He glanced back at Ivanka. 'And he's coming with me.'

'Shame,' she said, pulling her goggles back over her eyes. 'I was about to do some diving.'

Dammit. When she bent over the edge of the pool right in front of him...

'Come on,' he said, nudging Wyatt as he pulled himself away and toward the house. 'You can put your tongue back in your damn mouth now too.'

Despite his hard words, he was smiling as he spoke. He didn't care if guys ogled his wife. What was the point in having a woman on his arm who could have been a Miss World contender if no one got to see her? He'd happily have her walk around naked all the time. No man would ever have her apart from him. He knew it and she knew it.

Hardy sucked in the cool conditioned air as he stepped inside, and a cascade of goosebumps swept over his moist skin. A nice sensation, but he wouldn't get to enjoy it for long. They walked through to the east wing of the house – the guest annex – where a side entrance exited to a quaint manicured yard. Apparently the previous owners of the 12,000 square foot home had housed the mother-in-law over at this side of the property. Hardy rarely used the space, but Ivanka wanted him to turn it into a private health spa. And he would. If he gave her what she wanted, she always responded in kind. It's why they worked so well together.

Hardy and Wyatt continued across the yard and through a gate and into an open field, the barn 200 yards away from their destination, where Hardy spotted two big pickup trucks parked and four men standing around waiting, chatting. His men. They stood to attention as he approached and gave a series of acknowledgments that their boss had arrived.

'Where are they?' Hardy asked the biggest and ugliest of the group. Lyle.

'Still in the tank.'

'And my babies?'

'Hungry as hell.'

Hardy smiled. The beasts were always hungry as hell.

Jarrard, the youngest but probably bulkiest, opened the barn door and Hardy strode through and over to the cages in the corner where Rita and Sid roamed. They saw him coming and their little tails wagged like helicopter rotors.

'Good morning, my beauties,' he said, crouching down to the dogs who jumped up against the wire of the cages, panting and sticking their tongues through the gaps to try and lick him. Seeing them like this anyone would think the Bullies were the kindest, calmest, most caring of animals. And they were. Until Hardy needed them not to be.

Training. Dogs needed good training.

Just like people did, really.

He turned and walked away from the dogs, toward the hatch in the ground in the center of the barn, below which sat a concrete shell a near perfect ten-foot cube. He'd no idea who put it there, or why. Air raid shelter? Nuclear bunker? Storage space? It didn't really work well for any of those purposes given its small size and lack of staircase, electricity, anything.

Perhaps the last owner, some rich landowner from Arizona, had a strange fetish for locking people down there. Perhaps he'd secretly been a serial killer.

Or perhaps those dark thoughts were only prominent because of what Hardy used the place for.

The tank, he called it.

'Open up,' he said to Lyle.

The ugly bastard heaved and the metal hatch opened with a hefty scrape. Hardy and the others crowded around the edge, looking down into the dark space below where two figures hesitantly looked up, hands to their faces to shield from the sudden influx of light.

'How's it going?' Hardy asked them with a chuckle.

'P-please,' one of the captives said before mumbling, pleading, which Hardy didn't want to hear so he shut himself off from it.

'Get them both outside,' Hardy said before turning and heading to the exit. He pushed open the creaky wooden door and stepped back out into the sunshine. He looked out over the huge field. The Arizona guy had held livestock here. Hardy used it for sport. A unique kind of sport.

Moments later the two naked captives were brought out and tossed to the dirt ground. The dogs were brought out too. Jarrard had Rita on the leash, Nate had Sid. No wagging tails now – the dogs pulled and barked and gnashed their teeth. They knew what was coming.

'Easy,' Hardy said with a chuckle.

The muscles on both men's arms rippled as they did what they could to hold the dogs in place. Both were big guys. Each over six foot, over 250 pounds. But the dogs were big too. Jarrard at least had it slightly easier with the female Rita, at a little over a hundred pounds, but Sid was a true beast and nearly half the size and weight again. Still a lot less than the men holding them, but the dogs were quite simply pure animal, built for purpose: strength, aggression.

And the two men in the dirt knew it. Hardy could see the fear in their eyes. Heck, the dogs could smell it, which was why they were so hyped up.

'On your knees,' Hardy said to the prisoners. With their hands cable-tied behind their backs it wasn't the easiest maneuver for them to pull themselves up from the dirt and Hardy's guys naturally laughed and smirked and heckled, only making the process all the more humiliating.

Good.

'You've had plenty of time to think down in the tank,' Hardy said to them. 'So now it's time to—'

He stopped, cut off by more pleading and begging.

He held a hand up and left it there until the men got the message.

'I don't wanna hear another word until you're told to speak.'

Nothing. Hardy used the silence to take a good look at the two men in front of him. Two men who he knew a lot more about now than he had two days ago when they'd first been brought here and dumped underground.

Je'Von Evans, Carl Brogan. Carl was a loser in his late twenties who'd spent several years behind bars for various misdemeanors. A parasitic loser, basically. With what Hardy knew of him, and looking at him in the flesh... the guy simply had no redeeming qualities.

Je'Von, on the other hand...

The Black guy was six four, maybe six five and had a body that looked like it had been chiseled by gods. He should have been a college football star, or a track and field champion. Instead, at only twenty years old, he'd just fucked up his entire life.

'You know who I am?' Hardy asked them.

Head shakes, no answers.

'You can talk when I ask you a question. Do you know who I am?'

'N... no.'

'No, sir.' A more resolute answer from Je'Von who, despite his obvious fear, could at least hold Hardy's eye when he spoke to him.

'Do you like dogs?'

'W-what?'

'Dogs. Those things right there. Four legs, wagging tails, big teeth. Do you like them?'

One no, one yes. The answers didn't really matter much.

'I like dogs,' Hardy said. 'You know why? Because with the right training, you can get a dog to do whatever you want. You get it right, they obey their masters 100 percent. I only wish all humans were the same. Take you two, for example. Just like anyone else in this world, you had chances. Chances to do something good, productive with your lives. You fucked it all up instead. Why? Because you had no one telling you, training you otherwise.'

'We're sorry!' Je'Von said desperately, though he didn't yet know desperate.

'You don't even know what you're apologizing for yet. We're still talking about dogs. Now these two? American Bullies. XL Bullies, to be more specific because... Well, I think it's obvious, right? You know anything about this breed?'

Head shakes.

'They're fighters. I don't like dog fighting, but these animals, they're built for it. Pounds and pounds of pure muscle. Jaws strong enough to crush bones. And all that strength comes with a never-say-die attitude. If these guys were human, they'd be decorated Marines, damn sure of it. But you know what?'

Apparently not.

'They can also be the kindest, most caring dogs, if you know how to handle them. I know how, and so do my guys. Unfortunately, today, you won't see the loving, caring side of my dogs.'

Carl whimpered. Je'Von's eyes were wide with fear as he stared at Rita, her teeth bared.

'So let's talk about why you're here. You know that jewelers you robbed?'

No response.

'Do. You. Remember. Robbing that jewelers, you dirty stinking runts?'

Nods now.

'It belonged to my cousin, Alon.'

More head shaking, more mumbling. The men glanced at each other as though looking for an indication of what to say or do.

Hardy laughed. A couple of his guys did too even though he hadn't yet explained the joke.

'Come on, guys. My cousin, Alon? Do I look like a Jew to you?'

Je'Von and Carl looked really confused now.

'Of course he ain't my damn cousin! But do you know what he is?'

No. They didn't. They had no idea where this was going. Perhaps if they'd realized sooner they wouldn't be in this mess.

'Alon is a man who owes me a lotta money.'

'Please, we didn't know,' Je'Von said.

'Well that's pretty fucking obvious. And it's also a big problem. Alon owes me half a mil. The idiot wasn't making his insurance payments, and now his business is destroyed, and the guy is as broke as you two. So I have to ask myself, who's gonna get me my 500 g? Alon? Or you two?'

He got no response.

'Don't take too long, gentlemen, we're all cooking out here. So are you two gonna get 500 grand for me? Or do I need to hope that Alon gets his shit back together sometime soon?'

'F... five hundred thousand?' Carl said. 'But... we ain't got that.'

'You don't say? So back to my previous question. Where's my 500 grand coming from? You two or Alon?'

They stammered and they looked at each other several times but neither could come up with a good answer. Any answer.

'And that, my friends, is the problem. Even now he's broke, Alon's a better bet for me than you two, don't you think?'

Still nothing intelligible from Carl and Je'Von.

Hardy turned to Wyatt and nodded. Wyatt slipped behind the two men and cut the ties on their wrists.

'Don't get too excited, gentlemen. You're not in the clear yet, but I will give you a fighting chance at least.'

Not really. But it'd still be fun to watch.

'On your feet.' The naked men pulled themselves up. 'You see that fence?'

Hardy pointed behind them and both men looked that way.

'It's about... two, three hundred yards away. You get to it. And when you do, climb over, and continue running as far away from here as you can. You'll be free men.'

Hardy checked his watch. The men didn't move.

'Get to it! Your time's ticking and the dogs can't wait much longer for their morning run.'

Je'Von moved first, Carl a couple of seconds behind.

'Shit, look at him go,' Wyatt said.

And he was right. Je'Von looked like a damn Olympian, striding away. Within ten seconds he'd covered twice the distance of Carl who stumbled about, looking behind him every other step rather than concentrating on his freedom.

'Now?' Jarrard asked.

'Not yet,' Hardy said, focusing on Je'Von. Twenty years old. What a damn waste. Definitely an athlete. Two hundred years ago, around here, he would have been a slave. Hardy could have worked him so hard. He'd have been the most productive Black man in the state of Georgia. But... where was the fun in that? No, this guy should have been a gladiator in the Colosseum or somewhere like that. That way not only were his talents properly monetized, but it was simply a whole lot more fun to watch too.

'Boss?' Jarrard asked through gritted teeth, digging his heels in the dirt as Rita yelped and snarled and yanked repeatedly on the leash.

'Now,' Hardy said.

No sooner had he said it and the two dogs were released, and they bounded away across the field. Not the quickest dogs – they were way bulkier than spritely breeds like greyhounds, but they were still a lot faster than the men, even Je'Von.

Both men up front knew it too. The incoming hounds seemed to give Carl added impetus and for a few seconds he sped up some. Je'Von, on the other hand, completely lost his stride. He practically stopped, turned around to face the onrushing dogs. He waved his arms about, shouted at them as though he could scare them off that way.

Hardy's men were in hysterics.

Hardy was disappointed. He'd really thought Je'Von might make it. Carl closed the distance before Je'Von found a second wind. Then he was off again. Even faster than before, and Carl was going slower than ever now, all puffed out – it looked like he was running through treacle.

'He's actually gonna make it!' Wyatt said.

He meant Je'Von, because the next second Sid leaped through the air and caught Carl's upper left arm and dragged his prey down like a lion taking down a wildebeest. Dirt burst as dog and man tumbled. Rita joined in the fun, pouncing on Carl's neck and gnashing down.

Carl squealed like a pig. Cried out in pain and horror. Je'Von was all of fifteen yards from the fence.

'Go on, boy,' Hardy willed.

A couple of seconds later and Je'Von jumped up the fence, grasping the top. Then his body kind of froze a second before spasming, and even at distance Hardy thought he could hear and feel the pop and fizzle of electricity before Je'Von collapsed back down to the ground. A cacophony of laughter erupted as Je'Von's body twitched in the dirt.

Closer to them, Carl's pleading had quietened down. He was sucking his last breaths as the dogs continued to tear at him.

'Boss, there's someone here for you.'

A meek voice from behind Hardy.

'I told you, don't let anyone disturb m—'

Hardy stopped himself when he turned to see Lyle standing next to a smartly dressed man. Ridley. Not one of Hardy's guys. And not someone who was really welcome here either.

'Not to disturb you?' Ridley suggested, just those few words revealing the accent that agitated Hardy so much. Almost as much as the man's face. Clean cut, line free – everything about this guy was so damn... nice. On the surface. 'And why's that, Lance? You don't want people seeing your little hunting session?'

'What are you doing here?'

'Who are the two poor guys?'

Hardy looked back to the field. Je'Von's body lay crumpled on the ground. Carl was now silent. He was dead.

'Get the dogs back here,' Hardy said to Jarrard, who blew his whistle in response.

The dogs reluctantly pulled their mouths away from the flesh to look over, showing Jarrard had their attention.

'Come!' Jarrard shouted out.

And as soon as the word had left his lips the dogs raced back toward him. Quite a feat to get any dog to leave behind a kill when they had the taste of fresh blood in their mouths. But these dogs... these dogs knew. Forgoing their feed was a far better prospect than the beating they'd otherwise receive for disobedience.

Rita and Sid were soon back over, tails wagging, blood-dripping tongues hanging out of their panting mouths as Jarrard and Nate put the leashes back on.

'Gruesome,' Ridley said.

'Let's go inside,' Hardy said to him.

'Boss, what about Je'Von?' Wyatt asked.

Hardy stared back across the field once more. The guy's body continued to twitch, and not just because of an ongoing reaction to the electric shock, Hardy didn't think. He was trying to move.

'Put him back in the tank. See if he recovers. If he does, there must be something we can use a guy like that for.'

'Brutal yet resourceful,' Ridley said, quite snidely. 'A winning combination in my eyes.'

'Yeah, but who gives a fuck what gets you off?'

Hardy pushed past him and into the barn.

6

Hardy headed through the barn and out the other side, but paused in his step as he looked to the newly arrived black sedan, outside of which a man and a woman stood, staring at him. Like Ridley they were dressed in office wear, although he knew these were no accountants.

'You brought some muscle?' Hardy asked Ridley, who came up by his side.

'Muscle? I don't do muscle. But they're with me, yeah. Just balancing out the numbers a bit.'

He looked around at Hardy's entourage, a little accusatory. Although Hardy didn't quite know what he was being accused of.

'They stay out here,' Hardy said.

'I wasn't suggesting otherwise.'

'Let's go to my office.'

So they did. Just the two of them for this. Wyatt hung around somewhere outside the room. Hardy thought about offering his guest a drink, but that might imply the guy was more welcome here than he really was.

'You know by now that we have a problem, right?' Ridley said.

Hardy pondered before answering. Of course the answer was yes, but he had a difficult time admitting that things hadn't turned out as planned – particularly as he didn't know why or how things had gone wrong. Did Ridley? Probably. Hardy didn't know Ridley well, and what he did know he didn't like, but the guy certainly seemed to have tentacles that reached into all sorts of dark corners of society.

'Yes. I know.'

'Good. That's a good first step.' That damn accent and that damn smile. He clearly thought he was so superior to Hardy. 'So tell me what happened.'

'I don't know yet.'

'Then tell me what you do know.'

Hardy narrowed his eyes as he glared at Ridley, trying to figure out how much he'd say. The problem was the balance here was uneven. Ridley simply knew a lot more about Hardy than Hardy did about Ridley, and every conversation felt like a trap, as though this guy was testing how much of the truth Hardy would reveal.

From what he'd been told, and the little extra he'd gleaned from the digging he'd had more than one private investigator do, Ridley worked as a freelance security consultant. What that basically meant, as far as Hardy figured, was that Ridley was paid by the likes of the CIA to do dirty shit that agencies like that didn't want to do themselves over fear of the public backlash if such events got out.

Hardy despised men like Ridley. Men who truly sat above laws. The big problem was that Ridley had Hardy over a barrel. The only reason Hardy was a free man right now was because of this man, and the fact he'd buried evidence of some of Hardy's... overseas operations. For his own personal benefit, of course. But it meant Hardy owed him. He hated owing anyone.

Sooner or later he'd turn the tables. He was sure of it.

'I'm waiting,' Ridley said.

'What do you want me to say? You asked me to do a hit, make the body disappear. So I had my guys do the hit. You said I'd get paid once that happened. But I haven't been paid.'

'I thought we'd got past this point already,' Ridley said. 'Because where are your guys now?'

Hardy said nothing.

'You haven't a clue, have you?'

Hardy hadn't heard from them in over two days. So yeah, he knew something had gone wrong. He just had no idea what. How did Ridley know any of this?

'She's disappeared, hasn't she?' Hardy said. 'So now you owe me.'

Ridley smiled and nodded. What the hell did he have to smile about?

'What are you doing to resolve this situation?' Ridley asked.

'Until I find out what happened to my guys, what else am I supposed to do?'

'I heard the car they traveled in was last seen approaching the town of Prenticeville in Georgia. It's where Adam McGinty is from. He's one of your guys, isn't he?'

'No, he isn't. I've never met him. He's just a guy who works with my guys.'

'So you've no idea why they went there?'

'I've never even heard of that place.'

And he genuinely had no idea before now that Kittle and Huggins had headed up there. What the hell were they doing? He also had no idea how Ridley knew this. He wouldn't ask either, as it'd only confirm to Ridley that he was more in the know and Hardy hated that fact.

'I'd suggest you concentrate your search up there,' Ridley said. 'Make sure there's no unexpected hiccups.'

'Thanks for telling me how to do my job.'

'It's a shame I need to, but you have to understand this isn't just about me and you. There's more at play here and—'

'And you're gonna tell me all about what's really at play?'

Silence from Ridley. Of course the guy had no intention of revealing to Hardy who was paying him or why.

'Perhaps... you'd allow me to tell you a little story,' Ridley said.

'No. I wouldn't. Your stories suck ass.'

This guy sure liked the sound of his own voice. Every damn time they met. Hardy really didn't.

Ridley shrugged. 'If you'll allow me the courtesy? And then we can get back to discussing the most important matter here. Important to you, anyway, which is how and when you'll get paid. Because right now, you're getting nothing from me.'

'I'll hear your story,' Hardy said, clenching his fists as hard as he could.

He'd use the time to think of ways of slicing this guy up.

'Did I ever tell you about where I grew up?'

'Some shitty little town in England.'

He looked genuinely offended by the derogatory tone of Hardy's voice.

'Oxfordshire, to be precise, and it really wasn't that shitty. It's in the Cotswolds, which is really beautiful if you ever get a chance to visit.'

'I won't.'

'Back to the story. It's a nice town, but that doesn't mean everyone was nice. Like any place, there were good kids and bad kids. Quiet kids, loud kids. Kind kids, bullies—'

'OK, yeah, kids, kids, kids. You're into kids. Doesn't surprise me. Is that the story?'

'No. It's about one particular kid I knew. Elliott Savage.'

Ridley paused as though the name was supposed to mean something to Hardy. He was pretty sure it didn't. After all, this douchebag was the only Brit he knew.

'What does that name conjure to you?'

'Elliott Savage?'

Ridley nodded.

'It's a decent name. Savage.'

'Violence?'

'Yeah.'

'Except Elliott Savage was a nice boy. Kind, unassuming. But people teased the hell out of his name, because... it was almost like everyone wanted him to be savage. He got relentlessly bullied. Kids, older and younger, would try to pick fights with him all the time and he always came off worse. But then something happened.'

Another pause.

OK, Hardy was a little bit intrigued. 'What?'

'Puberty.'

Hardy scoffed. 'This story...'

Ridley shrugged. 'The point is, when puberty hit, little Elliott Savage wasn't so little anymore. He was a naturally big bugger...' Hardy had a passing thought about Je'Von. Some people were simply physically gifted. 'Elliott probably should have taken up rugby because he certainly had the physique for it. But he didn't. And despite his size, he still got teased, still got bullied, because he was such a pushover. A bit dim, if you ask me. And then... one day everything changed.'

'He fought back? Great story. Let's move on.'

'Fought back?' Ridley laughed, for way too long. What was this guy on? 'It was a bit more than fighting back. One morning before school, Elliott Savage used a kitchen knife to gut his own dad. Then he went into school and gutted a teacher and two of his classmates, and wounded another five in a rampage. He killed four people in the space of twenty minutes and if he hadn't been so dim-witted would probably have killed a lot more.'

'So?'

'You're not shocked by that?'

'I never met him, so no.'

'And this is all true, by the way. Elliott Savage. You can look him up.'

'Why would I do that?'

'Obviously this guy turned out psychotic, right? But he was only fifteen, so he went to a young offenders prison. Not exactly high security. Within his first year there he'd killed two inmates, and very nearly killed a guard too. Brawls that got out of hand, apparently. People still testing him, I believe. As soon as they could he was moved to an adult prison and he's been there ever since. Solitary confinement mostly because... the guy is a savage, after all.'

Ridley laughed. Hardy didn't find it funny.

'Remind me why I should care?'

Ridley shrugged. 'It's just a story. I'm just highlighting to you how reputations can precede people.'

'He didn't have a reputation before he went on a murder spree. The kid flipped because he was a head case.'

'No, I don't believe that. I think he finally fit into the space where people had always expected him to be. Savage by name, savage by nature. But he was forced down that path because it's what everyone thought he should be.'

'I still don't get your point.'

'Take you, for example. Lance Hardy. Your name... People only whisper your name around these parts because so many people are frightened of you. You've really done well to carve this role of ruthless demigod in this backwater shithole.'

Was this guy flattering him? Hard to tell.

'And I've seen some of the brutal shit you do. I mean, literally just minutes ago, that was some show.'

'Thank you.'

'So your reputation isn't just built on your name, it's your actions. What it comes down to? You're not a guy to mess with, right? That's why you do these things, so that you keep your place at the top, so nobody dares challenge you.'

Was that a question?

'I applaud you, Lance,' Ridley said with an almost silent clap.

'Thank you.'

'Your problem here is that you don't know my reputation. And why is that?'

Hardy didn't answer, because he wasn't sure how to.

'You don't know my reputation because I do everything I can to keep details of my life quiet. I'm not like you. I don't need to be seen to be brutal. It doesn't help me in my job, my life.' Ridley leaned forward and the snide smirk on his face disappeared, and his features took on a far more sinister edge. Hardy felt it, and it really wasn't pleasant. 'But believe me, Lance, whatever your reputation, if I need to crush you, then I will fucking crush you, and everyone in your life too. Your beautiful wife? – and she really is stunning – I'll tear the skin from her gorgeous body before I cut her head off in front of you. I'll get your own dogs to chew the flesh off your limbs and I'll keep you alive long enough to make sure you see it all, feel it all. I'll—'

'I think you've made your point.'

Ridley relaxed, the darkness in his eyes falling away. That damn smirk came back. Hardy still hated it with a passion, though he'd be lying if he said Ridley's little speech – the images conjured – hadn't made his insides twitch just a little.

'I'm glad,' Ridley said. 'So, shall we get back to business?'

'Let's get this over and done with.'

'Tell me what you know,' Ridley said.

'I already did. You asked me for a hit. My guys did it.'

'Who have now disappeared. Which makes me think... us both think, something has gone wrong.'

Hardy held his tongue.

'I've given you the lead,' Ridley said. 'Prenticeville. Get your men up there. Find out what happened. Clean up whatever mess there is to clean up.'

Hardy still said nothing.

'The reason I involved you in this is because I thought you were capable of something so simple, and because you're far enough removed that it made sense.'

Hardy gritted his teeth.

'You don't know her,' Ridley continued. 'You don't know what it means for her to be dead. But believe me, if any backlash from this reaches me... Just remember what I told you about reputations.'

Ridley stood up and smoothed down his nicely fitted clothes.

Hardy said nothing more in response before Ridley turned and ever so calmly headed out.

7

Peake made no more stops on the way back to Prenticeville. He'd already left the woman on her own for too long and as he approached the McGinty family home his anxiety levels ramped up. Had someone found her? Taken her? Killed her?

Had she simply passed away from his lack of care?

No cars on the property. A good first sign.

As he pushed open the stable door, he found her in exactly the same position as he'd left her in, lying on the pockmarked concrete.

He moved over. She was still breathing.

He sighed in relief and set about refilling her drip. The dressings would likely last a few more hours so he left those in place. Soon after, he was drifting to sleep, the heat of the stable and the non-stop day – and night – finally catching up with him.

Not a restful sleep, as it turned out, the hard floor providing no comfort, and after shifting positions several times to try to find something that worked he abruptly woke up, his whole body jolting, his eyes springing open.

OK. Maybe he'd been deeper than he realized, but something had roused him. Spooked him.

It only took a few seconds for his brain to recover and realize what it was.

Noise. Outside. A car. Someone was coming.

Peake checked over his handgun then slipped it into the back of his jeans before he crept to the door. He opened it a quarter inch to peer out.

Certainly not an all guns blazing attack, which Peake had feared and been ready for. The single vehicle that approached was a banged-up little thing. A Mitsubishi something or other. Silver paint peeling, cracked windshield, wheels that looked shopping-cart small.

Jenn's car.

Peake removed his gun and hid it under his backpack and took one last look at the woman – still unmoving – before he stepped out into the dwindling daylight.

'You weren't kidding,' Jenn said, closing the car door behind her. Even though she'd put some effort into doing so it clunked against the frame and remained ajar, something not fitting or catching properly. She glared at the car for good measure, showing her disapproval.

'Kidding?' Peake said.

'About sleeping in the stable. I thought maybe you'd had one too many last night.'

'No. I wasn't kidding. Like I said, I needed a place to stay. So thank you. For offering.'

'I didn't offer. I think you kinda talked me into it.'

Jenn closed the distance to him, her eyes searching the area around Peake as though she still didn't fully understand something. He pulled away from the door to meet her and gave her an awkward hug before she locked eyes on the stable once more.

'I know something's going on,' she said.

Peake said nothing.

'Is it because of—'

'It's nothing that involves you.'

'Except the part about you staying in my dad's stable block.'

Peake laughed. She didn't appreciate it.

'Seriously, though. I'm not having it. Frank gave me the night off. After the shit last night I really needed a break.'

He reached forward and touched her arm and she seemed to lift a little. 'What happened?'

'Those men at the bar last night—'

'The meatheads?'

'Meatheads? They were just regular guys enjoying a few beers, until you showed.'

'Did they hurt you?'

He'd asked Travis to look out for her, but—

'No, that's not what I meant,' she said her face souring. 'By the time the police had gone—'

'The police?'

'You didn't see the fight?'

'Not much of it. What happened?'

'Just the usual.' She said that so casually, like the police turning up on a Friday night was entirely the norm. 'I don't know who called them, but it was all over by the time they arrived. But it killed the night. Everyone left.'

'Including those two men?'

'They were gone by the time I'd locked up with Travis.'

'But you said they were giving you a hard time.'

'Did I?'

Hadn't she?

'They were pretty interested in you after you'd gone,' she said. 'Asking me all sorts of questions about who you are. Where you're from. Where you're staying.'

'And what did you tell them?'

He hadn't meant to say that with such a hard tone and her face took on a less friendly look in response.

'I didn't tell them anything. Told them it was none of their business. I certainly didn't tell them you'd turned up to ask for a place to crash. That you'd turned up asking me if I knew about some guy called Hardy.'

'So you never told them that name?'

'No, why—'

'And they never mentioned it to you?'

'No!'

'Thank you.'

'But are you gonna tell me what's going on now?'

'You really don't want to know.'

'Then why the hell do you think I'm asking?'

'I don't know those guys. Or why they were interested in me.'

'And my brother? Where does he fit into all this?'

'He doesn't.'

'I don't believe you.'

'I'm not lying.'

'But you're not telling me everything either, are you?'

'No. Not exactly.'

She rubbed at her eyes as though trying to force her doubts away or bury something painful.

'Forget about it,' she said. 'I only came by to let you know I have the night off.'

She surely could have called to say that, so he didn't fully believe the explanation. She'd come over to check on him. But he wouldn't question her further. The less said about his problems the better.

'You want to do something?' he asked.

'Yeah.'

'I'm guessing a night at Slug's isn't your preferred choice.'

She laughed. 'Never. Why don't... I'm pretty tired. We can get takeout and chill at my place.' She burst out laughing before he could respond. 'Jesus, that sounded so desperate. But I mean it. I want to chill. I just kinda need some company.'

'We can do that. I'll follow you over and get the food on the way.'

She smiled and looked over his shoulder to the stable one more time before heading back to her car.

* * *

They chilled for a while. Ate the pizza, drank the wine. They chatted. Banal stuff. Fun stuff.

They ended up in her bed. Whether or not that was the intention didn't really matter. Both were happy, both were content.

Peake didn't sleep well, though. Even if her place was nicely air-conditioned, his mind was all over the place with thoughts of the mystery woman in the stable, alone through the night.

He was fully awake an hour before sunrise. The room was faintly lit by the sliver of light coming in from the hall through the partially open door. She always slept like that, she said. She didn't like being on her own. Didn't like the darkness. He knew why.

He turned over onto his side to face her and watched her a few moments. She stirred, opened her eyes and her lips turned up in a satisfied smile.

'Is it morning?'

'Not quite.'

'Then why are you awake?'

He didn't answer.

'You're leaving?' she asked.

'I need to.'

'Why?'

'I have... to...'

'You can't even think of a good lie, can you?'

'I don't want to lie to you.'

He leaned over and pecked her lips.

'I wish you'd just let me in,' she said.

'You think you want that. But you don't.'

She shuffled up in the bed, a little more awake, a little more enthused, a little more angry.

'You know my darkest secrets,' she said. 'I've laid my scars out to you. Every last damn shitty thing that's happened in my shitty life, all of my vulnerabilities, you know about.'

'I know, and—'

'And... even after everything you've done for me... I still know so little about you.'

'You know enough. You don't want to know the rest.'

'How do you know?'

'Just trust me.'

'Trust you?' she scoffed.

He held her eye and eventually she slumped a little.

'I'm sorry,' she said.

'You don't need to be.'

'The thing is... I thought I'd be happier now. I thought after... you know, that I could move on. Have a better life.'

'You will.'

'When?'

He had no answer to that.

'Because the scars up here—' she tapped her temple '—are just as ugly as ever.'

He certainly knew a thing or two about that.

He reached out and put both arms around her and brought her closer, and they lay there for several minutes, their bodies intertwined, their heartbeats and their breathing in unison, calm and rhythmic.

She pulled away first.

'I thought you had to go.'

'I do.'

He kissed her on the cheek then got up from the bed and pulled on his clothes. She hadn't moved by the time he finished dressing.

'Last night was good,' he said. 'Exactly what I needed.'

'Better than sleeping alone in a stable, you mean? Yeah, I don't think I had to do too much to beat that.'

He smiled but didn't respond.

'But you did say it'd only be a for a few days.'

'I did.'

'And what about after that?'

'I don't know yet.'

'You're gonna leave town though, aren't you?'

'What makes you say that?'

'Just putting some of the pieces together.'

He sat down on the edge of the bed and took her hand in his.

'I'll do what I can to change your mind,' she said. 'Because I don't want you to leave. But it'd help to know what you're running from first.'

He kissed her forehead then left her there without saying another word.

* * *

'You goddamn piece of shit,' he said to himself as he drove away, back out of Prenticeville toward the McGinty home. He'd said it repeatedly. He hated the feeling that he was using Jenn. He wasn't using her, but it felt like it. And it must have really felt like it to her.

'You stupid damn idiot.'

And walking out of there like that, not even saying a goodbye or 'have a good day.'

'Yeah, because "have a good day" is exactly what a woman wants to hear after you've spent several hours in the night having sex with her.'

He shook his head in disgust.

'Running away. It's all you know.'

He slammed the heel of his hand against his temple. Enough of that. Enough of talking to himself. Enough of thinking about Jenn. He cared for her, and he really enjoyed the time they spent together, but he'd never led her on, never pretended to her that he was more than what he'd showed her.

The simple fact was that she deserved better than him.

He pushed thoughts of Jenn and self-admonishment as far away as he could. Time to refocus. He really needed to get back to the stables and check on the woman, but he was passing by the store on the way back so he may as well make best use of his time.

Early in the morning, the store was quiet and he soon had the food he wanted. He checked his watch as he made his way to his truck. He hadn't reached it before he stopped dead in the parking lot to stare at the vehicle which had just pulled in from the road.

A big black Cadillac Escalade. Expensive. Imposing. Not many people around here could afford a car like that. One man could.

Frank Booker.

'Shit,' Peake said under his breath.

8

No chance Frank turning up here was a coincidence. Especially with the way the SUV came to a stop facing Peake, engine idling, as though the driver was waiting for him to make a move.

Peake held his ground a moment, figuring how he'd react if a group of men charged out to ambush him.

No. Not this time. So Peake decided to carry on, as casually as he could, toward his truck. Except before he reached it he heard the SUV's door opening behind him and then Frank's angry voice.

'You're just gonna walk away from me, you fucking pussy scumbag?'

Peake stopped in his tracks, in two minds.

He turned to Frank. A big, imposing guy, tall and wide. In his prime – thirty years ago – he'd probably been quite a physical force, but these days the mass was mostly fat. He still had a dominating air about him, but Frank alone? Certainly not intimidating to Peake. Still this was a far from ideal situation right now.

'Frank, I'm really—'

'Sorry? You burned my house down, you piece of shit!'

'Not intentionally.' And his house? The guy had never lived there.

'I knew you were up to no good.'

Then why'd you let me stay there rent free and give me a job at your bar? Probably not the best time for a comeback along those lines.

'What were you doing? Cooking meth and got your mix wrong, you dumb fuck?'

Which certainly happened around these parts. There were plenty of meth labs and they did have a tendency to go kaboom every now and then.

'Nothing like that, I promise you,' Peake said.

'Doesn't matter now. You owe me.'

'Look, Frank. That house was falling apart. I—'

'What? You're gonna tell me you've put value on that farm?'

Well... it had crossed Peake's mind. He'd saved Frank the demolition costs at least.

But Peake didn't get a chance to argue that because his gaze diverted across the road where a pickup truck had pulled to a stop. He couldn't see the license plate from his position, but the Chevy was exactly the same model and color as the one from the bar the other night. The one that belonged to those two loudmouths. Frank's new business partners, apparently.

Who Jenn said had been asking a lot of questions about Peake.

A snide grin spread up Frank's face. 'Yeah, now you're in the shit.'

'Be careful, Frank. You don't need to start a fight with me.'

'That's where you're wrong. You don't get to disrespect me like—'

Peake turned back around to his Ford, had his hand on the door handle.

'Hey, Peake! Don't you—'

He climbed into the driver's seat before waiting to hear the rest of the threat or ultimatum or whatever it was. He turned the key and hit the throttle, and the truck shot forward out of the parking spot. Frank had dove back into his car too and the Escalade burst toward him to try to intercept and block Peake in, but Frank was too slow, or maybe too reluctant to get his nice motor into a smash. Peake shot by him and out onto the road. Frank would have to perform a U-turn before he could follow.

The driver of the Chevy had already figured that one out though and the truck was spinning around in the road as Peake sped away from the store. He took a couple of quick turns – a left then right – trying to avoid any roads with traffic. The last thing he wanted was an all-out chase across town, putting himself, other drivers, and pedestrians at risk. But as he took the next left onto a usually quiet road that led out of town, there was a queue of six cars at a standstill fifty yards ahead as a dump truck reversed into a side road.

Peake slowed, eyes mostly on the rearview mirror. He was a little surprised to see not the Chevy but Frank's Cadillac careen around the corner toward him. The guy obviously spotted the jam a second later because his tires screeched and the Escalade swerved as he battled to keep control...

Peake glanced forward. The driver of the dump truck was still making a meal of the maneuver. A couple of horns honked, the drivers getting antsy. Frank managed to straighten up the Escalade which continued to close in on Peake's Ford. Would Frank stop? Ram him?

No, he slowed as he came alongside on the verge.

Peake stared to his right as a darkened rear window slid down.

'Shit.'

Frank wasn't alone. Another guy in the rear. A guy who pointed a pistol toward Peake.

Peake floored it just as the gun boomed and a bullet smashed into the right rear passenger window.

He pulled the car out into the left lane, racing past the queue of traffic. The engine of his Ford whined and spluttered as he picked up speed, heading straight for the narrowing gap between the dump truck and the building at the corner of the street it was heading for.

Peake's knuckles turned white as he gripped the steering wheel a little more tightly, as though doing so would have any impact whatsoever on whether he made it or not...

He closed his eyes for a split second, braced for an impact that never came. He made it out the other side and raced away in the clear. Without slowing he risked a look in his mirror to see the Escalade burst through the now impossibly narrow gap, losing a wing mirror in the process. The vehicle must have brushed against the moving dump truck because the Escalade lost balance again, swinging left and right as Frank battled to control the lumbering beast.

Peake managed to pull away in the process. He took a right, then a left, heading for the freeway. Yet as he rounded a bend in the road he spotted the Chevy up ahead. They'd got lucky and got ahead of him somehow, and as he approached it the Chevy swung into the middle of the road, the driver aiming to block Peake off.

He tugged left on the wheel, aiming for the gap that way, knowing he'd have to mount the sidewalk to make it. The Chevy pulled further that way too to stop him...

Very kind.

Peake swung hard right. The Chevy driver couldn't react quickly enough. It started to back up but Peake wasn't stopping now. The front corner of the Ford smashed into the back corner of the Chevy with a thump and a crash of broken glass, but Peake raced away. He checked his mirrors again. Both chasers remained on him but the two near misses had helped him pull away.

One stop on the freeway, then he'd come back around toward town. He'd go to the stables for the woman. Did Frank know that was where Peake was staying now? The only person who could have told him was Jenn. She surely wouldn't have if she'd known Frank wanted Peake's blood.

Would she?

It didn't matter. He'd get the woman first. He'd take her out of town, then dump his Ford Ranger. They'd head into the wilderness while he figured out his next move. Frank Booker wasn't his battle right now. Figuring out who the woman was and who the men who were sent to kill her was bigger.

The traffic ahead on the freeway looked light. Peake had already hit seventy-five as the slipway ended. He'd hit ninety a few seconds later, still only a few cars dotted in front and behind.

Three miles to the next exit. Two hundred yards of clear space behind before the Chevy and Escalade, which raced side by side behind him.

Two hundred yards? No, they were closer. And they were closing all the time.

'Come on!' Peake shouted, pushing his foot harder on the already-floored pedal. Damn old motor had nothing like the power of the newer, more expensive vehicles in pursuit. He was pushing a hundred, but the engine had nothing left to give. The chasers... 120 mph or more, and likely nowhere near top speed yet.

His only hope was that he reached the exit before they reached him.

One mile to go. But they were only fifty yards behind now.

By the time the exit was only half a mile in front, the chasers were nearly on him.

He pulled into the middle lane, as though he might be able to trick them by making a late dive for the exit. The slipway started. The exit ramp rose up to meet an overhead bridge. The Chevy raced up his inside, only a couple of yards from him. They'd slowed down almost to his pace as though taunting him.

Nothing else for it. He tugged on the wheel and dove across in front of them. The Chevy driver did the sensible thing of braking rather than risk a hundred mile an hour smash that would likely end up with them all dead.

Peake's Ford bounced across the uneven shoulder and onto the verge that rose up to meet the exit ramp. He joined the slipway and pushed his foot down again, but as he looked to his mirror to check on the chasers, he hadn't realized the Escalade was already right on his tail – Frank must have gone straight for the exit. The Chevy wasn't far behind.

Nothing Peake could do this time. Frank nudged on his wheel, his vehicle cutting across the back corner of Peake's truck causing the rear wheels to lose traction and the back end swung out. He had no chance of correcting it and the Ford fishtailed, spinning around. Before he knew it, his Ford was heading down the grass verge and toward the huge upright for the bridge.

Bang.

The Ford smashed into the concrete. The driver's airbag smacked into Peake's face. Not a high-speed crash, but one which brought the Ford to an abrupt and final stop. He pushed the airbag away from him. Smoke hissed out of the crumpled hood. The engine whined and ground to silence. He tried the key, tried the throttle. Nothing. He was going nowhere.

'Get out of the car!' came a shout from outside. Not Frank. Peake looked in the wing mirror. The cracked glass made the man's body and face look crooked and sinister. No mistaking the object in his hand, though.

'OK!' Peake shouted back.

'And keep your hands where we can see them.'

Peake unclasped his belt. He released the door then brought his hands toward his head and kicked the door open.

He stepped out to be greeted by five men who'd fanned out in an arc around him. Nowhere to go. Frank stood at the center of the arc, flanked by the two from the bar plus two others Peake didn't recognize. All four pointed weapons toward him: three handguns, one shotgun.

'You made this happen,' Frank said, sounding as pissed as he looked.

'I made you chase me? I made you point weapons?'

'Get in my car before this gets out of hand.'

Peake said nothing.

'You ain't got a choice here, Peake.'

'No.'

Frank put his hands on his hips and threw his head up in exasperation. Clearly this wasn't how he'd wanted this finale to go.

'Someone grab him.'

'Any of you touches me...'

'And what?' the chief loudmouth from the bar said. Did that mean he saw himself as chief muscle? Or he was just the one who wanted the fight most?

Peake didn't bother with a macho response but kept his focus on that man.

'Peake. Move,' Frank demanded.

'Frank, seriously – I'm sorry about the farm. I'll make it up to you. But right now... I've got bigger problems.'

Frank laughed at that.

'Bigger problems than my guys being ready to shoot you to pieces?'

'Actually, yeah.'

'You wanna explain that?'

Peake really didn't. Although a thought did strike him.

'I'm in some trouble, that's all. With a guy named Hardy. You know him?'

A big risk perhaps to mention the name, but Peake was glad he did because Frank's reaction – and that of one of his goons – suggested the name meant something.

'Just get in the goddamn car, Peake,' Frank said.

'Actually, I don't think that's happening,' Peake said, allowing a smile to rise.

'If you think—'

Frank didn't finish. Something about Peake's demeanor must have given it away. Given away that he'd spotted something behind them, because the man on the right glanced that way first. Then the chief turned, then one nudged the other and within a few seconds all four goons had turned to see the approaching police car. Frank finally joined them.

'Put the fucking weapons away!' Frank hissed, and the four men sheepishly tried to cover up as they hotfooted toward their vehicles.

The police car hadn't come in sirens blaring and it casually rolled to a stop on the shoulder, adjacent to Peake's smashed Ford. A young officer stepped out. A tall, athletic guy who looked like he could have been Travis's younger, fitter brother.

Peake was surprised to see it was Travis's younger, fitter cousin – Shaun.

'Good day, gentlemen,' Shaun said. 'Everything OK here?'

'Had a bit of an accident,' Peake said.

The cop held his hands by his side, the fingers of his right hand primed, ready to grab his gun if this went awry.

'Swerved to avoid a deer,' Peake continued. 'Maybe I shouldn't have bothered.'

He glanced at his truck and tutted as though it was the old thing's fault.

'Frank and his guys were just passing,' Peake added.

'Is that right?' Shaun said to Frank, clearly not fully buying the explanation.

'Yeah,' Frank said. 'That's right. But now you're here, officer, we'll leave the situation in your capable hands.'

Frank retreated to his Cadillac, and for a moment Shaun looked uncertain – like he didn't know if this was how he wanted things to go down.

At least it told Peake one thing – Shaun wasn't in cahoots with Frank, otherwise there wouldn't have been any reason for the crew to back off so suddenly.

Within seconds the Chevy and the Escalade had disappeared up the slipway and out of sight.

'What did you say your name was?' Shaun asked.

'You know me from Slug's. I work with Travis.'

Shaun's face took on a sullen look.

'I need to see your license and registration.'

'It's that time of the day again, right?' Peake said with a chuckle. Shaun glared defiantly before Peake gave him the documents. Shaun disappeared into his car to do his checks. In the meantime Peake sent a text message and was pleased that whatever checks Shaun was doing took longer than expected. Not usually a good thing with cops, but on this occasion he decided it was.

Shaun came out of his car with an even more sullen look on his face.

'And Mr. Booker just happened to be passing by?' Shaun asked.

Peake shrugged. 'I told you, I work at the bar. Frank's my boss.'

'And those other guys he was with?'

'Business associates, he said. I don't know them. Do you?'

'They seemed pretty keen to take off when they saw me.'

'Frank's a busy man.'

'I know Frank. I know he's a big deal in this town. I know sometimes he sees himself above the likes of me, and I know men like him often ain't as straight up as they pretend to be. You in trouble with him?'

'What kind of trouble are you suggesting?'

Shaun didn't answer, just held Peake's eye a few moments as though should Peake had something to confess, that look alone would make him do it.

'And you live around here?' Shaun eventually asked.

'Have done for a while.'

'I can tell you're not from the States.'

'England.'

'New York license and registration though.'

'I used to live there. Haven't had time to change it.'

'You know you need to do that within thirty days of moving.'

'It's in the works.'

'Not according to the DMV. I'm gonna have to cite you for this. And you're gonna need to arrange a tow. Your truck can't stay there.'

'Understood.'

'And I need to take a sample.'

'I've not been drinking.'

'Yo, cuz!' came a shout from the roadside.

Peake had seen him arrive and park his car on the shoulder, but Shaun hadn't. Travis strode up the verge toward them, an easygoing smile on his face.

'You know that's Simon from the bar, right?'

'So he says.' Shaun fixed Peake a glare and a little of Travis's relaxed manner slipped away.

'I can take him back into town if y'all want?' Travis said. 'That truck looks like it's finished.'

'And I guess you just happened to be passing too, right? Like Frank?' Shaun asked his cousin.

'Frank?'

'You didn't know your boss was just here too?'

'Why would I know that?' He looked around him. 'I don't see him now.'

The two cousins stared at one another. Clearly Travis – the elder – held some sway here, but Shaun was an officer of the law. Peake was about to find out how much that meant to the young man.

'I'll take him back,' Travis said again. 'You write up whatever you need to about the accident.'

'I need a sample from him first.'

'A sample? Bruh, it's first thing in the morning and he's working soon. This dude ain't drinking. Never seen him drink, come to think of it.'

'You work in a bar, it kinda puts you off,' Peake said, but only received a glare from both men for his interruption.

'So you're refusing to give a roadside sample?' Shaun asked Peake.

'He ain't refusing. He just don't need to. Not today. Not for this.'

Shaun said nothing more. Travis took a step closer to his cousin and put a hand to his shoulder and whispered something that Peake couldn't hear. Shaun's head was bowed by the time Travis had finished, and he slapped his cousin on the back before looking over to Peake.

'Come on then.'

Peake followed Travis to his car, locking eyes with Shaun for a moment before he got in, and the look the guy gave was far from friendly.

'You watch your back around here, Simon Peake,' Shaun shouted out.

Peake kept quiet as he got into Travis's car.

9

'Thanks,' Peake said after they'd left the freeway and were heading back toward Prenticeville – the first time either of them had spoken since leaving the scene of the crash.

'Is that all I get? No explanation or nothing?'

Peake thought about it but then decided to change the subject. 'What did you say to him?'

Travis sighed. 'I just reminded him of a few things.'

Not a very forthcoming answer, but Peake wasn't exactly being forthcoming either and decided he didn't really need to know the details anyway.

'So how did the farmhouse end up a pile of ashes?' Travis asked.

'You heard about that?'

'It's a small town, Peake. What did you expect?'

'It's a long story.'

'Remember I just bailed you out, yeah?'

'Yeah. But this is a story where the less you know, the better it is for you. Trust me on that.'

Travis humphed. 'And now you're staying at the McGintys'?' he said, although Peake believed he only knew about that because it was where Peake had asked to be dropped off.

'Yeah. Just for a few days.'

'Does Thomas McGinty know about that?'

'I don't know.'

'So that's a no then. Jenn let you?'

'Yeah.'

'Shit, that woman would do anything for you.'

'She's helping me out, that's all.'

'But you do know McGinty Senior and Frank have all sorts of stuff going on together.'

'I heard.'

'So you ruining the farm and all... Probably gonna make McGinty just as mad as Frank.'

'Maybe.'

'Yet you're crashing at his crib. Eating his food. Drinking his wine. Screwing his daughter.'

Travis smiled a little snidely at the last sentence.

'You sure don't care much 'bout what people think of you.'

'I do, actually.'

'I see why Frank is pissed about the farm though.'

'That place was a shithole,' Peake said. 'In reality I probably haven't lowered the value of the land at all.'

'Maybe, maybe not. But you know 'bout his plans for that place, right?'

'I presume it's not growing corn.'

'Development. Golf course, condos.'

'Yeah. I heard something about that. But in Prenticeville?'

Travis shrugged. 'He and McGinty apparently got some backers from out of town. They think they can make it work. Something bigger than either of them's done before. If they pull it off... it could transform the town. Land is mostly dirt cheap right now. But that one development could kickstart a wave. Everything else those two owns – which is half the town – shoots up in value.'

'Losing the farmhouse hardly changes that plan.' If any of it was even feasible.

'It does and it doesn't. Still the same land. But if the police and the authorities think something crooked was going on out there, drugs, whatever, it's gonna make it a hell of a lot harder to get things moving.'

Why did everyone keep assuming the fire had something to do with drugs? Peake was almost offended. Almost. Because he did know that the police would certainly be very interested if they came to realize exactly what had happened out there.

'How well do you know Frank?' Peake asked.

'Everyone knows Frank.'

'But his businesses? His business partners?'

'I'm just a doorman. I only know what I overhear from guys who've had too many beers.'

'They're usually the most honest guys.'

Travis smirked at that. 'Look. What I know is Frank Booker is a self-made man. He lives in a mansion that cost over two million on the edge of a town where the average home costs less than two hundred grand.'

'What's your point?'

'My point is that he's made millions in this area, has businesses all over, connections to bigger businesses, politicians. The way I see it, no one gets to that position sticking to all the rules.'

Peake would agree.

'You know of any dirt in particular?'

Travis sent a glare Peake's way, as though he'd overstepped the mark.

'No. But I'm guessing the reason you're asking me these questions at all is because maybe you know something bad about Frank. And maybe you're worried about it.'

Peake didn't answer.

'You didn't just run off the freeway back there, did you?'

'No.'

'Those out-of-town guys involved?'

'Yeah.'

'They have something to do with the fire too?'

'No. Actually... I don't know.'

'Sounds like you're in over your head.'

Hardly. He just didn't know what he was in. But Frank and those goons didn't worry Peake that much really. He just needed to stay clear until he'd figured things out.

Travis pulled over at the edge of the drive to the McGinty home. He stared toward the house as though checking for any signs of trouble there.

'Not seen Thomas for a while,' Travis said. 'People are starting to wonder what the hell happened to him.'

'They are?'

'And here you are, crashing—'

'In his crib. Eating his food. Et cetera, et cetera. Yeah, we did that one already.'

'I'm just tryna figure where some of these loose threads I'm seeing join together.'

'You be sure to let me know when you do.'

Peake went to get out but paused when he realized Travis wasn't finished.

'You know I don't hold any loyalty to either of those men,' Travis said. 'They keep themselves at the top by keeping the rest of us down. So... if you need help, you know how to reach me.'

'Thank you. One question for you, actually.'

'Shoot.'

'You know a guy named Hardy? Probably a not so good guy. I don't think he's from around here but plenty of people seem to know the name. Think Frank Booker but several times bigger and nastier.'

Travis pursed his lips and shook his head. 'Means nothing to me.'

Peake really thought he was telling the truth about that, which surprised him a little.

'I owe you one,' Peake said, stepping out of the car.

'Yeah, you do.'

Peake shut the door and watched Travis's car disappear around the corner in front before he made his way along the drive to the stables. He found the woman in the same position as he'd left her the previous evening – still breathing but still unconscious.

He checked over her, refilled her drip, reapplied her dressings. The wounds were looking better each time he did so.

As he sat back against the stable wall, his eyes rested on her hand. He was sure he'd seen a finger twitch...

Perhaps not.

His gaze moved to her watch. A sparkly, gold thing. He moved closer and turned her wrist over. Rolex. He'd first noticed it even before he'd taken her out of the trunk. A real one or a fake? If it was fake, it certainly was a good one – it even had the telltale smooth-running second hand.

It surprised him that Adam or Kittle or Huggins hadn't stolen it from her. Perhaps that meant they knew it was a fake. Or perhaps they wouldn't risk stealing such a traceable high-value item in case it came back to bite them. Peake's job had been to dispose of her, dispose of anything that could help identify her.

Anyway, having a Rolex didn't tell him a whole lot about her, but it did suggest at least a certain amount of wealth. As did the other jewelry, unless it was all cheap knockoffs.

He sighed in frustration. The truth was, he had no clue what any of it meant.

And why did he even care, anyway? Over the past two days he'd just fallen further into the shit on so many different levels. He could just take this woman to a hospital and leave her there to be taken care of by professionals. He had ten grand cash. It would see him through a few weeks at least. He could leave this town, this area right now, rather than risk his hanging around and his asking questions getting him into more trouble.

More trouble... But really the trouble was inescapable already. And it wasn't just her that was in trouble, it was him. He'd killed those two men at the farm. He'd destroyed the farm. He'd got himself in the crosshairs of Frank Booker and Thomas McGinty's shady businesses. Not to mention Adam McGinty was somewhere out there still, the risk of his loose tongue perhaps the biggest threat of all to Peake.

Whatever was happening, he was now involved in whatever this woman was. The same people who'd wanted her dead would want him dead too. They'd come looking, if they weren't already.

'I will find out what's going on,' Peake said to her.

He put her hand down.

And then he saw it. And this time he was 100 percent certain.

Her eyelids flickered, half-opened.

She was finally waking up.

10

Peake was frozen to the spot, resting on his haunches as he stared at the woman's eyes. They flickered as though she was having a hard time forcing them open.

'You're OK,' he said after a few moments, feeling pathetic for his words – but what the hell else was he supposed to say or do in this moment? Putting himself in her position, even after overcoming whatever physical disorientation she was likely feeling, she was waking to find herself severely injured and lying down in a stable block with a man she'd never met before.

Yet his voice still did the job of getting her attention, of giving her something to focus on perhaps, as within a couple of beats her eyes were fully open and she ever so slightly turned her head toward him.

Fear. That's what he saw.

'You're OK,' he repeated, holding his hands up to show he wasn't a threat.

She didn't say anything, didn't move... then Peake flinched as she suddenly pushed her hands down to lift her torso up and shuffled – scuttled back – away from him, only stopping when her back was up against the wooden planks of the stable wall. Her eyes darted left and right, up, down, as though scoping out threats, exits.

'Please...' Peake said, hoping his calm voice would rub off on her.

'Who...'

'You're OK,' he said. 'You're safe. I'm not going to hurt you.'

She shook her head, looked over her body, the drip in her arm, confusion etched on her face as though nothing she was seeing made sense to her. Well, yeah...

'You were attacked,' Peake said. 'I saved you. You've been unconscious for... a few days.'

She squirmed and lifted a hand to her temple.

'Here,' Peake said. He grabbed a bottle of water from one of the bags next to him and edged toward her, but she shook her head and pushed herself even farther up against the wall. 'It's OK. You need this. You need water. You need food.'

'What... happened?'

She closed her eyes a moment as though trying to remember. But only for a split second before she fixed her fearful gaze on Peake again.

'Have some water. Just take a few minutes.'

He shuffled closer to her and stretched out his hand. She didn't move. He undid the cap and pushed the bottle toward her again.

'I'm not a threat to you,' he said. 'And you're not a prisoner here. But you're in a bad way. I'm here to help. To figure things out.'

She went to take the bottle but grimaced and groaned in pain. She put a hand to her gut.

'You were attacked,' Peake said. 'Stabbed. Do you remember?'

If she did, she gave no indication. She reached for the bottle again, this time taking it in a shaky grip. She brought the bottle toward her mouth, but liquid was already sloshing out of the top before the plastic hit her lips. She took two greedy gulps before pulling the bottle back down and she locked eyes with him a second before a renewed fear took hold on her face.

The bottle fell from her grip and bounced on the floor, sending water cascading over her, but she didn't seem to notice as she twisted onto her side and retched.

OK. The look she'd given him wasn't fear that time then.

The water she'd taken in came straight back up, but she continued to cough and gag until thick spit dribbled from her lips, and eventually she spat out a mouthful of bloody phlegm.

Peake went over to her and rubbed her back as though that would in any way help her.

'Take it easy. Your body's... still getting used to this. To being awake again.'

She wiped at her mouth with the sleeve of her – his – shirt, then turned back over and slumped against the wall. The movements had caused the bottom of the shirt to ride up, exposing her naval, and the dressing over the wound in her gut through which a patch of blood was slowly spreading out across the gauze.

'You... did this?' she asked.

'The bandages? Yes. Not the wounds.'

He waited to see if she had anything more to say. He had so many questions for her, perhaps even more than she had for him. After all, surely she knew who'd tried to kill her and why?

'What's your name?' he asked.

She didn't answer, just looked off into the distance, her mind clearly in turmoil.

'My name's Simon. Simon Peake.'

'Where...'

'Where are we?' He looked around the bare space. 'It's a stable. We're... The house out there belongs to a friend.'

She looked utterly confused.

'What I mean is—'

'No,' she said. 'Where are we?'

'Prenticeville.'

He could tell she had no clue where that was.

'Georgia.'

Even more confused now.

'You're not from Georgia?'

'I... No. I don't... think so.'

Don't think so?

'Do you remember what happened to you?'

She didn't answer. Didn't react to the question at all.

'Some people tried to kill you,' Peake said.

He thought about mentioning the names, seeing if they sparked recognition, but decided it might be too much, too soon.

She closed her eyes, squeezing them shut. Perhaps trying to remember or trying to forget.

'Three men brought you to me. They thought you were dead. They wanted me to get rid of... the body.'

Shit. Probably not the best way to explain it. Her eyes sprang open and the look of fear in her eyes intensified further. The sharper rise and fall in her chest showed her heart was racing as adrenaline surged. Perhaps the biochemical response would at least make her more alert, provide more focus to her addled mind.

He held his hands up once more. 'I don't know why they did that. I'm really sorry. And I don't know why the men came to me.' Not strictly true, but... 'I need to figure that out. But... you weren't dead. You were in a bad way, but you weren't dead. I saved you.'

'And... the men... they're...?'

'Evan Huggins. Tyler Kittle.' He paused, a little reluctant about the last name. 'Adam McGinty.'

She shook her head. 'I meant... what happened to them?'

'They... can't hurt you anymore.'

She said nothing to that. And he knew his words weren't strictly true. Adam was still out there and could hurt them both, either willingly or through coercion if the wrong people got hold of him.

'They told me they worked for a man named Hardy. Do you know him?'

She shook her head, no tell on her face. Hell, she couldn't have looked more confused if she were an Oscar-winning actress.

'You don't know why those men, or this Hardy, wanted you dead?'

She didn't react at all now. Except for looking petrified.

He reached out and put his hand to hers, trying to offer comfort.

'You're safe now.'

Still no reaction.

'What's your name?' he asked.

'I... It's...'

A tear escaped her welling eyes as she looked off into the distance.

'I...'

'You don't remember your name?' he asked.

Amnesia?

'I don't remember anything,' she said, almost shouted, despair in her voice before she pulled her hand from under Peake's and she turned away from him and sobbed.

'Nothing?' he said. 'You don't remember anything at all? Your name? Where you're from? The attack?'

'The attack?'

He had her attention again.

'What?' he prompted. 'What do you remember?'

'Just...' She put her hand to her chest. Then her neck. 'Pain. Noise.'

Her face turned white as a sheet. Her chest rose higher and higher with quickening breaths. She was hyperventilating, wheezing and rasping for air.

'It's so... hot.'

Within seconds her forehead, her neck, chest was covered in thick droplets of sweat. He placed the backs of his fingers against her cheek. She was burning up. Perhaps partly due to mental stress, partly physical stress, but the temperature of the stable in the blazing Georgia sun didn't help either. A hundred and twenty or more perhaps. Shit, he felt faint.

He turned and grabbed a new bottle of water. Not cold, but it was better than nothing. Hopefully.

He took the cap off, but she didn't have the strength or focus to take the bottle from him. He splashed some on her face, some sort of relief for her, before gently tipping her head back and slowly pouring the water into her mouth. It pooled and spilled out before she found the strength to swallow – or perhaps it was only a reflex reaction.

'We need to get you cooled down,' he said.

Stupid really, to ever think a seriously ill person would recuperate out here. But he'd had few options and this was the best he could do in the available time.

'Stay with me,' he said, pulling her head back up when it fell onto her shoulders. 'Have some more water.'

She found the strength to hold the bottle and took another glug.

'Can you walk?' he asked.

She didn't answer.

'Come on,' he said.

He reached under her shoulders and pulled her up. To start with she was nothing but a dead weight, but he heaved and propped her onto her feet once, twice, three times, like trying to stand up a wobbly ornament. Finally she engaged her muscles and took some of the weight.

'We'll go to the house,' Peake said.

He got no response. He pulled out the drip, she winced a little but didn't otherwise protest so he dragged her toward the exit, heat radiating off her and making him feel sickly from it. He kicked open the stable door and the sun beat down on them. She groaned and he lifted a hand to his face and nearly dropped her in the process.

'It's just over there,' he said.

Twenty yards. A few steps. Not so easy when half carrying, half dragging a delicate mass. His arms and legs and back ached from the awkward movements by the time they reached a door at the back of the house. A shaded spot, at least. He went to let go of her but she nearly toppled and he had to help prop her against the wall. It looked like a tiny breeze would knock her to the ground.

Peake had a flashing thought of Jenn. Her warning to him of the house – her family's house – being off limits.

But she'd understand. Wouldn't she?

Peake peered through the window of the door which opened out into a utility space. He tried the handle, just in case. No. Locked. Was the house alarmed? Time to find out. He smashed his elbow into the glass pane which shattered first time, then reached in and unlatched the lock. He pulled the handle down and opened the door and paused a moment.

No alarm. At least, no noise from one. Perhaps it wasn't set, or perhaps an alert had just been sent to the owner's phone.

Peake wouldn't dwell. He was doing this regardless.

'Come on,' he said.

He helped the woman inside. Whether by good fortune or whatever else, McGinty had left the air-conditioning on last time he'd left here. High seventies, or something like that. A world of difference to the stables, to Frank's farmhouse too. Peake hadn't enjoyed any interior – or exterior – this cool since he'd left New York all those months ago.

No. Not thinking about that now. He had enough immediate problems to deal with.

He helped the woman through the utility, into a hallway. The house somehow felt smaller on the inside than it looked on the outside. Perhaps that was because of the packing boxes which were in piles of various sizes here and there making the spaces look and feel cramped.

'Here,' Peake said, spotting a living room with a leather sofa and two armchairs.

The armchair was the nearest, so he stopped there and eased the woman into it where she slumped her head against the wingback.

'This is better, right?' Peake said.

She groaned and nodded in response.

He stood there like a chump for a few moments. What next? He could get her upstairs and dump her in the shower and run cold water over her...

No. Just the hassle of getting her upstairs was enough to put him off the idea, and would it really help her? Plus, he'd then have to help her change her clothes, which felt all the more awkward now she was awake.

But... at least there might be some more appropriate clothes for her – there was a chance some of Jenn's mom's things were still here.

He'd take a look. For food and drink too. Medicine. He'd bought the basics but a home would surely have a more wide-ranging and better choice, perhaps even some old prescription drugs that hadn't been finished off.

'Wait there,' he said before heading off.

Ten minutes later he walked back toward the living room. No clothes in hand, though he'd found the master bedroom and walk-in closet. Plenty of choice. Plenty of Mrs. McGinty's things remained. He'd let the woman choose when she had enough strength to get up there. Perhaps. Even though Peake had already taken the step of breaking into this house he still wasn't comfortable in simply rummaging and taking anything he wanted, even if he truly believed it was justified under the circumstances.

What he did have was a couple of cold, sugary sodas. Some cheese and salami out of the fridge too, which – other than condiments – were about the only foods left given the owner hadn't been around for a while. He'd picked up some chocolate too. Not exactly good nutrition, but the woman just needed sustenance. Energy.

He looked up and stopped in his step at the doorway when he saw the empty chair...

No, she hadn't made an unlikely run for it. She was across the room, by the fireplace.

'You OK?' he asked.

She whipped her fingers back from the photo frame she'd been touching and turned to face him.

'You know them?' Peake asked, noting the picture of the McGinty family. The four of them together. Much happier times.

She shook her head.

'You sure?'

The picture was a few years old. Adam was probably still in his late teens, but he was easily recognizable as the man he'd become. Had he been part of the attack on this woman or just the one charged with disposing of the body?

Peake really wanted it to be the latter.

'It's not them, but...'

'But what?'

'That... The picture.'

He moved over. A lake. He didn't recognize it.

'You know where that is?'

'I... don't know...'

'We can find out.' Jenn would probably know.

'No. It's not... the lake.'

'Then what?'

'I... I...' She put her hands to her temples and pushed hard. 'It's a memory. Water. But that's not the point. It's something... else. A face. A place.'

'What?'

He went to put his arm on her shoulder, but she shrugged him off, her stature, her movements so much more focused and considered now than minutes before. And then her whole demeanor changed in an instant – hyper alert and focused.

But also absolutely horrified.

'I... I have a son!' She grabbed his arm and squeezed hard, and he fought not to show the pain. 'You have to help me!' she shouted in despair. 'I have to find my son!'

She let go and her eyes rolled back, and she collapsed to the thick carpeted floor.

11

Hardy saw something overtly mocking in Ridley's choice of location for the meetup. Buc-ee's. A mammoth gas station with hundreds of pumps and a gargantuan store attached to it that was bigger than most supermarkets, and that specialized in – among other things – all manner of branded merchandise emblazoned with the famous and colorful Buc-ee's beaver mascot. The brand was something of a gimmicky attraction to people all across the south. To outsiders, Hardy felt it probably looked odd and insular. Exactly why Ridley had chosen it, most likely. A way of mocking, demeaning Hardy.

Sat in the back of his Mercedes S-Class, he balled his fists in anger as he awaited Ridley's arrival. Wyatt had parked them around the far corner of the store, as far away from the masses as they could be, but the whole place was heaving still.

'Here he comes,' Wyatt said, looking in his side mirror.

Hardy glanced behind and sure enough Ridley came striding over with a filled plastic shopping bag in his hand, the big face of the toothy beaver on the plastic grinning at Hardy the whole way.

Ridley opened the passenger door on the other side to Hardy and slapped his bag down on the leather in between them, then sank down into the seat.

'Nice motor,' Ridley said.

Hardy didn't respond.

'European? Honestly, I thought you'd go American. Something bigger, more in your face. Wearing your balls on your sleeve or whatever it is.'

'We're not all as simple and classless as you think we are.'

Ridley chuckled. 'Did I say anything of the sort? Perhaps that's your own insecurities calling out to you.'

'You're on your own?' Hardy asked.

'No. My friends are still shopping inside. Honestly, that place is a treasure trove.'

He opened up his bag and began looking through.

'It's amazing. You should see all the stuff they've got in there.'

'I've seen it.'

He took out a small plushy toy. A beaver, of course. 'For my niece,' Ridley said.

'Lucky her.'

He put the toy back and rummaged again. 'Jerky flavors galore. Unbelievable.' He grabbed a packet and tossed it into Hardy's lap. 'You have that one. A present from me.'

'Amazing. Thank you.'

Hardy pushed the meat off his lap. Ridley looked so damned pleased with himself. As always.

'So?' Ridley said. 'You told me you have some answers. Something to show me. Which is why we had to do this in person.'

Hardy said nothing but reached down and grabbed the leather bag by his feet. He thudded it down next to Ridley's shopping bag. The guy looked a little less pleased with himself all of a sudden, and he hadn't even seen the contents yet.

Hardy reached inside and took out the soggy, wrapped blankets. He lay the package on top of the now empty bag and peeled back the layers to reveal the chewed up, bloody mess inside.

Ridley looked a little taken aback. Not shocked or disgusted, just a vague confusion, as though he couldn't understand why he was looking at someone's severed arm. He pulled his Buc-ee's bag closer to him as though worried of cross-contamination.

'This is what we found of Tyler Kittle,' Hardy said.

'Your dogs did that?'

'No. My dogs sniffed it out, but the flesh was already chewed up by scavengers. Coyotes probably. But that's not the important part. The important part is this—' he pointed to the fingers '—and this.' He pointed to the cut end of the bone.

'The clean cut shows Tyler was dismembered. This arm wasn't taken off by critters. And the fingerprints are burned off to make it harder to identify.'

'Then how did you identify him?'

'Tattoos. Not on this piece. On some skin from his leg which we found not far from this.'

'So what's the story?'

'Good question. We found these pieces on farmland outside Prenticeville in Georgia. It's where Adam McGinty is from. Kittle and Huggins lived nearby too.'

'Whose farm?'

'Frank Booker. I don't know anything about him.'

Ridley rubbed his chin, thinking.

'Do you know him?' Hardy asked.

'No. I don't think I do. But I'll look into it. And Lucia?'

'No sign of her.'

'Which means what? Do you even know if she's dead or alive?'

'What I know is that two of my men were killed out there and cut to pieces and dumped all over.'

'Two men?'

'We found pieces of Huggins and Kittle. But not the woman. And not McGinty, either. And the farmhouse near where they were found was destroyed. A fire.'

'You think McGinty did this?'

'He's just a kid. A nobody. So I doubt it. But we also ain't found anything of him. So who knows.'

'But you don't know where he is now?'

'We're working on that.'

'If not McGinty, then who did this? I've had no word from Florida that anyone has any inkling that Lucia made it up this way.'

Hardy contemplated that for a second. Not the actual question, but the part about no word from Florida. He knew little of Lucia. Had never met her. Only knew what he'd been told by Ridley and that he was being paid to kill her and make her body disappear. But he knew a man like Ridley had a much bigger play going on than some disgruntled husband or whatever wanting his woman dead.

'So?' Ridley prompted.

'Word is Booker had a tenant staying on the farm. Don't know much about him. We're working on locating him.'

'Don't know much? Do you know anything?'

'No. Not yet. But I'm thinking he's a friend of McGinty's. It explains why my guys took Lucia there. Obviously something went wrong. I don't know what yet.'

'So this guy, this tenant, could just be another low life brought on board by your guys?'

Another low life. Ridley didn't even attempt to hide his contempt for Hardy and the people who worked for him. The sooner he was rid of this asshole the better. But not before he got his own back on him. If he could find a way.

'Whoever he is, he's nothing to do with me,' Hardy said.

'Whether he is or he isn't, it's your job to find him. And find out what the hell happened to Lucia. At the moment we've got bodies turning up all over the place, but none of them is her.'

'That was the whole point. You wanted her to disappear. If pieces of her were turning up I'd have failed.'

'So you're trying to tell me you've done a good job here?'

Hardy didn't bite back at that.

'Find McGinty. Find this other guy. Find out what the hell they did with the body. Don't make me go get someone else in to clean up this mess. You won't like how that ends for you.'

Ridley grabbed his bag and pulled on his door handle.

'Next time you want to update me? Leave the body parts at home. You've put me right off my jerky.'

He got out and slammed the door shut behind him. Hardy watched the guy saunter away. When he looked forward he caught Wyatt's grin in the rearview mirror.

'What's so funny?' Hardy said.

Wyatt wiped his smile away. 'Sorry. But that guy... What a douche.'

'Yeah.'

'So what do we do?'

'We do what he said. Prenticeville isn't a big place. None of the shitholes around there are. How fucking hard can it be? Find McGinty. Find his friend. Make them both yowl like a goddamn beaver having its nuts ripped off.'

His eyes fell on the big, grinning face of the Buc-ee's mascot above the signage outside. He picked up the jerky, opened his window and tossed the bag outside.

'Now get me the hell out of here.'

12

Adam's fingers moved at speed with the controlled precision of a state-of-the-art robot. The sounds of gunfire and the shrieks of his enemies as their insides splattered across the screen filled the small room.

'Take that, you piece of shit!' he said as a direct shot caused a head to explode into a fog of blood and brain.

One more to go.

Calmness, quiet now.

His heart drummed in his chest as he pushed open the door and entered the darkened room. His fingers stopped moving altogether, as did his on-screen avatar, and he quietened his breaths to strain his hearing for any signs of the big boss he knew remained somewhere within. He leaned forward on the couch, groaning in pain as he did so, the tenderness in his shoulder still agonizing if he made the wrong movement.

Footsteps at the door.

Not the door on the screen...

The actual front door a few feet from him. The lock released and the door inched open, and Adam cried out in pain as he pulled himself quickly to the side to draw the handgun from out under the cushion. He swiveled the barrel toward the figure...

'Damn it, Leo!'

'What?' Leo said, super casual.

'I thought... Doesn't matter.'

'You were gonna shoot me?'

Adam didn't answer as he put the gun back under the cushion. He looked to the screen. Dead. Damn it!

'You're still playing that dumbass thing?' Leo said as he pushed the door closed with his foot, his hands wrestling with the keys and a hefty bag of groceries.

'What the hell else have I got to do around here?' Adam responded. 'And it's your dumb game anyway.'

'Yeah. On the console my mom bought me when I was sixteen. Now I'm twenty-three and go out to work every day tryna get some money to live.'

'You stand outside the mall begging people to sign up for credit cards that'll end up sending them into a hell of debt. Hardly a career with prospects.'

'Fuck you.'

Leo dumped the bag in the kitchen and started to pull the food out, slapping each item onto the counter.

'Look, man, I'm sorry,' Adam said after taking a moment to calm down, recover from the irritation of losing that final battle, again, and the anxiety of the unexpected figure at the door. Although Leo coming home wasn't really unexpected given the time but Adam had been miles away, engrossed in the game.

'Whatever,' Leo said. 'You want pizza?'

'Sure.'

Leo grumbled something under his breath as he banged about putting pizza into the oven. He took two beers out of the fridge and popped the caps and came over and slumped on the sofa next to Adam.

'You want one?'

'Yeah.'

Adam took the beer. Leo downed most of his in one gulp.

'Anything happening?' Leo asked.

'Nothing. What about you?' Adam asked. 'You see anything?'

'Drove by your place this morning.'

'Everything OK?'

'Looked that way. Doors, windows still intact, so no one's broken in or anything. But I did see something.'

'Yeah?'

'Simon Peake's truck.'

'Outside my place?'

'Nah, I think he was at your sister's.'

'You saw them together?'

'No. But it figures.'

'Shit. That guy. He fucks everything up for me and has the balls to still be screwing my sister.'

Leo shrugged. 'Who is that guy, anyway?'

'Good question.'

Leo looked over at Adam's bandaged shoulder.

'He do that?'

Adam didn't answer straightaway. He hadn't told Leo everything. In fact, he'd told him virtually nothing. Leo only figured that Peake was somehow involved because of what had happened the other day when Adam had got all jittery when he'd spotted Peake arriving in his truck across the street. At first Adam thought Peake had found him. But actually it was Tyler's place he had his sights on. He'd gone up to Tyler's door. Spoken to the guy's wife. The audacity of that? He'd killed the guy only a few hours before.

He didn't know what Peake was up to. Perhaps searching for Adam to kill him like he'd killed Tyler and Evan. Or was Peake on Adam's side? He really didn't know, but, for now, it wasn't worth the risk of reaching out to the guy to figure it out. Better to lay low and see what happened next. Because he knew for damn sure that Hardy would want his blood given how things had panned out. And the prospect of Hardy catching up with him was a lot scarier than Peake.

Anyway, Peake had been confronted by Leo's dad, Gill, one of the local cops. Adam had got Leo to call him, although apparently he'd already known Peake was snooping around as he'd been to Evan's place right before coming over to Paleridge.

'Yo, you still there?' Leo asked.

'Yeah.'

'I asked you about Peake. You still haven't told me how he fits here. I thought you and him were good. Thought he helped you out.'

'He did.'

'So what changed?'

'I made a mistake. I thought he could help out with...' He wanted to say more, but he stopped himself.

'Shit, man, you know I'm good,' Leo said. 'Just tell me what went down. I ain't gonna rat you out. And you know my pops will help if he can.'

Adam sniffed and took a drag from his beer bottle. Gill Sanders was a stand-up guy. A career policeman. He'd worked around these parts for years. A stand-up guy? Yeah, he was well-respected. But around here there was no denying that the police were in a constant power play with the gangs who were given more than a little free rein to do what they wanted. As long as no innocents got caught up in their crossfire, at least. It wasn't as though there was a big, well-funded FBI field office anywhere near here to help tackle organized crime, so the best solution most of the time was to find some sort of harmony, side by side.

What Gill wouldn't like was the idea that Adam, Evan, and Tyler had got themselves involved with an out-of-town hard man like Hardy. But so far, Gill knew nothing about any of that, at least as far as Adam was aware.

'So?' Leo prompted. 'You know I don't have to let you stay here. You turn up on my stoop one night all bleeding and shit, asking for a place to stay? I ain't gonna say no to a buddy. But that was two days ago and you still ain't told me what went down, how you got shot. All I know is you're shit scared anytime anyone comes near this place, that Tyler and Evan haven't been seen in days, and somehow it all ties in with this Simon Peake.'

'You heard of a guy called Hardy? Down 'Bama way?'

'Fuck, yeah, I know 'bout him. The guy who feeds people to dogs, is what I heard.'

'Yeah.'

'Shit. He's after you?'

'Maybe.'

'Maybe?'

Adam sighed and finished off his beer.

'I never even met the guy. Like you say... he's got a bad rep. But it wasn't even my job. Tyler's the one who got the work.'

'Yeah. That figures. He started to get a big mouth when the money started rolling. But you only get money like that when you getting your hands real dirty.'

'He told me to go down Florida. We stayed there a few weeks, Evan,

Tyler, me. Just hanging. A few errands, dropping things, picking things up. We had to go snooping around these houses. Big mansions. Crazy rich people. We took pictures, that sort of thing. Then those two went off and told me to hang tight. Two days later I get a call to go meet them at the lake.'

'What lake?'

'Eufaula.'

'Thought you said Florida?'

'Yeah. They'd already left. So I go meet them there and...'

'And?'

'They had this woman.'

'What woman?'

Adam's hands were itching, feeling clammy.

'It doesn't matter. But... they'd killed her. For Hardy. And they wanted me to help get rid of her.'

Leo didn't respond but kind of made a weird grunting sound, as though he wished he'd never asked about any of this. And Adam kind of wished he'd never started talking, even if it felt pretty good to be getting some of this off of his chest.

'Why'd they ask you that?'

'You don't wanna know.'

The look on Leo's face suggested he really did.

'But I knew Peake could help.'

'Yeah? Sounds like you and Peake know a lot more about each other than you're letting on.'

They kind of did. But Adam really wasn't going to go into that with Leo. Not today.

Not ever.

'We rode over to his place. You know? Frank's farm. Except Peake attacked us. Everyone started shooting. I got away.' He put his hand to his shoulder. 'I've not seen Tyler or Evan since so... I guess they didn't make it.'

Leo said nothing but momentarily glanced to the front window, as though feeling sympathy for Tyler or his wife and kid or something.

'But why'd Peake do that?' Leo then said.

'I don't know.'

And that was the truth. Tyler and Evan weren't about to start a fight out there. They had the ten grand for Peake and they all just wanted rid of the body. So what caused Peake to flip like that?

Which was why Adam had no clue if Peake now wanted him dead or not.

'But you're saying Peake killed Tyler and Evan?'

'Yeah, but... they were fighting him too.'

'But he won. They're dead.'

'Yeah, I think so.'

'I could get my pops to—'

'No. Stay out of this. And keep your dad out of it. Best for both of you that way. Hardy... I don't know what he's gonna do.'

'Sounds like he just wanted that woman gone. As long as she's gone, does he really care what happened to Tyler, Evan, and you?'

Good point. Adam didn't know the answer. But he couldn't exactly ride down to Hardy's place and knock on the door, tail between his legs, to find out.

Leo got up and headed to the oven and pulled out the pizza. Adam grabbed another couple of beers from the fridge. He'd popped the caps when Leo's phone started buzzing on the counter.

The conversation didn't last long.

'Shay'na?' Adam asked.

'Yeah,' Leo said, sounding a little dejected about the fact his 'girlfriend' had obviously made another demand of his time.

Adam laughed. 'There's worse situations to be in. At least you'll be getting some action tonight.'

'Yeah, but she's gonna make me work for it again.'

They both had a laugh at that. Leo was forever in the bad books with her. His own fault, really.

'Looks like you get more pizza,' Leo said.

'And beer,' Adam said, nodding to the other opened bottle on the side.

'Don't wait up for me.'

Not long after and Leo was gone, so Adam got down to it. It wasn't the best pizza. Probably the cheapest they had, but Leo had paid for it. Damn, Adam really needed to get some cash together to give to his friend. Leo hadn't asked for a dime yet, but it was becoming clear even after only a couple of days that he didn't want this to become a long-term arrangement. Adam would pay him back, get out of his hair, just as soon as he figured a good, safe and cheap place to go.

He took a big bite of pizza, struggled a little to chew on it but then paused, mouth bulging when he heard the car pull up outside. But before he'd heard a door open, he heard footsteps out the back.

Shit.

Then footsteps by the front. 'Buddy, it's me!' Leo shouted out. 'Come on!'

Adam didn't hesitate. He rushed over to the sofa and grabbed the gun. He ran to the door, flung it open. Expected to see Leo there. Which was why he was off-guard, the gun nowhere near ready to shoot...

Not Leo. The hulking figure took up most of the space of the doorframe. Adam couldn't see his face because of the blinding sun behind him as it made its evening descent.

Adam let out nothing more than a pathetic whimper before the meaty fist caught him in the gut, knocking the wind out of him. He collapsed onto the floor, the gun fell free, and the half-chewed pizza spilled from his lips as the world around him spun.

13

It took several attempts for Adam to open his eyes and keep them open, and a little longer still to calibrate his brain and remember what had happened.

He was surprised to be waking up at all.

When he'd seen that figure at the door... he thought he was dead. The fist to the gut was the first of several strikes he'd taken. The rest came as he lay prone on the floor, boots to his face, his back, his ribs. Hardy's guys had found him and he thought they'd kill him there and then and bury him out in the sticks.

But he was alive.

He grimaced in pain as he tried to move from his position, crumpled on the cold concrete floor. Pain stabbed everywhere.

He wasn't tied down, wasn't shackled at all. Another surprise. He pushed back and his shoulder brushed the wall behind him. He looked around. A darkened room. No natural light except for a hazy glow coming from two plastic panels up in the vaulted corrugated metal roof. A warehouse. Not very big. Perhaps thirty feet long. Empty, except for him. He thought.

'Hello!'

He tried to shout but his throat was dry, hoarse, and he simply didn't have the energy, and the effort only sent a renewed wave of pain through his body and dizziness through his head.

'Hello!' He tried again, only a little more loudly than the first time.

No response.

He pulled himself to his feet, initially using his hands on the wall to help prop himself up while he overcame another head-spin.

He had a passing thought of Leo. What the fuck? He'd heard his friend's voice at the front door. So had the guy turned on him? Or had he been forced to trick Adam?

Certainly no sign of him in here...

'Hello!'

Still nothing.

He moved groggily across the floor, coldness greeting his steps. Only then did he realize they'd taken his shoes, socks, clothes. Everything but his underwear.

He pulled back the urge to sob at the indignity, the fear of what was still to come. He was stronger than that.

But they'd simply left him here. No ties or anything.

Perhaps they'd underestimated him.

If he was quick, he could escape.

He moved with a bit more purpose. Even in the dim light there was no mistaking the door in the opposite corner to where he'd woken.

He was a step from it when he stopped. He'd heard a noise outside. Not just that but...

He looked up to his left, where the corner of the room met the roofline. How the hell had he not spotted that before! The little red dot in the otherwise darkened room.

A camera.

They were watching him.

They knew he was awake.

The door swung open.

Two men burst in, towering over Adam who backtracked, squirming.

'No, please!' he screamed a moment before one of them swiped his legs and he crashed to the floor with a painful thud. The man grabbed his hair and dragged him along the concrete to the center of the room.

'Sit down,' the man said, his voice booming in the enclosed space.

'W-what?'

'Sit on the fucking chair.'

The guy practically lifted Adam and tossed him down onto the hard chair.

It took his confused brain a couple of seconds to figure the second man had put the chair there for him, because it certainly wasn't there before.

'W-why—'

The fist to his face halted whatever question Adam had tried to get out. His lip burst open and blood dribbled down his chin onto his lap as his brain swam. Dazed from that one strike, his body slid sideways until hefty hands pushed him back into place on the chair, held him there.

Thwack.

Another punch caught him on the side of the head. Strangely the pain that erupted was in his neck, as though the hefty strike had nearly torn a hole there such was the force. Adam winced and moaned and bowed his head, and took he didn't know how long to try and get his brain straight. When he finally had the strength to lift his head again his vision remained blurred, his left eye nearly swollen shut.

The man stood in front of him, an ugly sneer on his face.

'One more for good measure?' he asked.

'No, please,' Adam said.

Although he realized the question probably wasn't directed at him but the other guy holding him in position.

The fist caught his ribs this time and he was sure he heard a crack and was left gasping and rasping for breath. It felt like his heart had exploded into pieces.

'Please! No... more,' Adam coughed out.

Much to the amusement of the men who both cackled.

'You haven't even hit him hard enough to shut him up yet.'

'I don't want to shut him up. I want to hear him scream.'

The guy balled his fist once more and Adam cowered and found a strength from somewhere.

'I'm sorry!' he shouted out.

The beater paused.

'Tell... Hardy... I'm... sorry!' Adam said through gasps.

'Hardy? Who the fuck is Hardy?'

'A good question.' A different voice this time. Not as brutish. But also... familiar.

Adam focused on where the voice had come from, over by the door. A new arrival.

'He asked you a question,' that man said as he moved closer.

Frank Booker. What the actual hell?

'Frank,' was all Adam said in response.

'Who is Hardy?' Frank asked as he came up alongside his henchman.

'It's... not...'

'What? None of my business? I ain't so sure about that.'

He nodded to his man who reached forward and Adam tensed, expecting another pummeling, then relaxed a little when he realized a strike wasn't coming.

No. Something worse. Pain exploded in his shoulder when the man grabbed him over the gunshot wound then dug in his fingers. Adam's body convulsed, bucked back and forth, as the man behind him held him tightly in place.

'You're gonna start answering my questions now,' Frank said when the man released his grip. 'Or this is gonna get a whole lot worse for you.'

'OK!' Adam said. 'OK.'

'Start with how you got shot.'

But Adam didn't answer, just shook his head. He didn't even know where to start with that story.

'Why... am I here?' Adam asked.

Frank slapped him around the face. 'Hey, dickhead – I'm the one asking the questions here.'

'Y-yes.'

'I know something went down at the farm. My farm. You and Peake. Tell me about that.'

'I'm sorry,' Adam said. 'Peake fucked up!'

'Fucked what up?'

'It was just... business. He turned on me. He burned the place down.'

'And why would he do that?'

''Cause he's a madman!'

Adam pushed the twinge of guilt away. He didn't want to throw Peake under the bus, but in this situation... he just needed to get out alive. If he claimed ignorance, pushed everything away from him, maybe it'd work.

'So you two were up to no good on my property? Tell me about this business. That led to him shooting you, burning the place down. Him going into hiding. You going into hiding. And who the hell is Hardy?'

Too many questions. Adam's brain simply couldn't concentrate on any one of them properly.

Frank gave him time to respond but eventually stuck his hands on his hips and sighed.

'This is going nowhere,' he said. 'Beat him until he's on his last breath.'

Frank went to move away.

'No! Please!' Adam screeched.

Frank stopped.

'So you do want to talk?'

'Yes!'

'Good. Then let me back up. Do you know why you're here?'

'I... I...'

'Because you and Peake getting down to some horseshit out at my farm and the place burning down is one thing. But you know why I'm really here, don't you?'

'No!'

Frank rolled his eyes and sighed. 'Adam, where is your dad?'

'My... dad?'

'Jesus, this kid. Yeah. Thomas McGinty. Your father. Pops, whatever you call him. Where the fuck is he?'

'He's... in California.'

Thump.

The fist to the gut was powerful, but not as bad as before. More of a warning. Or an indication that the answer he'd given wasn't the right one.

'No. He ain't,' Frank said.

'But...'

'OK, Adam. Let's back up even more.' Frank sounded seriously fed up now, like a teacher unable to get something simple through to a dumbass kid. 'Let's make sure we're all aligned here before we carry on. You know me and your dad go way back, yeah?'

'Yes.'

'You know why?'

'W-what?'

Another sigh. 'Because we're about the only people around here who actually know how to make money. We've worked well together over the years. Best buddies? No. That's never been us. But we know that two of us side by side is better than the two of us working against each other, fighting for the same things.'

Frank paused, as though thinking or expecting Adam to say something. But Adam had nothing to say, largely because his brain was still processing the turn of events. Initially he'd felt relief that this wasn't Hardy holding him. Relief when Frank had opened up talking about the showdown at the farm, which really had nothing to do with Frank. But now the conversation had taken this latest turn... Adam feared things were about to get real messy after all.

'And we do work well together, mostly,' Frank continued. 'But quite honestly, I never really liked Thomas. I never fully trusted him. Never thought he was my equal. For example, I know about his temper. The beatings I'm sure you took, because I know for sure your mom took them. I know he had a drinking problem. I know more than once he lost stupid amounts of money on stupid bets, because he'd come whining to me asking for loans. So maybe I'm a dumbass too because last year when he offered to help me out with my tax problem...'

Frank shook his head and looked down at the floor. He took a few moments to compose his thoughts.

'Ask me how much he owes me.'

'How... much?'

'Two million. I gave your dad two million, straight up, so he could put it away, keep it out of view of the IRS. You know what happened?'

'No.'

'Liar. You know. Have you seen him lately?'

'No.'

'Exactly. The motherfucker's taken my money and run.'

'No... he's...'

'In California? Bullshit. I hired these guys to track him down out there. Know what I found?'

Adam shook his head.

'The last address he gave me? He hasn't been seen there for more than two months. Tommy upped and left one day, several weeks behind on rent.'

'I... haven't seen him.'

'Bullshit. He came back here a few days after that. Seven weeks ago yesterday. We've got him on a flight to Atlanta. And he was seen in Prenticeville the day after that. Then… poof. Gone.'

Adam shook his head.

'I've searched everywhere. Even thought maybe you and Peake had him hiding out at the farm.'

'He's in California,' Adam said. 'He messaged me from there! Not… even a month ago.'

Frank looked to his guy who shrugged.

'I can prove it!' Adam said. 'Get me… my phone.'

Finally the man behind let go and Adam's body slumped. He hadn't even realized the guy had been taking his weight like that. But now… he had no one holding him. Yeah, he was beaten, dazed, but this could be it. His chance. He could make a run for it…

Except he didn't move a muscle as his phone was pushed in front of his face.

'Unlock it,' Frank said.

Even with the bruising, Face ID did the rest.

'Show me.'

'In voicemail.'

Frank tapped away, his face souring as though he didn't like what he saw. He pressed something and held the phone out, and Thomas McGinty's voice came through the tinny speaker.

'Adam, it's Pops. Sorry to let you down, but I'm still in SoCal, something came up. I'll… I'll get over to you as soon as I can. Speak soon.'

'What the hell is that?' Frank asked, but the question seemed not directed at Adam, but more at his guy who simply shrugged. 'It's from four weeks ago,' Frank added.

'I told you…' Adam said. 'As far as I know, he's still out there.'

'You're a lying piece of shit,' Frank said.

'I'm not lying!'

Frank balled his fist and smashed it onto Adam's nose. Not the heaviest hit he'd taken recently but still painful enough, and fresh blood dribbled down to join the caked stuff around his mouth and chin.

'Guess we'll have to beat the truth out of you after all.'

The man behind took a hold of Adam again. No chance for escape now.

Next up came the big guy. He laid fist after fist into Adam's ribs, onto his chin, the side of his head. Everything blurred. Blood poured. Gashes opened up. He could barely see from swelling and pooling blood.

Then pain in his shoulder exploded again as fingers gouged at the wound there. Adam shrieked liked an animal. But at least the shock had somehow made him more alert as he'd been drifting moments before.

'Please!' he begged.

'You want this to stop!' Frank yelled in his face, spittle covering Adam. 'Tell me where he is!'

'OK!' Adam shouted in response, and just like that the beating stopped. But not the pain. 'OK.'

Frank gave him a minute. It didn't help much. Adam had never known pain like it. A big part of him wished he was already dead.

'He came back... two months ago. Like you said. But the truth is... he never... left.'

'So where the hell is he?'

'He's dead!' Adam bellowed. 'My dad is dead.'

Frank seemed to consider that, calming all the time, before, 'You killed him?'

Adam shook his head. 'No. Not me.'

'Then who?'

'Peake! Simon Peake killed my dad.'

'You're lying.'

'I'm not lying! I was there. We... we agreed to cover it up.'

'Why?'

'Because... because my dad was an animal! You said it yourself. But... it didn't really end there, did it? It's why me and Peake had a run in. The fire, you know?'

Shit. The words, the lies, were just pouring out now. But he had to do – say – what he could to get out of this mess.

Frank snorted. 'So Peake killed him?'

'They got into a fight and... yeah. Peake did it.'

'And he convinced you to cover it up?'

Adam nodded. 'I should never have agreed to it.'

'So where is he? Your dad?'

'Where do you think?'

Frank's face screwed up in disgust. 'You buried him on my fucking farm?'

Another nod.

'You stupid piece of shit. Do you know where?'

'Yes.'

'Then this is what's gonna happen. You're gonna take me there. You're gonna dig him back up. You're gonna go put his stinking, rotting corpse some other fucking place! Then you're gonna get me the money he owed me.'

'Two million? How the hell—'

'You figure it out. Collect on his death. Sell the house. Whatever. Get him off my land. Get me my money. Or you'll be maggot food right by him.'

'OK,' Adam said.

The room fell silent, as though everyone expected someone else to make the next move, to say the next word.

'What the hell are you waiting for?' Frank said to Adam. 'Get up.'

The hands behind him helped Adam to his feet. He needed it, given the beating he'd taken, and was a little surprised that when the hands released him, he was able to stay upright.

'Come on,' Frank said. 'You take any longer and you'll still be digging in the dark.'

He turned and moved for the door.

Survival instinct. That was the only way Adam could describe what happened next. He didn't plan it, didn't think it through. Everything happened subconsciously, a part of his brain he had no control over directing his body through the movements, desperation and a deep desire to survive spurring him on.

The metallic sheen caused the initial reaction. A sheen from the handgun stuffed into the waistband of the guy who'd been smashing Adam's face. He really should have had it in his hands.

Adam burst forward. He took hold of the gun, whipped it out, threw his elbow up into the face of the man who reeled back. Adam spun and let rip with the gun. Three shots to the man behind him. At least one hit, he thought. He turned back the other way and fired again and the bullet hit the big man in his lower leg and he crumpled to the ground. Adam got a bit more recompense by stomping on his face. He would have done it several more times if he could, but instead he turned the gun toward Frank, fired two more rushed shots to keep him at bay as Adam raced for the door.

He pulled down on the handle, kicked the door open, took an inhale of fresh air... then ran for his life.

14

Several hours had passed since the woman had collapsed to the floor in Jenn's parents' house. She hadn't been out for long though, only a few seconds before she'd groggily come around. Groggily being the key word as she'd been far less with it than before, her words slurred, her body listless. Peake had helped her to drink a can of sugary soda and given her time and eventually she'd started to brighten. Since then he'd tried more than once to talk to her but she'd fobbed him off with excuses of tiredness and the like several times. He'd let her nap. He'd given her medication, more food and drink. Time was passing. He wanted more answers as sitting here waiting did little good for either of them as far as he was concerned.

'Do you remember anything else yet?' he asked as they sat in the living room, her slumped in a sofa, him on the armchair opposite. 'About yourself, your son?'

She looked up at the mantlepiece once more. To that picture of the McGintys at the lake.

'Do you remember where it is?' he asked.

She shook her head.

'Anything else at all?'

She looked down to the floor and squinted as though trying to find the answers. 'Xavi. That's my son's name.'

'And yours?'

'I think… I think it's Lucia, but…'

'But?'

'Maybe it's not me. But someone I know. I have this face, an image of a face in my head. Someone… important to me.'

She clenched her teeth, tensing up as though the struggle to recollect was taking a physical toll on her.

'I just don't know. Anything!'

'It's OK,' he said. 'It'll come back.'

'How do you know?'

He didn't. He had no clue, actually.

'If you think that's your first name, I'll do some searches online. You've got a son, and judging by the ring on your finger, you've got a husband. Or had one. But someone close to you is missing you. There might be a notice that tells us who you are.'

Even without her name he'd already tried searching what he could of recent missing persons reports but had found nothing of anyone matching her description in this or neighboring states.

But he also didn't fully believe that she could recall so little. He had no real experience of amnesia, how common it was, how severe or short-lived it may or may not be, and it all seemed a little too… convenient.

'I still don't understand how I ended up here,' she said. 'With you.'

'You want the truth?' he asked.

'Of course.'

No reason to hold back. It was her life. 'The people who attacked you… they wanted you dead. And gone. They thought they'd killed you. They brought you to me. For me to get rid of the body.'

'But… why…'

'Why did they come to me? Because they thought I'd help. They were wrong. Especially when I realized they'd made a mistake. That you weren't actually dead.'

She shook her head. Her eyes welled. Not for the first time. Her emotions were all over the place, but he guessed that had to be expected.

'The thing is… because I saved you, I'm now a target too. Whoever wanted you dead will be after both of us.'

She said nothing.

'Lucia, who tried to kill you?'

'I don't know.'

'A man named Hardy?'

'Who?'

The quizzical look on her face certainly suggested she didn't know the name.

'The men who came to me were called Tyler Kittle, Evan Huggins. Adam McGinty. Do you know any of them?'

'I… don't think so.'

They'd been through all this before, and she was repeating the same unhelpful answers.

He stood up and she shuffled uncomfortably in her seat as though she couldn't read his intentions. He took his phone from his pocket and found the pictures and moved over to show her. To start with, her face was unmoved, but then that same look of fear returned, and she slowly nodded her head.

'That's Huggins and Kittle,' he said.

'They… they…'

'They attacked you?'

She nodded.

'And your son?'

'I… He was there. When they came to the house. I think. I remember him shouting…'

'The house. Your house? Do you know where it is. Can you describe it?'

'I… No. A big place. But… maybe it's not even my house.' She closed her eyes and pushed her fingers against the side of her head. 'Water. There's water.'

'You mean the lake? It's a lake house?'

'No. I don't think so. But… maybe.'

'Your son was calling, shouting. Then what?'

'I don't know what they did to him…'

She sobbed and held her head in her hands and he put his hand to her shoulder as though that would in any way bring her comfort.

'Those two won't hurt you anymore. You can be sure of that. But we need to find out who ordered you dead. Because I'm sure the men who brought you to me were just two chumps given some cash in hand for a hit.'

She shook her head. 'I can't do this! I… just want my son back.'

He was about to respond when his phone rang. Jenn.

He answered it as he moved out of the room and into the hall.

'You OK?' he asked.

'Are you? I heard about the car crash on the highway.'

He paused a moment. Not because of the question but because of the echo to her voice.

He looked at the front door. Moved that way. He pulled the door open and there she was, over by the stables. Her car was further beyond, by the road – no wonder he hadn't heard it when she'd arrived. Had she done that deliberately?

'And there you are,' she said. She brought the phone down and pushed it into her back pocket and folded her arms as she glared at him. 'You're a real piece of shit, you know.'

She went to turn away but he rushed over, intent on holding her back. As he reached out she whipped back around.

'How dare you betray me like that.'

He stopped and stared and tried to think of something good to say. He had nothing really so chose that instead. Better than digging.

'I heard about the fire at Frank's farm,' she said. 'He's been asking everyone in town where you're hiding. He even asked me at the diner.'

'Did you tell him?'

'Of course not! Otherwise don't you think it'd be him here now, not me?'

'Thank you.'

'But I kinda wish I had told him now that I've found you sneaking around my parents' house. I told you—'

He took her hands. 'Jenn, I'm sorry.'

'Just tell me what's going on.'

'Perhaps… perhaps it's better if I show you.'

* * *

Jenn stood in the doorway of the living room, speechless. Lucia stared over not knowing what to say either.

'I couldn't leave her out in the stable,' Peake said. 'She would have died out there in the heat. I'm sorry, Jenn, I had no choice.'

'Yeah, you keep saying sorry, but I'm not really feeling it. And choices? You had so many, but to me it looks like you chose all the wrong ones.'

She spun around toward the door.

'Jenn!'

He went after her. She'd made it outside before he caught up.

'I'll explain.'

She turned back to him and the look she gave was pure anger.

'I don't even want to hear it.'

'Please. Let me try.'

'This involves Adam, doesn't it?'

He paused for a moment, thinking about exactly how much of the story he could tell.

'Yes.'

'Tell me everything. This is your one and only chance. Otherwise I'm outta here, and I'm calling the police.'

'You know that won't help any of us,' Peake said. 'Trust me on that.'

'Trust?' she scoffed.

OK. Perhaps the wrong time to use that word.

'Your brother's got himself mixed up in something bad,' Peake said. 'A guy named Hardy. Do you know him?'

She shrugged. 'Maybe I heard Adam or someone else use that name. I never met a guy called that.'

'Me neither. But Adam and two lowlifes were doing a job for him. They turned up at the farm two nights ago with a bag full of cash and a body in the trunk. The money was for me. To get rid of the body for them.'

Jenn gulped.

'You can take a guess why Adam chose to come to—'

'Jesus, Peake, I get it! Move on,' she said, squirming with unease.

'The body in the trunk was Lucia. Only she's not dead, is she? I couldn't do anything else. Digging a grave for a corpse is one thing but I wasn't about to bury someone alive, or murder someone I don't even know.'

'Where's my brother?' Jenn said, the words all garbled with distress.

'I don't know. That's the truth. The other two... they're dead. Gone. But Adam? I didn't want to hurt him. I didn't want to hurt the others, but it was them or me. Adam ran. I haven't seen him since.'

'So you burned the farmhouse down to cover your tracks. And that's why Frank is after you.'

'Seems that way.'

'And Frank and this Hardy guy?'

'I've no idea if they know each other or not.'

'Who are you?' she asked him, not hiding her disgust. 'Killing people. Burying bodies...'

'I didn't ask for any of this.'

'But it's not new for you either... is it?'

He didn't answer. It wasn't as though he was some serial killer with a history of dispatching of bodies. But still...

'Is Simon Peake even your real name?' she asked.

'Yes.'

He took out his wallet. Pulled out his driving license. She scrutinized it as though checking its authenticity.

'I've never lied to you about who I am.'

'Just what you are?'

'No. Not that either. But my past is... messy. I needed a new start here—'

'New York license. Is that stupid English accent even real?'

He laughed at that; she didn't. 'It is, but I haven't been to England in a long time. Before here, I was in New York.'

'So you're running?'

'Like I said, I needed a new start.'

She pulled out her phone and angrily tapped the screen for a few seconds and stared at it a while longer. He knew it wouldn't be hard for her to find the grim basics about him. His most recent past, at least. Not the part of his life that defined him, but an ugly blight that most 'normal' people would have a hard time moving on from.

When she finally looked back up to him she seemed so... disappointed.

'Five years in a state penitentiary?'

He nodded.

'You assaulted and permanently disfigured two teenage boys.'

He squirmed at the way she said that. Why did so many people always see it for something that it wasn't?

'The teenagers in question were bigger than me. And they were armed. I saved a girl from being raped by two vicious scumbags.'

She opened her mouth to respond but stopped herself.

'It says you were in the army.'

'Yes.'

She held his eye a moment, as though searching for answers.

'I'm not making excuses,' he said, 'but... I've been through some shit, Jenn.'

She scoffed. 'Then go see a fucking therapist.'

He didn't respond to that.

'So you got out of prison and...'

'And came here. Like I said, I was looking for a fresh start.'

Which was only partly true, as there'd been an intervening period in New York after his release from prison when things had gone really bad for him. His old past catching up with him in a damn nasty way. That was the real reason he'd left there so hastily several months ago. But he wasn't about to open up about all of that now, even if those events were the real reason he'd headed south.

Shit, if she knew the whole truth about him, what he'd seen and done over the years, she'd never have spoken a single word to him. Some things were best left out of mind. Most of Peake's life, really.

'You saved a teenage girl,' she said. 'Kinda how you saved me that time at the bar. Now it's Lucia's turn. So that's it? You go around towns searching out vulnerable women to help out. Lurking in the shadows, waiting for the right time. Then after... you get to sleep with them, right?'

'No. Not right. Not even close.'

'I'm not some little girl that needs your protection.'

'I never said you were. And I never thought that either. Jenn, I—'

'I want you out of my parents' home. Both of you. I want you gone from here and gone from my life.'

'I understand,' Peake said. 'But... you heard about the crash, right? My truck's totaled. Just give me the night. I'll get another vehicle tomorrow. Then I'm gone.'

'You really have the balls to ask me for anything more?'

'We have no other options.'

She thought a moment. A good sign. 'I'll come back tomorrow, before my shift at the bar. If you're still here, I'm calling the police.'

'Understood.'

She went to walk away. 'One more thing,' he said. 'Please? Wait there.'

He rushed off to the house without awaiting a response. He grabbed the photo frame from the mantlepiece and headed back out to her.

She looked even more unimpressed when she saw what he was carrying – if that was possible.

'Lucia thinks she recognizes this place,' Peake said. 'It might help to figure out what happened to her.'

Jenn kept her eyes on the photo, a whole host of emotions likely going through her at that point, not just about everything Peake had just told her, but about what the picture itself represented. Happier times for the McGintys, perhaps. Or perhaps just uglier times that were glossed up to appear happy.

'It's Lake Eufaula,' she said. 'At least that's what we call it. Walter F. George reservoir.'

'You're sure?'

'I'm sure.'

Peake knew of the place, but there were no landmarks in the picture that he'd recognized. Lake Eufaula was a huge manmade reservoir a couple of hours drive from Prenticeville that stretched along the state line between Georgia and Alabama.

'She was looking at this?' Jenn asked. 'Lucia?'

'Yeah.'

'So you two have just been snooping around?'

'It's not like that.'

'Sure it isn't. She's been around the house, scrutinizing our family pictures, and she doesn't think it strange that she's now staying in the home of one of the guys who tried to kill her?'

Peake had asked himself the same question. 'I think she's struggling to connect the dots. But maybe... Adam wasn't actually involved in trying to kill her.'

He really hoped Adam wasn't.

'Yeah. Maybe. I just know... If I was in her position, I'd have run the first chance I got. Anyway, that's your problem. Not mine.'

She turned and walked off. Peake stayed there until her car was out of sight. He hated the whole conversation. He especially hated that he'd let Jenn down. That had never been his intention.

For now, he had little choice but to do as she'd asked and disappear.

He found Lucia exactly where he'd left her. He replaced the photo above the fireplace.

'That woman... She's the girl in the picture?' Lucia asked.

'Yes.'

'She's your girlfriend.'

'No.' Certainly not anymore.

'But you two are close.'

'We were. I'm not sure we will be now.'

'Because of me.'

'Not directly.'

'I'm sorry.'

'It's not your fault.'

'I heard some of the conversation. I mean, some of it was pretty heated.'

'Yeah.'

'So her brother...' She looked up at the picture.

'He was one of the men who brought you to me.'

So she had recognized Adam after all. Or perhaps just had figured things out because of what she'd overheard.

'That's pretty fucked up,' she said. 'That you want to help me, but you think this is a safe place for me.'

'You think I'm lying to you about something?' he asked. 'That I have an ulterior motive for helping you?'

'I don't know. But...'

'Whatever happened to you, I know Adam. I'm not hiding that fact from you. He and the other two brought you to me. I already told you how that ended for Kittle and Huggins. But Adam... He's young, he's made some stupid choices in his life, but he's not a killer.'

'Lucky for me.'

'That's not what I meant. What I meant is... I don't know how this all started but he was pulled along with whatever happened to you.'

'Seems like you really think you know him.'

'Yeah.'

'And he knows you too. Which is why he thought you were the right guy to... you know.'

'Yeah.'

'Why'd he think that? Why you?'

'You don't need to worry about that.'

'But I do worry about that. Because just like your girlfriend I have no idea who you really are. What your intentions are.'

He glared at her but said nothing. She should have been thanking him, but she was accusing him. Of what though?

'Anyway. I found out where that lake is. Lake Eufaula. You know it?'

'I... don't think so,' she said.

'We'll go there tomorrow,' Peake said. 'It's not that far.'

Although he'd have to find a new set of wheels. Which was the only reason he wasn't immediately going there. He had two choices – steal a car or use some of the ten grand to buy one. He hadn't yet made up his mind which would be easiest, nor which had the potential for causing the most problems long-term. He'd prefer to take the legal route, but he didn't have an endless supply of cash and buying a car legitimately also led to yet more records in his name. Given the way things were going around here at the moment, perhaps it was best to avoid that.

She went to shuffle up on the sofa but grimaced in pain.

'I can check the wounds if you—'

'No. I don't want you checking me anymore. You're not a doctor and I can do it myself.'

'Understood,' Peake said. 'So you're happy with the plan? Rest tonight, head out tomorrow?'

'Happy? I'm not really happy about anything here.'

'Fair enough. I'm gonna go fix some food. Do you have any preferences or dislikes?'

'I haven't a clue what I like.'

He headed to the kitchen and spent a few minutes rummaging. Little fresh food other than the odds and ends he'd bought at the store earlier, but the pantry and freezer had supplies too.

He settled on a frozen lasagna for four – he was damn starved – and had the packet in the oven when a rumble somewhere outside in the distance caught his attention. At first he thought maybe Jenn had returned, had changed her mind and wanted him gone immediately. Or maybe she'd called the police.

No. Neither of those. The engine noise was too deep to be her car. And it was more than one vehicle, he was sure. And the police? No sirens, so...

Peake slammed the oven door shut and rushed back toward the living room. Lucia was on her feet, a strange glint in her eye as though she thought he was about to go for her.

He carried on past her and to the window.

'This is a problem,' Peake said as he peeked out to see two hefty vehicles barreling toward the house. One was a black SUV – a GMC. The other... a Ford F150. Riding high on a beefed-up suspension and oversized tires. A pretty damn distinctive vehicle. 'A big fucking problem.'

15

Peake spun around to Lucia. He looked down at the knife in her hands, the blade pointed at him. A kitchen knife, though he had no idea when she'd picked it up.

'We need to go,' he said.

She didn't move.

'Lucia, we need to go.'

Was she about to attack him?

He strode across the room and grabbed her arm and pulled her toward the door.

Apparently not.

The vehicles had stopped outside. Peake heard car doors opening, closing.

He slowed in the hallway.

'Who are they?' Lucia whispered.

Peake didn't answer.

'Simon Peake!' came a shout from outside and Lucia gasped. 'We know you have her. Send her outside. That's all we're asking from you.'

'You know that voice?' Peake asked Lucia. She shook her head in response. 'We go out the back. But we need to be quick.'

Peake took her hand and pulled her along again. She groaned in pain at the quick movements, but she'd have to put up with the discomfort if she wanted to live. Peake opened the back door and took a quick look out. Clear. For now.

'This way.' He went right to the far corner where a door led to a tool room. Not the best of hiding places but Peake didn't have time for anything better and he wanted her to stay close.

'In there,' he said, opening the door. 'Keep the knife. See whatever else you can find. If anyone else opens this door but me—'

'You can't leave me alone!'

'I'm not leaving. I'll be back soon.'

He closed the door and rushed back into the house. He slowed again as he reached the hall and spotted movement beyond the frosted windows at the front. A knock on the door.

'Peake, open up. We won't ask nicely again.'

'OK, OK!' Peake shouted. 'Back up and I'll come out.'

'And make sure your hands are empty, or you're not gonna take more than a step.'

'I'm not armed,' Peake said.

Although his handgun and shotgun were both in the little cubbyhole under the stairs, not far from the front door. He really wanted to grab them, but...

They wanted the woman. She was leverage. They'd somehow tracked Peake here but they had no idea where Peake had hidden Lucia. It'd buy him some time, and not knowing where she was – if she was even at this house or somewhere else – they wouldn't shoot him dead the moment he opened the door.

At least that's what he tried to convince himself as he stepped forward and turned the handle.

He opened the door slowly, both for caution, but also to allow him more time to scope out the threats before he fully revealed himself.

Two vehicles. Four men, one woman on their feet. All were armed. A couple of handguns, a couple of shotguns and what looked like a semi-automatic rifle. A mini army.

And he had nothing but his wits.

He brought his hands up as he took a step out.

'Hold it there,' said the man who'd earlier shouted. A squat but broad guy with shaggy hair up top, dirty jeans and a checked shirt. He looked like a stereotypical yokel, as did his younger buddy next to him. The other three all looked Hispanic and Peake assumed they'd come out of the Ford truck he'd seen the other day.

The two white men, one with a shotgun, the other a handgun at the ready, came up to Peake and patted him down.

'Where is she?' the oldest of the Hispanic men asked in a gruff, heavily accented voice. He had gnarled features, and Peake knew he was the boss here, even if he didn't understand the dynamic between the two sets of people.

'Who?' Peake asked, and received an elbow to the gut from the eldest country bumpkin for doing so.

'You know who.'

'The woman? The one Hardy's guys wanted me to make disappear?'

No response to that.

'I did what I was asked. I made her disappear.'

No one said anything. The two white guys finished checking Peake and retreated to the line of defense. Or maybe offense.

'If she's not here, why are you?' asked the elder yokel.

'Look, things went a bit... sideways. There was a minor disagreement with your friends. They tried to withhold payment. I eventually got my money, but... that farmhouse kinda got torched.' They weren't buying it. 'But you don't need to worry about that. I did what I was asked to do. She's gone.'

'Bullshit.'

'I only came here to lie low for a few days. The guy who owns that farm? Frank Booker. He's pissed at me. I'm sure you can imagine.'

'So you're saying she ain't here?'

'She isn't anywhere anymore.'

'So you won't mind if we take a look around the place then?'

'Knock yourselves out.'

The bumpkins went to move forward again but the chief grabbed the shoulder of the mouthy one to stop him.

'No,' he said to Peake. 'We know she's alive. So you tell us where she is. Save us the trouble. This doesn't have to end badly for you.'

'She's not here,' Peake said, shaking his head.

'OK, Jay.' The chief guy took his hand back and the older white guy – Jay? – and his friend approached Peake once more.

They headed past him and into the house. He turned to follow. It would take them all of a few seconds to find the medications, the clothes. Peake could obfuscate about those too but sooner or later he needed to take action here.

'No. You stay right there,' Chief said.

But Peake only paid heed to those words until he'd counted to five. Just long enough for the yokels to have moved inside, out of sight. Past Peake's weapons stash so he had a clear route to get there.

He dashed that way.

'Hey!' came the shout from behind him, a moment before a bullet zinged by his ear. He ducked and darted inside. Damn. Jay's friend hadn't moved on at all. He was crouched down in the hall, pulling out Peake's shotgun. He sensed Peake behind him and spun around, swinging the butt of the gun in an arc.

Peake ducked and dove into him, slamming him to the floor. The shotgun blasted and the man screamed. Peake twisted the gun from his grip, smacked him across the side of the head with the butt then jumped up to his feet.

Silence. A strange silence. Obviously everyone had heard the shot but there was no sudden onrush either from the other guy inside, or from the three by the vehicles.

They were readying themselves. Perhaps taking better positions.

Peake crept toward the living room doorway, the kitchen adjacent.

Then he flung himself forward when rat-a-tat gunfire boomed and echoed from outside. Bullets pinged and thwacked all around him. Plaster dust and wood splinters burst through the air. Peake threw himself up against the wall to the living room, pulled himself into there for cover.

'Don't move!'

Jay. He had his handgun pointed at Peake's head.

'I got him!' Jay shouted out in a momentary respite from the barrage of gunfire before he set eyes on Peake again. 'Drop the weapon.'

Peake looked at the shotgun in his hands. Damn thing was empty, but it was still a chunky tool.

'I said, drop it!' Jay shouted before pulling his trigger. The boom so close to Peake's head caused his brain to swim and his vision to blur for a few seconds. Only a warning shot – the bullet had lodged harmlessly in the wall next to Peake's ear.

He tossed the shotgun and didn't resist as Jay grabbed him around the throat from behind and pressed the barrel of the handgun against his skull.

'Walk,' Jay said, shoving Peake forward to get him started.

They moved out into the hallway. Jay's friend remained on the floor, awake but looking seriously groggy.

'You alright, Lee?'

'Do I look alright?' he said through clenched teeth. He grasped at his ankle, below which his shoe, his foot probably too, was riddled with holes from the shotgun pellets.

'Can you walk?' Jay said.

Lee nodded and growled as he dragged himself upright.

'We have him!' Jay shouted to the outside. 'Coming out.'

He jolted Peake forward again and soon the threesome outside came into view, all with their weapons trained on Peake. One wrong move from him, one nervous twitch from any of them, and he was dead.

Lee hobbled past, momentarily distracting the woman, who held the rifle, as though she was questioning whether the injury was down to her.

'Where's Lucia?' Chief asked.

'I told you already.'

In response to that, Lee, with a sudden rush of adrenaline spun around, strode up to Peake and slammed his meaty fist into Peake's gut.

He would have doubled over from the blow had Jay not got such a tight grip around his neck. Peake coughed and spluttered.

'Liar,' Lee said. 'I saw the shit inside. Bandages. Meds. She's here. Just like we knew she was.'

Having said his piece and dealt his blow, Lee's face twisted in pain again and he lifted his wounded foot off of the ground like a dog would with a sore paw.

'I'll ask you one more time,' Chief said, 'and then we'll start making this real personal for you.' He holstered his handgun and pulled out a mean-looking hunting knife. Several inches of serrated blade. He took a couple of steps forward. 'I'm thinking which piece of you to take first.'

Peake wrestled for a second, testing Jay's grip. The guy was strong. Chief looked really damn pleased with himself as he stepped further forward.

'So?' he asked, a smile creeping up his face. 'Where is she?'

'I'm right here.'

Peake slumped at the sound of her voice from behind him. What the hell was she doing?

He didn't hesitate for long though. The unexpected turn had taken everyone's attention, even if only for a second. Peake reached up and grabbed Jay's wrist with both of his hands and pushed the barrel of the gun toward the sky. He roared with effort as he drove forward, only a couple of steps needed before he lifted his foot and sent Chief stumbling backward with a push kick to his chest. Then Peake pulled his body down, hard and fast. Jay didn't release his grip on Peake's neck. Not straightaway. Not until Peake twisted around, twisted the arm he was still holding too until he heard and felt a snap.

Jay shrieked. Peake slipped free of the arm around his neck. He took the gun from Jay's limp grip, dropped to his knee, fired two shots at the onrushing Lee. Two hits to the chest. He fired off against the woman with the rifle and hit her in the leg. She collapsed to the ground. He twisted and fired at the other Hispanic guy with the shotgun who retreated behind the pickup truck without getting a shot off.

Peake looked back at the chief who was dragging himself along the ground, dazed. He lifted his gun toward Peake...

Two more shots. Hand, shoulder.

'Ahhh!' Peake roared as pain rushed up from his ankle. He spun to see Jay on the deck behind him, blood-dripping knife in his hand. Peake kicked him in the face. Stomped on his skull.

'Lucia, get in the car!'

He looked around. Three down, two still up but hiding behind the truck.

'Lucia!'

He glanced at her. She looked shellshocked, wide-eyed and scared as she crouched at the side of the house.

'Go!' he shouted at her.

She did, but movement in the opposite direction caught Peake's eye. The woman. She bobbed up with the rifle and Peake pulled his trigger in response. A rushed shot. The bullet pinged into the side of the truck. And now he was out of bullets.

He raced for the SUV, tossed the spent handgun at the truck. Chief was trying one last time to get his foe, the gun in his left hand now, pain and desperation etched on his face.

Peake diverted toward him, kicked the gun from his grip before he'd had a chance to fire. He bent over and scooped the weapon up. The guy with the shotgun now took a chance and revealed himself.

Peake fired. Three shots. The first two hit. Chest. He was done for. The third shot burst the truck's front tire. A deliberate move from Peake.

He dove into the SUV where Lucia was in the passenger seat. Start button. The engine roared to life, just as he knew it would with the key fob now in his pocket. The one he'd pilfered from Jay's jeans as they came outside. The woman bobbed up again and Peake fired off more warning shots through Lucia's open window before he tossed the gun to her.

'Cover us!'

But she looked bemused. Or too shocked to act.

He put the SUV in drive and hit the throttle. He tugged the wheel and the vehicle shot forward, spinning as it did so, dust billowing. Jay, just about with it after the blows to the head, saw the monster bearing down on him and rolled out of the way as the SUV swept past. Peake adjusted the steering wheel and thumped the throttle, and they shot off toward the road.

No braking as they approached the turn. Peake lifted his foot and pulled on the wheel again and the tires screeched as they tried in vain to keep traction. The back end swung wildly, the SUV rocked on its hefty suspension, but Peake kept the vehicle on the road and soon had it straightened up and them moving away from the McGintys' home at speed.

He checked his mirrors.

No one chasing them. They had no chance with the front tire of the truck shot out.

'You OK?' Peake asked, glancing at Lucia. Her face was streaked with tears, the handgun still in her lap. She looked in shock. And in pain. Probably from the sudden movements, rushing into the car like she had.

She nodded meekly in response.

'Are you sure?'

'I said I'm fine!' Fine, but not happy apparently. Neither was he, to be honest.

'Why did you do that?' he asked.

'What?'

'I told you to stay hidden. I was dealing with it.'

'Didn't seem like it to me.'

'I asked you to stay put. So why'd you come out?'

'I heard shooting! I... thought you were in trouble. You were in trouble.'

'And your plan was to come out and rescue me?'

She tutted and huffed. 'Why are you being so shitty with me?'

He didn't answer, instead took a few moments to think. 'I'm trying to help you.'

She said nothing to that and he looked over and realized the agitation she'd shown moments before had ebbed away. Now she looked scared. Of him?

'You... killed them.' Disappointed as well as scared.

'Not all of them. Maybe only one of them.'

'But... Who are you?'

She asked the question in such a critical way, as though she was disgusted by what she'd just witnessed.

'And you said yourself you killed the two men at the farmhouse, and...'

'You're actually bothered that I killed people who were coming to end your life?'

She shot him a scathing look. 'I don't know anything about you. About your past, your life, but this? Shooting, fighting, killing, blood and... It's not normal for me so I'm sorry if—'

'How do you know?'

'What?'

'How do you know violence isn't normal for you? You don't even remember who you are.'

She tutted. He probably hadn't needed to sound so petty.

'I'm sorry if you think I'm overreacting but I'm...'

She didn't finish the sentence.

'In shock,' Peake suggested.

She didn't reply, just looked away and out of the window.

'Did you know those people? Any of them?'

She hesitated before answering. 'I don't think so.'

'I don't know how they found us.'

The only people who knew Peake was staying at the McGintys' were Jenn and Travis. Had one of them tipped off Hardy?

He really couldn't believe they would, and how would they even know Hardy? Peake still had no clue who that guy was.

But rather than running and hiding, again, perhaps it was time to find out...

'Has anything else come back to you?' Peake asked. 'Anything at all.'

Perhaps the trauma of what she'd just witnessed would give her some flashes of memory.

But she simply shook her head.

'I'm going to ask you one more time, Lucia. Do you know who's trying to kill you? Did you know any of those people at the house just now? Do you know Hardy?'

She locked eyes with him, looked irritated by his questions more than anything else.

'No,' she said. 'To all of those questions. I don't know them. I don't know why they're trying to kill me.'

He huffed. 'Then we're going to do everything we can to find out.'

16

'Is this journey ever going to end?' Greg asked from beside Ridley in the back of the car. Katie sat up front driving and had been for the last three hours. If anyone needed to complain about the toil, it was her. But she remained diligent, focused.

'It's not that long, really,' Ridley said to Greg, who grumbled and looked out of his window.

Maybe the guy was just anxious about what was to come. He hadn't met Jorge Ramirez before, only knew him through the information Ridley had provided – both the factual, written down stuff and the more flavorful anecdotes.

Most likely it was the latter which had got the normally unflappable man uptight.

'You know this probably won't go well,' Greg said. 'And there's nothing you can say to him in person that you couldn't have said to him over the phone.'

'The simple fact is that I need to keep on Ramirez's good side. No different to any client relationship in many ways. It's more courteous to meet him in person. Especially given it's bad news we're delivering.'

Ridley caught Katie's eye in the rearview mirror before she looked back at the road. A slightly knowing look from her, though he wasn't sure why.

As different as Greg and her were, one thing he knew: he'd rather have them by his side right now than be going to Ramirez's alone. The world he occupied – as a go-between, sitting in the middle of secretive government agencies and their rivals – was fraught, dangerous. Brawn was one thing which helped in many situations, which was why he had the likes of Greg. He wasn't the biggest guy ever at a shade over six foot. But he could handle himself and more. He would have done well in the special forces, Ridley believed – he'd met plenty of those men and women before and they all had a certain je ne sais quoi about them that set them apart from regular people. But Greg hadn't wanted that life. He wanted something closer to home, to family, so after a few years of trying to find a job that fit, he had eventually ended up as part of the FBI's SWAT team at its field office in Detroit. He'd been part of some pretty all-out operations there and would have still been there had it not been for government cuts.

Ridley had picked him up two years ago. The stop-start life Greg now had as a self-employed consultant to Ridley suited him, he said, as it gave him long bouts of time to spend with his wife and young son up north in between assignments. But, not for the first time, it was as though the further Ridley took Greg from that safe life, geographically and mentally, the more sullen he became.

'Anyone want one last rest stop?' Katie asked from up front. 'We're coming off the freeway in five miles. Then we're nearly done.'

'All good here.' Ridley said.

'Same.' Greg added.

Ridley kept his focus on Katie a few moments longer as his mind dwelled. She was quite a different beast to Greg. No family to speak of, no ties to anywhere in particular. Having been a math whiz her whole life she'd ended up as a junior analyst at the CIA but had been turfed out in a cloud over suspicions that she'd been tapped up by Russian agents. He'd asked her about it only one time, the first time they'd met when he was feeling her out to see if she was suitable to take on.

'Did you do it?' he'd asked her.

'Do you think we'd be sitting here having this conversation if I'd taken money from the Russians?'

A good point. More likely if there was any convincing evidence of foul play she'd have ended up in a jail cell or dead in a ditch somewhere after a 'carjacking' gone wrong.

'So why did they say that?'

'Because what do powerful men do when they don't get what they want from young women who they expect to be docile and compliant?'

He didn't ask any more. He got the point. She'd been screwed over. Either she'd refused the sexual advances of some dirty bastard higher up, or had simply been too keen, eager and confident – and female – for her lowly position. The CIA was no different to any other big organization in that regard. The only difference was they sometimes had much more elaborate ways of getting people out of the business.

Katie was clever, a good negotiator, a good strategist. She could also handle herself just fine from her training days, even if her skills were far less utilized in the real world than Greg's. But she and Greg complemented each other well and they both added skills to Ridley's repertoire.

Yes, he was perfectly confident going to see a man like Jorge Ramirez on his own. In fact, he'd met with the guy alone in the past.

But today was not that day.

There was no other chat in the car before they were winding toward Ramirez's luxury seafront villa. Out here on the Gulf Coast, a couple of hours south of Tampa, the super-sized properties sat on large plots of land with walls and hedgerows that screened them from the roadside. As they arrived at their destination the only indication of what lay beyond was the white-painted wall and the big, blocky security gate.

Katie stopped by the intercom and after a brief intro the gate slid open to reveal the villa over fifty yards away. She took them through and parked up on the poured concrete drive in front of the villa. Poured concrete everywhere, really. The villa was sleek and modern and angular with exposed concrete walls, big windows, smatterings of cedar here and there to add warmth to the look. The whole thing hugged the edge of the low dunes which gave way to the sea beyond.

Greg whistled as he looked out of his window before they all got out of the car.

'Now this, I could get used to,' he said on the outside.

'What, you'd actually leave Detroit?' Katie said. 'I mean, other than this big-ass mansion, what else does this place have? If you ignore the year-round sunshine and the ocean and the infinity pool and the—'

'Yeah, yeah,' Greg said, waving away her teasing. 'And year-round sunshine? Kinda, if you forget about the hurricanes.'

A fair point. Even if the weather was glorious today; they'd heard about the next incoming storm several times on the radio while driving, and every electronic road sign on the highway gave warnings, details about evacuations.

Two days to go until the growing hurricane in the gulf smashed into Florida's west coast. Which probably explained why there were piles of sand bags all around the property, ready to be put into place before landfall to try and prevent the storm surge from flooding out the mansion.

Would sand bags be enough?

Katie took in a big inhale. 'Still, gotta love the sea air.'

Ridley looked back at the gate which was now rolling closed behind them. He spotted the sentry there, standing by a little security hut tucked away behind the wall, out of sight. The guy wore neat suit pants, white shirt. Obviously a gun or two on him. Ramirez had plenty of guys like that around. Not hugely overt security, but it was there.

'Come on,' he said before moving for the villa.

The large oak front door opened just before they reached it, and they were greeted by another nicely dressed soldier. Ridley appreciated the efforts of their attire at least. Unless they needed to be more discreet, he and his workers always dressed smartly too. You are what you present to the world, he remembered an old mentor saying to him many years ago. Ridley agreed. And what Jorge Ramirez presented to the world was not just a man of wealth and power, but one of class and dignity too.

Ridley liked him. Even if he was hellishly wary of him. Especially today.

'Señor Ramirez is waiting for you. Go to the left.'

Ridley nodded at the instruction and he and Greg and Katie made their way across the airy interior. Glossy marble floors covered the expanse and monstrously big ornaments and paintings struggled to fill the space. They ended up in a huge living room, big fireplace taking up one wall, windows at least twelve feet high adjacent giving a breathtaking view of the sea.

'Wow,' Katie said as the three of them stopped inside the room.

Ridley had noticed the sumptuous view too, but his focus was soon on the man they'd come to see. He got up from the cream leather sofa and beamed a smile. Jorge Ramirez was forty-six years old, but with his dark, wavy hair, designer stubble, and nice skin he looked ten years younger. Actually, he looked like he wanted to be on the cover of a fashion magazine. With dark linen pants and a white shirt his clothes weren't that dissimilar to those of his entourage, but his attire was clearly a lot more expensive, set off by the chunky gold watch, the gold bracelets, the gold necklace.

Ramirez wasn't alone in the room. He had another guard standing in the far corner, doing his best to look inconspicuous, and a little boy sat on the big rug in the center of the room messing with toy cars.

'Jorge, how are you?' Ridley said, moving up to his host and giving him a handshake and a friendly slap on the shoulder.

'You made good time, my friend,' Ramirez said, all smiles. For now. 'And these two are?'

He looked at Katie and Greg, who both had their game faces on.

'These are my colleagues, Greg and Katie.'

Ramirez went to Katie first and shook her hand then pecked both her cheeks. Ridley noticed the slightest of squirms at the friendliness, but she was a good actor and kept her cool.

'Wow, you are a looker,' Ramirez said, still holding her hand as he took her in, his stare moving up and down her. 'You should be a model. You know, I have some contacts—'

'I like my job,' she said. 'This is more my thing, you know?'

Ramirez glanced at Ridley and winked. 'Oh yeah, I imagine. I'm sure he's a charmer when he wants to be. All aloof. And that accent? A shame, about you though.'

He let her hand go and went up to Greg who stood tall and stiff as a goal-post. Ramirez shook his hand then crumpled down and shook his fist, making a real meal of it.

'Man, now that is a handshake!' he said. 'Wow, you are something.'

Ramirez slapped Greg's back then ducked and bobbed and weaved and threw a couple of air punches Greg's way.

Greg didn't move a muscle. Ridley really wished the guy would just relax a little.

'I bet it'd take something to knock you down,' Ramirez said, still shadow-boxing. 'Where'd you find him? MMA cage?' Ramirez threw a fist that landed less than an inch from Greg's nose. To Greg's credit, he didn't even blink. 'Pow!'

Ramirez was done with his mocking. He moved back toward the sofa, smoothing his hair back. He wiped his brow and panted hard for a couple of seconds, obviously putting it on.

'Remind me not to get on the wrong side of those two,' he said. 'You spooks always have some dirty tricks up your sleeves, right?'

No one said anything to that.

The boy had stopped playing with his cars and looked around the room expectantly, as though he knew he didn't belong.

'I've heard a lot about you,' Ridley said to him, hoping to deflect Ramirez's attention away from his crew.

'Yeah?' the boy responded.

'I was told how big and brave you are. But I didn't know you would be so big.'

The boy blushed.

'How old are you?' Ridley asked.

'Eight.'

'What! I thought at least ten.'

'You sound funny,' the boy said.

'He's from England,' Ramirez said.

The boy's face brightened a little. 'Have you met the King before?'

'Actually, I have,' Ridley said, and was about to carry on the conversation – one of his favorite stories – but Ramirez held his hand up to stop him.

'That's a story for another day. The adults have some things to discuss. You go play in your room.'

The boy didn't need to be told twice. He grabbed as many cars as he could in his arms and shot off.

Almost as soon as he had gone, Ramirez's smile faded.

'You wanted to talk to me,' Ramirez said. 'So talk.'

And Ridley was about to, had his mouth open to speak, but Ramirez cut him off a second time with that damn hand. The smile came back too.

'You know what?' he said. 'You guys must be so tired after that drive. You want coffee?'

'I'm good,' Katie said.

'Not for me,' Greg said.

'I think we're OK,' Ridley confirmed.

'Nonsense. You need coffee. Let's go to the kitchen.'

Ramirez strode off. Greg and Katie both glanced at each other and then at Ridley with what the fuck? faces. Ridley said nothing but gave them an imploring look before they followed their host to the obviously huge and expensively fitted kitchen, the guard from the living room, and the one from the front door propping up the rear.

Ramirez quickly dismissed the two cooks. A large pot bubbled away on the stovetop. Ramirez went over to it and looked in before setting about prepping the fancy-looking coffee machine. Once he was done he went back to the pot.

'Bunuelos,' Ramirez said as he picked up a large mixing bowl, stirring the mixture inside with vigor. 'You like them?'

'Donuts?' Ridley said. 'Yeah, I guess.'

Ramirez shot him an unfriendly smile. 'Not donuts. Bunuelos. I know it kinda means donut, and there's so many types, but this type. This is the right kind.'

He poured some batter into the hot oil in the pot and began working it with two skewers.

'You know my mother was from Spain?'

'No,' Ridley said. 'I didn't.' Actually, he did know. He knew everything about this man, but he also knew Ramirez hadn't personally told him such details.

'From Andalusia. In her hometown, at the weekend, you walk around and some of the people set up bunuelos stalls on the street. Huge pots much bigger than this and they just sit there and fry all day for everyone who passes. And it costs pennies. Unless you're a tourist. Then it costs you a bit more.'

He laughed at that then a few seconds later brought one of the skewers out of the oil. A series of stringy donuts dangled off the end, which he slid onto some kitchen roll ready and waiting on a serving plate. He dusted the donuts in sugar and offered the plate around. Katie and Greg looked to Ridley for approval. He nodded and each of them took one. He did too.

'Wow, these are so good,' Katie said through a mouthful. Ridley forced his way through the overly hot morsel as Ramirez finished making three coffees. He handed them around. All three of them left the drinks on the counter.

'Now we're all satisfied, right?' Ramirez asked.

'We are,' Ridley said. 'We appreciate the hospitality.' Greg and Katie murmured their agreement.

'You wanted to talk, so talk.'

'You know we have a problem. It seems we've got a—'

'Is she dead. Yes or no?'

Ridley paused a moment. 'No. We don't think she is. That's the problem.'

'You don't think she is?'

'Correct.'

'You don't even know?'

'I'm doing what I can—'

'No. You're standing in my home, in my kitchen, eating my bunuelos and drinking my coffee. This is doing what you can?'

'I thought it—'

'Remind me, who's the guy you brought into this?'

'Hardy.'

'The redneck thug.'

'A man who's far enough removed from you to ensure you come away from this clean.'

'If he'd done the damn job properly, yes.'

'We're sorting it.'

'And what's he doing right now?'

'I don't—'

'Tell me I don't know, or I'm not sure one more time and see what happens.'

Ramirez didn't speak the words forcefully but the tone in his voice and demeanor had changed.

'So I'll ask again – what is Hardy doing right now to resolve this situation?'

'He's got his guys searching for her.'

'But they haven't found her.'

'Not yet.'

'And what pressure are you putting on this inbred asshole to get the job done?'

Ridley didn't answer. Ramirez sighed.

'You want another bunuelos?' he asked Ridley who politely declined. Katie did the same.

Ramirez turned to Greg, standing closest to him, but Greg didn't get the chance to answer the question before Ramirez picked up the pot and tossed the molten oil at him. Katie and Ridley reeled back as the amber liquid sloshed over Greg. He squealed like a feral animal as his skin sizzled and smoked. Katie jolted, as if to respond to the attack, but Ridley, trying everything to stay calm, put a hand out across her to hold her back. The gun barrels pressed to the backs of their heads by Ramirez's minions only helped confirm that decision.

Greg writhed and fell down on one knee and whipped out the gun from his waistband, but Ramirez saw it and wrenched a cleaver from the magnetic strip behind the stove. He swung the knife down and the metal slashed through skin and flesh and bone. Greg's squeal turned to a howl as his severed lower arm dropped to the floor, fingers still clutched on to the weapon he never got the chance to use.

His body crumpled down on the side, blood pouring from what was left of his arm, the skin on his face and neck bubbling and bleeding.

'Wow! Get a look at that!' Ramirez said, crouching down for a second as if he needed to get a proper look. 'His flesh... It's mush!'

Greg's cries died down to a whimper, then nothing more than a strange rattling noise as he tried in vain to breath. Ramirez, still enjoying himself, kneeled right by Greg's face.

'Holy cannelloni! The dude really just melted right in front of us. Cannelloni. That's what he looks like! Look at that...' He pointed to Greg's mangled face. 'That white drippy stuff is like the pasta, and the red oozy stuff is the fill —' He stopped and looked up at Ridley, dropping the forced smile as if he'd made a faux pas. 'Sorry. I forgot. He was your friend. My bad.'

He leaned further down and put his ear close to what was left of Greg's mouth.

'He's still breathing, you know. I'm not kidding. He's still breathing as though he actually has a chance of getting himself back together after this! I knew he was a fighter. I just knew it.' Ramirez paused and his face went solemn and he shook his head. 'Man, this is sick. That poor bastard. I don't like to see an animal suffer like that.'

He unpeeled Greg's gun from his fingers, pointed the weapon at his bulging eyeball – the flesh all around it melted away – and pulled the trigger.

Katie and Ridley both winced. Ramirez dropped the gun and wiped away his smile.

'Do I need to explain the point to you here?' Ramirez said.

'No,' Ridley said. 'I got the message.'

'You sure? What about you, honey?' he asked Katie.

'You want us to put more pressure on Hardy,' she said. 'Get nasty if we have to.'

Ramirez laughed and clapped his hands. 'Give her a fucking pay rise. She got it. Time to get results. Time for you two to get nasty. Yes?'

'Yes,' Ridley said.

'Good. Now both of you, get the hell out of my house.'

Ridley and Katie turned but Ramirez wasn't quite finished.

'Oh, and don't worry, I'll get rid of this body. It's not actually that damn hard.'

* * *

Five minutes later and Katie was driving them back north, Ridley in the front next to her, the back seats morbidly quiet.

'It was just a power play,' Ridley said.

Katie said nothing but her hands were shaking. He was sure she'd never witnessed anything like that before. Hell, it shocked him and that was saying something.

'I get that,' she said. 'But are you really just gonna let him get away with what he did? What if it was me lying there with my flesh all melted into the floor?'

She glared at him.

'No,' he said. 'I'm not letting him get away with it. But we did well to walk out of there alive, don't you think?'

'Then what do we do now?'

'We go to Hardy. Just like Ramirez said. We put more pressure on, just like he said. But we don't forget. When the time is right...'

'I'm going to give that motherfucker exactly what he deserves.'

Ridley thought that one over a moment. The whole reason they were here at all was because Ramirez was a very important cog in something much bigger for Ridley. But that didn't mean the cog couldn't be replaced with another, when the time was right.

'Yeah. He'll get what's coming. You can count on it.'

17

Jenn was still agitated when she arrived at the bar. How had she ever fallen for a man like Peake? Yet another guy who'd let her down, but at what point did it switch from being their fault for being assholes, to her fault for getting close to them?

An hour to opening. An hour to get not just the place straightened out but her head. One other car was parked up in the lot. Travis's. A couple of times recently she'd found him in the unit above the bar. A one-bedroom apartment, technically, though Frank hadn't had a tenant in there as long as Jenn had known the place, and it didn't even have a full working kitchen or bathroom up there anymore.

She unlocked the main door of the bar, moved inside and flipped on the lights. She took in the familiar smell of cleaning fluid that only barely masked the odor of stale alcohol and last night's guests.

'Hey, Trav?' Jenn shouted out. 'You up there?'

She heard a bit of banging about above her but no response. She went behind the bar and opened the washer and started to take out and rack the clean glassware. She was only partway through when she heard thuds coming down the stairs out back in the storage area, then Travis rolled into the bar, all bleary eyed, his hair a mess.

'Jesus, you pull an all-nighter or something?' Jenn asked him.

'Nah. Didn't get home till after three. But Mom was snoring like a rhino. I had to get out of there. Didn't actually get to sleep until after midday.' He glanced up at the Georgia-shaped clock on the wall. 'Shit, is that the time?'

'Yeah. Just getting things sorted. Your mom OK, though?'

She knew his mom was ill. A degenerative lung condition that would eventually kill her. Not cancer, but it was likely caused by smoking – and it meant her lungs were slowly failing. Eventually, her heart and brain simply wouldn't get the oxygen they needed, and one night would simply stop working. The doctors had originally suggested she had less than two years, but that was over three years ago. As far as Jenn knew, she wasn't getting any worse, but she would also never get better.

'As OK as she can be,' Travis said. 'But I feel so useless. Like there's literally nothing I can do to help.'

'You help by being there for her.'

Which meant having her stay with him permanently in his one-bedroom condo. Not the best set-up for a guy in his mid-twenties, but they had no other options.

'Not much help when I'm not even there, though, is it?' he said.

'Don't beat yourself up. You're doing what you can. You wanna drink?'

'Yeah. Double whiskey please.'

She caught his eye and only then realized his joke.

'Or plain coffee,' he said.

'I'll get a pot on,' she said, and paused on the glasses while she got the machine working. They didn't get many coffee orders in the bar, but the machine was a useful companion for the staff at least.

'Thanks.'

He stretched his hands to the ceiling and yawned.

'You seen my brother recently?' she asked him.

'Not in days. Why?'

'Because I'm worried about him.'

'Is this the shit that Peake was talking about?'

'What shit?'

Travis waved it away like it was nothing but the look on his face showed he knew it was more than nothing.

'Don't know much about it,' Travis said. 'Just that Peake's got Frank all riled up about something at the farm. Thought Adam was involved in it too somehow.'

'And you know anything about this something?'

He went rigid in the face of her hostile tone.

'No. I don't. Do you?'

'I know Simon Peake is a liar.'

'Why, what's he done?'

'I don't want to talk about it.'

She fished out two mugs and found some milk – still in date – in one of the fridges.

'I thought you were into Peake?' Travis said.

'Yeah. 'Cause I have a real good record of picking nice guys, right?'

'Peake's a straight-up guy.'

'Oh, Trav, you're too goddamn kind. Always seeing the good in everyone.'

She meant that as a compliment, but he looked put out.

'Did you know he was in prison?' Jenn asked.

The twitch on his face and the lack of a response suggested not.

'Five years for assault.'

Travis still said nothing.

'You still think he's a straight-up guy?'

'Plenty folk make mistakes,' Travis said. 'I also know he was once in the army. Some of those guys see some bad shit. Messes with their heads when they come home. He wouldn't be the first ex-soldier to struggle to adjust to civilian life.'

'Now you're making excuses for him?'

Jenn picked up the coffee pot and poured them both a cup. Although he thanked her for his, there was no doubt it was a little forced, the tone of their conversation bordering on hostile. Why was Travis so keen to stick up for Peake?

'Look, Jenn, I don't know what went down with you two, but sometimes you just get a sense for people. Peake... You can depend on a guy like that.'

Travis took a sip of his coffee as Jenn went back to the glasses.

'And I know he helped you out before,' Travis added.

'Excuse me?'

'That night here. Out back. The bikers.'

Now she was really pissed – with Peake. 'He told you about that?'

'Yeah, he—'

'He had no right to.'

She set down the glass she was holding, harder than she'd intended. Luckily it didn't break. She just wanted this conversation to end. She knew Travis was only trying to make her feel better, but he wasn't.

'And there was that other time too,' Travis said.

'What other time?'

She froze, glass in one hand, tea towel in the other, and Travis straightened up and held her eye but didn't respond straightaway. Likely well-aware he'd hit a nerve but was trying to think what he could say to smooth things over.

'You know? That night you and him were getting cozy up in here. It was a Tuesday and there were no games on, so it was quiet as shit. Peake got a call from Adam. Some problem. The two of you shot outta here and I had to hold the fort. The first time I'd been asked to stand the wrong side of the bar.'

Jenn said nothing. Of course she remembered that night. She hated that night. She wished she could forget.

'I didn't see you for a few days after that. I sensed it was something about your dad because he'd been back in town, but... I never asked you or Peake about it.'

'That's because it's none of your damn business.'

Travis held his hands up. 'You're right.'

'Damn it!' Jenn yelled in pain when the glass cracked in her hand. Blood dribbled from her finger and down onto the towel. Way to go, letting out her frustrations on an inanimate object.

'Jesus, you OK?' Travis said, coming toward her.

'I'm fine!' she shouted at him. 'I'm fine.'

She tossed the broken glass in the trash can and went over to the sink and flushed the gash in her hand with cold water.

'Sorry, Jenn, I didn't mean to upset you.'

'Travis... just go. Please. I've got a lot to do.'

'I'm sorry, I don't know what—'

'Travis, just get lost, will you!'

'Yeah. You got it. See you around.'

He slapped his half-finished coffee on the bar top and strode out of there, slamming the door for good measure.

Jenn turned off the water and found a Band-Aid and was soon carrying on with her prep, but she couldn't shake the conversation out of her thoughts.

Yeah, Travis was only trying to make her feel better, but he really had only made the turmoil in her head even worse than before.

And it didn't get any better when her phone rang and she saw who was calling.

'Frank? How are you?' she answered.

'Jenn, where are you?'

'At the bar. I'm working tonight. We're opening in twenty minutes.'

'Yeah, well, I need to speak to you.'

'But—'

'It's urgent. I'll send someone else over. Lock up and come see me.'

'Come see you where?'

But the call was already dead.

Jenn stared at her phone for a minute then headed for the door. She locked it behind her and was halfway across the parking lot to her car when she spotted Frank's big black SUV on the road outside. The passenger window slid down.

'Come on,' Frank called over to her.

'What the hell is this?'

'We need to talk. About your brother.'

'Adam? What the hell has he done now?'

'That's what we need to talk about.'

She hesitated and reached behind her where her finger brushed the form of her phone in her back pocket. She'd never been scared of Frank before but after everything that had happened recently?

Damn she wished Travis was still here.

Or Peake.

'Jenn, you're wasting my time. Get over here already. The longer this takes, the longer you're not getting paid tonight.'

His window glided back up. Jenn moved around the other side, glancing up and down the street as she went. No sign of Travis at all now. No sign of anyone.

She pulled open the passenger door and crouched down to get in and...

Expecting to see two empty seats next to Frank she instead saw a big bald guy right there in front of her. She knew him. One of the two who'd been in the bar that other night when Peake showed up.

She went to turn and run away but his enormous hands grabbed her. She screamed but there was no one else to hear it as he dragged her into the car.

The next moment they were moving. She bucked and writhed trying to get out of his meaty grip but had no chance of shaking him off.

No chance either of freeing herself from the pungent rag that was smothered over her mouth and nose.

Soon, she had no fight left in her at all.

18

Dusk approached as Peake and Lucia traveled south and west, away from Prenticeville – perhaps for the very last time, although Peake certainly hoped there'd be an opportunity to see Jenn again. Under better circumstances than how they'd left things.

That was a worry for another time though. Right now he needed to figure things out with Lucia. Getting away from Prenticeville was the first priority, but Peake wasn't heading off aimlessly, running as far and as fast as he could. Doing so would bring no answers.

Lucia stirred next to him. She opened her eyes and stretched out and then grimaced, the movement clearly causing her discomfort.

'I was asleep?' she said.

'You drifted off. Not long ago.'

She glanced at the clock on the dashboard and groaned as though disappointed that she'd been asleep for all of twenty minutes rather than several hours.

'Where are we even going?'

'To the lake. That picture sparked something in your mind. I'm hoping that by going there, seeing it in the flesh will help you even more.'

She didn't say anything but stared out of the windshield, then out of her window, then she craned her neck to look out of his window.

'The lake's here? I thought it'd be more... rural.'

'No, we're not there yet. And we're making two other stop-offs first.'

Which explained why they were driving through Granton in Morrison County, heading back to Evan Huggins's house for a second time.

The street was as quiet as the last time Peake had been there, with no one in sight at all.

'Do you know this area?' Peake asked as he slowed the car.

'It... could be anywhere.'

'But if this was where you were from, you'd surely know it.'

Though perhaps that was just him being hopeful more than anything.

He stopped outside Huggins's house. Last time no one had answered Peake's knock on the door, but it certainly looked like someone was home now as he could see a light on in the front room.

'That's where Evan Huggins lived. He was one of the two men who brought you to me.'

Lucia shook her head, looked frustrated with herself.

'This could be anywhere,' she said.

'Last time I came here, I didn't stay long. It didn't feel like I could. Even though I spoke to no one, I felt under watch. This truck came cruising past me. A big Ford truck on big wheels.'

He studied her for a reaction, but she only looked confused.

'I'm pretty damn sure it was the same truck that turned up earlier.'

'What are you saying?' she asked indignantly.

'Isn't it obvious?' Peake said. 'Like I said, maybe you're from around here. People around here certainly know you.'

'Want me dead, you mean.'

Peake shrugged.

'I didn't know those people at the house. And I don't see anything here that I recognize. In fact, I'd go further – this is not where I'm from. I just... know.'

She certainly seemed confident enough about that idea. His eyes rested on her Rolex a moment before she covered it up with her sleeve.

'What?' she said.

He didn't respond.

'I didn't mean it like that,' she said.

'Like what?'

'Like this place is beneath me.'

'Come on,' Peake said before putting his hand to the door.

'But—'

'We have to try this.'

Peake stepped out and was pleased to see Lucia emerge the other side only a few seconds after.

They made their way up to the door side by side, Lucia moving a little awkwardly, nervously.

'What the hell are we doing?' she whispered.

He didn't answer before knocking on the door. He heard footsteps. The door opened. A woman. She looked a bit like Lucia. A few years younger but with the same dark hair, dark eyes. Except although younger, she had a weariness to her look, as though life had treated her hard.

Or because she was maybe drunk or stoned.

'Hey, is Evan home?' Peake asked. Lucia shuffled at the question as though even more uncomfortable now.

'Who are you?' the woman asked, not trying to hide her hostility.

'Acquaintances. Hardy sent us. Evan's been ignoring him. We're trying to find out why.'

'Yeah? Well, I ain't seen him neither.' She seemed more angry than worried.

'What did you see say your name was?' Peake asked.

'I didn't.'

She fixed her eyes on Lucia, a disapproving look.

Any recognition? Peake couldn't tell.

'Just tell him we came looking,' Peake said, already edging away.

The woman didn't shut the door until Peake and Lucia were back in the car. And they didn't speak until after that.

'So?' Peake prompted.

'Nothing.'

'You didn't know her?'

'If I did I have zero recollection now. Surely if I knew... Seeing her would have sparked something?'

Which is what he'd thought, hoped. And it really didn't seem like Huggins's wife or girlfriend knew Lucia at all either.

'Kittle lived—'

'I'm not doing that again,' Lucia said.

'What?'

'That was horrible,' Lucia said. 'Horrible for me, and for her. You killed her husband!'

'She doesn't know that.'

'Now you're knocking on his door, pretending you're his friend.'

'He didn't deserve any better than what he got.'

'But what if she did?'

Peake didn't answer that.

'I'm not doing it again. And you can't force me to.'

'Can we at least drive by there? It's not far. Just see if the neighborhood looks at all familiar.'

She sighed.

'Please? It'll help me help you.'

'I'm not getting out of the car.'

'Fine.'

It didn't take long to reach the street in Paleridge. Last time Peake had come here he'd been questioned by that policeman. Thankfully he hadn't been bothered by the boys in blue since. Not that the last couple of days had been trouble free, but at least they'd been cop free. Well, except for Travis's cousin...

OK, so the last few days had been nonstop problems, but hey...

'It's that one there,' Peake said, nodding to the house, which – like in Granton – had lights on inside with twilight now upon them.

'I'm getting nothing,' Lucia said. 'Can we just go?'

Peake thought for a moment as his eyes stared into his mirror at the two vehicles that had pulled into the street. As with the last time, there was definitely more activity here. A more ominous feel about it too.

The two vehicles moved on past. He didn't recognize either. Definitely not the Ford truck from his last visit, but he didn't like it here. His eyes rested on one of the houses across the street. He'd noticed movement in one of the windows at the front. Nothing there now.

'Are we done here or what?' Lucia asked.

'Yeah. We're done here,' Peake said. 'Let's get over to the lake.'

* * *

Full darkness arrived soon into the journey, but rather than nighttime bringing a chance for rest, Lucia had become even more fidgety and restless. Perhaps overtired, perhaps just full of anxiety. He'd let her have his phone so she could do some 'research'. He'd take a good look through his phone's history later to see exactly what that entailed. Although she was good enough to give him some of the basics through conversation.

'I don't see any news reports that look like they could be me,' she said.

'No. I didn't find anything either.'

She tutted.

'What?' he asked.

'Perhaps... I don't know. Perhaps it's being kept quiet. For a reason.'

'What reason? Like ransom or something?'

'Yeah. But then—'

'Nobody ransoms a dead person. They wanted you dead and buried, remember?'

She squirmed, a common reaction to his direct way of pointing out her predicament.

'You said before something about remembering water. But you don't think it's the lake?'

'Did I say that? I'm not sure. I think I meant... I didn't live at the lake.'

'But you definitely recognized it from the picture.'

'Yeah. But it wasn't the lake itself, but a building on the lake. It wasn't in the picture but... I remember it.'

'It could be any lake then, couldn't it?' Peake sighed. 'You said it was this lake. Lake Eufaula.'

'No, you told me it was Lake Eufaula.'

'That's not what I mean.'

'Then what do you mean?'

'It's a damn big lake. I'm just trying to figure out where we should head to.'

'Yeah, well, I think I found the building on a map. An old pump house or something.'

Which sounded like a positive step.

'And you think you were actually there, or was it just something you saw?'

'I... I don't know for sure if it was that building. But I have no recollection of being in a house. I told you that already. It was something more... industrial.'

'OK. We'll go to the pump house. Put it into the GPS.'

It wasn't that much farther anyway.

They fell into silence for several minutes as she carried on her searches. The highway at night in this part of the world was dark and quiet. The whole area was dark, quiet, isolated, with few big towns around. A great place to bring a kidnap victim. A murder victim.

'The lake covers 46,000 acres,' Lucia said, breaking Peake's dark thoughts. 'It has over 600 miles of shoreline.'

'Let's hope we're going to the right place then, otherwise we've got a really long night ahead.'

She gave him a sullen look. He wasn't sure why.

'The lake was built in the fifties,' she said, eyes back on the phone screen. 'They evacuated numerous towns. Ended up flooding all sorts of historic sites, apparently. Native American sites.'

She looked off, out of her window into the darkness, obviously deep in thought.

'What?' Peake said. 'Does that sound familiar to you? You think you might have some Indigenous blood in you?'

She shot him a scathing look. 'No,' she said. 'What are you talking about?'

'I'm sorry, I thought that's where you were going.'

'I wasn't.'

'I'm just trying to help you figure things out.'

He couldn't understand her irritability. Had he said something out of hand?

'You're pretty certain you're not Native American? Fine. But that suggests you're probably certain where your origins actually are. So...'

'Mexico. I'm Mexican. But I don't know if I was born there, or if that's just my family.'

He said nothing to that. Given her looks and her name, it kind of fit. But knowing she was Mexican didn't on its own help much.

'This is the turn coming up,' she said.

He took it and they continued along a single-track road, nothing but blackness now reaching out into the distance beyond the GMC's headlights. To Lucia's side the inky black ripples of the huge lake undulated ominously in the thin illumination.

'There's stories about people going missing out here,' Lucia said.

'Yeah?'

'I don't mean like me – people who were kidnapped or anything. I mean people who were out on the lake who never made it back alive. Swimmers, boaters. There's an urban legend that it's the spirits of the Indigenous people who used to live here, the ones who refused to move. According to some people, the developers had heavies lock them in their homes and they were drowned. People claim they can hear their screams still. That the spirits rise up from the depths and pull people under as revenge.'

She looked up from the phone screen, concern spread across her face as she first looked out over the dark water, then back at Peake.

'What?' she said, challenging in her tone.

'Like you said, it's just an urban legend.'

'Yeah, well, you didn't almost die out here. And you've got to admit... you wouldn't want to be stuck floating out there right now, would you?'

Her eyes fixed on the water once more. Peake didn't answer. He really didn't know what to say to her pensive, unnerving thoughts.

'Is this it?' Peake asked as they rounded a bend and the looming structure came into sight, its outline silhouetted against the moon.

'Yes. I think it is.'

Peake took the car off the road and up to a set of metal gates. He shut down the engine and stepped out. The temperature had dropped since nighttime had arrived, but only to the low eighties, yet it still felt more chilly here with a hefty breeze coming across the water, and perhaps given the isolated, almost eerie surroundings. Lucia seemed even more unnerved than before as she came up to his side, eyes fixed on the pump house.

'I remember this,' she said. 'It was a night just like this. I remember thinking... it looked like a ghostly castle or something.'

She was right – it kind of did. The gray stone structure had been built in something like a mock-Gothic style, with turrets and buttresses. Quite why, he had no idea.

'This way,' she said.

She led them off and around the side of the wire mesh fence which eventually came to an end on a small bluff which fell to the inky water several feet below. Peake didn't question her as she stepped out onto the rocks, holding on to the fence to swing herself around and to the inside of the small compound.

Not the best security, but the fence was at least a basic deterrent for a building like this, in a place like this. He couldn't think of many reasons why anyone would bother to trespass or break in.

Although he did wonder why the hell the men from Morrison County had chosen this place to bring Lucia.

They walked across the tarmac and to a sturdy-looking door on the water's side of the building.

'In here?' Peake said, glancing around as though there might be a sudden ambush from somewhere.

Of course there wasn't. No one else was out here in the middle of the night.

Lucia nodded and tried the handle, but the door didn't budge.

'It's not locked,' she said, heaving. 'Just stuck.'

Peake tried it, then threw his shoulder into the door and sure enough it creaked open, the bottom scraping along the concrete.

They walked into a pitch-black room, the smell of damp permeating all around. Peake turned on his phone's torch and shone it across the floor and the ceiling and the walls which glistened with dark, slimy spots.

'This is it,' Lucia said, holding a hand to her mouth before she slid down onto her haunches.

The room was empty. Perhaps it'd been a basic storage room at some point as there were no other internal doors, and it certainly didn't take up the whole footprint of the building, just one small part.

'You're remembering?' Peake said.

He didn't get a response from Lucia. She'd zoned out as she stared across the room to the far corner.

'Your son's not here,' Peake said. 'There's no sign anyone was here.'

'I was here,' she said, shooting him a scathing look. 'We arrived at night. Just like this. I was in the trunk of their car.'

'Huggins and Kittle?'

'I think so.'

'But they hadn't hurt you by then?'

'I was... bleeding. But not hurt bad. I was scared. Petrified. Gagged, my hands tied. They pulled me from the trunk and dragged me in here. One of them tossed me onto the floor, then...'

'Then what?'

She stretched up and composed herself. Her words were mostly monotone, a little robotic as though she was trying to be as emotionless as possible about the whole thing.

'I don't know how long we were here. Several hours maybe. There was no food, water. The two of them talked outside. Always outside. I could only hear their muffled voices. Until... until...'

'Until what?'

'The third one arrived.'

'Adam?'

'He was younger than the other two. It seemed odd to me. That he was with them. One time I was in the room with just him. He stared at me the whole time. I... spoke to him.'

'What did you say?'

'I asked him, why are you doing this?'

'And he said?'

'Shut up, or I'll shut you up, bitch. That was the only time I spoke. And the only time he said anything to me.'

Peake clenched his fists in anger. Adam had so much to answer for.

'Then later, they were all in the room. One of them was on the phone. I... couldn't hear the other side of the conversation but the whole thing felt different. The fact he was in here talking at all.'

'Do you remember what he said?'

She closed her eyes as though thinking. 'We'll get it done tonight. Maybe not the exact words, but it was something like that. He said, McGinty knows a guy. We'll be back in the morning.'

Peake could guess what those words meant, and Lucia obviously had too.

'As soon as the call finished they all turned to me and I knew that was it. They were going to kill me. So as they came forward, before they'd even said a word to me... I attacked.'

She wiped her eyes then stood defiantly, hands on hips. Peake remained still and waited, gave her the space he felt she needed.

'I had no plan,' Lucia said. 'I just knew I wouldn't sit there and let them kill me. I jumped on one, bit his shoulder as he tried to throw me off. I felt this... not pain, but warmth in my side. I only knew I'd been stabbed when he tossed me off him and I felt down to the blood pouring out. I put my fingers there and there was just this... hole to my insides. I was desperate. So I got up and I went for the door. And I managed it. I was outside, running. One of them jumped me from behind, we both ended up on the ground. He hit me. He stabbed me, again and again. I remember the sound. The horrible sound as the knife slipped through my flesh. Then he grabbed my neck. Choked me.'

Tears rolled and she broke off and turned from him. He left her for only a moment before moving up to her and putting his hand on her shoulder. After a few seconds he wrapped his arms around her. She didn't move from him.

'I didn't even know what to think or to do,' she said. 'Part of me wanted to fight. But the rest of me just wanted it to be over. I didn't want to be there, suffering anymore. I went still, I couldn't move. He stopped attacking me. I knew I was still alive but I didn't know if I wanted to be, or if there was anything I could even do about it. Then I just drifted. The next I remember is when I woke up with you.'

She shuffled in his grip and he loosened, thinking she was trying to get away, but instead she turned around and buried her head in his chest.

'I'm sorry,' Peake said.

'For what?'

'For what they did to you. And for making you relive it like that.'

She said nothing for a good while before eventually peeling from him.

'But it worked,' she said. 'Just like you said, coming back helped me remember. If we keep going to places I know... maybe it'll all come back.'

'What about before?' Peake asked. 'You arrived here in the trunk but what happened before that? Where were you? Where was your son?'

She shook her head and looked out of the door, then silently went that way and stood looking out over the dark water.

He came up by her side.

'Lucia? What else can you tell me? You said before about water—'

'I don't know!' she yelled at him. 'Don't you think if I knew, I'd tell you?'

He didn't answer that. Gone was the robotic retelling now, she was firing out conflicting emotions, her head likely in turmoil.

'Just get me the hell out of here,' she said. 'I don't ever want to come here again.'

She turned and stormed off.

They were walking across the tarmac to the fence when Peake's phone buzzed in his pocket. Lucia, a couple of steps ahead, glared at him as though the thrumming device had offended her.

Peake checked the screen. Jenn. He was in two minds whether to answer. Most likely she was calling from her parents' house. A team of police officers would be swarming around her, blue and red lights flashing everywhere, an ambulance or three there to take away the dead and the injured. Several rolls of police tape would be laid out around the grounds. A big old shitstorm would be coming Peake's way if anyone figured out he was involved – if Jenn told the police he was involved.

All the more reason why they needed to dump the GMC they'd ridden out of town in sooner rather than later.

'Are you just gonna stare at it or answer it?' Lucia growled as though his deliberation had annoyed her even further.

It wasn't like he needed any more hassle tonight...

He pressed the green button.

'Everything OK?' he asked Jenn, but even before she spoke he realized he'd pictured the scene wrong. Something about her breathing told him that.

'Peake, please, you need to—'

Thud.

Follow by a muffled cry of pain. Then a moan and a shriek of terror.

'You get the idea,' came a man's voice. Peake recognized it.

'Frank, if you hurt her—'

'What? You'll bury me on my farm, like you did with Thomas McGinty?'

Peake held his tongue.

'You know where to find us,' Frank said before the call ended.

19

'I have to go back,' Peake said to Lucia, stuffing the phone in his pocket.

'Back where?'

'Prenticeville.'

'But—'

'You can come with me, or you can stay here. But I've got to go—'

'Someone else needs your help.'

Peake said nothing. He didn't like her sarcastic tone.

'Your girlfriend?' But then Lucia's snideness ebbed away as though a realization had hit her. 'She's in trouble because of me?'

'Yes, it's Jenn. No, it's not because of you. But I have to go.' He looked across to the pump house. 'It's quiet here. Safe enough. I'll be back in the morning.'

'You think. Unless your plan doesn't work out. Then what?'

'Your choice.'

'I'm not staying here.'

'Come on then, let's go.'

* * *

All thoughts of Lucia's past and who wanted her dead and why were put to the back of Peake's mind as he raced back north toward Prenticeville on the quiet night roads. Lucia did the right thing of not asking him any more questions. He didn't want to talk. He only wanted to be there and get in front of Frank and do whatever he needed to do to get Jenn safe.

'You don't think it's risky going back in this car?' Lucia asked dubiously, as they approached the outskirts of the town in the stolen GMC.

Of course Peake knew it was a big risk, but what other choice did he have? In the middle of the night, they'd barely seen another car on their journey through rural Georgia, but there'd be a police presence somewhere or other around here. Would this car be on a wanted list? Possibly, if the owners had called it in stolen, or if the police had figured out there'd been a shootout earlier in the evening and this was the getaway car.

But Peake felt neither of those things were likely, given how things had turned out. This car belonged to an armed gang who'd turned up at the McGintys' to take Lucia by force. They were hardly likely to call 911 themselves. And, as doubtful as it seemed, he didn't think the police were even aware yet of the earlier shootout. Because he was sure it was the McGintys' home where he'd find Jenn and Frank.

'Here?' Lucia said as Peake brought the car to a stop at the roadside. The house still wasn't in view from this point but the corner of the stables were. Everything looked quiet enough...

'Yes,' Peake said. 'You don't need to worry. This isn't about you. Wait here. If you see anything you don't like... take off.'

'And how would I contact you again if I did that?'

He thought a moment. There weren't many options. 'Go into town. Slug's Tavern. Find a guy called Travis. He'll help. Lay low until I get there.'

He got out of the car without waiting for a response and made his way up the drive, the early morning sun rising up behind the small hill to his east. He soon reached the driveway to the house. Two cars parked up there, but neither was that big Ford truck that he'd sped away from hours earlier. Gone too were the bodies – both live and dead. He walked slowly along the gravel, stopping at a dark patch. He crouched down and touched it. Dried blood. So whoever had been alive when he and Lucia had escaped had cleared out, but not cleaned up.

'OK, you get up real slow now, hands where I can see them,' came the gruff voice from over by the door to the house.

Peake did as he was told, eyes fixed on the shotgun in the hands of the man standing ten yards from him.

'Is she in there?' Peake asked him. He recognized the man's face. He was one of the two who'd been in the bar a few days ago. Who'd chased him along the freeway. Frank's 'business' partners.

'Yeah. She's in there. And for now, she's fine. But you do anything stupid and my friend'll put a bullet in her head.'

'Thanks for spelling things out for me.'

Peake moved forward, slowly pulling his hands from above his head and down to his sides to test how the grunt in front of him would react.

No reaction.

'You armed?' the guy asked.

'No,' Peake said.

'I'm gonna check you anyway. Hey, Chris!' he yelled, half turning his head back into the house.

Peake paused a moment as Chris sauntered out, a cigarette dangling from his lips. Chris was the younger, shorter, slightly skinnier of the two, with straggly light hair, a short but unkempt beard, and tattoos which covered his arms like sleeves and poked out from above the neckline of his white T-shirt.

He came over to pat Peake down.

'So he's Chris; what do I call you?' Peake asked the guy with the shotgun. He was a good ten years older, perhaps early forties, with a buzz cut that didn't hide the fact he was almost entirely gray and heavily receding. He had a meaty face and only speckles of tattoos around his arms rather than the full-on sleeves of his friend.

'You don't call me anything,' the guy said unhelpfully.

'Mr. Nobody,' Peake said. 'Seems apt for a washout like you.'

'Who the fuck you calling a washout?' the guy bit back.

Peake received an extra rough hand from Chris around his kidney as the guy dug his fingers into a tender spot as if in retaliation for his insolence. But then he was done and he stepped back and pulled a gun from his waistband.

'Fine,' Peake said, still concentrating on the guy at the door. 'I'll just use your real name, then. Anton.'

OK. He really didn't like that. The two of them glanced at one another as if to question what to do next.

'You think I didn't try to figure out who you two were since the first time you were out in Prenticeville, asking about me?'

And it hadn't been too hard really. Peake had only needed to use one old contact to get what he needed.

'Just get in the fucking house,' Anton said. He took a step forward, looked around the grounds as though worried that Peake had more surprises up his sleeves.

He didn't. Yet. So he headed on into the house and made his way through to the living room at the back, Chris and Anton closely following behind.

Peake spotted Jenn as he entered the room, sitting and looking forlorn on a dining chair, her mouth covered in tape, blood caked on her nostrils and spots of the red stuff on her T-shirt. Her eyes looked at him pleadingly and he knew what was coming – he sensed the movement behind him – but he decided to take the hit. The blow with the butt of the shotgun sent him stumbling forward and to one knee as Frank and Chris and Anton took up their positions in the room.

It was the main reason Peake had taken the hit in the first place, rather than fight back immediately. He wanted to weigh up the dynamic more first.

He achingly got back to his feet. Frank settled into an armchair which he'd pulled up alongside Jenn, a real satisfied grin on his face. Chris took up position behind Jenn with the handgun, Anton stood to the right, the shotgun aimed at Peake's gut.

'Ever eager to be the hero,' Frank said. 'I knew—'

'You OK?' Peake asked Jenn. She moaned and shook her head but then nodded too.

Peake turned his attention to Frank whose face had soured from Peake's interruption.

'Just so you know, whatever you do to her, I'm doing to you tenfold.'

Frank looked even madder at the threat, but Anton smirked then chuckled and Chris followed suit too until Frank glared daggers at them.

'Time to get back to reality, Peake,' Frank said. 'This is my town, and here we do things my way.'

'If you say so. You wanna tell me why she's here? She had nothing to do with what happened at your farm.'

'The farm? You think I'm going to all this effort because you burned down that old shack?'

'Then what?'

Peake found Jenn's eye again. She looked even more worried now.

'Actually,' Peake said, stopping Frank just as he'd been about to answer, 'it's been a long night. I'm shattered. I could really do with coffee. Anyone else want coffee?'

He turned to leave the room.

'You're not going anywhere,' Chris said.

But Peake took another two steps to the door. He stopped when the gunshot boomed and a bullet thwacked into the wall in front of him.

'I said, you're not going anywhere.'

Peake swiveled back to them. Chris turned the handgun back to Jenn. Frank looked all the more pleased with himself now as though Peake had been put back in place.

Not even close.

'OK, so no coffee,' Peake said. 'What are we doing here?'

'Where's Adam?' Frank asked.

'I've no idea.'

'Here, take this.' Chris palmed off the handgun to Frank and pulled out a serrated knife. He grabbed Jenn's hair and pulled her head back and she yelped before the knife was pressed up against her neck.

Peake did his best to show no reaction at all, but inside he raged at seeing Jenn's distress.

'This is real,' Frank said. 'So drop the cuteness. We're not playing and no one's coming to your rescue this time. I want to know where Adam is. And I want to know what you did with Thomas McGinty. And I want to know how you're going to get me the two million dollars I'm owed.'

'If you'd just asked nicely...'

Frank huffed, his agitation growing. 'You really want to—'

'You want to make me talk?' Peake said. 'You have to try a bit harder than this. Where's the pressure, Frank? The real pressure? You hit me in the head one time with a gun? You think that's enough?'

'Peake, you're really—'

'If it were me? I'd get your guy Chris there to actually hurt her. You need to show me what you're all capable of rather than just this tough guy standoff.'

'You don't think—'

'I'd start by cutting pieces off her. No messing around with slaps to the face or anything like that. Just get down and dirty. Perhaps a finger or a toe first. That knife is plenty sharp enough.'

Jenn's moans heightened and her pleading stare bore into Peake's skull. He ignored it.

'Who the fuck is this guy?' Anton asked, grinning as though amused. He looked to Frank for affirmation but got nothing. Frank was incensed.

'Yeah, see, you brought me here under this threat to Jenn, because you know I care for her, but I need to really believe the threat. These two guys... They look tough enough. But I know who they really are. Anton Jacobsen. Chris Dumont.'

The two grunts sent each other a questioning look.

'That's right. Like I told you outside, I've been checking up on you two. And you've probably checked on me, yet you still decided this was your best option.'

'Peake, you need to shut—'

'Frank, you shut up. I'm talking. Anton, you joined the army when you were eighteen. You wanted to be a marine, but you got a nasty spinal injury on a training exercise. After that, you weren't much use to them. A shame, but life's a bitch. You were a security guard for a while after that before you joined up with a bounty hunter operating out of Fresno. Mostly low-level bail bond stuff until a couple of years ago when you set up shop on your own. You look mean, and I'm sure with your size you pack a punch but... sometimes you need more than muscle.'

Anton sneered and renewed his grip on the shotgun, but said nothing.

'And Chris? You're more of a wildcard. You trained as a police recruit in Oakland but you never made it through, and since then you've been working here and there for various PIs. I don't know why you dropped out of the police, but looking at you... Don't take offense but I'm thinking drugs or violence or some other shit got you booted out. You fucked up, basically. You've had a chip on your shoulder ever since. Out on your rounds you probably enjoyed giving a beat down to losers who wouldn't fight back, but are you really about to torture Jenn, to take things to another level? Because when you do that, you don't get to turn back. You never get to turn back.'

'Listen to you,' Frank said. 'You really think a lot of yourself, don't you?'

'I just know what I'm capable of. What I've had to do to survive. Anton and Chris here would weep if they knew.'

'You're doubting me?' Chris said, teeth bared like an angry dog. Peake had got under his skin.

He didn't bother to respond to the question. Instead, Peake stooped low and drove forward at Anton. He swiveled then threw his elbow out and up, catching Anton on the side of his head before he could decide whether to pull the trigger of the shotgun. A shotgun he no longer had control over after Peake ripped it from his grip a second later. He threw the butt up and it cracked under Anton's chin, and Peake swiped his legs and he plummeted to the floor.

Chris raced at him with the knife. Real fight in him and pure anger on his face. Yeah, this guy was a fighter. But he was someone who fought with rage and spite.

Peake went to dodge left but then spun to the right, catching Chris off-balance as the blade punched air. Peake dropped the shotgun, grabbed Chris's arm and twisted it until it snapped. Chris screamed in agony. Peake took hold of the knife and kicked him to the floor then swung the knife down and straight through Anton's hand as he reached for the shotgun. The knife sank through flesh and through the floorboards beneath him, pinning him in place, the shotgun less than an inch from his grip.

Peake picked the weapon up again and turned it on Frank, and was facing down the barrel of the handgun. Peake took a couple of beats to get his breathing back under control.

'You're an animal,' Frank said.

'Yet you decided to provoke me. Jenn, get up.'

'She's not going anywhere.'

'Frank, learn when to shut up.'

'You broke my arm!' Chris yelled.

Frank looked over at Chris and Jenn sprang to her feet and dove on top of him.

Now that was unexpected.

Frank fired the gun in panic, but the bullet thwacked into the ceiling and Peake was on him in a flash. Jenn rolled away onto the floor with a thud. Peake kicked the gun from Frank's grip then pushed the shotgun barrel onto his eyeball.

'Don't think I won't do it.'

Jenn yanked the tape off her mouth and picked up the fallen handgun.

'You OK?' Peake asked.

She nodded. Peake quickly glanced behind him.

'Point the gun at them. Either tries to get up, shoot them both.'

'I hope they try it,' Jenn said.

'So what now?' Frank asked.

'Now Jenn and I walk out of here. Whatever beef you thought you had with me is over. And if you bother Jenn or her brother or me ever again, next time I'll kill you.'

'Like you killed Thomas McGinty.'

Peake's mind stuttered.

'I didn't kill McGinty.'

'That's not what Adam said.'

Peake looked at Jenn but she was just as confused as he was.

'And what the hell did Adam say?'

Frank's confidence was growing again. Peake had to resist the urge to knock the rising smile from his face.

'That you murdered Thomas McGinty. And you killed two other men out on my farm. A drug deal gone wrong or something. The pressure is piling up on you, Peake. Perhaps it's you who needs to stop with the idle threats. You're gonna have to kill us all here tonight, because if you don't, I'm coming back after you. I'll ruin you.'

Jenn grabbed his arm. 'Peake, no.' As if he'd really been contemplating just executing the three of them.

'Adam's full of shit,' Peake said to Frank.

'And then some,' Jenn added.

'Yeah? So where is your dad, then?' Frank asked Jenn. 'And where's your brother too?'

'Adam was lying,' Peake said. 'Thomas McGinty is dead. But I didn't kill him.'

'He couldn't have done,' Jenn added. 'Peake was with me that night. We only found out after.'

'After what?'

'After Adam killed my dad,' Jenn said.

'But we did help Adam that night,' Peake said.

'What the hell are you two talking about?'

Peake thought for a moment.

'Why don't we show you?' he said. He held a hand out to Frank who glared at it suspiciously as though he couldn't understand how the night had taken yet another turn. But Peake felt he knew the way out of this now. And it wasn't through putting a bullet in any of these three. Not unless he really had to.

Frank eventually took the hand and Peake hauled him to his feet.

'And where are we going?'

'Back to your farm, of course.'

20

Peake drove the GMC. Frank sat up front next to him. Chris and Anton sat in the middle, quiet and sullen as they dealt with their pain and embarrassment. Jenn and Lucia sat in the third row of the SUV, a handgun and shotgun in their hands respectively, ready to shoot Anton and Chris in the backs of their heads if they found the strength or desire to fight back.

They were still quiet ten minutes later when Peake brought the car to a stop. They'd traveled less than three miles, but it'd all been off road, traipsing and bouncing across the fields that rolled away from the McGintys' and eventually intersected with Frank's land.

'This is it,' Peake said, and he got out first and they all assembled at the front of the vehicle.

'You OK?' he quietly asked Lucia and she nodded in response.

He was sure she didn't want to be here, doing this – her physical frailty among many reasons why – but Peake felt it was better this way. He didn't know how long they'd be out here and the longer she was sat out front of the McGintys' by herself, the more she was an open target for the people who were still looking for her. Plus, he really appreciated the extra pair of hands.

'You're sure this is the spot?' Frank asked, looking around as though he couldn't understand how Peake had navigated to this seemingly indistinct section of land. And it looked like any other field in a sea of fields.

'This is it,' Peake said. 'And it's already hot as hell out here. No need for us to all get heatstroke. So why don't you start digging.'

Peake grabbed the spade and dumped it at Frank's feet.

'And why the fuck would I do that?'

'Because I don't think Anton and Chris are really up for it, eh guys?'

Nothing but scowls and growls from those two. Most likely they just wanted to be back in California, sitting on the sand by the ocean, waiting for a call to go pick up a junkie who'd forgotten to turn up at court because they were too baked.

'Damn flies,' Frank shouted, swatting away at nothing. 'I can't dig in this, I'm—'

'We got water. And the sooner you start, the sooner you get to finish and go take a cold shower.'

Frank grumbled again but then picked up the spade. 'Fine. But you two need to start talking to me. And who the hell is she anyway?' He swooshed the spade at Lucia.

'She has a name, hijo de puta.'

'But you don't need to worry about her,' Peake said. 'Just get digging.'

So Frank did. Not particularly quickly, but he kept at it, slowly, slowly working his way down through the soil.

'Adam told you Peake killed my dad?' Jenn asked.

'Yeah,' Frank said.

'When did he say that?'

Frank didn't answer.

'For all his faults, I know my brother. He wouldn't have said anything about that night willingly.'

Frank again didn't answer as he puffed and panted, trying his hardest to dig through the compacted soil. Fitness and physical strength were not this guy's forte.

'Did you two beat it out of him?' Jenn asked, flashing the gun toward both Anton and Chris. They looked to Frank as if for approval to answer.

'Yeah. We beat it out of him,' Frank said, taking a break to mop his brow. His arms, his shirt were covered in dirt already and as he peeled his fingers from the spade's handle to inspect them, Peake could see he had some nasty blisters forming, even though he'd only dug through three or four inches of soil.

'And where is Adam now?' Peake asked.

'I don't know. And that's the truth. I want to know where he is, but no one's seen or heard from him.'

'But Adam told you Peake killed my dad?' Jenn asked again.

'He did. But why don't you tell me your side of the story?'

Frank said that with a certain malice, as though relishing the dirty secrets that were about to be revealed.

Or perhaps he just wanted a longer break from digging.

'You know what my dad did to us, don't you?' Jenn asked.

'I know he was an asshole.'

'An asshole who beat Adam black and blue ever since he was a boy. An asshole who beat my mom too. But worse were the other things he did to her. He used her like a fucking plaything. One minute he'd be slapping her around the face, the next minute the bedroom door'd be locked and he'd be fucking her. Raping her. He was a sadistic animal.'

No one responded as Jenn took pause, but she had all eyes on her now, and all eyes were both sympathetic – to her – and horrified by her revelations.

'Did you know?' Jenn asked Frank.

'I knew he had problems. I knew he had a temper. And I knew when he'd had a drink that he lost all his senses. I guess I never knew how bad it was. For any of you.'

'Oh, I got off lightly,' Jenn said. 'Adam hated me for that. For so long, he despised me because dad never laid a hand on me like he did to them. But that didn't mean… it didn't mean there was no abuse.'

'Jenn, you don't need to do this,' Peake said, putting a hand on her arm but she shrugged him off before wiping at her eyes.

'I was twelve the first time. I woke up one night and he was just standing there, over the bed, staring at me. Doing you don't even want to know what. That was just the start. He'd come and watch me get dressed. Or taking a shower. My doors had no locks and if he couldn't get in when he wanted it'd just make him mad, and I knew he'd take it out on Mom or Adam, so what other choice did I have?'

'My God,' Lucia said, hand to mouth in shock. 'He was your father?'

'He never once touched me. As though everything he did to me was OK because of that. But it was never OK.'

'I get it,' Frank said, going back to digging as though it was easier than listening to Jenn's harrowing secrets.

'No. You don't,' she said. 'Because you're an asshole too. Not like him, but you're about as selfish as a person could be. You only care about yourself and your money. That's all my dad was to you. Business. It's why you have beef with Adam and me, right? Two million dollars?'

'I thought... I admit, I made a mistake,' Frank said. Break time again, apparently. 'I thought you two were in on it. I thought you and Adam had helped your dad run away. It's why...'

'It's why we're here at all,' Anton said.

'No. I would never have helped him like that,' Jenn said. 'I've never been more relieved than the night I saw his dead body. He destroyed our family, our lives. My mom...'

'I knew her a long time,' Frank said. 'She was a good woman.'

Jenn hung her head.

'Wait... you think... there was more to her death?' Frank said. He was reading between the lines, but he'd hit home. Jenn had confided the exact same thing to Peake. Yet he just wanted this conversation to end now. He could see the toll it was taking on Jenn.

'Maybe she killed herself,' Jenn said. 'Or maybe, somehow, my dad caused that crash. Or maybe it really was just an accident. But with her gone... I knew something would give. Me and Adam, we no longer had the ties to him we did before. Dad knew it too. I think it's one reason he wanted out of Prenticeville. Not to get away from you, with your damn stinking money, but to get away from us.'

Frank jabbed the spade into the dirt but then paused and everyone looked down into the hole. Everyone had heard it. A different kind of thud to the hefty thwack of the metal hitting rock-solid dried-out clay soil. Frank glanced up at Peake as though to question what he should do next.

'Keep going,' Peake said.

So Frank did, although more carefully than before. Or maybe he was just worn out.

'What really happened?' Lucia said, her question surprising not just Peake but the others too judging by the raised eyebrows and questioning looks.

'Dad came back from California. He was in a mess. Debts were piling up and his drinking was out of control. He and Adam were at the house, arguing. Dad wanted to sell the house, Adam hated the idea because that was our home. Dad was drunk and he... I only know what Adam said. That he defended himself when Dad attacked him with a knife.'

'You don't believe him?' Frank said.

'It doesn't matter what I believe. Dad is dead. Adam isn't. What choice did I have?'

Frank dropped the spade and got down on his knees and brushed at the soil with his already dirtied and bleeding hands, moving dirt away to reveal the upper torso of a man, the side of his head too. The smell was bad, but the dry heat at least meant it wasn't as bad as it otherwise might have been, the body shriveled and dehydrated like a mummy, rather than a festering, putrid mess.

'So Peake's grand idea was to bury him out here,' Frank said, looking down on his 'friend', almost with sympathy for the dead man.

'Yes,' Peake said. 'Because Adam and Jenn deserve the chance to move on. He'll go down as a missing person. We already made sure his last movements are recorded as being in California.'

Anton and Chris shared a look as though they had no clue what he meant by that. Clearly their PIing hadn't figured this out yet.

'His phone's now somewhere out in the Pacific Ocean,' Peake said. 'But—'

'But not before he left a voicemail for Adam a couple of weeks back,' Frank said. 'How'd you do that? A copy of a voice note or something?'

Peake nodded. Frank looked kind of impressed.

'You had someone out in California doing that for you?' he asked. 'For the location record?'

'Yeah,' Peake said. 'Add a few ATM transactions into the mix too.'

Frank glared at his accomplices.

'We were looking here,' Anton said. 'We were working forward from the dates you gave us.' He hung his head in shame. 'We never got that.'

'Who cares,' Peake said. 'The point is that Thomas McGinty went missing in California, and he'll stay missing. At some point Jenn and Adam will have him declared dead. Then they get to finally move on.'

'You're telling me I have to wait to get my money back?' Frank asked, all pissy again like he still had a big say in what happened here. 'It could be years!'

'You don't have to wait at all,' Peake said. 'Because they owe you nothing.'

'You think—'

'There's two ways this can go from here. One is that Thomas gets three buddies to join him in the afterlife.' Anton grunted, Frank kind of squirmed like he finally felt threatened. 'The other is you pay Anton and Chris what you owe them for their services. Give them some extra for their medical expenses and for their trip back home.'

They both nodded as though that sounded a good deal to them.

'And me?' Frank asked.

'And you just carry on your life here as the big boss of Prenticeville.'

'What about the—'

'Two million dollars? You don't need it, Frank. And you certainly wouldn't need it if you're dead.'

'Adam murdered someone,' Frank said. 'And you two helped him cover it up. You'd all face life if I went to the police with this. Not to mention the two men he told me you killed out at the farm. Which I'm sensing has something to do with her.'

He shot a scathing look at Lucia, but she remained looking calm and surprisingly assured with the shotgun in her hands.

'You kidnapped me,' Jenn said. 'I'm pretty sure you did something similar to Adam. You hired these two to threaten me, held me and Peake at gunpoint. For those things alone you'd be looking at a long stretch. Not to mention the fact you have this body buried on your land. The body of a man who owed you two million dollars. And what about the other two guys killed and buried on your land? You think the cops aren't gonna see you as suspect number one?'

'Particularly as your DNA is all over this spade,' Peake said, holding the tool aloft. 'And all around the burial site, what, with you dripping sweat and blood everywhere. And didn't you just touch the body?'

'You fu—'

'Save the insults,' Peake said. 'I've heard them all before.'

Frank rose to his feet. Yeah, he was mad. But he had no play here.

'I think we all understand where each other stands. Are you two good?' Peake turned to Anton and Chris who mumbled their agreement. 'Great. And Frank? We leave Thomas out here, and the rest of us get on with our lives. Yeah?'

Frank paused as though still desperately trying to think of a different way that would benefit him more.

'Don't forget the alternative,' Peake said, and as if on cue Jenn and Lucia renewed their aims on the forlorn businessman.

'If I never have to see your damn face around here again, it's a deal,' Frank said.

'You'll only see my face if you fuck this up,' Peake said. 'Now cover McGinty back up and let's get the hell out of here.'

* * *

Peake pulled the GMC into the parking lot outside Jenn's condo unit. Lucia remained inside the car as Jenn and Peake both got out. The sun was fierce as ever now and even after only a few seconds made him feel woozy. He and Lucia, and Jenn too really, had been on the go all through the night. He wanted and badly needed rest somewhere nice and cool and knew that Lucia did too. But not just yet.

He took Jenn's hands in his. He had so much he wanted to say to her, but he didn't even know where to start.

'Thank you,' she said to him before she pecked him on the cheek.

'It wasn't quite how I expected to see you again.'

'Me neither.'

'Do you really not know where your brother is?' he asked.

'I haven't heard from him in days. You're worried about him?'

He was, and he could tell she was too.

'It's because of her, isn't it?' Jenn said, momentarily flicking a not-so-friendly look toward Lucia.

'Yeah. But I'll find him. I'll do what I can to help him.'

'Sometimes... I think maybe Adam's made his choices already. I'm not sure your help is what he needs.'

'The point is, you could be in danger too. You saw how tonight played out, and that was just with a local thug like Frank. Adam's involved in something bigger. Something worse. And that means you're a potential target for anyone who wants to get at him, or me.'

'What are you saying?'

'You should leave town for a while. Go up to Tennessee or something. You said you had an aunt up there. Anywhere but here right now.'

'OK. I will,' she said to his surprise. He'd expected more pushback.

'And you know I'll always help you if you need me.'

'I do.'

'I do have to ask you again though,' Peake said. 'Do you know who your brother was working for? A man called Hardy.'

He'd ruined the moment. Her face soured and she shrank a little.

'I already told you,' she said.

She pulled out of his grip and moved away, only giving him a momentary glance over her shoulder before she was out of sight.

Peake got back into the car and sighed.

'So that was an eye-opening evening,' Lucia said, an unusually bright smile on her face. 'Or morning.'

Peake could only smile at that, hoping doing so would erase some of the bubbling doubts and regret.

'Yeah.'

'But who are you?' Lucia said.

She received a raised eyebrow to the question.

'Seriously. For whatever reason, I've trusted my life to you. And it looks like I'm not the only one. You're not just a good guy drawn into a mess, it's almost like...'

'What?'

'I don't even know. But... Who are you, Simon Peake?'

'You really wanna know about me?'

'That's why I'm asking.'

'Then I'll tell you,' he said, taking them back onto the road. 'We've got another long drive ahead.'

21

Ridley and Katie spent the night in a roadside hotel on the outskirts of Tallahassee, not far from the Florida state border with Georgia. In the morning Katie remained somber, a little rattled too. They hadn't spoken much since leaving Ramirez's villa, since leaving behind what was left of Greg. Ridley decided to drive for the remainder of the northerly journey. Generally when he had any crew with him, Ridley would get them to chauffeur but today felt a little different. He liked Katie – she had a lot of potential by his side and he wanted to make sure she remained on board, not just for this assignment but in the future too. His driving was just a little sweetener for her.

He cringed at his own thought. A sweetener? She'd seen her colleague brutally killed so her reward was getting the morning off driving?

Whatever.

He needed a new Greg, though. He had several other guys who routinely did grunt work for him, but the nearest of them was up near DC. He wouldn't wait for reinforcements. They were going to Hardy today. Time for Katie to step up.

'Will you tell Greg's wife what happened to him?' Katie asked from the passenger seat. It annoyed him she'd decided to bring it all up again, as though she'd been stewing on the question all night. He only wanted to move on now.

'You know I can't do that,' he said.

'Then what?'

'Everything you do for me is off the books. It's what you signed up for. Greg was no different.'

'What happened last night is not what I signed up for.'

Ridley disagreed but wouldn't force the argument. 'The point is I never met his wife. She knows nothing about me.'

'You're assuming Greg never told her anything then.'

'Of course I'm assuming that. Unless you're telling me otherwise?'

'No. I'm not. But... what? You're just going to ignore the fact he has a family who are waiting for him to come home?'

'I'm not ignoring it. There's just nothing I can do about it.'

'Same difference.'

'Do we have a problem, Katie?'

'No.' Defiance in her tone now. He didn't mind that. Better than moping.

'Good. Because I can cut you loose right now if you're not up to the job.'

'I'm up to it.'

'I said last night, I don't like what happened to Greg. And I will make it right. But now is the time for focusing on what lies ahead.'

'If you say so.'

Ridley slammed his foot onto the brake pedal and the wheels skidded and screeched as the car jolted to a stop on the highway. He'd set himself, pushed back hard against his seat but Katie was caught unawares and her body shot forward, catching on the belt before tossing her back against the seat.

'Yeah, I say so,' Ridley said. 'This isn't a game. It never was a game. This is real life and sometimes we're dealing with real bad people.'

'I get it. I'm a pawn in your dangerous games. I sold my soul to you for a few dollars.'

'Several hundred thousand dollars, actually. For this one job.'

They glared at each other, neither blinking as though it were a contest. She was angry, he was too. Quite honestly, he didn't actually mind that much that she was blowing off on him. She needed that fight in her, that feeling of injustice if she was to get through this.

'I'm not the enemy,' Ridley said.

She didn't say anything to that.

'I'll get some money to Greg's family. Everything I owed him for this assignment times two.'

Everyone who worked for him did so on a freelance basis. He had a churn of LLCs that he used to pay them money through, and which he used to receive money from his clients. All of it just far enough removed to not raise too many questions. Although obviously questions would be asked by Greg's wife when he didn't show up at home, and the money would look suspicious as hell, but Ridley wasn't the kind of guy to balk on his word. If Ramirez was as clever as he thought he was, Greg's body would never be found. Greg would join a long list of missing persons, which from Ridley's point of view was far better than him being on a list of homicide victims. He'd have to deal with the fallout as and when Greg's recent movements were linked to him, but it'd take a while, and this assignment would be done and dusted and the related LLCs dissolved so that the paper trail didn't lead too far.

But all those were issues for another day.

'You happy with that?' Ridley prompted.

'I'm happy with that.'

'Then let's get this done.'

They talked little on the onward journey, only a brief conversation to go over the plan. As with any plan in Ridley's world, it required a large amount of fluidity as he never knew exactly how things would pan out. But they had one clear objective: Pressure Hardy.

They arrived at Hardy's ranch a little before midday and the sun blazed in the deep blue sky. Getting out of the car was like stepping into an oven and Ridley squinted and panted and—

Katie shot him an unfriendly look across the hood of the car, as though she'd read his thoughts, the linkage he'd made in his mind to the extreme of the heated air and the burning oil that had caused so much agony for Greg.

Perhaps the Alabama heat wasn't so bad after all.

'Come on,' he said, before indicating the array of parked cars, a pristine-looking Mercedes S Class among them. 'It looks like he's home.'

Indeed Hardy was home, as were a number of his brutish guys. Nothing sophisticated about this rabble, not just in their ragbag clothing but in their attitudes too. A couple of those guys escorted Ridley and Katie to their master out the back.

'We need to talk,' Ridley said to Hardy when he arrived by the pool. Hardy was lounging with a beer while his wife swam. Ridley did a double take. Yeah, she was naked in there.

'Like what you see?' Hardy sneered.

'I tell you what I don't like. I don't like how you've fucked up something so simple.'

Hardy huffed but said nothing as he chugged from his beer bottle. He glanced at Katie then back to Ridley.

'You're down on numbers today,' Hardy said.

'Katie's plenty enough company for today. Why don't we go inside? Better doing this in private.'

Hardy's sneer only grew. For some reason he didn't like the idea, but it was really no different to last time.

'OK,' Hardy said. 'You can come to my office. Your little bitch can stay out here with mine. She can go for a swim too if she likes.'

'No. She's fine,' Katie answered. 'Didn't bring my costume.'

'I think you can see, you don't need one here, honey.'

'You lead the way,' Ridley said to Hardy, nodding to the house.

Hardy huffed and pulled a silk robe from the back of his lounger and he and Ridley retreated inside. A couple of his henchmen followed but were left the other side of the office door which Ridley closed and quietly locked as Hardy went for the decanter.

'You want one?' he asked.

'A big one.'

Hardy raised an eyebrow as though not expecting that response.

'Ice?'

'Not with scotch.'

Hardy shrugged and dumped some ice in his nonetheless. Ridley wouldn't bother to explain to him the wrongs of that, but the Scots would be appalled. Ridley took the glass and a decent measure of scotch in his mouth which he worked around his gums before swallowing.

'Cheers,' Hardy said a little belatedly, and the two of them clinked glasses.

'No need for any more small talk,' Ridley said. 'Tell me what the fuck is happening.'

'What's happening? You're in my home. Drinking my scotch. So watch your damn mouth.'

Ridley placed his glass on the corner of the desk. Not on the coaster, just on the nicely polished wood, and he could tell Hardy didn't like that by the way he sucked in air through his nostrils.

Hardy didn't see the move coming. He'd always underestimated Ridley. The stiff posture, the aloofness. The overt Britishness that made Hardy see Ridley as some sort of uptight Victorian gentleman rather than the clandestine operator that lay beneath.

He went for the glass in Hardy's hand first. A distraction more than anything as he knew Hardy's first instinct was not to make a mess in his plush office. Ridley swiped the glass away and it clattered against the bookcase, shattering and sending liquor over them both. Ridley hauled his knee into Ridley's groin, grabbed the guy's wrist with one hand. He twisted the wrist up above Hardy's head as he took hold of the man's hair with his other hand, then slammed Hardy's face down onto the thick mahogany desk.

He pinned Hardy's head there, his nose dribbling blood from the impact, his arm up above him and pushed to bursting.

'Move or make a sound and you'll be jerking off with your left hand the rest of your life. If you've got anything left to jerk off when I'm finished with you.'

Hardy squirmed and grimaced but did the right thing of not shouting out. The whole move had taken only a few seconds, but it had been far from silent. At least one of Hardy's guys was right outside the room. Ridley had made sure to lock the door, but still. No indication of a sudden onrush from out there at least, but a moment later there was a knock on the door.

'You OK in there?' the guard the other side asked.

'Tell your man you're good,' Ridley said to Hardy, quietly. 'That you dropped the glass.'

No response.

'Tell them you're good,' Ridley said. 'Tell him to clear off.'

Hardy didn't say anything, so Ridley tested the arm again and Hardy let out a little yelp.

'Yeah, er, this dipshit smashed one of my glasses. He's cleaning it up. You go check on the guys in the barn.'

'Check for what?'

'Just... go and make sure everything's OK in there!'

'Sure thing.'

And that was that, apparently. Ridley had got away with it.

'You'll fucking pay for this,' Hardy said through gritted teeth.

OK, well maybe not long-term, but for now at least.

'Shut up,' Ridley said, before thumping his knee up between Hardy's legs, into Hardy's groin once more. 'This is how we're going to do things...' He eased the pressure on Hardy's arm a little, pulled on his hair to move him around the corner of the desk. 'You see your wife out there?'

He gave Hardy just enough room to turn his head toward the double doors that led outside, the pool twenty yards away across a patio. His wife was out of the water now, robe on, standing on the poolside with Katie right by her.

'You fucking touch her and—'

'Ah-ah,' Ridley said, pushing the arm once more and causing Hardy to grimace in pain. 'Katie might look sweet as pie to you, but don't buy it. They're going to come over here. You're going to unlock the door right there and they're coming in to join us. Then we'll see how much you've got to say when there's a knife up against that nice face of hers.'

As he finished the sentence, Katie and Ivanka were already strolling over, both of them smiling, Ivanka blissfully unaware. But being married to a man like Hardy, her whole life probably relied on her being like that, even if she had to force herself to fake it sometimes.

'Move,' Ridley said as he pulled Hardy's head from the desk and twisted his hand up behind his shoulder blades. He used his own sleeve to wipe the blood from Hardy's nose – not ideal, but needs must – before he pushed Hardy toward the double doors so he could unlock them.

'You even think about shouting out, and you both die in here,' Ridley said.

He pulled Hardy back from the doors and a few seconds later Ivanka opened up. She'd barely taken a step inside, still in mid-conversation with Katie, when she realized she'd been duped.

Katie gave her no chance. She hauled Ivanka to the floor and smashed her in the gut with her boot. Another one to the face got her complete compliance before she pulled Ivanka onto her knees, a knife now in Katie's hand which she pressed to Ivanka's throat.

Hardy moaned in protest but once again did the right thing of not trying to alert his soldiers.

'Now do I have your attention?' Ridley asked Hardy.

'Baby?' Ivanka said to her husband through a mouthful of blood.

OK. He was still being too nice. Hardy was still doubting him.

'I asked you a question!' Ridley shouted, wrestling Hardy down to his knees so he was face-to-face with his wife before Katie slapped her hard across the cheek – hard enough to crack her bottom lip and leave a red hand imprint across her nice skin.

'Yes!' Hardy responded.

'Which piece of her do we take first?' Ridley asked.

He got no response from anyone in the room.

'Katie, cut her ear off.'

Katie caught his eye with an imploring look. But what else did she think 'pressure' was going to entail?

She pulled the knife away from Ivanka's neck. Placed the blade on the top of the ear. Pushed until a dribble of blood snaked down the side of Ivanka's face.

'No!' Hardy said. 'Please! No!'

Katie paused.

'Where is she?' Hardy asked. 'Where's Lucia?'

'I don't know!'

'Wrong answer. Katie?'

She moved the knife down a fraction more and Ivanka's eyes bulged and her sobs heightened.

'Is she still alive?' Ridley asked.

'Yes! She is. I don't... understand... but she's still alive.'

'Where?'

'I already said, I don't know! But she's... got help.'

'Help?'

'Some guy. We don't even know who the hell he is! Simon Peake. He's not a local. But he's... he's the one. He was supposed to bury her but... my guys fucked up. She was still alive and Peake the bastard decided to save her! He's got her.'

'You decided to wait for me to have your wife's ear cut off before telling me this?'

'I only just found out! We're still figuring out what happened. Where he came from. Who he is.'

Ridley paused a moment to think. The explanation had caught him off guard. Yeah, the situation was screwed up, he knew that already, but he'd put it down to the incompetence of Hardy's guys, the nonchalance and arrogance of the man himself. But... perhaps there was more at play than he'd realized. A rival faction?

'Who is Simon Peake?' Ridley asked.

'Exactly!' Hardy asked. 'We don't... we really don't know.'

He twisted the wrist again causing a renewed tension in Hardy. 'If you know so little, what good are you to me?'

'Check the desk drawer!'

Still holding Hardy, Ridley shuffled that way, opened the drawer. The piece of paper was on top. A picture, some basic information about Simon Peake. New York driver's license, but a British passport. A news article...

An ex-con. An ex-soldier ex-con at that.

Ridley didn't like the connections one bit.

'Take Ivanka back to the pool,' he said to Katie. Both women looked at him bewildered. 'Take her back to the damn pool, will you! And put the knife away.'

Katie didn't question him and the knife was soon sheathed. She helped Ivanka back to her feet, her legs all shaky. The two of them edged out.

'You bastard,' Hardy crowed. 'You—'

Ridley smacked him in the groin with his knee. Just because he wanted to, more than anything.

'Save it,' Ridley said. He let go and Hardy shot up and to his feet to face him off. But he didn't make a move. Just glared daggers, his face not hiding his utter confusion at the sudden change in atmosphere.

'This doesn't mean I'm finished with you,' Ridley said. 'But it is an unexpected turn. Now sit down.'

Hardy did as he was told. Ridley kept his eyes on him as he pulled out his phone and made the call. He checked his watch. Early evening back in England.

'Yeah?'

'Hinch, it's me,' Ridley said.

A pause before Hinch answered. Ridley knew why. Genuine surprise, first of all, because they were hardly allies these days. But for a guy like Hinch – a highly experienced asset handler at MI5 – that surprise wouldn't last more than a flash. Next he'd need to set up a trace, find out where Ridley was calling from, followed by a need to pass on a message to his team to reveal who he had on the phone. He could have done both those things while speaking to make it less obvious but he didn't care about the delay. Hinch knew that Ridley knew what he was doing.

'Now this is unexpected,' Hinch said once he'd done what he needed. 'How have you been?'

Small talk. More delay.

'Never better.'

'I doubt that. Given you're calling me.'

'Yeah. I need a favor.'

Hinch laughed at that. A deliberately antagonizing laugh. 'Seriously? You're asking me for a favor? Wait... OK I've just had a text from the director himself. Pretty quick reaction from him. He knows you're on the line with me. Now I'm asking him if I should send a team out after you, picking you up in... middle-of-the-fucking-nowhere Alabama? OK, maybe you'll get a head start on us this time, but—'

'You don't need to send a team after me,' Ridley said.

'Maybe I get to decide that.'

'I just need some information. A quick data search.'

'Right. Boss says... nah, actually you don't need to know what he says. But looks like he's in a good mood today. Lucky for you.'

'Glad to hear. A name's come up over here. I need to know where he sits. Simon Peake.'

'And what do I get in return for this?'

'Next time one of your assets comes up on my hit list, perhaps I'll look the other way.'

'Perhaps? Yeah, right. Simon Peake? And his name came up because...?'

'He's causing me some problems.'

'What kind of problems?'

'Just see what you can find.'

For a man like Hinch, it wouldn't take long. Ridley gave him the scant details on Peake from Hardy's data. There was no more chat for the next two minutes. Ridley kept a close eye on Hardy, but the guy didn't move a muscle. He looked intrigued more than anything now.

'Yeah. He's here,' Hinch said. 'And he's Cat X.'

Ridley sighed.

Category X. Every man and woman profiled on databases held by the UK intelligence services were put into one of several categories depending on their status, their history, their risk. Categories A through F. Then X. X sat all on its own, a unique group of people. Xers had previous either as part of the UK's armed forces – most commonly special forces – or as employees or assets of MI5 and MI6. They were people who'd taken part in the most dangerous, highly secret and sensitive missions, but who'd since left official service, generally under not so good circumstances.

Xers were often extremely clever, conniving, physically talented, but also about the most unstable group of people you could imagine. Often riddled with PTSD, many of them turned to vices, drugs, alcohol, and spiraled into oblivion. Suicide rates were high. So too was violent crime, which definitely seemed to be Peake's case, given the five years he'd apparently spent in state penitentiary in New York. But occasionally, those whose ideas were more political would turn antagonistic. Rebels who wanted to get back at the system that had broken them. Sometimes they were cajoled into working for less friendly states. Whatever their path, every Cat X was a big political risk – a big societal risk, really – because of the things they'd done and the things they knew and the things they were still capable of doing.

In Ridley's mind the safest thing would be to assemble an elite team and go out across the world and eliminate them all. But Cat Xs were likely too savvy for that. If they knew they were targets, they'd fight back with everything they had. It'd be chaos.

So as it was, they were left to roam the world as ticking time-bombs.

An imperfect system if ever there was one.

'You said he's causing you problems?' Hinch said.

Ridley now wished he hadn't said that and also knew there would be a definite change in tone now from Hinch, from reluctant to helpful. He'd be keen to know more and likely want to be involved.

'If you want I can get a team together to come and—'

'You don't need to send anyone,' Ridley said. 'This is a problem for me, not anyone else. This conversation never happened.'

'Yeah. But it did. And the director knows it did. And he knows you've got a Cat X on your tail.'

'He's not on my tail. He doesn't even know I exist. He's just got himself mixed up in something I'm running, probably because he thinks he's still a hero.'

Silence from Hinch. Which meant he didn't agree.

'Seriously, Hinch, this guy is my problem. It's not something that's about to come back and bite you or anyone you know.'

A sigh from Hinch now but nothing else.

'I'll deal with him,' Ridley said. 'Don't come stepping on my toes.'

'OK. I'll lay off. But this is going on record. You have a good day.'

The call ended.

'Now that was interesting,' Hardy said, confidence returning in his demeanor. 'And who was that?'

'You don't need to know.'

'But the guy on the other end knew this Simon Peake?'

'You don't need to know that either. But you need to tell me how you found out about him.' Hardy folded his arms to show he wasn't going to answer. 'Just because the knife isn't to your wife's throat still doesn't mean you're in the clear for the mess you've caused. How'd you know about Peake?'

'Because I'm not the hillbilly hick you think I am.'

Ridley wasn't so sure about that.

'So who is he?' Hardy asked. 'A spook like you?'

'No, he isn't. But he's not someone to underestimate. What I don't understand is how he got involved here.'

'Looks like I'm one step ahead of you then,' Hardy said smugly.

Ridley thought for a moment. On the face of it, having Peake out there running amok with their target was a disaster. But, looking at it another way, perhaps Peake's involvement could actually help Ridley. A man like that wanted to fight. Wanted to stand up for what was right. At least what he thought was right. A moral crusader who was prepared to get his hands very bloody.

Peake wasn't Ridley's enemy. Ridley just needed to help point Peake in the direction of the bad guys.

One of them was sitting right in front of him.

'I'll only ask you one more time. How'd you find out about Peake?'

'Why don't I just show you?'

Hardy got up and walked to the patio door. Ridley had one hand to the gun stashed in the waistband of his pants as Hardy moved outside, waiting to see if he'd do anything stupid. But he didn't.

Ridley followed and signaled to Katie who left Ivanka's side. The three of them headed around the back of the house, across the grounds and to the barn. A couple of guys stood there chatting, oblivious to what had just taken place in the office. Ridley tensed nonetheless and waited again to see if Hardy would raise the alarm, or if the men would notice the blood caked in the boss's nostrils.

No. Nothing. The three of them headed on past, into the barn which stank of piss and sodden straw. The sound of barking dogs filled Ridley's ears and he pushed away the doubt that perhaps Hardy was about to set a trap. He'd seen what those dogs could do...

They stopped at a hatch in the ground.

'Hey, Nate, open up,' Hardy shouted and one of the men from outside jogged over and pulled the hefty door open.

Ridley tentatively stepped toward the opening, making sure he kept Nate and Hardy at least in his periphery so they couldn't push him down into whatever lay below.

Once again, there was no ambush, and as Ridley's eyes adjusted to the dark he spotted the outline of the barely clothed, dirty-skinned young man in the concrete shell.

'Who the hell is that?' Ridley asked.

'That is Adam McGinty.'

22

Adam looked up at the clutch of men standing above him around the edge of the pit. He recognized most, but not all. The well-dressed businessman-type was the one his attention lingered on but then he and Hardy moved out of sight before Je'Von dangled the wooden pole down into the hole.

'Get out,' he said.

Adam grasped the pole and grimaced and groaned as he clambered out and to the top.

'Take him outside,' Hardy called over. 'And get the dogs ready.'

Rough hands grabbed Adam. He tried to find his feet but was too weak, disoriented, and ended up being dragged across the concrete to the outside. They tossed him to the ground. He rolled off the edge of the wooden decking and landed in the dusty red dirt below with a thump. Much to the amusement of everyone around him.

The blazing sun beat down, causing Adam's eyes to water and his vision to blur, and it took him several seconds to adjust and focus back above to the men crowding over him.

Hardy. Je'Von. Wyatt. Jarrard. The businessman.

'Adam, I'd like you to meet my acquaintance, Ridley,' Hardy said, slapping the guy on his shoulder, although it really looked like Ridley didn't appreciate that. 'Like me, he's real interested in your buddy, Simon Peake.'

'I told you, Peake isn't my friend.'

'Yeah, sure he ain't,' Hardy said before turning his attention back to Ridley, but Ridley looked distracted, a little confused by something. 'What?'

'Your man over there,' Ridley said, nodding to Je'Von who was standing arms folded staring off into the distance.

'What about him?' Hardy asked.

'I saw him last time I was here.'

Hardy laughed. 'Yeah, you did. Get that, Adam. Just a few days ago Je'Von was in the tank, like you. But I gave him a simple choice. Show me why I shouldn't kill him. He did that.'

'I've already told you everything I know!' Adam shouted.

'Well you can go ahead and tell it all again,' Ridley said. 'For my benefit.'

'I hardly know Peake!' Adam said. 'He's just some drifter who turned up in Prenticeville one day. He was asking around about work. Frank took him on at the bar.'

'Frank being Frank Booker,' Hardy said to Ridley. 'A local big man, apparently. He's also the one who put all those cuts and bruises on Adam, in case you thought that was us.'

Ridley raised an eyebrow at that but said nothing.

'Apparently Booker has beef with Peake,' Hardy continued. 'He had some guys go to town on Adam asking about him. Seems Peake's not too good at making friends.'

'Frank Booker?' Ridley said. 'Is this guy a problem to us?'

'No,' Adam said. 'He's not.'

'Who the hell asked you?' Hardy said before turning back to Ridley. 'I'm kinda undecided, but I don't think so. The guy certainly won't be helping Peake anytime soon.'

'He could be useful in tracking Peake down though.'

'We won't need him. We have him.' Hardy glanced back down to the dirt. 'Adam?'

'W-what you want me to say?'

Hardy sighed. 'Let me fast forward through the dull stuff. Adam was working with my guys to snatch Lucia, and... deal with her. Adam's bright idea was to take the body to Peake for him to dispose of it. Except the idiots hadn't actually killed her. And Peake, being some goddamn hero or something, decided to save her and kill my men. This guy here ran away like a little bitch. Have I got all that right so far, Adam?'

Adam sank his head, eyes fixed on the dirt. 'Yeah. That's right.'

'Now Peake is protecting Lucia,' Hardy said.

'And you know where he is?' Ridley asked Adam.

'No. I don't.'

Another sigh from Hardy. 'And this is where we got to with him. Like most idiot wannabe heroes, he thinks he won't talk—'

'No!' Adam shouted. 'I'm not holding out! I don't know anything else! I'm not projecting Peake. Why would I? Look at the shit I'm in because of him!'

Hardy glared down at Adam but said nothing, as though the silence and the look he gave was enough to warn Adam of his displeasure at the interruption.

'But I'm not about to play around with any will-he, won't-he bullshit,' Hardy said to Adam. 'I'm gonna give you a test instead. Except... we're missing something here.' He put a finger to his lips and looked off into the distance as though deep in thought. Everyone looked confused by the gesture. Everyone except Ridley who just seemed a little irritated. By Hardy, more than anything else. Then Hardy became more animated as he stared over at Je'Von. 'Hey, big guy – why don't you tell Ridley how we got Adam here?'

Je'Von stuttered, struggling to find his words.

'He ain't much of a talker,' Hardy said, waving away Je'Von's poor attempt at an explanation. 'Not much of a thinker, either. Honestly, it's harder to find good workers around these parts than you'd think.'

'Is this the story?' Ridley asked, sounding as bored as he was irritated now and Adam could see that Hardy was struggling not to react to the guy's pissy attitude.

'No,' Hardy said. 'The story is about how Je'Von got that big black eye. Adam, you wanna tell us?'

But Adam really didn't, and he kind of realized Hardy wanted to do the talking anyway.

'So we're scouring Georgia, Alabama for this guy. Going to all his old haunts, tapping up all his old friends, but we're getting nowhere. So I get a couple of guys to do the most basic of stakeouts. One outside, one inside Adam's condo.' Hardy paused and chuckled to himself. Wyatt and Jarrard looked amused too. Je'Von looked spaced out as always. 'You remember the movie, Pulp Fiction?'

'I do,' Ridley said.

Hardy chuckled again. 'You know that scene where Bruce Willis arrives home, he's on the run and he's looking around the place trying to be in and out as quick as he can?'

'Rings a bell.'

'He spots a big old gun just sitting there and realizes someone's in the house. It's only John Travolta taking a dump. He flushes, opens the door, and Bruce is right there. Something in the toaster pops up and boom! John Travolta's dead. Only he's only kind of dead because the timeline is all screwed up, but you get the point.'

'Do I?' Ridley asked.

'You don't?' Hardy kept his eye on Ridley a moment as though expecting a response to that. He didn't, so carried on. 'Adam, the doofus, was hiding out here and there, doing a pretty decent job of evading us, but maybe he'd burned all his bridges or something, or maybe no one likes him much and wouldn't take him in any longer, so he eventually wound up going home. Why the fuck did you do that?'

Adam shrugged. The truth was he'd been desperate. As Hardy had said, he'd burned all his bridges and then some. He needed money. Clothes. Food.

'Except Adam walks in there, not realizing Je'Von's already inside. But Je'Von isn't just sitting there waiting, like he should have been. He's taking a dump just like John Travolta. At least, for him, he didn't leave a weapon lying around for Adam to blast him full of lead with. But he did get one hell of a fright when he came off the shitter to find Adam standing there with a baseball bat. Bang, crash, whatever. Je'Von gets a smack around the face with the bat. Adam runs for it. Maybe would have got away for a while had it not been for Wyatt on the outside.'

'OK. Nice story,' Ridley said. He checked his watch.

'Don't worry, we're nearly at the end. The moral? Some guys are just not much fucking use to me. Wyatt, go get the dogs. Je'Von, get down in the dirt with Adam.'

'W-what?'

Hardy went over and grabbed Je'Von by the back of his neck and pushed him forward. Je'Von was several inches taller, full of muscle, but he didn't resist Hardy at all.

'Get down there and get ready for the one thing you're actually any good at.'

Hardy shoved Je'Von forward and he landed in a heap next to Adam. The two of them shared a fearful look, then both focused on the barking dogs as they came outside, gnashing their teeth, spittle flying everywhere as the men holding the leashes struggled to keep them at bay.

'On your feet, both of you,' Hardy said.

Adam and Je'Von both did as they were told.

'Je'Von, you're not new to this. Adam, for your benefit, the aim is simple. Don't fucking die.'

'You don't have to do this,' Adam said.

'But I want to,' Hardy said.

Adam looked at Ridley as though for some sort of help, but the guy did and said nothing.

'Please!' Adam said. 'Please, I'll do anything!'

'Adam, don't beg,' Hardy said. 'It shows your weakness.'

'I told you everything I know! I don't know where Peake is, I swear!'

'All the more reason why you're not much use to me anymore. Unless you show me something right about now.'

'Hardy, no!' Adam yelled, his throat hoarse from the effort.

'Now run. Both of you.'

Je'Von moved first. Adam didn't wait long. He spun and sprinted away, Je'Von already pulling from him. The guy was fast. Seriously fast. No way Adam could keep close to him all the way to the fence, which was... two, three hundred yards away?

As soon as Hardy released the dogs, they'd be on Adam in seconds. That's what Hardy was planning, wasn't it? Unless this whole thing was some sick joke.

Je'Von didn't seem to think so. Hardy said he'd done this before. Clearly he'd not lost the last time.

'Ten!' Hardy shouted out. 'Nine!'

No. This wasn't a joke.

'Je'Von!' Adam shouted. 'Behind you!'

The guy actually slowed and turned. Then stumbled. Nearly lost his balance. Adam strained every muscle, sinew, tendon, whatever, to close the distance and launched himself forward. Je'Von turned again, perhaps sensing Adam behind him, but it was too late with Adam midair, arms outstretched like a football player making a last-ditch effort to save a touchdown. Not a perfect tackle by any measure, but with them both moving at speed over the uneven ground it didn't need perfect contact to send Je'Von way off balance and tumbling. Adam cried in pain as his shoulder cracked onto the hard surface. He rolled over twice, dirt billowing around him.

But he fought through the pain and the disorientation and bounced back up and launched his foot under Je'Von's chin to keep him down.

'Four!' Hardy called out.

'No!' Je'Von screamed, sensing what Adam was about to do.

Nothing stopping him now, though. Adam lifted his foot again and slammed it down onto Je'Von's prone lower leg. The sound of snapping bone was more sickening than Je'Von's harrowing scream.

'Two!'

Adam sped off, ignoring the pleading and the begging from the fallen man.

'One!'

Nothing for it. Adam didn't look back as the sounds of the dogs barreling forward filled his head. No barking now, just the thud-thud-thud of their paws on the ground, so loud to Adam he was sure he could feel the ground beneath him shake, as though a whole herd of wildebeest was stampeding toward him.

He winced when that sound abruptly halted to be overtaken by Je'Von's even more heightened screams of anguish, accompanied by the growls and chomps of the dogs.

The fence was fifty yards away. Thirty. Twenty. Ten. Adam would propel himself up and over. After that? He had no clue. At least he wouldn't be a meal for the dogs.

He was about to leap up onto the fence when he skidded to a stop… He'd spotted the thin wire trailing along the mesh of the fence.

Electrified.

He glanced behind him. The dogs were still ravaging Je'Von but he was quiet and surely dead now. How long before the beasts wanted another kill? The men in the distance were too far away for Adam to see the looks on their faces and he could only just hear their heckles and calls now. One thing he knew for sure: they weren't about to come to his aid.

'Shit, shit, shit!'

He looked around. He needed something. Something to attack the dogs, to at least fend them off.

He spotted it.

A metal rod. An old fence post or something. It lay partially submerged in dirt, all rusted over. Adam ran to it, yanked the four-foot pole out of the ground. The surface was mottled with splintering sharp edges where the metal was falling apart and as he gripped the rod tightly, two-handed, pain shot through his hands where loose shards broke through his skin.

He held the rod like a bat. Swooshed it through the air, trying to think through a method of attack. One of the dogs, sixty, seventy yards away, looked up from Je'Von's corpse, blood dripping from its mouth.

Then it raced forward, bouncing over the ground, five, six yards at a time.

No chance. Adam knew he had absolutely no chance!

'Think, think!'

He turned back to the fence, his brain scrambling for something. He'd lived on a fucking farm his whole life! No doubt Hardy had made this fence more powerful than a simple cattle fence but—

'That's it!'

He jammed one end of the rod into the ground, a few inches from the fence, then kicked the top of the rod forward where it dropped down onto the electrified wire.

Adam jolted at the crack and the sparks that flew as the rod grounded the electrical circuit running through the fence, shorting it.

He didn't dare look behind to see how close the dog was and made a leap of faith for the fence...

Nothing! He was fine! He clambered to the top and swung around and dropped into a heap on the other side as the dog launched itself against the metal. The fence shook and clattered but held firm. The dog yapped and barked, throwing blood and saliva onto Adam as he achingly pulled himself to his feet.

'Yeah, you stupid mutt. Now what?'

'Now we take you back.'

Adam spun but the fist caught him on his ear and sent him back to the ground. His vision blurred a couple of seconds before he could make out Wyatt's face above him. The guy was smiling. 'What, you thought Hardy was just gonna let you walk away?'

Was he supposed to answer that?

'Now get up.'

Even without the added persuasion of the gun in Wyatt's hand, Adam wasn't sure he'd have fought back. He simply didn't have anything left in him, his confused brain as mushy as his depleted muscles.

They walked all of twenty yards before Wyatt shoved Adam onto the back of the flatbed truck. Soon they arrived at the barn. The dogs were already back in their cages. Adam was taken out into the sun once more. Across the field Jarrard was busy scooping up Je'Von's remains onto a small trailer attached to a quad bike.

'I liked that,' Hardy said. 'Ingenious. Not just with Je'Von but the fence too. Although you owe me if you've caused any lasting damage.' Despite the last comment he actually did look pretty damn pleased, as though he'd gotten exactly the entertainment he'd hoped for. That Ridley, on the other hand… he showed no emotion at all. 'Perhaps I underestimated you,' Hardy added.

Adam said nothing.

'You have anything else you want to tell us yet, about Peake?' Ridley said.

'I already told you everything.'

Ridley sighed.

'It's OK,' Hardy said. 'I believe you. This isn't just about what you know anymore. It's about what you're prepared to do. To help. So tell me, Adam, just how far are you willing to go?'

'I'm pretty sure I already showed you that. I'll do what I need to survive. I always have done.'

Hardy nodded as though he got it. He really didn't.

'Good answer, Adam. So let me explain exactly what I need you to do.'

23

As he drove, it didn't take long for Peake to explain the basics of his life to Lucia, how he'd come to be in Prenticeville, and how he'd become involved in the death of Thomas McGinty. Largely because keeping it basic was his natural tendency. He could tell by the suspicious, almost disappointed look on her face that she wanted more. Much more.

'So you were in the army?'

'Yeah.'

'The British Army?'

'Yeah.'

'You still have family over there?'

'My mum. That's about it. No siblings. We never had a big extended family so there's probably others, but no one I ever knew well.'

'What made you join the army?' she asked.

'There was nothing else that fit. I dropped out of school at sixteen because I saw nothing good there for me. It'd got to the point where I hardly went anyway. I didn't have a hard time there really, I wasn't bullied or anything like that, but I just didn't... get it. I knew I couldn't take another two years knowing that I'd get nothing from it. My mum hated that I wasn't trying, but...'

'But what?'

'But that's just how it was. The truth is, she struggled with me. My dad died when I was young and even if she loved me and meant well she just didn't understand how to steer me. Like a lot of kids I gave her grief. I regret it. She never said so, but I think she was relieved when I signed up for the army at sixteen as it meant most of the parental burden was taken off her.'

'I'm a mother. Parenting isn't easy but "burden" isn't the word that comes to mind.'

Except she could barely remember a thing about her life, so how did she know that? He decided not to challenge her. He wasn't a parent, he knew nothing of it.

'I had a friend whose older brother had joined the air force and he had all these tales of heroics and excitement, and knowing the army would take on a sixteen-year-old like me, pay me, house me, show me the world… It made sense.'

'And that's what they did? Showed you the world?'

'Showed me all of the good and all of the bad. And until you've seen the bad, you really don't know just how fucked up it can be.'

Although as he glanced over at her, he was sure he saw a certain knowing in her look, as though she did understand the bad. He was about to ask her about that, turn the conversation back to her and what she could remember, but she jumped in first.

'But how'd that sixteen-year-old boy get to where you are now?'

'Well, that really is a very long story.'

'One that I thought you were going to tell me. Now you don't seem so sure.'

He sighed. He'd set this up so couldn't hold back now. Not everything, anyway. 'At twenty-one I was invited to test out for a new unit. I was still young and naive, and I didn't even ask what the unit was, why they'd picked me out, and I just went with the flow. I always enjoyed testing myself physically, my limits. Apparently I did good. But this unit… I mean, there really isn't much I can tell you—'

'Like, special forces?'

'Something like that. We worked in small teams, often deep behind enemy lines, often completely unofficially in territories we had no right to be in. It was hard, often brutal, always nerve-shredding, always only one slip up from being captured, killed or just from causing outright chaos.'

'And were you? Ever captured?'

He shook his head. 'You don't need to know the details.'

She tutted as though already fed up with his evasive answers.

'I spent over ten years there,' Peake said. 'With virtually no time back on home soil. Really it felt like I had no home. No girlfriend, friends even. The job was my life, all I knew.'

'It broke you?'

'No. A lot of the time, I loved it. I enjoyed the danger and I enjoyed the idea that I was doing good.'

'OK, then I'm getting more and more confused as to how it all fell apart for you. Because I know it must have done.'

'I guess I just got too used to being that guy. The one who could operate beyond normal rules, because that's exactly what I was supposed to do. Until one time I came against a superior I clashed with.'

'Clashed?'

'Again, you don't need to know the details, but the end result was that I flipped and broke his arm in anger. Payback for him having toyed with the lives of me and my team.'

'Now we're getting to it. They kicked you out?'

'Dishonorable discharge. And like I said, the job was my life and I'd never had a plan of what would come next. I had no home, no friends, as an adult I'd never had to live a civilian life. I couldn't have gone back to live with my mum, we'd just... Our lives had moved apart too much.'

'You had PTSD, you think? Because of what the army put you through?'

Peake scoffed. 'No. In some ways I wish I could claim that, but it wouldn't be true. Like I said, I saw some bad things, truly horrific things, and I had to do some horrible things too. And it probably says a lot about me that I don't have PTSD from it.'

'Perhaps you do, but you just never talked to anyone about it properly. Because I'm sensing, based on what I already see in you, that a man like you who thinks he's indestructible never looked to anyone for help.'

He glanced at her again, initially unsure what to say, a little taken aback that she thought she had such a good read on him. And also not sure if she was teasing him about him thinking he was indestructible. Actually, he knew exactly how breakable he and every other human being was. He'd broken plenty.

'Anyway, after I got kicked out I had no job, nowhere to go to or to be. I had an old friend—'

'I thought you had no friends?'

'Not a friend as most people would define it. Someone I'd worked with, trusted my life with. Except he'd got himself a life after leaving, a wife, kid. I knew we weren't about to be best buddies as there's no way he'd want me invading that life, bringing back all the old memories of what we did together. But I also knew he'd at least help me.'

'He was British too?'

'He was from New York. I'd never lived in a big city before and I thought why not give it a go? Land of opportunity and all that.'

'And was it?'

Peake shrugged. 'I had no qualifications, no work visa, social security number, so it wasn't like I could apply for anything official. But anyone can find work in a city like that.'

'Doing what?'

'Whatever pays. I made it work for a while. But for a guy like me... New York is a city where if you hang around on any street long enough you'll see something untoward. And let's just say I have a habit of not looking away.'

'Yeah. I see that in you.' She laughed at that although he detected only warmth in it rather than any kind of snideness.

'You heard about the prison thing from Frank,' he said. 'I made a mistake, but I'd lived for so long under a different set of rules, rules where I got to make decisions on the fly to get to a beneficial end result.'

'You said you saw a girl being raped?'

'And I reacted in the only way I knew how.'

'Did you know the attackers were only teenagers?'

'In the moment, no. Would it have made a difference in what I did? Possibly. But I neutralized the situation quickly, definitively. It's what I'd been taught to do. It's how I'd lived for years. In the moment I didn't even think about whether I'd gone too far.'

'And now?'

'I understand there was another way.'

'You spent five years in prison because of it.'

'Yeah.'

'How was that? For a man like you?'

He wasn't sure what she meant by that. A man like you. He didn't ask; he wasn't sure he'd like the answer.

'Prison was prison. I didn't get involved in any shit in there because even if I was still struggling with the outside world, prison is definitely not where I belong. It was long, hard, it definitely changed me in some ways. And gave me a couple of bad habits too.'

'Like what?'

'For one, I started smoking.' He lifted up his shirt to show the nicotine patch. 'Only realized when I got out how damn expensive it is in the real world.'

She shook her head in disbelief as though she really still didn't know what to make of him.

'And then you came down south for a new start?'

He snorted. 'No. I stayed in the city a while longer. Got a new job which turned out to be not so good.'

'Doing what?'

'Add ex-con to everything that I already said before, and you can probably imagine the type of person that would take me on.'

'Yeah. I guess so.'

'But that wasn't the problem. The problem was my old life catching up with me.'

'How'd you mean?'

'It's hard to explain, but let's just say I made a lot of enemies over the years. Some in high places in this country and others. I've never intentionally gone into hiding, but there are people out there who, if they found out where I am now… they'd come after me for my blood. That's what happened in New York.'

The conversation paused and he could tell that the more he'd talked, the more confused and perhaps wary of him she'd become by it all.

'Are you a wanted man there?'

'I don't think so,' Peake said. 'Not officially, at least. But I needed to get out. And I also realized that maybe a big city like that really isn't best for me after all.'

She laughed at that. 'Yeah. Too much trouble going on around you that could suck you in. Unlike around here.'

He smiled and shook his head. 'Yeah. Like I said, maybe I just have a habit of coming across trouble, wherever I go.'

'But I have to be thankful for that. Perhaps it was fate.'

She signaled a cross on her body as though thanking a higher power for Peake's intervention. It was the first religious overture she'd shown. Peake himself had never believed in such things, not after what he'd seen and done, but really hers was as good an explanation as any he could come up with as to how his life always came to these points.

'And together with what you heard last night already about Thomas McGinty, and Adam coming to me for help with that, and then with you... that kinda brings you up to date.'

'I guess it does,' she said. And she seemed more relaxed now, knowing more about him, although the reality was that he'd kept full details of the darkest parts of his life entirely out of the conversation. Lucia stretched and yawned. 'How much farther? I could really do with a break.'

'We'll be back at the lake in less than an hour.'

'The lake?'

'I think we should go back to the pump house.'

Her face screwed over with distaste. 'Why are we going back there?'

'Because it's secluded, safe.'

'It's where they tried to kill me!'

'You want to go and stop at a motel? Hide in plain sight?'

'Yes! But it's not hiding. No one's following us right now.'

She looked behind as though to confirm that. Certainly Peake saw no cars in sight in the rearview mirror, but that didn't mean there weren't people out there searching for them, hunting them down.

'I still think the familiarity will help,' he said. 'Last time you were there, it brought back memories—'

'Bad memories. The absolute worst moments of my life!'

'I'm not doing this to upset you, but surely anything that helps you remember is better than you not knowing. And the more we know, the more I can help.'

She said nothing to that, but Peake carried on turning over the point in his head.

'Do you remember anything else?' he asked her.

She shot him a glare.

'Lucia, I can only help with what I know. Anything at all that you remember could mean—'

'I don't know anything other than what I've already told you. But please… I don't want to go back there right now.'

He thought about that for a while. 'OK,' he said. 'We can find a motel. Rest up for a while. But the lake… It's somewhere that hardly anyone who's still alive knows about. You might not like the idea, but if we get separated for whatever reason, that's where you go. That's where I'll find you.'

Lucia still looked anything but convinced, but before she could confirm or oppose Peake's suggestion his phone vibrated with an incoming call.

'Who is it?' she asked as he looked between the road and the phone screen.

The number wasn't saved, but he thought he recognized it as he answered the call.

'Yeah?'

'Peake, it's—'

'Adam.'

'Yeah. I need your help. Please, Peake, you have to help me.'

24

The request from Adam was simple. A time and a place to meet up. A few hours to kill for Peake and Lucia as they were relatively close already given the decision to move south from Prenticeville. So they took the opportunity to rest at a basic motel about twenty miles east of their intended destination. Except Peake didn't sleep too well on the stained armchair in the shoddy room. Perhaps better than he would have done in the car or on the cold concrete floor of the pump house at the lake, but still not good. And not just because of the uncomfortable chair, but perhaps mostly because of his edginess which meant he never quite achieved deep sleep. Every car that went by, every creak of the building's fabric, had caused him to stir and renew his attention on his senses.

But the time had wound on without incident and when he checked the time on the bedside clock and realized he only had a few minutes before the alarm on his phone went off, Peake decided to give up on any further hope of shut-eye. He shuffled in the chair, which was enough to rouse Lucia on the king-sized bed. She'd stayed on top of the covers, clothed. She'd offered that he could sleep next to her, and he knew there'd been no hint of anything suggestive in that, but he'd still said no. Even if the bed was undoubtedly more comfortable, he'd wanted to not sleep deeply for the very reason that he had to be alert if someone had turned up at their door.

'How are you feeling?' he asked when she groaned and winced in pain.

'A little better, but still not too good.'

He got up from the chair and grabbed some painkillers and a glass of water.

'To take the edge off,' he said as he passed them to her.

She took the pills and went to the bathroom to freshen up, and when she came back out she did look a bit more lively, the creases of pain on her face mostly gone for now.

'At least we had AC,' she said, looking about the room with distaste as though only now realizing how shoddy it was.

But it was a fair point about the AC. The daytime temperature had crept beyond a hundred but in here they'd set the thermostat at seventy-five. The few hours in the cool had been about as comfortable as they could have hoped for, all things considered.

'We're meeting Adam at six?' Lucia asked.

Adam. Probably not just Adam, though. Peake wasn't that stupid.

'Yeah.'

'It's only four fifteen now.'

'Which gives us plenty of time to eat first, then get where we need to be ahead of time.'

'Then let's do that.'

* * *

They ate at a café off the highway. Even though they were heading to a diner afterward to meet Adam, Peake didn't want to miss the opportunity of them both filling up on calories – they'd missed too much sleep and too many meals the last few days. As they approached the outskirts of Hazelwood, he spotted a roadside sign proudly displaying the name and the year it was established – 1934. The decorative sign also included a large, bushy tree which Peake assumed to be a hazel although the paintwork on it was all scratched, virtually no green left in the canopy. Before they got to any of the town's residential buildings they passed by a damn big, old factory, rusted wire fence, weed-filled grounds, a looming but falling apart structure in the middle. A much bigger sign than at the town's entrance sat atop the partially caved-in metal roof of the building, some of the lettering faded to nothing, but still clear what it would have once read: Hazelwood Nut Company.

'That explains the town's name,' Lucia said.

'I guess so.'

As he drove on he saw a lot of familiarity in Hazelwood to the Georgian towns he'd been to recently, just on a bigger scale. A once industrial town – perhaps the nut company its primary employer, originally – which had fallen on harder times. As they neared the center they passed by strip mall after strip mall, each of them drab and functional. The town also had a few low-end chain hotels. A few high-rise condo units, some newer looking, others looking on the verge of abandonment.

Soon they came to what looked like a traditional old main street, buildings clustered either side that had once held all manner of businesses, cafés, restaurants, but about a third of the units were now empty and of those that remained open many were thrift shops and the like.

But as they carried on, Peake noticed signs of recent development and perhaps attempts to bring the town back to a former glory. A large shrub-lined square took center stage with a pristine-looking church on one side, and a handsomely and obviously recently renovated redbrick town hall opposite. Posters hanging from ornate streetlights announced the Hazelwood Historic District. Peake slowed the car a little. Next to the town hall stood a police station. Three squad cars sat outside it. A couple of uniformed police officers stood there talking, with coffee cups in their hands. Neither paid Peake any attention as he rolled on past.

'You OK?' Lucia asked.

'Yeah. Just thinking,' he said as he quickly checked the GPS map on his phone.

'About what?'

'About how that police station is less than half a mile from where we're going.'

He said nothing more than that before he took the next right, moving out of the historic district and onto a street with more plain-looking buildings, most of them single story.

'There it is.' He pointed to the diner in front, on a corner on their left-hand side, and kept moving slowly past it, a hundred yards until he swung a U-turn and then crawled forward to park on the roadside between two large pickups.

He shut the engine down.

'Did you see him inside?' Lucia asked.

'No.'

Silence from them both for a few minutes, though Peake knew Lucia was intermittently sending questioning glances his way.

'Are we just sitting here?' she asked.

'Yes.'

'Because?'

'Because Adam called me late last night, out of the blue, to tell me he needs my help and to come meet him here.'

'You don't trust him?'

'Of course I don't. We know he was working for Hardy, the man who wants you dead. And we know Adam hasn't been seen in days. Either because he was lying low or because the boss has already caught up with him and now has him under duress.'

'You didn't think to tell me before now that you think this is a setup?'

'I thought it was obvious.'

She scoffed. 'Not to me. You helped Adam out before and... Didn't he say he was in trouble? With Hardy? That's why he needs your help? That could be true?'

'Exactly. Which is why we came here. Because we want to find Hardy, and Adam's our best way of achieving that. But make no mistake, I don't owe Adam anything. He's the reason we're both in this mess.'

'You think Hardy's near here?'

'I'm sure of it.'

'So what is the plan? Because I'm sensing you're not about to suggest a second dinner.'

'We wait. We watch. We figure out who's coming to meet us here. Adam? Others? We make our next move based on what we see.'

She seemed apprehensive about that but didn't say why and he didn't bother to ask. They'd arrived fifty minutes before the planned meet with Adam and in the thirty minutes that followed, Peake paid close attention to every car and every pedestrian that went past. With the engine – and AC – off the temperature in the car rose quickly, despite the windows being partially down, despite them being shaded from the sun. For now at least, but not for much longer. Even just sitting there doing nothing Peake's skin glistened with moisture.

Still no sign of Adam as the clock on the dashboard continued to close in on 6 p.m.

'He's still not here,' Lucia said.

'No.'

'And what about everyone else you've seen? You've not said a word.'

'You haven't asked.'

She tutted. But he hadn't meant to be facetious, he'd just been busy, in his own head, as he watched.

'There are thirteen customers in the diner,' Peake said, although from their position about fifty yards away he could only see seven of those through the windows, but he'd kept a tally of who had gone in and come out since they arrived. 'There're four of those I don't like.'

'In what way?'

'In my naturally suspicious way. The four turned up within five minutes of each other. One in the black Ram truck you see right by the exit, the other in the brown sedan on the street, facing us.'

'And that's suspicious why?'

'Just the way they were. Not enough chat between the men. Too much looking around as they went inside. Since they sat inside, too. The ones from the truck are in the booth by the entrance and they've had nothing but coffee and are spending all their time looking out. The other two took an inner table the other side. I can only see one of them, but I don't think they're eating either. And the way they parked their cars? Covering off the parking lot exit.'

She nodded but said nothing, as though processing what he'd said and trying to figure if she agreed or not.

'My best bet is that Adam's going to arrive any second,' Peake said. 'He wants to get there before time so that he can choose the table, and he'll take one directly between those pairs. And I bet he'll arrive on foot. Most likely one of those two vehicles brought him over here and dropped him around the corner, so that if I happened to be in there early, I wouldn't get jumpy when I saw he wasn't alone.'

And Peake had barely finished the words when out of the side road, coming from the historic district, a man strode across the street, looking left and right as he moved. Adam. Looking a little disheveled and hobbling on his right leg. He was hurt. And he was clearly nervous by the constant swiveling of his head.

Sure enough, he took a window seat a couple of booths away from the pair at the door, equidistant to the other two.

'So what now?' Lucia asked. 'We wait for them to leave and follow?'

Peake thought about that one for a moment.

'No,' he said.

'No? Then what? Accost them here?'

'Definitely not. The numbers are way out of our favor. And I still don't like that the police are right there, around that corner.'

'Adam and his friends don't seem to care much about that.'

'Which is something else I don't like.'

'You think Hardy and these guys have the run of the local cops?'

'I wouldn't bet against it.'

'Fair enough, but would you please just tell me what the hell the plan is then!'

Instead, Peake started the engine and pulled another U-turn, heading farther away from the diner.

'We're leaving?'

'No.'

He took three left turns, coming onto the narrower road that led along to the side of the diner. He pulled over thirty yards from the junction.

'And we did that because?'

'Because I'm not so bothered now about what happens inside. From here I can still see the truck and the sedan those men arrived in, so I'll know when they leave. But it's that blue car there I'm locked in on.'

He gave her a moment to hone in on the Ford Fusion sitting at the end of the street, right before the diner, facing away from them and toward the main road.

'That car arrived not long after we did. I can't say 100 percent, but I'm pretty sure there's only one person inside. A woman. And she never got out.'

'Why the hell would she do that if she's with them?'

'Good question, isn't it? Perhaps she isn't with them. But I'm banking that she's here because of them. Because of us.'

'So she's now our target? What if she's a Fed or something?'

'Maybe. But whoever she is, the numbers look a lot better for us going after her. Two against one rather than five.'

Lucia said nothing more. They waited. Waited. Nearly an hour without much happening, other than a couple of missed calls from Adam, and a voicemail asking Peake where he was. The woman remained in her car. Plenty of other customers came and went but the four men and Adam didn't.

Not until Peake spotted the two from the sedan sauntering toward their car. They headed off, no interaction with the woman at all. Less than two minutes later and the other two – Adam tagging along by their side – came out and up to the Ram truck. Adam looked lost, a little forlorn, his head bowed as he stepped into the back of the truck followed by one of the guys. For the briefest moment Adam locked eyes in Peake's direction but then the door closed and seconds later the Ram pulled out onto the road and moved out of sight.

Peake and Lucia continued to sit there, both of them silent, both of them with their gaze directed to the blue Ford. Less than five minutes later and the brake lights flickered as the engine was turned on. Peake went to turn on his engine too to follow but then paused, because the next moment the blinker flashed and the car pulled out and swung a U-turn and headed straight for them.

'Get down!' Peake said. Lucia moved her head out of view more quickly than he did, mainly because her smaller frame allowed her to sink toward the footwell easily. Peake would rather have stayed up to get a better view of who sat in the approaching car, but that could wait.

He listened for the sound of the car moving past then waited a few more seconds, pulling his head up just enough so that he could see the Ford in his side mirror. It took a right.

He turned on the engine and the tires skidded as he swung out into the road and turned to follow the Ford. He gunned it to the end of the street then slowed as he took the right. The car was only fifty yards ahead. Peake followed the car across town, keeping what he hoped was a safe distance. At least in this slightly larger town there was plenty of other traffic to help them blend in.

'No sign of the other two cars,' Lucia said.

'Nope.'

'So she wasn't with them.'

'Doesn't look like it.'

'And she's not following them. So who the hell is she?'

'That's what we need to find out.'

They followed for about three miles until the Ford turned off the road into the parking lot of a condo unit. The single building had six stories. Dark-blue-painted wood siding and white-painted edges and trims gave it a pleasant traditional look.

'Not a hotel or a motel,' Lucia said. 'You think she's a local?'

'Possibly. Possibly not.'

'It's weird that she's staying here, right in the same town that Adam and Hardy's men lured us to?'

'It's not at all weird. It means we're close to where Hardy lives. Either in this town or very close to it.'

She looked dubious about something, but she didn't say what.

Peake parked the car in the far corner of the lot, watching the Ford in the rearview mirror. The woman emerged. She was alone.

'Do you know her?' Peake asked.

Lucia sighed as she shuffled in her seat to get a look out of the side mirror.

'If you'd parked head on I might have had a better chance of knowing. But... I don't think so. And I don't think I know this town either.'

Peake said nothing to that.

'I'm sorry,' Lucia said, as though sensing his frustration.

'It's not your fault.'

After moving to the stairwell the woman appeared again on the fourth floor and headed along the exposed walkway to the third door along. She stopped there, looked around, opened the door then walked inside.

'Come on,' Peake said. 'Let's go.'

He opened his door and stepped out.

25

'Wait, you don't want to take the guns?' Lucia said as she got out of the car.

The handgun was in the glove compartment. He'd hidden the shotgun from view under the passenger seat.

'No,' Peake said. 'Save them for when we might really need them. Like I said, this is two against one. We already have the upper hand.'

'And if she's armed?'

Which Peake was certain the woman was, given the bulge he'd noticed on her right hip.

'Then we might get a third gun to add to the collection.' He winked at Lucia and she opened her mouth to say something but then didn't before Peake set off for the building.

They moved quickly. As quickly as Lucia could, at least. Peake saw nothing suspicious around them but at least their angle of approach meant the woman – and anyone else in the condo on the fourth floor – wouldn't have spotted their approach.

Peake took the stairs with a bit more caution, always prepared for the unexpected, but nothing happened before they arrived at the front door. Peake held back to the side while Lucia stood in full view of the peephole and knocked.

'Housekeeping,' she called out.

A simple enough ruse, even if it was a bit late in the day. Would the woman open up? Perhaps unlikely if she felt at all threatened, but the only aim was to get her close to the door.

No response after a few seconds so Peake gave the nod for Lucia to try again.

'Housekeeping. Is anyone home?' Lucia shouted out with a set of three harder knocks.

Peake studied her reaction as Lucia kept her eyes fixed on the door. Her eyes widened ever so slightly a split second before she turned to Peake to give him the signal that she'd seen the glass of the peephole fog over – someone was approaching the door.

Lucia edged out of the way and Peake moved in front, lifted his foot, and crashed his heel into the door, which splintered around the lock and caved in first time. The woman the other side cried out in shock and pain as the door smacked into her face, knocking her back a couple of steps. Even as she reeled she whipped her hand to her hip to reach for the holstered weapon.

Peake pounced. He grabbed her wrist and turned it around and peeled two of her fingers from the grip of the gun and pushed them back until they snapped. The woman screamed again, even more loudly than before, and the gun dropped to the floor.

Lucia pushed her way into the condo behind Peake and closed the broken door as best she could. Peake left the gun and pulled the woman's wrist up behind her shoulder blade, a hammerlock. He used the resistance to push and guide the woman through the corridor into the open plan living space of the basic unit. Once there he let go of her and shoved her forward and she bounced off the back of the sofa and crumpled to the floor, clutching at her broken fingers.

Lucia followed them into the room, the gun now in her hands and pointed at the woman. For the second time now, she certainly looked confident enough in her new role as chief weapons holder.

'I'm guessing you already know who we are,' Peake said to the woman on the floor. 'Given you were staking out that diner waiting for us.'

'You broke my fingers!' the woman yelled.

'And he'll break more if you don't tell us what we need to know,' Lucia said, her strength and resolve surprising Peake – in a good way.

'I've no idea who you are!' the woman said. 'Please!'

'Let's not play that game,' Peake said.

He spotted a purse on the kitchen counter. He picked it up and pulled out the driving license.

'Katie Embleton. Virginia. What brings you to Alabama?'

Peake waited for an answer while his brain worked over the possibilities. Katie said nothing.

'Virginia makes me pretty damn suspicious. Who do you work for?'

Still no answer.

'If you were FBI you'd have a badge. So I'm thinking some offshoot of the CIA perhaps, although nothing mainstream as the CIA has no jurisdiction on home soil, right?'

He noted Lucia's shocked reaction to this suggestion, but Katie didn't react at all.

'So is it me or Lucia you're here for?' Peake asked.

No answer, so Peake crouched down by her and as he reached out she did the right thing of opening her mouth.

'I don't know what you're talking about!' she yelled. 'I don't work for the CIA. You're crazy!'

Peake sighed and moved back over to the counter and grabbed Katie's phone from by her purse.

'Tell me the code.'

She said nothing. So he crouched back down and she cowered once more before he grabbed one of her broken fingers. Katie squealed and writhed.

'Just open it,' he said, pushing the phone out to her and although initially reluctant, she eventually reached forward with her good hand and pressed across the screen to unlock the phone.

Peake quickly rummaged through the phone's contents. Not a lot to look at, really.

'This is what I want to know,' Peake said. 'Who's Hardy? And why does he want Lucia dead?'

Once again Katie decided not to answer, despite the obvious threat.

'I don't see a Hardy in here,' Peake said. 'And put together with the fact that you weren't with Adam McGinty and the welcome crew at the diner earlier, I'm sensing it's because you don't work for him. But you do know him, right?'

Still nothing but a defiant glare.

'You really want me to break some more bones?'

'No!' Katie said. 'I don't work for the FBI, the CIA, and I don't work for anyone called Hardy! Why are you—'

'Then who?' Peake asked. 'This guy called Ridley, perhaps?' He turned the phone to show her the messages from the contact saved as Peter Ridley. One of the few contacts she had.

She didn't answer, but the hostile stare kind of gave the answer.

'And who does Ridley work for?'

She pursed her lips. Peake's irritation grew rapidly. He was getting closer and closer to bringing out his bad cop persona. One of the only reasons he hadn't already was because he didn't want Lucia to witness that.

'Who. Does. Ridley. Work. For?'

'I don't know! And that's the truth.'

'This is bullshit,' Lucia said, renewing her grip on the gun. 'She must know who I am. Why Hardy wants me dead.'

Katie shot a glare that way but then her face mellowed, and she looked almost a little smug. 'Do you really not know what's going on here?'

The slight quake in Lucia showed she didn't like the question, as though she felt weakness in what she knew was the answer.

'I... don't—'

'She doesn't remember,' Peake said, matter of factly. 'Because of the brain trauma they caused her when they tried to murder her. Hardy's guys. And now we're looking for Hardy so we can find out why, and so we can kill him and anyone still alive who was involved.'

Katie said nothing but gulped, rightly recognizing that Peake's threat was real.

'So if you don't want to tell me what you know freely, we'll just go back to the other way of doing things.'

'No,' Katie said, shaking her head. 'Not that.'

'Why does Hardy want Lucia dead?'

'Because he's being paid for the hit,' Katie said. 'That's it.'

'Paid by who.'

'I don't know that. Honestly, I don't.'

He didn't believe her, but there was another thread he wanted to pull.

'So Hardy doesn't know Lucia?' Peake said. 'Other than for this hit?'

'I don't know who he does or doesn't know!'

'OK. So why does anyone want Lucia dead? Who is she?'

Katie shrugged, looking really pleased with herself now despite her predicament, as though enjoying that she obviously knew more than Peake and Lucia did.

Peake went to grab her fingers again but she squirmed away.

'OK, OK.' She shuffled again. 'If you... let me get up. I just want you gone. So ask me what you need, and I'll tell you what I know. But it really isn't much. You must see I'm not any kind of top dog here.'

Peake straightened and took a half step from her to give them both space.

'Why were you at the diner?' he asked.

'Because we're looking for Lucia too.'

'You and Ridley?'

Katie nodded.

'Why?'

'It doesn't matter to me why so I don't ask questions like that. I get paid to do what Ridley asks. Lucia is missing... or was. My job is to find out where she is. Was. You know what I mean. Ridley told me you had her, that you were supposed to meet Adam McGinty at that diner.'

'And how did Ridley know about that?'

'I don't know!'

'And I don't believe you. So if we'd showed our faces at the diner, and Hardy's crew had attacked us, taken us – which I'm pretty sure was their plan – what would you have done? Sitting in the car all on your own. Taken some nice pictures for your boss?'

She scowled as though offended. 'I would have reported back what I saw. Which is exactly what I did anyway. Like I said, finding Lucia – observing – was my only job.'

'How'd you even know to be there?' Peake asked.

'I said. Ridley told me.'

'And how did he know?'

'You'd have to ask him.'

The conversation was going nowhere fast.

'If you were one of the good guys here,' he said, 'you really would be trying a bit harder to win me over.'

'Are you sure you're the good guy?' Katie asked. 'Because you're the one who forced your way into here and broke my fingers. Who killed two men in Prenticeville. Maybe more.'

Peake held his tongue.

'The way I see it, you're in a lot more trouble than I am in all this. Of course, if you don't believe me, why not call 911 and get them over here so we can go through everything with them?'

Enough. Peake went to go for her, and she flinched as though knowing perhaps she'd done the wrong thing in taunting him... but then he paused. Because he'd heard the car door down below. Only one car door at least, so not a full on counterassault, but still, the look in her eye told him she knew what was happening.

'Don't let her move,' he said to Lucia.

He moved quickly to the window, pulled back the drape to look below. A smartly dressed man walked toward the unit, gazing up in Peake's direction.

'I'm guessing this is—'

Ridley, he was about to say, but the word never fully formed in his mouth before Lucia yelled out to alert him. The next moment the gun fired as Peake whipped around and ducked down. Katie, undeterred, raced across the room for the exit. Lucia fired again. Peake spotted the object in Katie's hand. He had no idea where she'd pulled it from but as she moved she rolled the small canister toward him and Lucia and it bounced along the carpet between them.

'Get down!' he shouted to Lucia as he threw himself to the floor and buried his head in his arms, his eyes squeezed shut.

But he hadn't moved quite quickly enough and the explosion from the flashbang sent his head into a spin and turned everything into a wall of white. He groaned and rolled out flat on the floor, head lolling as he battled through the disorientation and the throbbing pain in his ears.

'Lucia,' he called out, the focus on speaking somehow helping to bring him back to reality at least a little.

She only groaned in response. As the wall of white slowly turned into a spinning room, he managed to pull himself onto his haunches. With the smoke clearing he spotted Lucia on the floor right by him, awake but out of it, the gun on the carpet nearby.

He heard car doors outside. The noise provided him greater focus to get back to his feet and he rushed to the window and looked outside again to see the car that had arrived moments before speeding out of the parking lot toward the main road.

'Damn it!' Peake shouted.

He spun and went to Lucia and helped her up.

'You OK?'

She nodded in response, the simple gesture an effort as she battled for control of her senses.

'She's... gone?' Lucia said.

'Yeah. And we need to go too. We don't know if there's a secondary team on the way.'

'A secondary team?'

'Come on.'

He pulled on her shoulder to help her get moving. Peake hesitated a moment at the front door before stepping out into the open. There was no one there. No sirens, no other signs of an impending assault either.

'Keep going,' he said to Lucia, and the two of them moved as quickly as they could, Lucia regaining her balance more and more with each step before they were both back in the car.

'What the hell happened?' she asked.

Peake took them out onto the road before answering.

'My best guess? She and this Ridley are connected to some agency or other. I don't know what that means yet.'

Lucia seemed really unsure about that.

'Anyway. She sent an alert to this Ridley guy. Either when we knocked on the door or when I got her to unlock her phone.' Although if it had been the latter, she'd done that incredibly quickly and deftly.

'We found out nothing,' Lucia said, sounding dejected. 'Who the hell is Ridley? Is he working with Hardy or not?'

'We've got a lot more questions than answers, that's for sure. But we found more than nothing.'

'Did we? I've still no idea who I am. Why Hardy, why anyone wants me dead. Why there're people from a government agency involved in all this!'

He held the phone aloft. 'But we do have this.'

Lucia huffed. 'And what good is that?'

Peake allowed himself a smile. 'It might not have had Hardy's name in this thing, but it does show her search history in the maps data. And several times over the last few days she's gone to the same place not even an hour from here. Looks like it's out in the middle of nowhere.'

'You think that's where Hardy is?'

'I think very soon we'll find out.'

26

Peake and Lucia talked little until they were out of Hazelwood, as though both needed the time to process what had happened, at the diner earlier and then when they'd accosted Katie Embleton in the condo. Darkness fell as they headed further west, the sun dipping below the seemingly endless fields on the horizon.

'We have no idea what we're going to find out here,' Lucia said.

'Answers, hopefully. Hardy, hopefully.'

'At the diner, you were concerned about being outnumbered. It's why you wanted to go after that Embleton woman instead. Now you just want to drive into the unknown like this?'

'I never said I was concerned, just that it made more sense to take the path of least resistance, given we had the option to.'

'And what if we turn up at this place and there's a whole army of thugs waiting to attack and kill us? There were five of them at the diner. What if it's all of them and more here?'

'Well, at least we have three guns now, remember?' He winked at her. The tut she gave in response showed she didn't appreciate the gesture much.

'I'm not joking, Peake,' she said. 'You might enjoy fighting and going up against bad guys, but I don't.'

'Or maybe you do, but you just don't remember,' he said.

He'd intended the quip to be lighthearted, but she pretty much snarled in response and to show his words had landed more than flat.

'I'm sorry,' he said.

She didn't respond.

'But are you sure there's nothing else you can tell me yet?' he asked.

She glared at him but still said nothing.

'That woman, Katie Embleton – you didn't recognize her?' he asked.

'No.'

'Nor any of the men at the diner?'

'No. You asked her if she was CIA. What made you even think that?'

'A few things. Firstly, because I thought for a moment that perhaps I'd read some of the situation wrong. That she, and whoever she worked for, were out here looking for me, not you.'

'Because of your past?'

'Yes.'

'So the CIA are your enemy?'

'It's not as simple as that. But the organization as a whole was never my enemy. Individuals within it? That's a different matter.'

'But now you don't think that she was there for you?'

'Not according to her.'

'You believed her?'

'About that, yes. Not about much else.'

'You need to explain that to me, because I couldn't be more confused right now.'

'The fact she lived in Virginia is one red flag to me. FBI headquarters, CIA headquarters, and countless other government agencies are all up in the vicinity there. She claimed not to be working for an agency, but for this Ridley, who I assume you've never heard of.'

'No.'

And she hadn't been at the window when Peake had spotted the guy, so he couldn't ask if she recognized him either, although he guessed it'd be another no.

'And she said Ridley was paying her to find us. You, really.'

'Yes, she did.'

'So perhaps Ridley is an agent of some sort, or at least, perhaps he's working alongside an agency. The big question is what that all means for you.'

'I wish I knew.'

'I know a lot about how that world operates. Particularly the dark, murky world right at the depths of the CIA and the like that most people never hear or see anything of.'

'And?'

'And I'm not saying they wouldn't get involved in a kidnap and murder plot. But I'm saying they wouldn't do it just for the hell of it either. I don't know if Ridley and Hardy are in cahoots somehow, but I do know there's more to someone wanting you dead than what you've told me.'

She didn't say anything and it was only when he glanced over as they passed under a streetlight that he noticed the streaks of tears.

'You think I'm lying to you?' she said.

'I didn't say that.'

'You didn't have to. You know, I never asked for your help.'

'It's irrelevant. My primary aim here is to eliminate any threat to myself.'

Lucia huffed. 'And there was me thinking you were trying to do the right thing.'

'I am,' he said. 'And I will help you as far as I can to achieve my aim. Then I can move on.'

'Some hero you are.'

'I never claimed to be a hero.' Though the truth was that her comment still annoyed him. Hurt him a little, actually.

The conversation ended. He knew he'd annoyed her, upset her as well, but the reality was that doing so had been partly his intention. Perhaps not a nice thing to do to her, but he had so many questions and so few answers that it was inevitable that he'd have to push her. He wanted to believe that she could remember next to nothing about her life, but the more that was revealed of the other parties involved, the more he came to question why these people wanted her dead, and why so much effort was going into it.

Peake took them off the highway five miles from their destination, onto a single unlit track. Initially tarmac, that road soon turned into a dirt trail.

'There's nothing out here,' Lucia said, eyes fixed on the outside.

And she was right. The crescent moon hung in the cloudless sky directly above them, providing some illumination to go with the twinkling stars. But the fields all around them were black and seemingly lifeless. No towns, villages, farmhouses out here. No other vehicles at all since they'd left the highway.

'Who is this guy?' Lucia asked.

Peake didn't answer, and he didn't really know what she meant by the question either.

With only half a mile to go to their destination the road wound right, the moon disappearing out of view, but a flicker of light replaced it in the near distance.

'That must be it,' Lucia said.

Peake turned off the headlights and slowed his speed, the thin glow from the moon just about good enough to help him navigate the track, the growing light in front drawing them in.

They were about a hundred yards out when Peake pulled the car to the side of the road.

'We're walking from here?' Lucia asked.

'Not we.'

'You want me to wait here?'

'No. I want you to go.'

She hesitated, before, 'You're serious?'

'There's more at play here than you or I know. Even if I'd like an extra pair of hands for whatever's to come tonight, I'd rather know you're safe.'

She scoffed. 'So now you care. You're a confusing man, Simon Peake. Do you have a plan?'

'Get inside. Find Hardy. Make him talk.'

'And if there're fifteen other people in there ready and waiting to attack you? You have to at least think that's a possibility, given how things ended with Embleton. If she and Ridley are working with Hardy, then they'll have alerted him.'

'You're right, that's a possibility.'

'You're not worried? Scared?'

'Yes,' he said. 'Which is why I want you nowhere near here.'

She didn't respond but he could sense her reluctance.

'Go back to the lake,' he said. 'I told you before, it's a safe place. No one will expect to find you there.'

'Honestly, I'd kinda rather take my chances sticking with you.'

'I'm not giving you a choice,' he said. He stuffed one of the two handguns in his waistband, filled his pockets with the few shells he had, and pulled the shotgun from under her seat. 'Go to the lake. I'll be there before morning.'

'And if you're not?'

'I'll be there.'

He got out of the car and walked away into the dark.

* * *

The taillights soon faded out of sight behind him. In front, the outline of the home was more distinct now. Not exactly a farmhouse, even if the building did obviously come with a vast swathe of land. Built in a traditional antebellum style, with a wraparound veranda to both stories, Peake imagined the home had originally been put up for a rich landowner. A plantation here perhaps, slaves working the land for the further enrichment of the master. The slaves were long gone, but not the disparity in wealth and power between the rich and poor. Peake had no clue how Hardy had come into his money. Maybe it was generational, maybe it was built from crime. Whatever it was, the guy had money.

No slaves anymore, but Hardy definitely had company here. Even at the roadside, he could hear voices outside somewhere, and Peake was sure the many cars parked up weren't all the homeowners: for starters he could see the two vehicles from the diner earlier.

No security wall here, only a small picket fence at the property boundary before a sprawling lawn that led to the house. A collection of cars and pickup trucks clustered outside a garage block. A huge barn sat the other side of the house. Peake headed toward the garage, aiming to come up to the house at the side. The voices became louder with each step he took through the dark. Soon the sounds of the men were more dominant than the cicadas even. At least three people. Hearty chat and laughter. No red alert here, which suggested Embleton and Ridley hadn't sent a warning to Hardy.

Interesting.

Peake reached the garage block. He peeped around the corner. Blue lights twinkled in a curvy pool. String lights lit up the patio around it. He caught a glimpse of the veranda at the back of the house where overhead fans whirred and where men were sitting, drinking, talking.

Peake went back around the garage the other way and then made a dash for the side of the house. He pulled up against the wall, but as he did so he heard noise from inside the house. Thudding footsteps. A booming voice getting louder. The door three yards away swung open and a bulky man stepped out, pulling a cigarette from a packet. He turned back to the house to say something to whoever was inside, cupping his hands to his mouth as he did so to light his smoke.

He locked eyes with Peake.

Peake launched forward. He threw his fist out. His knuckles smacked into the man's clasped hands, and through sheer misfortune – for the guy, at least – the lighter flew from this grip and into his now open mouth. He coughed and choked and did the stupid thing of going for his gun rather than dislodging the lighter. A vicious uppercut from Peake sent him down to the ground, still rasping for air. A heel to the face shut him up.

He'd live. Possibly.

But Peake had already made too much noise and the conversation at the back of the house had stopped. He turned, lifted the shotgun just as a man darted into view.

Boom.

Peake fired and the man's body flew two yards back as it was bombarded with lead shot. Peake raced for the corner, reloading the shotgun as he went. He ducked down as he peered around and fired off another shot. The pellets splattered all over the veranda, sending wood splinters flying. He hit one of the two men there in the leg and he collapsed to the floor shouting in agony. The other man fired off a wayward shot with a handgun as he dashed for the house.

Peake again reloaded the shotgun and headed up to the man bleeding on the wooden planks of the veranda. A handgun lay just out of his reach.

'Are you Hardy?' Peake asked as he pointed the barrel of the shotgun to the man's face.

Peake already thought he knew the answer. The guy looked like a basic thug. The man who'd run into the house with a gold chain bouncing around his neck was more likely to be the rich guy. Either way, the man below him said nothing in answer before he did the stupid thing of making a move for his weapon.

Peake twisted the barrel of the shotgun to the side and pulled the trigger.

The man's hand was all but obliterated. He screeched like an animal before Peake smashed his face with the butt of the shotgun.

He only had enough for one more reload. Peake got the weapon ready before he edged to the back door of the house. No one in sight in the large dining room he entered. No sounds from anywhere in the house now but he knew there were at least two men somewhere – the one cigarette guy had been speaking to and the one who'd fled the veranda.

In front, a double-sized doorway led to the main hall. To his right, a narrower doorway led to another room.

Peake heard a creak from beyond the latter. He ducked down and fired off the shotgun. The pellets ripped through the wall. A man, hunkering, dashed across from one side to the other. Peake dumped the shotgun and pulled out the pistol, but then gunfire erupted from out in the hall and he dove for cover behind the wedge-like dining table. Bullets thwacked all around him, but he wasn't hit. He crouched low and took aim and fired several shots to the doorway. It was enough to cause whoever was there to halt their fire and hopefully backtrack, and Peake took the chance to run for the door to the hall. He slapped up against the wall there. He risked a quick look into the space outside. No one there, but he caught sight of movement on the staircase. He fired two more shots that way. Was about to move out into the hall when whoever was up there returned fire, and Peake cowered as the bullets zinged into the floorboards right by him.

A lull. Peake listened. Could hear their muffled voices.

'Hardy!' Peake yelled out. 'You know who I am. You know why I'm here.'

He got no response.

'Lucia's alive. And she's gonna stay alive.'

Another shot came his way, but Peake barely flinched this time as the bullet hit right by the others. The shooters upstairs didn't have the angle to get him.

'Hardy! I know you were paid to kill her. But you don't know her, she doesn't know you. So her living or dying means nothing, right?'

No response but he could still hear their voices.

'This was only money for you. Now I don't know if you've been paid already or not. But this is what we can do. Tell me who hired you. They're the ones I want. Tell me what I need to know, give me your word that me and Lucia aren't your targets anymore, and you get to live.'

'Fuck you!' came the shouted response. 'You're a dead man. My dogs will finish off what's left after I've torn you to pieces!'

Peake sighed. He supposed he had just forced his way in here, shooting up the place and Hardy's crew. The guy was hardly going to want to bargain right now. But it'd been worth a try.

'Now!' someone else shouted from out in the hall. Not upstairs. Ground level. The next moment a man burst into view. Also one in the doorway across from Peake where he'd earlier fired. A third man rushed down the stairs.

Peake did the only thing he could. He fired at each of them in turn as he jumped up and raced for the door to the outside. His covering fire gave him a couple of seconds but as he neared the exit they opened fire on him. Bullets flew all around as he dove for the outside and rolled across the veranda and bounced down the steps. He pulled himself up and fired off at the house, causing the men – already nearly at the door – to cower back. In fact, he was pretty sure he hit one, but didn't hang around to make sure before he jumped up and raced away. He moved into the dark of the garden. Past the house. Into the barely lit space between the house and barn. He heard the men behind him, but they didn't fire. For now, they couldn't see him.

Not until he was only five yards from the barn and caught in the light attached up by the door.

'There!' one of them shouted.

Peake spun and used the sound of the voice to help take aim to the men he couldn't see. He fired two more shots. He only had one bullet left.

He flung open the barn door and raced inside. Spotted the cages almost immediately. Two cages. Two huge bulldogs who barked and gnashed their teeth, rattling the cages with ferocious force.

Now he understood Hardy's earlier threat, and he had no doubts those dogs would rip him to shreds given the chance.

Rip anyone to shreds?

Peake looked around. Not many places to hide in here. A mezzanine level sat in one corner.

He heard the men's footsteps outside. He only had seconds before they ambushed him.

He took one more look at the cages. One bullet in his gun.

He sprinted toward the dogs. Their barks became even more frenzied. He passed the first cage, then in fluid motion he unclasped the door to the second cage before dashing the final few steps and flinging himself for the ladder that led upward. The freed dog launched itself for him and Peake managed to haul his feet out of the way a split second in time. He made it halfway up the ladder before he turned and fired the last bullet.

The shot was perfect, tearing through the clasp that held the door to the other cage closed. The dog in there burst free too. Peake clambered the rest of the way to the top and rolled along the wooden planks to get cover from the door as one of the men charged in. He shouted in shock when the dogs spotted him.

The man cowered and lifted his gun and fired, hitting one of the dogs, but it didn't stop either of them and they leapt for him, one taking him around the neck, another his upper arm to drag him to the ground. The man screamed and shouted and fired his gun again until one of the dogs ravaged his arm. Two other men ran in. More shouting. They were trying to get the dogs to heel.

But there was no chance. Perhaps it was the taste of blood. Perhaps the gunshots had spooked them too much and they knew they were fighting for survival. Soon the dogs had turned on the new arrivals and more gunshots boomed and bullets clanked around the barn. The dogs yelped, one after the other, and then everything went quiet for a few seconds.

'Peake! I know you're in here and I'm not even going to kill you anymore!' Hardy shouted. 'I'm going to skin you alive and I'm going to cut off your balls and feed them to you!'

Right, so Hardy was still OK. Peake lay flat on his stomach and ever so slowly pulled his body along toward the edge so he could see down below. One of the dogs was already dead. One was still breathing, its chest rapidly rising and falling as it lay on its side bleeding out. The first man the dogs had attacked was finished, a gaping hole in his neck. Two men remained on their feet. One clutched at his leg, blood pouring out from the teeth holes in his jeans. And Hardy, who looked unscathed and absolutely raging. Peake slithered back out of view.

'Peake! You have no idea how much I'm gonna make you suffer!'

He slid further the other way. To where a square hole in the mezzanine sat toward the far corner, another ladder there leading down. The men roamed, searching, pulling everything upside down, inside out to check where Peake was hiding. They'd learn he was above them soon enough. There really weren't many places he could be.

So he only waited until he spotted the shoulders of the bleeding man directly below him as he came to look behind the boxes in the corner. Then he jumped down. The man had no clue until Peake wrapped his arm around the guy's neck as he plummeted. He yanked the man to the ground with him, swiveling as he did so, causing the man to turn, his hip and shoulder smacking down first, Peake on top of him.

The guy was dazed and Peake took the pistol from his grip and twisted and fired, hitting Hardy in the knee. Hardy initially tried to stay on his feet, tried to turn his gun on Peake before Peake fired again. The second shot hit Hardy in the lower arm and he dropped the gun and stumbled back and onto his rear. Peake dragged himself to his feet, ignoring the aches and pains that shot through him.

The man below him mumbled something but two stomps to the head quietened him down.

He moved toward Hardy who, despite his injuries, remained looking defiant and vengeful.

'You should have taken my offer,' Peake said.

Hardy said nothing.

'Where's Adam?' Peake said. He certainly hadn't been any of the men he'd taken down, which most likely meant he wasn't now working for Hardy but was being kept somewhere under duress.

Hardy didn't answer the question but Peake spotted the hatch in the ground not far from where Hardy lay sprawled.

'He's in there?' Peake asked.

No answer. Peake didn't really need one.

'You're a sick fuck,' he said.

Hardy looked almost complimented.

'Who's paying you?' Peake asked.

Hardy said nothing.

'I can still make this a lot worse for you.' Peake lifted his foot and pressed it down onto Hardy's shot leg and the man yelped in pain. 'Who's paying you? Ridley?'

Hardy's eyes flickered at that name but then Peake's attention was diverted to a distant sound outside.

Sirens.

'Get up,' Peake said to Hardy.

'You shot my leg, asshole! I can't walk.'

'You can if you want to live.'

Peake grabbed him under the armpit to help him up then moved to the hatch in the ground. He kept one eye on Hardy as he heaved the lid up.

'Adam,' Peake said and gave a little salute.

'Peake, fuck, I am so, so—'

'Save it.'

The concrete pit below had no ladder to get in or out. Peake looked around. Spotted some rope.

'Don't move,' he told Hardy.

He dragged the hefty rope over and dangled one end into the pit and strained to hold it as Adam clambered out.

'What the...?' Adam said as he surveyed the carnage.

The sirens outside grew louder, the police closer all the time. 'We need to go. Get us the keys to one of the vehicles.'

Adam nodded and rushed off, but no sooner had he moved out of sight than tires screeched. Doors opened. Shouting erupted.

Peake went to turn to Hardy and the idiot actually found the strength to launch himself in some sort of desperate, suicidal moment. Peake side-stepped and ducked down and grabbed Hardy's shoulder and twisted to fling him...

And it was nothing but bad luck that the guy thudded on the ground and rolled over the edge of the pit and went down head first. He yelled out before...

Crack.

Peake looked over the edge. Hardy lay in a heap, blood poured out of the back of his head which hung at a crazy angle to his twisted body. His glassy eyes stared back up at Peake.

And Peake was out of time. Before he could move, the shouting had moved inside the barn and he did exactly as he was told, dropped the gun, fell to his knees with his hands clasped above his head.

The next moment he was cuffed and forced to the ground as several pairs of feet gathered around him.

27

Ridley looked up at the clock on the wall in the windowless room. 4.20 a.m. He'd arrived at the police station in Hazelwood around ten, not even an hour after Simon Peake had been brought here by the local police. Still, Katie had beaten him here, although it wasn't until he'd arrived and the sheriff had taken the call from Ridley's current paymasters that he and Katie had been allowed inside. A little while longer before the sheriff and the others here had finally realized that tonight they really weren't calling the shots.

Peake had been brought to the interview room next door a little after midnight and he hadn't left since. So far Detective Browning – Hazelwood's top detective, apparently – had tried his hardest to rattle Peake, to get him to say anything really. But Peake wasn't playing, and as the night wore on, Ridley's patience wore down.

Twenty minutes ago, Browning had left the interview room to leave Peake stewing. For the whole of that twenty minutes, Peake had stared up at the camera in the corner of the room, no perceptible movement from him at all except for the very occasional blink. As Ridley watched on the screen in the adjacent room he had more than one doubtful moment where he thought perhaps the feed had glitched and frozen, or somehow Peake had hacked into the system and paused the tape so he could escape, even if Ridley knew that was absolutely ludicrous.

'What is this guy on?' Katie asked. 'Is he drugged up or something?'

Ridley didn't answer, holding Peake's eye as though the two of them were having a silent conversation through the wall.

A knock on the door. Katie opened it and Browning stood there, coffee mug in his hand, looking weary, his eyes bloodshot. Ridley guessed the look was probably because of the hour, but maybe it was just the way he always came to work.

'You two OK in there?' Browning asked.

'We're fine,' Ridley said.

'You want coffee or—'

'We're good. I just want to see you put some more pressure on this guy.'

Browning sighed and looked at his watch. 'We'll make him talk. But we have plenty time, and by stalling we're only arming ourselves better. We're still hearing new news every now and then from over at Hardy's place. It's a real shit show down there.'

'A shit show that I'm not interested in. What I want to know is where is Lucia Vasquez?'

Browning's face turned sour now. 'Yeah. You told me that already. Except I've no idea who she is, or how she fits into what caused this guy to turn up in my town tonight shooting and killing. What I'm dealing with is—'

'I'll give you another half hour, then I'm going in there myself,' Ridley said.

'You have no authority to—'

'Are you really going to make me prove to you again exactly how much authority I have here? Haven't you and your boss been humiliated enough for one night?'

Browning clenched his jaw shut and Ridley could tell the guy was grinding his teeth in anger. He didn't say another word before he turned on his heel and slammed the door shut on his way out. The noise caused Peake to move too, finally breaking eye contact with the camera and looking at the door of his room. The next moment Browning walked in.

'You really want to put yourself in front of Peake?' Katie asked.

'Why wouldn't I?'

'Because don't you want to be more... secretive than that? Peake's doesn't know who you are. Perhaps you're better off keeping it that way.'

'You think I'm afraid of him?'

'That's not what I meant.'

'I want to see the look on his face when I press him. I want to study every minute flinch and muscle twitch.'

'You know you can't do anything in there other than talk to him.'

He glared over at Katie, it was quite clear what she was insinuating.

'I know that. Having Peake here is far from my preferred option. But don't forget things have gone as they have tonight largely because of you.'

'And what does that mean? The way I see it this is exactly what you wanted. Hardy's been dealt with. He's out of the picture.'

'And we have no idea where Lucia is.'

'We know where she was. She was in my apartment barely three miles from here. You made the call for us to leave them there.'

He grumbled but didn't respond and turned his focus back to the screen.

'I just had a call from the hospital,' Browning said. 'The man you shotgunned in the chest didn't make it. So that's now four dead men from your rampage tonight.'

Peake didn't say anything – there wasn't even a question anyway – but Browning paused as though giving a chance for a response. Then he sighed and shuffled the papers in front of him a little.

'You know you're looking at the death penalty. I can't put it any plainer than that.'

Another pause.

'Look, I know Hardy wasn't a good guy. Don't you think in a place like this we don't know all the bad apples? If you wanna tell me a story, of how you ended up there tonight, fighting for your life, I'm willing to listen to it. Just try me. Because right now I can't figure out why you were there at all, and there's a chance… there's a chance we read this all wrong. And you're the victim.'

'Fuck me, this is how their elite investigator is putting pressure on Peake? By trying to give him a way out?'

'Maybe it's—'

'Get him out of there.'

'Peake?'

'No, Browning. Get him out of there, so I can go in.'

'You think he's gonna listen to me?'

Ridley turned to Katie, the look of disgust at her questioning him enough to get her to see her error. She left the room and moments later Ridley heard the knock on the door. Browning looked really pissed at the interruption but was soon heading out of there. Ridley got up and moved out into the corridor just as Browning closed the interview room door behind him. He looked ready to explode with rage, and the two uniformed cops who were standing on guard seemed eager for the prospect as though in the middle of the night they needed a bit more action to keep them entertained, or even just awake.

'You said thirty minutes,' Browning said to Ridley.

'And I changed my mind. You've had plenty of time with him, and you've got plenty more to come. But let me see what I can do.'

'You know what? I'm so fucking tired of your shit already... it's four thirty in the morning. I'm going home to get into bed with my wife while she's still there. But as soon as I get back here later this morning? I'm going to watch every second of what you say and do in that room. And if I see anything I don't like... I don't give a crap who you think you have pulling strings above me. I'm going after you.' Browning jabbed a finger Ridley's way as though to add weight to his paltry threat.

'You got it,' Ridley said. 'Say hello to Mrs. Browning for me.'

Browning turned and stormed off. Ridley's sneer remained even if inside he was smiling at having rattled the guy and gotten his way.

'You want me to come in with you?' Katie asked.

'No. Stay out here and come and get me if there're any more developments.'

Ridley headed inside and paused, standing over the table to study Peake for any kind of reaction to his presence. Without a word, Ridley sat down and continued to hold Peake's eye. The guy looked disinterested more than anything.

'Do you know what a Cat X is?' Ridley asked.

Peake didn't answer.

'You might have heard that term before in your old life.'

'You must be Ridley,' Peake said.

A surprise that he'd spoken so soon into the conversation, and even if Ridley didn't outwardly react, inside he was berating Katie for having given Peake his name earlier that night, even if – at least according to her – she hadn't given Peake much of the truth. Regardless, this was the first and last time he'd be using her.

'Yes,' Ridley said. 'But I'll ask you again, do you know what a Cat X is?'

Once again, Peake didn't answer.

'You are,' Ridley said. 'And at first, when I found out you were somehow involved in this... mess... I wondered if there was something I was missing. If there was another party's involvement here that I'd not been informed of or had just overlooked. But do you know what I think now?'

Peake sighed, said nothing.

'I think you stumbled into my path by sheer stupid chance. You're just a washed-up has-been, probably drinks too much, regularly gets into bar fights with idiots who should know better. I bet you hang there at the bar just scouring for poor women who've had one too many and who're now vulnerable to the redneck assholes who frequent those places.' Ridley paused then laughed. 'Yeah. I got you pegged. Because beating the crap out of losers is an easy way for you to still feel alive. But Peake, seriously? You've gone way too deep with this one. And it's why you've made so many goddamn awful mistakes and left such carnage everywhere you've stuck your stupid nose where it doesn't belong. You're not that man anymore. You're a nobody.'

An ever so slight twitch in Peake's right eyebrow. He was trying damn hard not to show it, but Ridley was getting under his skin.

'Does it worry you that I'm here?' Ridley asked. 'Someone who knows about your past?'

He gave Peake a chance to respond but got nothing.

'It should worry you. Because the fact alone that I know you should tell you what type of person I am. Right now, your life is in my hands. You realize that, don't you? That detective's already spelled out to you the mess you're in. Four brutal murders, witnesses still alive, to go along with the ton of forensic evidence you left riddled around the place. Have no doubt, the death penalty is coming your way. Unless I intervene.'

Ridley reached forward and took a sip from the glass of water in front of Peake.

'This is cute,' Ridley said. 'The whole no talking thing. Very cute. But I know you're dying to ask me really, aren't you?'

Peake didn't.

'Seriously, Peake, just ask me already.'

Still nothing.

'You want to know what happened to Adam McGinty, don't you? Whether we captured him. Killed him. Although an idiot like that is definitely more threat to you alive, and blabbing, than dead.'

Peake continued to hold his tongue.

'I bet part of the reason you went to Hardy's tonight, like you did, was to save Adam. Simon Peake, the wannabe hero strikes again.' Ridley smirked and even if Peake still didn't respond, Ridley knew his taunting manner was making him mad. So he'd push more.

'I heard you have a thing for Adam's sister. In that backwater town in Georgia.' Ridley paused and then laughed. 'Yeah, I know about her. Jenn, isn't it? What do you say I find some rednecks to go up there and do the most unspeakable things to sweet Jenn? You won't be around to save her this time. And you know I can make something like that happen.'

'Actually, I know nothing about you,' Peake said. 'Other than you seem like a real up his own ass prick.'

Peake actually had the audacity to smile at that.

Ridley slammed the table with his fist. Peake didn't flinch at all.

'Tell me where Lucia is,' Ridley said, quickly pushing his anger deep down inside once more.

Peake made no attempt to answer.

'You know that's why I'm here. And finding her is all I want from you now. I'll ask one more time. After that? I leave you to the hounds. You'll die here, in Alabama, knowing the pain, the suffering, you caused to Jenn McGinty.'

Peake slowly shook his head.

'Do you even know who Lucia really is? Katie told me she's got amnesia. That she claims to have amnesia, I should say. Do you really believe that? Haven't you asked why someone like me is involved here?'

'Why someone like you wants her dead?'

'Who says I want her dead? That's your poor assumptions showing through, telling me once more that you really are so far out of your depth here. Peake, you're not that man anymore. I told you already. Now tell me where Lucia is. You do that, I'll make sure you get out of here. You and I... We don't have to be enemies.'

Peake sighed and looked away. Ridley didn't get a chance to probe him again before a knock came at the door.

If that was Browning back to interrupt things...

Ridley got up and went over.

'What?'

'We need to talk, now,' Katie said from the other side.

Ridley balled his fists with frustration. This had better be good.

'Are we done already?' Peake said. A big smile on his face now. 'I was just starting to enjoy your company.'

'No, Peake. I am nowhere near done with you.'

Peake gave a nonchalant shrug before Ridley opened the door and stepped out. Katie wasn't there, so he went to the room next door, found her inside, standing hands on hips, looking anxious.

'Close the door,' she said.

Ridley did so. He turned back to Katie but before she said a word, banging from out in the corridor grabbed their attention. Ridley's eyes jumped to the screen next to him.

Peake. At the door, fighting the guards.

'No!' Ridley bellowed before hauling open the door. The noise amplified but as he went to dart out gunshots pinged his way and he scurried back inside. More banging, shouting. More gunshots. A lull a few seconds later and Ridley poked his head out again, but an explosion sent him reeling backward. Flames shot along the corridor, the hairs on his arms and face singed. The initial flare-up quickly died down but the sound of a roaring fire, hissing wood and whatever ever else that was burning, took over.

How the hell did Peake do that?

Ridley pulled himself to his feet, then flinched when a uniformed police officer, screaming in shock and pain, rushed past him, flames leaping out from his back. He collapsed to the floor further down the corridor, rolling around to put himself out.

'What the hell is happening?' Katie asked, sounding as scared as she looked.

Ridley said nothing. He fought against the heat and moved along the corridor. Further ahead he noted doors and windows were blown out and fire was quickly taking hold, the main exit out more or less blocked.

He reached the interview room. The door was open. He peered inside. Two uniformed officers lay crumpled on the floor, both alive but unmoving.

But they were the only people in the room, because Simon Peake was already gone.

28

Peake didn't like good fortune much. It made him unusually nervous, like he'd missed something big and was about to be blindsided somehow. And he'd definitely had a big slice of good fortune back at the police station. Perhaps it was just the world – fate – evening things out after the mishap which had earlier seen Hardy accidentally fall down into that pit to his death. Or maybe the balancing-out was still to come and Peake would have to remain alert and wary for things going badly wrong.

The good fortune? He'd never expected that explosion. Not part of his plan at all. But he had planned the escape. They'd had him sitting in that interview room for hours, most of the time alone and in his own thoughts. Actually, even with that detective in there, he'd mostly been in his own thoughts as he'd hardly listened to a word the guy was saying, having already made his mind up to keep his mouth shut as much as possible.

The escape had already been planned even when that Ridley guy showed his face. His doing so hadn't changed Peake's actions, but it did once again throw up an array of questions that Peake had no answers to.

The main element of the escape was simple enough. Work the cuffs, wait for the door to be opened, tackle the guards. Really such a basic plan took guts as much as it did skill. As he'd disarmed the first of the two policemen in the corridor, the second had opened fire on him. Peake had fired back with the gun he pilfered from the first guy. Somewhere in that melee – which had lasted all of five seconds and saw the policeman hit in the shoulder and leg – a wayward bullet had sunk into an old HVAC unit. Peake didn't know the science, but the bullet – the bringer of his good fortune – had caused one heck of a bang. Maybe the bullet had ignited a refrigerant. Maybe it had punctured a highly pressurized part of the system. It didn't matter. The ruckus caused by the explosion had given Peake a huge advantage, and when he'd shot a more deliberate round into an exposed gas pipe to add fuel to the fire...

The ensuing inferno made his getaway all the more easy, every person inside more concerned with getting themselves and whoever else they could out of that building alive.

Peake hoped they managed it. He hadn't intended to kill anyone in there.

He'd taken the car keys from one of the policemen he'd felled but had dumped that vehicle at the other end of the city, near to where he and Lucia had accosted Katie earlier in the evening.

He drove out of town in a battered old Toyota Corolla that he'd been able to hot-wire. Not many such cars existed anymore, modern electronics and security systems making it virtually impossible to start a vehicle in that clichéd way. Good recon, rather than good fortune on that occasion though, he decided.

By the time the sun was rising up across the vast swathes of cornfields to his east, Peake was already approaching Lake Eufaula, the journey carefree, despite the mess of a night which had preceded it.

So many questions tumbled in his mind, but two in particular. Firstly, would he find Lucia here? Secondly, what was the truth about her?

He'd hardly seen a car for the last half hour as he pulled off the highway and onto the twisting road that wound toward the lake. Every now and then as the road veered close to the water he caught a glimpse of the pump house in the distance, its shape becoming larger and more distinct each time, and his anxiousness rising with it.

If she wasn't here, he really didn't know what his next move would be. Possibly to just cut his losses and run.

No. Not that. Even if it was perhaps the safest option for him, given the increasing heat building up because of his actions, Peake had one more roll of the dice after this one if he didn't find Lucia where he'd told her to be.

He rounded the final corner, the road now hugging the lake tightly for the final half mile approach to the pump house. Peake initially kept his speed steady, until he spotted the two vehicles parked on the inside of the security fence there.

He slowed up, surveying the scene with renewed rigor. His initial thought was that perhaps the vehicles belonged to an official maintenance crew of some sort. But the vehicles – one a truck, one an SUV – were both unmarked, no company insignias. Not a full confirmation of anything, but what he saw next was. Two figures, lurking at the fronts of the vehicles, casual clothes, both armed and on the lookout.

Peake floored the throttle. He was a hundred yards away when the two guys took notice. They signaled to each other. One called back to the pump house. Before long another armed man appeared. Then three more people who stayed closer to the building. A man, two women. One of the women Peake didn't recognize but one, looking forlorn in the middle, was Lucia.

Peake didn't let up on the speed. Not until the last moment when he had to twist the steering wheel to veer off the road and through the open gates. He lost traction of the back tires and had to fight to keep control before he thumped the pedal again. The engine whined. The car shot forward. The three men at the front rushed to take up positions around their vehicles. One took cover behind the truck's hood, one behind the back end of the SUV. But one was caught in no-man's-land in the middle.

Even as that man lifted the assault rifle up, Peake still only went faster.

Then he ducked down to hopefully protect him from any gunfire, and from the impact he knew was inevitable. He tugged on the steering wheel as hard as he could, and the back end of the Corolla swung out wildly. No way for him to properly control the spin or to even stop it, but at least he'd set the car on the right trajectory.

The spinning hulk smashed into the man with the rifle a moment after he'd let rip with the weapon. His body was sent flying into the SUV and was then caught wedged when the Corolla smashed into the larger vehicle. Even if the SUV was larger than Peake's car, the sheer force of the impact sent it flying from its position and the man who'd been hiding behind it found himself buried under the weight.

Peake was dazed, his world blurry for a second but the sounds of shouting and gunfire soon brought him around.

At least the smash had caused the Corolla's out of control spin to stop.

And he was now facing the right way.

He thumped the pedal. Somehow, despite the already hefty damage, the dependable motor still had life. The Corolla lurched forward to the man who'd been hunkered by the truck. He did manage to dive out of the way before he was run down, but found himself still on the floor as Peake threw open his door and jumped out on top of him.

A fist to the face. Then a knee to the groin. Peake tore the rifle from his grip. He slammed his elbow into the man's face then rolled away, looking out under the Corolla toward the pump house to where Lucia and the final two attackers were.

Four shots. Three hits into the man and woman either side of her. Peake jumped back to his feet and slid over the Corolla's hood.

'Lucia, come on!' he shouted as he raced to her. She was crouched down, hands covering her head, and when she peeked out she hesitated. The man and woman writhed on the floor next to her.

'I'll finish you both here if I have to,' he said to them, to keep them down.

Neither looked willing to fight on.

He grabbed Lucia's hand and pulled her up and toward the truck. He didn't need to look for the key. The vehicle was already unlocked, the fob sitting in one of the central cupholders.

Lucia clambered in by his side and before she'd closed the door he'd released the brake and was swinging the vehicle around for the exit.

He glanced in the rearview mirror as he headed for the road. Another scene of carnage behind him. Four of the attackers were in various states of agony as they tried to pull themselves up. The one who'd been wedged between the Corolla and the SUV lay unmoving.

No one looked like they'd be making an attempt at following.

'You OK?' Peake said as he took a sharp left onto the road.

'No. No, I really don't think I am,' Lucia said as tears rolled.

* * *

'You don't have anything to say?' Peake asked as they drove south toward the highway.

'I... I don't know what you want me to say.'

He humphed at that. He hadn't expected to feel so agitated by their reunion.

'Are you OK?' he asked, trying to find his sympathetic side.

'You asked me that already.'

'But I mean are you hurt? Physically.'

'No.'

'Who were they?' Peake asked.

'I don't know.'

'Then what did they say to you?'

'That they were taking me.'

'Where?'

She looked over at him, her whole body trembled. 'Home.'

'And that's where?'

'I don't know!' she yelled.

'I don't believe you anymore.'

He thumped the brake pedal and the car slammed to a stop. Lucia's nerves ramped up even more and she twisted to look behind a couple of times as though worried someone would catch them up.

Except there was no one out there.

Perhaps it was him she was scared of.

'You need to tell me what the hell is going on,' Peake said, trying to rein in his agitation, his anger.

She shook her head but didn't say anything.

'OK,' Peake said. 'How about this? I'll explain what I know, what I found last night, so we're on the same page. Then maybe you can help me out with a few things. That sound good?'

'I... guess?'

'Last night, I went to Hardy's place, just like I'd planned. And just as we thought, he had a whole gang of men in there with him. I fought them off. I had Hardy. I was ready to find out what he knew... then next minute cops descended. They took me.'

'And Hardy too?'

'No. He's dead. I got nothing from him.'

She sank down a little as though despondent. She should have been happy, relieved.

'The police took you, but—'

'But I got away from them. Not before I got to meet the mysterious Ridley face-to-face.'

He paused, taking his thoughts back to their one-sided conversation.

'And?' she asked.

'He's English. Like me.'

'So... he's... after you, not me?'

'No. Not at all. This is definitely about you, Lucia. And even if he didn't tell me, I know exactly what type of person he is.'

'And that is?'

'A spook. Most likely freelance. He's working alongside or at the call of a government agency. Because how else would he get access to me in a police station like he did? And how else would he have the power, authority to have me released from there if I'd given you up? Which is exactly what he offered me.'

He noticed a flicker of fear as though she wasn't convinced that Peake hadn't taken that deal and was now working with Ridley.

'But the biggest question is why would a spook like him, why would any government agency, be interested in you,' Peake said. 'And this isn't anything like official business. This is something murky, grimy.'

She said nothing, just gave him the doe-eyed look he'd gotten so used to from her. He reached over and grabbed her wrist and squeezed hard to get her full attention. She writhed in pain but he didn't let go.

'I bought it to start with, the whole amnesia thing, and maybe it was even true at the start. But I'm not buying it now. You know more than you've told me, and I'm not moving from this spot until you tell me everything.'

He let go of her arm and she rubbed at the reddened flesh there, but she didn't say a word.

'Lucia Vasquez. That's what he said your name was.'

She frowned. But despite his doubts about her, he really did believe her confusion at the name.

'What?' he said.

'That... doesn't make any sense.'

'What doesn't?'

'The name. That's not... that's not me. That's... it's...'

'Lucia, you need to start explaining.'

But she didn't. Instead she looked behind them again, to the clear road that lay there.

'OK. I'll talk. But please, can just we go from here?'

He weighed that up for a few moments but then got them moving. The destination he had in mind was a long, long way. And the sooner they got there, the better. Not just because he wanted this over with, but because, as they'd driven back and forth, he'd heard several times on news reports the last few days of the incoming storm down south. A big one. Catastrophic. And hitting exactly where they needed to go.

But he wasn't quitting now.

'This is...' Lucia sighed and put her head in her hands then rubbed at her temples as though she was really struggling to find the words. 'I wasn't lying to you. And that's the truth. When I woke up in that barn... I had no idea who I was or what had happened. But things have come back to me. More than I've told you.'

He gritted his teeth at that rather than respond. He was angry with her. But he'd hear her out first before deciding what it all meant for him.

'I didn't know what else to do. I don't know you, and I really didn't know if you knew me! How could I? And... the memories I have. Some of them don't even make sense, like they're not about me but perhaps people I know.' She growled and pushed her hands to her temples again. 'I don't even know where to start when everything in my head is such a mess.'

He said nothing, just waited for her. If she wanted or even deserved his sympathy, she wasn't going to get it right now.

'My name isn't Lucia Vasquez. When you first said that name I had this image of someone. My mother. Vasquez was my family name. But I'm Lucia Ramirez. My husband... he's Ramirez. Jorge Ramirez.'

She paused there as though he was supposed to react to the name. But he'd never heard of it.

'But he's not my husband through choice. And this... this is where my memories are blurred. Because at first I thought I was remembering about someone I knew, not me. I was a nobody. I was just a girl from a small town in Mexico. I came here alone, like so many people I knew, looking for work and a better life. I don't even know how long ago that was.'

Peake kept his eyes on the road, and kept his mouth shut, awaiting more. He wouldn't push. Not until he was sure she was done.

'For someone like me, there wasn't much I could do here. I cleaned houses for cash. Down in Florida. I had... a really good friend and she got so lucky getting to work in all these huge mansions on the sea. One day I had to cover for her and... that's how I met Jorge. He was married, and his wife seemed to like me, and it didn't take long before I was not just cleaning but looking after their house all on my own. I made enough money just from that one job to start feeling like I had a life. But... maybe I should have known it was too good to be true because I always knew Jorge wasn't... wasn't normal. And, like every woman, I've known men like that my whole life. Predators. Men who get what they want from women, no matter what.'

She paused there and took a few moments to compose herself. Peake still didn't take his eyes from the road even if now his agitation was rapidly dissolving, and he felt maybe he did need to offer her some comfort. Because he sensed what was to come next wasn't going to be pleasant.

'He raped me. Not once, but many times. He threatened me and I knew there was no way I could ever tell anyone. And I couldn't stop going there because I... The money wasn't important, but he told me if I ever left he would find me and kill me. And I believed him. A year after I first met him, my son was born. He couldn't have children with his wife, and he knew Xavi was his. He had the son he always wanted, but not the marriage and so... something had to change.'

She wiped at the tears on her face.

'His wife disappeared, but I know he killed her because he told me so. He enjoyed telling me. When Xavi was three, when the mystery of his wife's disappearance was far enough in the past... I married him. I wasn't given a choice. I've lived as his wife, his property for years. And my son? I had to stay for my son. I love him more than anything and I'd do anything to protect him.'

She broke down sobbing. Peake still didn't say anything, just gave her the time.

'I guess I pushed him too far,' Lucia said. 'He knew I wanted to leave, but that I'd never go without Xavi. And, in the end, when I threatened him about his son one time too many... this is what happened.'

She stopped there. Neither of them talked for more than ten minutes. Until Peake finally bit the bullet.

'So he's what? A gang leader?' Peake said, trying to put some of the pieces together. Lucia said nothing. 'A drug dealer. Or smuggler, more likely. That's why Ridley is involved. My hunch was right. Perhaps he's not with the CIA but it's why they or someone like them are involved here. Right? Because it's long been known that by having some control over the cartels in South and Central America, the CIA and the American government get proxy control over so much more. Not just income, but politics too.'

'Yes, it's drugs. From Colombia. Jorge is Colombian. But you're saying he's working with the CIA? I really don't know. That is not my world. All I know is Jorge is a monster and he wants me dead.'

'Because you know too much about him. His crimes. And because of that you have the potential to expose the people in the CIA or whoever it is that he's working with too.'

'I can't expose what I don't know about! And I never cared about exposing Jorge! I just wanted my son away from there.'

'To a man like the one you've described, the two things are the same. The only power you had over him is in what you knew about his criminal activity.'

She pursed her lips, shook her head, like she didn't agree. Or like something still didn't make sense.

'So Ridley is most likely working with your husband,' Peake said, thinking out loud again. 'Ridley probably was responsible for bringing in Hardy to have you killed so that it was a step removed from Jorge. But... those men at the lake earlier. They didn't just shoot you dead the second they saw you. You told me they said they were taking you home.'

'That's what they told me.'

'Why would they do that?'

'Do what?'

'Take you back to Jorge if he's the one who wanted you dead in the first place?'

'I don't know!'

Peake thought about that some more but couldn't find an answer that stuck.

'You should have told me this sooner,' he said.

'I couldn't. For so many reasons. I already said I really didn't remember at first. And it didn't all come back at one time. But more than that... I didn't trust you at the start. How could I?'

'You do now?'

'Since very early on. And please forgive me, but one of the reasons I didn't tell you what I just have...'

'What?'

'It was because I didn't want you to run. I saw what you were capable of, but I didn't want you to decide I was too big a problem for you. So I decided to see how far I could make you go.'

'You manipulated me?'

'No! Please don't say that. I'm not explaining it right. But I thought... you'd help me figure things out. And, even as I remembered who I was, I thought it better to let you figure it all out for yourself, and that eventually... you'd help me get my son back because... because it's the right thing to do.'

'You mean, you thought I'd help you kill your husband?'

She didn't answer at first and he knew she was glaring at him.

'It's not such a bad thing,' she said, 'when you know who he is.'

Peake said nothing to that, just carried on driving.

'So?' Lucia asked after a while.

'What?'

'You don't have anything else to say to me.'

'No.'

'But... are we...?'

'Going to your home? Yes. We are.'

'And are you going to kill my husband?'

Peake didn't have to think too long. 'If that's what it's going to take to end this, for both of us, then yes, I will.'

29

The journey down the western coast of Florida to Tampa and beyond was long, tiring. Quiet. Peake and Lucia chatted little. Both took turns driving, both snoozed, but only for a few minutes at a time as though they were too wired, too edgy to allow themselves deep sleep.

The radio helped keep them focused and alert, but after the latest round of news – not so new anymore, the incoming hurricane the sole focus – Peake reached forward and pushed the knob to turn it off, as though doing so would stop reality from coming to fruition.

'What?' Lucia said as though sensing a problem.

'I've heard enough of the forecast now. I get it. It's going to get bad. Very, very bad, very soon.'

The heat and humidity had been building for days. In this part of the world it was inevitable that it'd end with a storm. The temperature outside had already dropped some from the recent highs, down to the low eighties, even if humidity was so high that even walking a few yards from the pump to the gas station not long ago had left Peake covered in a thin film of moisture. And even if the sun still beat down on them in a sky with only wisps of clouds, he knew how quickly things could – would – change. Pop-up thunderstorms often appeared suddenly on otherwise hot sunny days and were as fierce and potentially damaging as they were simple normality.

But this was no pop-up storm on the horizon today. For the last three days, the news reports had been awash with fears over the tropical storm, hovering across the Caribbean, veering northward and strengthening as it did so.

That eventuality was now without doubt. Tropical storm Bertha had been upgraded to a category three hurricane, and before nightfall it would strengthen further. Its projected path would see it tear through the gulf coast of Florida only a few miles north of Tampa. The city itself could even feel the full impact of the storm if conditions changed ever so slightly, leading to widespread devastation not seen in the state for many years. Peake's and Lucia's destination, not far south of Tampa, near Sarasota, likely wouldn't be the worst hit, but it would be hit, and hard.

'There's a reason there's so little traffic heading in this direction,' Lucia said.

'And so much heading against us.'

'We can do that too,' Lucia said. 'Stay somewhere low-key and make our move in a couple of days.'

'No,' Peake said. 'We're too close now.'

'He might not even be here. Given the storm.'

'From what you've described, Jorge doesn't sound to me to be the type of man to run from bad weather.'

Lucia sighed. 'No. You got that right. He thinks he's indestructible.'

Many people did. Even as they stared death in the face. Peake had seen the sad realization of reality spread across such faces too many times.

It didn't take much longer for clouds to fill the sky around them. Not even 6 p.m., but the outside turned nearly black as night. They were skirting around Tampa when the wind picked up. It battered against the Corolla, nearly tossing it off the highway on several occasions.

The heavens opened, dropping a torrent of water onto them and the road. Peake had no choice but to slow to a crawl on several occasions. They passed flashing lights every few miles, both precautionary crews on alert, but also responders to drivers who'd succumbed to the foul conditions when they should have listened to the many, many warnings and either sought shelter or evacuated long ago.

Peake wouldn't admit it to Lucia, but by the time they were out the south side of the city, the weather still worsening with the storm officially not even making landfall yet, he was beginning to doubt his earlier bullishness.

Yet he wouldn't quit now.

'This is it?' Peake said as he pulled up outside the closed solid gates set in a tall wall that showed nothing of what lay beyond. Not that they'd be able to see much anyway – visibility was all of twenty yards because of the sheets of rain.

'This is it.'

'You ready for this?' Peake asked.

Lucia looked unsure but nodded anyway. Peake wound down his window and pressed in the code for the gates and they whirred into action, opening up to reveal little of what lay beyond. But she'd explained the layout as best she could. They were coming in through the service end of the sprawling property. This way, they'd come around to the side of the coast-hugging mansion. A little bit more discreet than the main entrance. And she'd explained to him the security here. Jorge nearly always had some crew on hand, much like the smaller-scale Hardy back in Alabama, but there'd be no waiting army.

The mansion, the home, wasn't a fortress. It had a traditional security system, cameras and the like, but nothing extravagant or particularly high tech. And the fact that the PIN code that Lucia had given Peake for the gates still worked suggested Jorge had done nothing to update the system since putting out the hit on his wife. So getting inside the house wouldn't be a problem. Getting to Jorge without incident might be.

The mansion only came into view through the swirling rain when they were a few yards away. It would probably be glorious on a sunny day. But in the midst of a hurricane and with the swelling, turbulent sea right behind it, the home looked gloomy and... kind of sinister.

They got out of the car and battled their way through the wind and the rain to a side door which had a keypad for entry. Again the code which Lucia gave Peake worked and after closing the door behind them they each shook themselves down, water cascading onto the tiled floor beneath them, in a utility room bigger than most people's living spaces.

Peake checked over the two handguns they had and palmed one over to Lucia.

'You OK?' he asked her.

She nodded in response and he got moving. The longer they dwelled, the more doubt would creep into their minds.

They moved through various anterooms, eventually coming out into an expansive and expensive kitchen. Spotless. No sign of recent activity, but lights were on further through the home and Peake could now hear soft, muted voices.

They kept on moving, every quiet step taken with caution. Outside, the wind howled. Rain pelted the windows, sounding like a murder of crows, tapping their beaks on the glass as though warning the homeowner of the intruders. Or warning Peake and Lucia that they were about to come unstuck.

They passed into a hallway, a grand staircase off to their right. Lights were on up there but Peake heard no sounds. Lucia paused a few moments, as though debating whether to go up or not. At this time of night, Xavi was most likely in his room already. But her going up there now wasn't the plan.

They'd nearly made it across the hall when Peake heard a creak through an open doorway to their left. He signaled to Lucia to carry on across the hall while he pulled up alongside the wall by the door, waiting.

As soon as he saw the gun barrel poke out he ducked down and darted forward, reaching over the threshold. He twisted the man's wrist quickly, sharply, and then smacked his gun down onto the bones of the lower arm on a limb that was already pushed to bursting. The man's howl of pain, and the noise of the ever-worsening storm outside, drowned out the sound of breaking bones but Peake knew the damage was done. Dislocated elbow, snapped ulna and radius. The guy's gun clattered to the floor. Peake took the man's good arm and pushed it up behind his back into a hammerlock.

'I'll do the same to this one if you try anything stupid,' he whispered into the man's ear.

He got no response, which he took to mean the guy understood.

Lucia, wide-eyed, stared over at Peake, her chest heaving. Adrenaline was wreaking havoc with her nervous system. Peake remained calm, even if he knew there was a good chance the man's shout of pain had been heard by others in the house.

No onrushing attack, though.

'Move,' Peake said, pushing the man forward.

They headed on past Lucia and toward the lights beyond a partially open door at the far side of the hallway.

Peake glanced behind at Lucia.

'Ready?'

She nodded. Peake shoved the guy forward as hard as he could and the man banged into the door, sending it crashing open and sending him rolling across the carpet into a heap. Peake followed him in, gun switching from target to target across the dining room beyond. But he didn't fire, because he realized no counterattack was coming. So instead he and Lucia fanned into the room, each taking up a position either side of the door.

Four people were already inside. Two were seated. Jorge Ramirez and Peter Ridley. Katie Embleton stood behind her boss, and a goon Peake didn't know stood behind Jorge.

'Welcome home, darling,' Jorge said, his eyes fixed on Lucia. She had her weapon pointed at her husband. Her grip was solid, no hint of a tremor. 'We've been expecting you.'

'Certainly looks like it,' Peake said.

Both Jorge and Ridley looked smug, as though this turn was unexpected to Peake and Lucia, but it really wasn't. As she'd already told him, Jorge thought himself indestructible, even as he stared down the barrels of two guns.

'You want a drink?' Jorge asked, indicating the trolley of spirits in the corner behind him. On the table stood a decanter filled with rich amber liquid. A glass each for Jorge and Ridley was already poured. Jorge lifted his drink from the table, two thick gold signet rings clinking against the glass.

'I'm—'

'I'll take one,' Peake said. 'A large one.'

Lucia glared at him. Jorge looked even more amused now.

'Where's my son?' Lucia said, hatred but also intense worry in every word.

'Our son is upstairs. Where he should be. So I'd appreciate it if we can keep this quiet and civil.' Jorge laughed. 'As if he can sleep through this storm.'

As Jorge went to get up Lucia shrieked and pulled on the trigger.

Click. Click. Click.

With each pull the realization on her face deepened. She looked at the weapon first, as though angered by the object for failing her, before she set her angry eyes on Peake.

'Oh... oh!' Jorge called, having to work hard to stifle a laugh. 'Did that really just happen! Shit. Lucia, baby, you were just gonna walk in here and shoot me! What the fuck?'

'What did you do?' she said to Peake.

'He set you the hell up, that's what!' Jorge crowed. 'My man. I was going to offer you this cheap as shit bourbon like Ridley's drinking.' He slapped Ridley's shoulder and the guy looked really put out. 'But you deserve the absolute best.' Jorge moved over to the trolley and perused for a second before taking a bottle and showing it to Peake. 'Thirty-year-old Macallan OK for you?'

'I'll give it a go. Neat, please.'

'Peake, what the hell!' Lucia said.

He shrugged. 'Didn't I tell you? I'm in this for me. So before I start shooting anyone, I need to know the truth first.'

'Holy shit,' Jorge said as he poured nearly a full glass of scotch for Peake, which he set down onto the table. 'Isn't it obvious? He didn't trust you, you bitch. So what bullshit did you tell him?'

'Apparently she claimed to have amnesia,' Ridley said, receiving Lucia's death glare for daring to join the conversation.

'I'm sorry,' Peake said to her. 'There were too many things that didn't add up.'

'You'll have to explain those to us,' Jorge said, hovering over his seat as though at the ready. 'What lies has she been telling you about me?'

Lucia gave Peake an imploring look, but it was a little late for that. If she'd been honest to start with, or at any point, they wouldn't be standing here like this.

'She told me you're a Colombian drug smuggler,' Peake said.

'Well, yeah?' Jorge said with a nonchalant shrug.

'And that she was a Mexican immigrant. A cleaner.'

Jorge nearly spat out his mouthful of scotch.

'That you were married when she met you. You started an affair with her. No, she said you raped her.' The amused look on Jorge's face dropped some. 'You got her pregnant. You killed your wife because she couldn't provide a child for you. Then you made Lucia marry you so you could legitimize your claims to her son. Your son.'

Jorge said nothing, but the mood in the room had definitely changed; none of his joviality remained now.

'She thinks you wanted her dead because she was making noises about leaving you. So you had your mysterious friend Ridley organize the hit with some clown up in Alabama. But that all went to shit and I somehow got involved and... here we all are, trying to figure out what's next.'

Ridley looked more uncomfortable now, as though mention of how a seemingly simple plot to murder one person had turned into such a clusterfuck. But then even if the mood in the room had darkened, Jorge somehow found some amusement in the situation once more.

'I guess the last part of the story, you wanting her dead, is probably true, given events,' Peake said. 'But the rest of it?'

'Steaming crap,' Jorge said, his eyes locked on to Lucia. 'You actually tried to pass off Maria's story as your own?' He still looked mad, but he clapped in mock congratulations. 'Clever girl. Manipulating him like that.'

'I'm not a fucking girl.'

'But you did try to manipulate me,' Peake said. 'And even as I started to doubt the amnesia, even when I told you my doubts, you only lied to me more. But so many other little things didn't add up, especially when I look back. First to those people turning up at the McGintys'. Remember?'

She gave no response at all.

'I thought they were Hardy's crew, there to kill you. Same with those four at the lake today. But they weren't, were they? They were your people. Coming to find you.'

'You have no idea how hard it was for me to reach them,' Lucia said. 'Because they're all in hiding now too. Jorge would kill each and every one if he found them. And you killed some of them trying to save me.'

'I'm impressed you saw through her,' Jorge said to Peake. 'From what I heard from Ridley, you were just some loose cannon, a wannabe hero.'

'I'm no hero,' Peake said before turning his focus back to Lucia. 'You want to know what else struck me? Even though you really should have known that gun was empty, I see how relaxed you are around weapons. How relaxed you are around violence, in a way that's hard to describe. I even doubted the whole Mexican thing because your English accent... it's not like any I've heard from a Mexican before. But the real misstep? When I mentioned the name Vasquez to you. The name for you that Ridley gave me.'

Lucia said nothing but Jorge gasped in mock shock and turned to Ridley and smacked him on the shoulder again.

'You sneaky bastard,' Jorge said.

'Thought I'd throw a curveball into the mix,' Ridley said. 'See just how much of that story of brain fog was real when Peake gave her that name as hers.'

'Not much was real, I'm thinking,' Jorge said.

'She stumbled,' Peake said. 'Then told me Vasquez was her family name.'

'Then she sold you a big, rotten red herring there, Simon Peake. Vasquez. Maria Vasquez. She was the maid. The one I fucked, over and over because... because I could. And because my wife is a shit fuck anyway. Maria is the one who disappeared without a trace one day. The one I'm pretty damn sure my lovely wife here had murdered.'

No denial from Lucia.

'Just tell me who you really are,' Peake said to her.

But she didn't. Instead Jorge did.

'My wife is the daughter of David Fuentes. If you don't know him, you should, because he was one of the biggest cartel bosses of this century. He sent her here as a fresh, young thing to run his stateside operations.'

'Fuentes died, fifteen years ago,' Ridley added. 'But not before Lucia married Jorge.'

Lucia scoffed. 'Not everything I told you was a lie, Peake! And I had to tell it like that because I really believed in you! I believed you'd help me, and my son.'

'But you did lie to me. You did manipulate me.'

'I did, but Jorge really is the monster I told you about! He didn't have an affair with Maria, he raped her! And our marriage? It's a sham. We're only glued together by our son and my father's dying wish that I have a husband who could help grow the empire.'

Jorge looked really self-satisfied at that last statement.

'I would never have let a man like him anywhere near my family's business, and certainly not near my son. My father was a great man, but his one fault was not seeing my true worth. His belief that I needed any kind of man to steer his ship.'

'You'd be nothing without me,' Jorge said.

'No, it's the other way around. Which is why you're sitting next to a loser like him.' She jabbed a finger Ridley's way and he coughed on his bourbon as though struggling to understand why she was insulting him. 'The only way for you to cling on to power was by removing me, and pandering, begging, tail between your legs to the CIA so you'd have their protection. You're weak. You're a coward. You always were, you always will be.'

For the first time in the conversation Peake saw anger, bloodlust anger in Jorge's eyes. Lucia was poking the tiger and it was working.

'But you made a mistake,' Lucia said, focused on Ridley. 'Because you bet on the wrong horse. If you'd come to me first, we could have figured out a way forward without Jorge in the picture. A way forward that truly would have benefited all parties. You have no idea how useless he is once you get past his hopeless arrogance. You know what? We still can work together, you and me.'

Peake saw the flicker of intrigue in Ridley's eyes. But it was only the merest of flickers, and it was gone a split second later when Jorge whipped a gun from his waistband and pushed the barrel to Ridley's temple and pulled the trigger.

A whole mess of red spray and skull and mushy brain matter cascaded out of the other side of Ridley's head. Katie lurched back to scream in shock, grotesque horror. Lucia had the opposite reaction and rushed forward. The goon by Jorge knew a fight was coming too and readied himself as Jorge turned his gun to fire again...

All hell broke loose.

Jorge fired. His man fired. Peake fired. Katie screamed again. Another man rushed into the room behind Lucia as she charged toward her husband.

Peake bundled into the goon nearest to him and they both hit the floor. Peake smacked him around the head with the gun and would have put him out of his misery there and then except the other man who'd rushed in had his weapon trained in Peake's direction. He lifted up the torso of the man by him and ducked down and the bullets thwacked into soft flesh. Not Peake's soft flesh. He lifted his hand up and fired off without looking then darted for the shooter, firing as he moved. Hit home, but another attacker rushed in too and Peake had no chance to take aim, instead barging into him and slamming him against the wall. Peake sent a vicious headbutt onto the crown of his nose. Blood erupted as Peake spun.

Lucia lay crumpled on the floor several feet away.

Jorge?

Rushing for Peake, a war cry bellowing from his lungs.

Jorge shoved into Peake and sank his teeth into Peake's shoulder and gnashed down. Peake roared with pain, tried to find an angle with the gun in his hand but one, maybe both of the goons who were still alive, were soon on him too. They punched him, gouged at his face, wrestling for control of his weapon, his arms. Jorge released his jaw. Peake's blood covered his face and made his smile look even more maniacal.

Peake tried to move but the two men holding him had him pinned. Jorge flung a fist into Peake's gut and he would have doubled over in pain were it not for the men. Jorge hit him again, cracking a rib, knocking the air from his lungs, and Peake's world spun.

'Keep him there,' Jorge said. 'He can watch this, before we figure out what to do with him.'

Peake's vision returned, blink by blink, as Jorge retreated to where Lucia lay dazed. He still had a pistol in his hand and lashed it down onto the side of her head and her body juddered. He did it again then launched a foot into her stomach. Another. Another. Peake writhed and wrestled but the men held firm.

'I should have done this myself to start with,' Jorge said.

He turned Lucia over onto her back, her head lolled. He straddled her and slapped her around the cheeks as though to rouse her. Then he dropped the gun and put his hands to her throat and squeezed, and at that point she woke or at least found some last-gasp survival instinct and she gasped and spluttered and bucked to try and get him off her. He snarled, squeezed her neck even more tightly, his knuckles white, Lucia's face turning deep red. He pushed his face close to hers, Peake's blood dripping down onto her.

'I always wanted to—'

'Dad?' came the meek voice from the doorway.

Jorge couldn't take away his animal quickly enough. Had he done so it might have made a difference. But Jorge's hands remained squeezing, his face snarling, even as he locked eyes with the petrified boy.

'Xavi,' Lucia said, although the name was slurred and garbled.

'Mom!' the boy answered, on the verge of a breakdown.

'Don't you fucking move!' Jorge said to him, hands still choking the life from the boy's mother.

And to start with Xavi didn't move, just nodded his head as he sobbed. But then a thunderous boom at the other end of the room caused everyone to flinch. A window blew out, sending glass shards flying and a barrage of wind and rain billowed in.

The boy turned and ran.

Jorge jumped up from his wife and went after him.

The men holding Peake were too distracted, perhaps unsure whether to go with their master or not, or by whether there was more devastation to come from the storm outside. Peake reached behind and grabbed the scrotum of one of the men and yanked down hard until he felt something snap, and the man squawked like a demented parrot. Peake pulled from his grip, grabbed the other man's arm with both his hands, and bent at the knees. He twisted around and pulled the man from his feet, and as Peake dropped down and spun he tossed the man over his shoulder. But he didn't let go of the arm. He was surprised it didn't cleave right off, such was the force of the throw and the weight of the man pulling on it. It didn't come off. It definitely snapped, though. And the man howled, his voice echoing with the pulsing wind before Peake stamped on his neck. After that, his last-gasp coughs and splutters were entirely muted by the storm.

Peake glanced across the room at Katie. She'd slumped up against the wall, looking on in horror, but was stunned into inaction. Peake left her and the injured but not dead men and rushed to Lucia and knelt and cradled her limp torso.

'Lucia,' he said, and she blinked a few times, trying to find the strength for something more.

And she did. 'He's got my son!'

Peake helped her to her feet.

'Can you move?'

'Please!' she shouted. 'Don't let him—'

'Come on,' Peake said.

He rushed off into the hall. To the front door. He flung it open just as a huge thunderbolt cracked down in the ground not even fifty yards from them. Sparks flew from the car it'd hit by the garage. And it wasn't the first strike nearby, or the first damage from the pounding winds as the flash of light illuminated a huge pine tree collapsed across the driveway, a car crushed beneath it.

What Peake saw no sign of at all was Jorge or Xavi.

Nothing. But he did hear something mechanical above the din of the storm. From the other side of the house.

'The water!' Lucia shouted before running off into the house.

Peake followed her through and then out of the back door into the darkness of the garden, the churning sea surrounding them. Lucia carried on, as if oblivious to the deadly hurricane, heading onto a narrow wooden jetty that swayed and rocked. She didn't make it all the way to the end. There was no need. Peake could already see there was no boat moored here. Not now.

As his eyes scanned the water, he saw the small craft bobbing, so small on the giant waves that he had no clue how it hadn't been swallowed up already.

'Peake! He's got Xavi! You have to save my son!'

Except as he stared out at the vengeful sea from the now boat-less dock, her desperate words dripped with a harrowing impossibility.

30

Even if there'd been another boat on the jetty, Peake wouldn't have gone out onto the water. Doing so was nothing but suicide. Although he was sure suicide wasn't Jorge's intent.

'Where's he going?' Peake shouted to Lucia, who'd shrunken down, not just because of the hammering wind and rain, not just because she was so badly beaten, but because she was distraught at watching her son being taken out to his near certain death.

'I don't know!'

'Then think. That dinghy can't be your and Jorge's only boat. What else do you have? A yacht?'

'Yes, but it's...'

She looked out to the water. Nothing else was out there.

'The marina!' she said. 'He's going to the marina.'

She moved off for the house at speed but her impetus didn't last long. However much adrenaline she had left in her veins, and however desperate she was, there was no mistaking her physical frailty. Peake had to guide her around the side of the house toward the cars, ever wary of any more threats appearing from inside the house. None did.

They reached the car and were soon traveling north. Neither of them spoke as Lucia fiddled with the radio, looking for weather updates, as though they needed to be told that outside the car's windows everything was simply horrendous.

The hurricane had made landfall a hundred miles north. As bad as the storm was here, they were lucky not to be experiencing the eyewall where the wind speeds were gusting at more than 140 miles an hour. At those speeds the moving car could well have been sucked into the air.

But hearing the almost good news also gave them the slimmest of chances of Jorge and Xavi making it off that boat alive, and Lucia seemed to grow in strength a little at realizing that.

She turned off the radio. 'You hate me—'

'I don't hate you.'

'Then you should do.'

'You shouldn't have lied to me.'

'Perhaps not. But... would you have ever helped me if you'd known the truth from the start?'

'That you're a drug smuggler? A cartel boss?'

She sneered at him. 'You watch too many movies. You have no idea what my life is.'

Movies? Except he'd actually come up against his fair share of cartels in the past. They were vicious entities, the people who ran them used to ordering bloodshed to further their aims.

'You used me,' Peake said.

'You chose to help. You could have walked away at any point.'

Peake scoffed. 'You did everything to make sure I would stay involved. And I'm only here right now for your son. Because he deserves better than to be used as a pawn like this.'

'Thank you.'

'I already said, I'm not doing this for you. Not now.'

'Still, thank you.'

He gripped the steering wheel more tightly.

'The truth is, it was either Jorge or me,' she said. 'It's been that way for a long time. The conflict was inevitable because he always wanted sole charge, and I was his way to the top. The only thing stopping me from making the first move was because I wasn't sure I had enough backing. And... I underestimated him. I had no idea he already had the help of Ridley, another head to concoct his master plan with.'

Peake didn't say anything, and he wasn't sure if he even wanted to hear this or not. Was Lucia trying to justify herself to him still, or just spouting thoughts at will?

'I'm not a bad person,' Lucia said.

'Define bad person.'

'You think you're better than me now, don't you?'

'You're the head of a drug cartel. You're telling me you do good in this world?'

'In the few days I've known you, how many people have you killed or permanently maimed?'

'To help you.'

'And everything I've done is to help my family.'

He really didn't think they were the same thing at all.

'And what really happened to Maria Vasquez?' he asked. 'The maid your husband was sleeping with?'

'You think I had her killed?'

'That's what I'm asking.'

'I gave her 5000 dollars and had one of my guys drive her over the border back to Mexico.'

Peake said nothing but glanced over and the look she gave him showed she was disappointed. In him.

'I'm not the person you think I am.'

'It doesn't even matter who I think you are. I'm going to help save Xavi. Then you'll never have to see me again.'

'Jorge really is the monster I told you he was.'

Peake didn't respond to that. He had nothing more to say. They arrived at the deserted marina not long after. Along with several rows of boats and yachts of various sizes and expensiveness, there were also three mammoth boatyards. The whole area was lit only by a series of dim gangway lights. Every few seconds the choppy sea water smashed up against the pier at the end of the marina, sending frothy waves and spray tens of feet into the air. The moored boats bobbed and swayed and clanked and crashed into one another. Several had broken free from their moorings and had been thrust further out into the water. Some were on their sides, some were upside down.

'Xavi!' Lucia cried out as they made their way toward the boats.

'There's no way he came here to get onto another boat!' Peake shouted, and the lack of reaction meant he wasn't sure at first that she'd even heard him over the pounding wind. Which meant if they'd actually made it here alive, they were coming ashore.

'There!' she screamed.

She rushed forward and Peake went with her, and she stopped right by the water's edge, nearly toppling over. 'Xavi!'

Peake saw him. Right by an upturned dinghy. He had a life jacket on, but the ferocious swell was still dragging him under.

No sign of Jorge...

Lucia flinched as though about to dive into the water, but Peake held her back.

'No.'

In her weakened state, she'd have no chance.

'Find a pole or a rope or something.'

He palmed her his handgun then dived over the edge without waiting for a response.

The first thing that struck him was just how warm the water was. It somehow didn't match with the vicious wind and rain, and he'd braced his body for a chilly impact, an initial shock that for many people plunged unexpectedly into cold waters ended up costing them their lives.

No such shock. But no time for respite either as within seconds, and not helped by his water-sodden clothes, the force of the swelling water was pulling Peake under. He fought against it, pushed on with everything he had to close the distance to Xavi. He went to take a big breath of air but only sucked in a face full of water and coughed and spluttered and for a few seconds was left flailing, trying to keep his head above the churning water.

'Xavi, reach out... to me!' he shouted.

The boy had seen him and was batting his arms around, slapping the water as though trying but unable to get into a front crawl, the life jacket hampering him as much as the choppy water. Despite his effort he drifted further away, nudging up against the capsized boat. Peake continued to power across the water, and he wasn't sure if it was his effort or the roll of the waves that suddenly sent him hurtling toward the boy.

'Xavi! Take my hand!'

The boy reached out and Peake grabbed him and pulled him close.

'You OK?'

No response.

'Where's your dad?'

He shook his head.

'Come on.'

Peake turned him over, kept Xavi's face above the water as he tried to track back to the marina. As he looked up there... No sign of Lucia. Was she still searching for something to help them out?

Xavi's life jacket gave them both some much needed buoyancy, but the extra weight on top of Peake made it even harder for him to keep his own head above water and to move through the churn. His muscles ached and screamed at him as lactate built up, and he didn't know how long he could continue to push without stopping. The marina was all of ten yards from him but no matter how hard he strained his muscles he wasn't getting closer.

He took a pause, shifted Xavi across him so his left side was doing the bulk of the work. In the few seconds it took him to achieve that, the waves pushed him closer and closer to the edge.

'Nearly there!' he yelled, as much to himself as to Xavi.

And with one final, brutal effort, Peake made it, and he grabbed hold of the floating jetty above him as Xavi clung to him like a koala.

Still no sign of Lucia.

'I'll help you up,' Peake said.

Xavi nodded and Peake worked his legs as hard as he could to tread water while he pushed Xavi to lift him higher. The boy grasped the planks and strained and groaned to pull himself up. He accidentally smashed Peake's face with his trailing foot and Peake let go and was sent flailing under the water. He could see nothing. He battled against the swirling current, tried to find the surface. But he didn't even know which direction was which.

Then he crashed up out of the water, opened his mouth to take in air but smacked his head against the jetty and was soon under again, dazed. He sucked in water and tried, tried as hard as he could not to panic and to give in to the temptation to suck in more.

He winced when he hit his head. Something hard. A support for the jetty?

No. Too thin. He grabbed at the wood and the next moment his head thrust up out of the water and he coughed and spluttered and water spilled from his lips as he gasped for air.

'Arrghhh!' Xavi screamed, holding on to the pole and pulling with all his might, but it looked like if he held on much longer Peake's weight would drag him into the water.

One last effort from Peake. He kicked and reached up and grabbed the wooden planks and roared with effort to pull himself out of the water. He rolled onto his back as his chest heaved and...

'My mom!' Xavi screamed, shaking Peake to alertness.

He jumped to his feet.

'Where?' Peake asked.

Xavi didn't answer. He didn't need to because even above the sound of the wind and the rain and the crashing waves, he heard her scream.

The boatyard closest to them.

'Come with me,' Peake said. He really didn't want the boy coming inside, coming anywhere near where Jorge might be, but he also couldn't just leave him out in the middle of the storm either.

Another shrill scream pierced through the night. They reached the metal wall of the boatyard. Some sort of shelter here at least.

'Stay down,' Peake said. 'Don't move from this spot. If you see your dad, scream, as loud as you can.'

The boy crumpled down onto the floor, shivering like crazy. Nothing Peake could do about that right now.

He moved off, up a metal staircase at the side of the building. With each step he took his position became more exposed and the wind more severe, and the whole structure creaked and swayed.

Relief when he reached the top and the door there without being blown off.

Unlocked. Yet he still struggled to open it, such was the force of the wind slamming into the side of the building up high. He eventually heaved it open enough to slip through, but as soon as he moved inside the door banged shut with a huge crash, any hopes he'd had of a quiet entry obliterated.

He stood and listened. Could hear nothing but the storm and the groans of the building. Not a storage yard in front of him, but a workshop, a factory perhaps with various metal gangways on different levels and vessels in various states of build dotted around the expansive space. Peake had entered on a mezzanine in one corner, and he crept to a railing to peer down below. He could see no one but heard a bang and a muffled groan beneath him.

Peake moved for the nearest stairs, eyes scanning. He picked up a crowbar from a workbench. Moved down the stairs, senses primed. With no lights on in the building he had only the merest sliver of moonlight coming in through the few windows to see around him.

Until a flash of lighting from outside lit up the space in front of him.

He spotted the outline of a darkened figure, crouching behind the bare hull of a partly built yacht fifteen yards in front. Peake went around the yacht the other way, treading carefully across the metal gangway, trying not to make a sound.

He made it to the front of the boat and leapt out...

Nothing there.

A crash came from above and Peake looked up to see a piece of sheet metal from the roof peel away from the force of the wind, and debris crashed down toward him.

'Look out!' came Lucia's shout from his left.

And not to warn him of the debris but of Jorge. Not Jorge, specifically, but the hoisted engine hanging a couple of yards from where Peake stood. He could do nothing as Jorge hauled the hefty machine Peake's way and it glided or slid or just fucking flew through the air and smacked into Peake, taking him off his feet and slapping him up against the hull of the boat.

Peake was dazed. But not too dazed to see Jorge lunging at him, an axe in his hand which he arced through the air toward Peake.

He ducked down and swiped with the crowbar, catching Jorge solidly in his leg. The impact was enough to cause him to stumble. The axe-head flew past Peake's ear and wedged into the hull. Jorge tried to pull it free but couldn't and Peake hit his leg again with the bar before rising up and coming up behind Jorge and pulling the metal up against the guy's throat.

Peake yanked back and took Jorge off his feet and twisted to slam him down onto the metal floor. He lifted the crowbar and was about to smash it into Jorge's face, but another bolt of lightning cracked down onto... something. Wood and plastic shards flew and shrapnel dug into Peake's shoulder, and Jorge found an impetus. And the knife that he must have had stashed somewhere. He slashed at Peake's arm and threw him off, and before Peake could react the guy was up on his feet and rushing for Lucia. He took hold of her around her neck, pressing the knife against her throat.

'You really want to help her?' Jorge said. 'She lied to you. Brought you so much trouble... And for what? To satisfy her own twisted fantasy?'

Peake didn't answer. He had no interest in a conversation here.

Another thunderclap caused all of them to cower, but Peake reacted first and rushed forward. Lucia stomped on Jorge's foot and sank her teeth into his arm, and it was enough to allow her to slip from his grip.

But not to get away from him.

Jorge grabbed her shoulder and flung her into the railings, and she toppled over the edge. Screamed.

Thud.

Peake couldn't see where she'd landed but it hadn't been a long fall.

He'd have to worry about that later. He roared and took Jorge off his feet and drove him into the boat. Peake slammed him a second time and the whole craft wobbled and swayed, the props holding it in place creaking and straining. Peake hit Jorge with a headbutt. Even more brutal than the one Peake had earlier delivered to one of the goons. Jorge's head lolled, and Peake hit him again. Then he thrust his thumbs into Jorge's eyes and took the man off his feet as he pushed as hard as he could. Jorge screamed. But then Peake winced and his eyes shot wide and his whole world paused for the briefest moment as he tried to figure out why...

His side. The knife. Jorge grimaced with effort as he pushed the blade deeper and Peake simply couldn't hold on. He slumped to one knee, hand to the wound as blood poured. A knee to the face sent him onto his back and he rolled off the gangway and to the platform below, underneath the hull of the boat.

Jorge jumped down and straddled him. Kind of like how he had with Lucia earlier. Except this time he still had the knife in his hand.

'I'm gonna enjoy this,' he said.

The knife came down. Peake caught Jorge's wrist. He added his second hand on top but when Jorge did the same, both men double-handed, pushing against the other's strength, Peake knew he couldn't hold out for long, he was already too depleted. The blade edged toward his ribs.

'No! No!' Peake shouted out.

The tip of the blade pierced his skin.

Bang.

Peake didn't understand at first. He'd thought it was lightning. Or some other part of the weakened building failing.

No. A gunshot. And in that moment, Jorge's strength failed him. A patch of blood opened up on his shoulder.

Peake let go of the guy's wrist and reached up and grabbed his hair and yanked to the side as he rolled them both over. He jumped to his feet, grabbed the edge of the gangway above and rolled up onto it. Saw the axe. He took hold of it and swung out at the prop nearest to him. Not with the blade, but the back of the axe-head. The already strained wood faltered and caved and the whole boat crashed down.

Jorge screamed. The hefty craft splatted onto him, his whole body under the weight except for his head and one shoulder which poked out.

His eyes flickered as his life faded.

Within seconds he went completely still, his eyes staring up aimlessly as rain cascaded onto him from the hole in the roof.

Peake dropped the axe and it clattered on the metal. He turned to where he was sure the gunshot that saved his life had come from.

A surprise.

He'd expected to see Lucia.

'Katie.'

She had the pistol in a double-handed grip, the barrel pointed at Peake's chest.

He paused a moment, unsure of her intention.

'Thank you,' he said to her.

'Shit,' she said when Peake collapsed down to his knee again, holding his side.

She rushed over.

'Lucia,' he said. 'She's... down there.'

'No,' Katie said. 'She's not. She's already outside with Xavi. She's fine. They're both fine.'

But Peake wasn't. He slumped onto his back, staring up at the hole in the roof again, like he had moments earlier, and like Jorge had in his final moments.

He blinked a few times, unsure if he was hallucinating because the flashes he saw in the sky now weren't the bright white of lightning, but blue and red.

'You're gonna be OK, Peake,' Katie said, and only then did he hear the whir of sirens above the storm, and it all made sense. 'You saved them both and you're gonna be OK.'

Peake said nothing as he closed his eyes.

31

Peake sat on the side of the gurney in the back of the ambulance, the doors wide open as he surveyed the scene outside. Three ambulances in total, four police cars. A whole host of responders went back and forth, battling through the wind and rain which were only just starting to ease. He still hadn't seen Lucia or Xavi but had been assured they were both fine, no major injuries. Not compared to him, at least. The stab wound to his side had taken multiple stitches and they'd put him on a drip to replace lost fluids but at least the blade hadn't damaged any organs, or he'd have been in a whole other mess.

He pulled the cannula out of his wrist and groaned as he got to his feet. He ducked down and made a bit of a mess getting off the ambulance and onto the ground, stumbling and grimacing in pain until a paramedic rushed up to him.

'Hey, what are you doing?'

'I'm... fine. I'm fine.'

'You need to be—'

'I said I'm fine, please.'

The paramedic didn't look convinced, but Peake shrugged him off and spotted Katie through the rain, over by one of the police cars, talking to two plain-clothed men. She found his eye and a moment later was coming his way.

'You shouldn't be—'

'Save it,' he interrupted. 'What's happening?'

She said nothing, looked reluctant to speak.

'You're on the inside with the cops here?' he asked. 'Who are you?'

'Don't go getting all conspiratorial on me,' she said. 'There's no play here. What you heard from Ridley and Jorge at the house is all you need to know. I was helping Ridley but had no idea how out of control he was.'

'Yeah, but I'm talking about how you're in with the cops here. You're not just some average Joe that Ridley picked up.'

'I just... happen to know a few people with a bit of sway. From my old job.'

'You need to explain that to me.'

She sighed, as though to show her continued reluctance, but then decided to speak anyway.

'I was a CIA analyst. It's as simple as that. But I went freelance for reasons you don't need to know. I only just started working with Ridley.'

She looked around her, as though making sure no one was within earshot.

'I honestly didn't know what his game was here, please believe that. When he brought me in, it was to help find Lucia. I swear I didn't know the full story.'

'And now?'

'I helped you, didn't I?'

'How'd you even know we were coming here?'

She shrugged. 'What does it matter to you? Perhaps just be content with how it ended.'

'No. I'm anything but content here.'

'I'm not a bad person,' Katie said. 'If I'd known what Ridley was up to, I would never have signed up for this.'

'And what exactly was he up to?'

'There're still some big unanswered questions. I'd be lying if I said he was a lone wolf here. So most likely there's a connection to the CIA or another agency who was in on his scheme to get Jorge Ramirez to the top of the Fuentes cartel. But I've spoken to people back at Langley who I trust and they've all told me this wasn't anything official.'

'And now... what? You're back on the inside again? Because you're looking pretty cozy with the Feds over there, or whoever they are.'

'You're talking to me as though I didn't just save your life.'

Peake scoffed.

'I don't work for anyone anymore,' she said. 'But I'll help out here as much as I can, and you want to know why?'

'Why?'

'To save my own ass. Because I can't exactly hide my involvement here so the best I can do now is to tell the police, the Feds, anyone else with authority who asks, everything I know.'

Peake didn't know what to say to that. Did it make her a moral beacon of truth, or just a coward?

'What's going to happen to Lucia?'

'I have no idea. You do realize her organization is well known to—'

'Yes, I imagine the cartel is well known to the CIA, the FBI, whoever. Although so far no one has had a go at dismantling it, have they? Only swapping out one boss for another who'd provide more benefits.'

'What are you trying to say?'

'I wasn't saying anything. I was asking you about Lucia.'

'It's possible she's an asset for some party I don't know about. But she's not my problem.'

'Is she anyone's problem here?'

'As far as I know, no. I expect she'll be given the all clear here tonight and be sent on her way. But there's a big mess to sort through, not least the dead bodies at her home.'

'And me?'

'That's a good question, isn't it? Did I just mention the dead bodies?'

Peake didn't answer. He didn't like the smug way she said that, as though she was still holding way more cards than him.

'Peake, we don't know each other well, but I think we'd both rather move on from this shit pretty damn quickly.'

'You got that right.'

'If you were to... slip between the cracks here tonight... You never know, with the friends I have, maybe your name never comes up, maybe no one ever comes looking.'

She held out her hand and pressed a key fob into his palm.

'To help make those cracks a bit easier to slip through. Just... try not to cross paths with me again. Yeah?'

'Yeah. And thanks for... you know what.'

She didn't say anything more before she turned and walked off.

Peake pushed on the key fob and the lights on a black sedan across the way flashed.

He went that way but then paused when he spotted Lucia and Xavi, both of them wrapped in shiny emergency blankets, hot drinks in their hands as a uniformed policeman stood talking to them beneath a makeshift shelter. Peake went over and the cop looked wary at first.

'Can I get a minute?' Peake asked.

The cop said nothing but took a few steps to the side, arms folded as he glared at the three of them.

'You OK, kid?' Peake asked Xavi who nodded in response but wouldn't look Peake in the eye.

'Thank you,' Lucia said. 'For saving him.'

'Sure,' Peake responded.

An awkward silence followed, neither of them sure where to take the conversation.

'I am sorry for how this worked out for you,' Lucia said.

'Yeah.'

'Just know that—'

'You don't need to say anything more,' Peake said. 'This is where we go our separate ways.'

'Probably for the best.'

'It is. But... you do have the choice, you know.'

'Choice of what?'

'Of what kind of person you want to be. You told me you only ever did what was best for your family. He's your family. So do what's best for him. For his future.'

Lucia didn't respond. Xavi remained looking at the ground. An uncertain future for him, whatever path his mother chose. But it'd be a path and a future that Peake had no involvement in.

He nodded to the policeman, signaling that he was done, then he turned and walked to the car.

32

The hurricane two days ago had long since passed over Florida, Georgia, the Carolinas, the remaining remnants now nothing but torrential rain upon the northeast Atlantic seaboard. The devastation in Florida, north of Tampa and around the Big Bend would take months, possibly years to fully overcome with some communities all but wiped out. Record levels of flooding would continue to wreak havoc and hamper aid and rescue efforts.

The chaos south of Tampa, near Sarasota which had seen several people killed – including a drug kingpin from Colombia – was low-key, small-scale in comparison and hadn't made any kind of news headlines even in the local area, Peake only finding online articles through targeted searching.

Altogether it was a welcome result for Peake, whose name wasn't mentioned at all in any of the articles he'd found.

He was sure Katie Embleton had a hand in making that happen. He'd never know for sure. At least not unless the CIA, or whoever, tracked him down at some point in the future looking for payback on their 'favor'.

A bridge to worry about crossing when he arrived there.

The skies in Georgia were clear, little more than a gentle breeze out, but the weather felt almost fall-like, the high summer temperatures of the last few weeks not yet recovered after the battering of the storm.

Peake arrived back in Prenticeville not long after midday. He'd debated multiple times on the drive north whether to stop here at all. He'd decided yes, but he wouldn't stay long.

Slug's Tavern was open but the only car already in the parking lot as Peake drove in was Travis's. Peake watched the street for a few moments before he made his way inside.

Travis was alone, not a customer in sight, and it looked like there hadn't been any yet today as the guy was laid out across the bench of one of the booths, taking a nap.

Peake closed the door with a thud and Travis jolted and jumped up to his feet and Peake burst out laughing. Travis eventually saw the funny side.

'Lucky it wasn't Frank walking in to see you like that,' Peake said.

'Shit, man, you know I was working here until 3 a.m. last night? Barely made it up the stairs without falling asleep. Was back down here at nine.' He shook his head as though he couldn't believe the toil. 'But it's good to see you, man. A surprise, but good.'

Travis came forward and he grabbed Peake and wrapped his arms around him. He slapped Peake's back and Peake groaned and grimaced from the pain in his side.

'Shit, sorry,' Travis said. 'You OK?'

'I'll be fine.'

'So it's all done? I'm guessing you wouldn't be back here otherwise.'

'I think so.'

'Didn't think I'd ever see you back here.'

'I wasn't sure I'd come. But you know why I'm here, right?'

'To see me,' Travis said, thumping Peake's arm.

'Yeah, other than that.'

'Jenn? She ain't here.'

'Not Jenn. Adam. You heard from him?'

'Nah, man, not seen, not heard. Not for a long time.'

Except Peake didn't really believe him.

'Well, if you do see him... just tell him I hope he's OK. Tell him... look out for Jenn. And to sort his fucking life out.'

Travis laughed at that and Peake couldn't resist either. He heard a creak upstairs and the smile on Travis's face dropped a little.

'You got lucky last night?' Peake asked. 'Is that why you're so tired?'

But he didn't even try to pretend that was the case. Peake got it.

'Like I said, just tell Adam I get it. I get why he did what he did.'

Peake headed for the door. He didn't make it outside before he heard footsteps coming down the stairs. He turned and Adam appeared at the far end of the bar, looking sheepish as hell as though he still wasn't sure if Peake was about to attack him.

'I'm sorry,' Adam said.

Peake nodded.

'You know they gave me no choice? I had to make that call to you.'

'I understand,' Peake said. 'I'm just glad you're OK.'

'I caused so much shit for you. For Jenn.'

'Then make sure that's the last of it,' Peake said.

Adam nodded. 'We're gonna sell the farm. Now that... you know, everything's sorted with Frank.'

'Probably for the best.'

'Me and Jenn'll share the money. It'll start something good for the both of us.'

'Make sure it does. When you see her, tell your sister I said hi.'

Travis scoffed. 'Yeah, as if you ain't on your way to her right now.'

Peake said nothing, but both Travis and Adam were grinning.

'See you around,' Peake said, before heading on out.

He hadn't made it to his vehicle when he spotted the police car across the street. He got into his car anyway but Shaun was out of his and blocked Peake's exit so he stopped and wound down his window.

'Didn't think I'd see you around here again,' Shaun said, coming over.

'Just passing through.'

'You better make sure about that. You know, I still got stories going around here about dead bodies on one of the farms. And you know what else I heard?'

Peake shook his head.

'Apparently there was some sort of shootout over in Hazelwood, Alabama. You know one of my cousins works out there?'

'No, I didn't know that.'

'Yeah. Small world, eh? Anyways, if I found the time, wonder what'd happen if I compared notes with him, swapped DNA samples, that sort of thing.'

'No idea,' Peake said. 'I already told you, I'm just passing through here. What happens here and... Hazelwood, you say? None of my business.'

'Damn right. This is my town. I don't want to see you here again.'

The guy stomped off to the bar. Perhaps Travis was about to get an earful too. Did Shaun know Adam was hiding there? About his involvement in the whole mess?

It didn't matter. Peake wasn't lying to Shaun – he was done in Prenticeville. He hit the gas and headed out onto the highway.

* * *

Dusk wasn't far off as Peake wound the car up the twisting mountain roads above Sevierville, Tennessee, the peaks of the Great Smoky Mountains rising around him. The log cabin home looked exactly as he'd expected it to look – brown wood exterior, a veranda on all four levels of the thin but tall home that was built on a rise at the edge of a forest clearing. The views down into the valley several hundred feet below were spectacular.

He walked up the steps to the porch deck and knocked on the front door. A woman opened. Mid, late fifties with loose, wavy fair hair that fell down past her shoulders. Her green eyes sparkled, a clear family resemblance not just to Jenn, but Jenn's mother too.

Peake was about to open his mouth when a man appeared behind. Tall, pudgy, but his broad shoulders and thick arms showed he was a beast. He had one hand behind his back but just poking out from the side of his knee was the tip of the barrel of a shotgun.

'Sorry to disturb you,' Peake said. 'I'm looking for Jenn.'

'Sorry, sweetie,' the woman said, with a forced smile. 'There's no Jenn here.'

'Tell her it's Simon Peake. Please?'

'She told you, there's no Jenn here,' the man said, and he pulled the shotgun out and pumped the barrel. His wife moved aside as he came toward the threshold.

'Time for you to back up, boy.'

Peake took a half step back.

'You better keep on steppin'.'

Peake didn't. Not until the barrel of the gun was pressed against his chest.

'I'm gonna count to five, then I'm blasting you into the dirt. Now step back and keep on goin'.'

Peake did so. Tentative, slow steps. Down off the porch and onto the compacted dirt path.

'Did I say stop? You keep moving now. And keep it real slow.'

Peake took three more steps then stopped. Because from this position he was now in view of the windows upstairs. And he was sure he saw a curtain twitch up there.

The next moment he saw the face. Saw the smile. Jenn banged on the window and then disappeared from view, but the next moment he heard her pounding down the stairs.

'It's OK, Robbie, it's OK! It's him!'

Jenn brushed past her aunt and up to her uncle, who still didn't look too convinced – at least not until his niece put her hand to his shoulder and helped guide the gun down.

'Damn lucky for you, boy,' Robbie said, before huffing and turning and walking back into the house.

'Excuse my husband, he gets a little antsy when he's hungry,' the wife said. 'I'm Caroline. Come on in. I was just putting some supper on.'

Peake headed in behind Jenn and they kind of hung back in the hallway, both of them seeming a little unsure what to do next.

'Are you staying?' Caroline said as she came out of the kitchen, drying her hands on a towel.

'I don't—'

'Course you're staying. You look tired and it's late. Robbie! Go make up the bed for our guest. Or are you two...'

She looked really uncomfortable.

'Oh... you two decide,' she said. 'You're both adults. But Robbie, go make up the bed!'

The big guy grumbled as he came out into the hall then stomped up the stairs.

'Outside, you two, I'll bring you some drinks.'

Wine, and beer, it turned out. Peake and Jenn sat on chairs on the deck looking out over the view to the west, the evening sun casting a warm glow over the forest around them. Birds chirped. Cicadas hummed. Bigger creatures roamed and rustled nearby.

'Are you gonna tell me what happened?' Jenn said.

'You don't want to know it all. But it's finished.'

'But... you've seen Adam?'

'He's not been in touch with you?'

'I heard from him once. That was it.'

'I saw him earlier today. He's fine. You'll both be fine now.'

'And you?'

She glanced at his side as though she'd sensed he had pain there.

'I've had worse.'

Jenn held his eye and looked pensive, like she wanted to say something, but...

'I'm glad she's gone.'

'Who?'

'That woman. Lucia. I didn't like... the way she was with you. The way you were with her.'

Peake smiled although Jenn didn't seem to appreciate it. 'You're jealous?'

'Yeah, I'm jealous. But also... something else. Like... I like you better when you're not the tough guy. When it's just you like this.'

'Yeah. Me too.' He drank to that. Downing most of his bottle.

'But you're finished with her?'

'Yeah. We figured things out. I won't be seeing her again. Nor any of the people who were causing her trouble.'

Because they were all dead, he could have added, except he didn't think Jenn would like to hear that.

'So what next?' she asked.

'I don't know.'

'But... you're moving on?'

'Yeah.'

She sighed. 'Thought so.'

'Adam said you'll sell the farm. So you get the chance to move on too.'

'I will. There's nothing for me in Prenticeville anymore.'

'Look at you two!' Caroline said as she came outside with a tray with more drinks and a basket of bread. 'Isn't it glorious out here tonight?'

'It is,' Peake said.

Caroline disappeared inside and Jenn shuffled closer to Peake and took his hand.

'Seems like she was expecting me?' Peake said.

Jenn blushed. 'They kinda realized I was looking for an escape up here, so I had to tell them something. Uncle Robbie's a decent protector. But I said maybe you'd show up when things quietened down back home, so don't just shoot anyone turning up unannounced.'

She laughed at that. Peake said nothing.

'But I'm glad you came,' she added.

'Me too.'

'I know you'll be gone soon enough, but... you should stay a little while at least. It's pretty peaceful up here. Maybe you need it even more than I do right now.'

He sipped from the fresh bottle, enjoying the feel of her next to him.

'So?' Jenn said. 'You'll stay a while, won't you? At least until you're all healed up?'

She nuzzled further into him and he wrapped his arm around her shoulder and held her tight, enjoying her closeness, and the tranquility, as he watched the deep red sun drop below the horizon.

'Yeah, I guess I could stay a little while,' he said.

* * *

ABOUT THE AUTHOR

Rob Sinclair is the million copy bestseller of over twenty thrillers, including the James Ryker series. Rob previously studied Biochemistry at Nottingham University. He also worked for a global accounting firm for 13 years, specialising in global fraud investigations.

Sign up to Rob Sinclair's mailing list for news, competitions and updates on future books.

Visit Rob's website: www.robsinclairauthor.com

Follow Rob on social media here:

facebook.com/robsinclairauthor
x.com/rsinclairauthor
bookbub.com/authors/rob-sinclair
goodreads.com/robsinclair

ALSO BY ROB SINCLAIR

The James Ryker Series

The Red Cobra

The Black Hornet

The Silver Wolf

The Green Viper

The White Scorpion

The Renegade

The Assassins

The Outsider

The Vigilante

The Protector

The Deception

Angel of Death

The Enemy Within

The Enemy Series

Dance with the Enemy

Rise of the Enemy

Hunt for the Enemy

The Simon Peake Thrillers

Dead Reckoning

Deadly Mistake

Standalone Novels

Rogue Hero

www.ingramcontent.com/pod-product-compliance
Lightning Source LLC
Chambersburg PA
CBHW011128050326
40690CB00024B/5234
9781806353217